Julius Müller, Adolphe Monod, Friedrich W. Krummacher

Select Discourses by Adolphe Monod, Krummacher, Tholuck and Julius Müller

translated from the French and German, with biographical notices, and Monod's

celebrated lecture on the delivery of sermons

Julius Müller, Adolphe Monod, Friedrich W. Krummacher

Select Discourses by Adolphe Monod, Krummacher, Tholuck and Julius Müller
translated from the French and German, with biographical notices, and Monod's celebrated lecture on the delivery of sermons

ISBN/EAN: 9783337264536

Printed in Europe, USA, Canada, Australia, Japan

Cover: Foto ©Andreas Hilbeck / pixelio.de

More available books at **www.hansebooks.com**

SELECT DISCOURSES.

SELECT DISCOURSES

BY

ADOLPHE MONOD, KRUMMACHER, THOLUCK, AND JULIUS MÜLLER:

TRANSLATED FROM THE FRENCH AND GERMAN,

WITH

BIOGRAPHICAL NOTICES, AND DR. MONOD'S CELEBRATED
LECTURE ON THE DELIVERY OF SERMONS.

BY REV. H. C. FISH, AND D. W. POOR, D.D.

With a fine Steel Portrait of Dr. Monod.

NEW YORK:
SHELDON AND COMPANY.
BOSTON: GOULD & LINCOLN
LONDON: TRÜBNER & CO.

———

1860.

W. H. TINSON, Stereotyper.

PREFACE.

The object in the preparation and publication of this volume, has been to render accessible to Christian readers generally, some of the rich literary and religious treasures which lie hidden in the writings of the good and great men here represented. Several of the Discourses here presented, have long had the reputation, in Europe, of being among the *chefs-d'œuvre* of their respective authors. This is true, for example, of the two of Dr. Monod on WOMAN, and his three on THE TEMPTATION OF CHRIST; and those of Dr. Krummacher on the same subject; which, for deep penetration and lofty eloquence, are not excelled by anything that this celebrated author has ever published. It is believed that these two sets of sermons on the TEMPTATION OF OUR BLESSED LORD, coming as they do from two of the ablest and most eloquent preachers of this age, contain a more touching, instructive, and exhaustive discussion of this deeply interesting subject than is elsewhere to be found.

Professor Tholuck's Discourse on the CHRISTIAN LIFE AS A GLORIFIED CHILDHOOD, is a precious gem; and each of his sermons here furnished will enhance his already distinguished reputation. Those of Professor Müller will be the more gratefully received, from the fact that none of his Discourses, with a single exception,* have ever appeared in an English dress.

* In PULPIT ELOQUENCE OF XIX. CENTURY.

The sermon of Krummacher entitled THE BELIEVER'S
CHALLENGE, is a remarkable specimen of bold and abrupt
rhetoric, the peculiarities of which it was difficult to
preserve in the translation.

It has been a delightful task, thus to be the means
of extending the acquaintance of these honored and
beloved servants of God—now ripening off for heaven,
and one of whom has, of late, already 'gone up higher.'
In a very few instances advantage has been taken of
former renderings, but not without the most careful
revision.   The part which the translators respectively
have performed in the preparation of the work, is indicated by the order of their names on the title-page, taken
in connection with the order of the sermons in the
volume; the first named being particularly responsible
for the French department, and the last named for the
German.

NEWARK, N. J., *April* 20, 1858.

CONTENTS.

———•—

ADOLPHE MONOD.

F. W. KRUMMACHER.

AUG. F. G. THOLUCK.

ADOLPHE MONOD, D. D.

BIOGRAPHICAL NOTICE.

Dr. Monod* was a son of the late Rev. John Monod, of Paris. He had seven brothers and three sisters, all of whom, it is believed, survive him. Three of his brothers are in the ministry of the gospel—all evangelical, faithful, and most highly esteemed brethren. The oldest is the Rev. Dr. Frederic Monod, who is pastor of one of the churches in Paris, connected with the Free Church of France. The Rev. William Monod, another brother, is now pastor of a Protestant Church in Paris. The youngest brother is the Rev. Horace Monod, one of the French pastors at Marseilles.

Dr. Adolphe Monod, as well as his brothers, was educated mainly at home, under private teachers and professors, and then, according to the liberal practice which prevails in France, he underwent an examination in one of the colleges of Paris, and, paying the usual fees, received his diploma as Bachelor of Letters. His theological studies, we believe, were pursued in Geneva, in the Theological department of the Academy (or University, as we should call it) of that city. For two or three years he preached to a French congregation at Naples, holding the post of chaplain to the Embassy of Prussia. From that city he was called to be one of the pastors of the National Protestant Church in Lyons, in France, when his great pulpit talents soon made him widely known. He was even chosen president of the consistory of that church.

But he had not long been settled in the church in Lyons, before his mind was led by the grace and Spirit of God to embrace heartily the evangelical system. As soon as he had clearly apprehended Christ as the Son of God, as well as the Son of Man—as the only Mediator

---

* Pronounced as if the *d* were lost: thus, Mono.

between God and man—his preaching began to partake of the glorious change. At first, and for a while, the rich and worldly church of Lyons, to which he (with two other pastors, men of a very different spirit) ministered, were astonished. Soon dissatisfaction with truth began to manifest itself, and in a few months the distinguished but humble servant of Christ was compelled to resign his place, and open an independent chapel, on truly evangelical principles. About seventy people, mostly poor but pious persons, followed him. He commenced his labors in a large room in the third story of a private house. Soon it was filled to overflowing. It was again and again enlarged, until it held nearly four hundred people. As it could be enlarged no more, it was resolved to build a chapel or church in a more central part of the city.

From Lyons, Dr. Monod was called, in 1836, to the **Theological Seminary** at Montauban, where he became Professor of Sacred Eloquence. This appointment he received from the hands of Baron Pétit, a Protestant nobleman of **evangelical sentiments, who was** for a considerable period Minister **of Public Instruction in the reign** of Louis Philippe. **For several years Dr.** Monod filled with great **ability the** professorship **which he held in the only theological institu**tion of the National Reformed Church of France. During that period he wrote several of his most valuable publications. **In his vacations** he visited Paris and other important cities, and was always heard, when he preached, **by** great crowds of **people ; or else he made** missionary tours **in the** ancient provinces of **Saintonge, Poitou, or** other districts in southern and south-western France.

The last seven or eight years of the life of Dr. Adolphe Monod were spent at Paris, where he preached the gospel with great effect, **to** large **and** delighted audiences. His labors, and those **of Dr. Grandpierre and other** distinguished brethren of the same school, have done much **to make** the evangelical doctrines known and re-spected **among those who attend the** churches of the Reformed body in that great and important city.

It was on Sunday, April 16, 1856, that this honored servant **of** Christ ceased from his labors. His death-bed was one of intense suffering, and, at the same time, of glorious and gracious triumph. In the full and perfect assurance of his salvation through Christ, **and in peace,** he commended his spirit into the hands of **his Heavenly Father.** A few days previous to his decease, he was heard **to say :**

"*My ministerial labors, my works, my preaching. I reckon all as filthy rags; a drop of my Saviour's blood is infinitely more precious.*"

At the time of his death he was not far from fifty-six years of age; and to show how deeply he was beloved among the pious men and women of France, it is only needful to say, that while he lay dying in Paris, in the remotest extremities of the nation the dispersed Protestants were holding circles of prayer for him. French Protestantism universally wept at the news of his death.

As a preacher, it would not be asserting too much to say, that Adolphe Monod occupied the first rank in France. Although not a large man, or a man of commanding appearance, he was nevertheless a prince among preachers. His voice is said to have been melody itself, and ever under perfect control. As to his discourses, those which he delivered in large assemblies were almost invariably prepared with great care, written, and committed to memory. And yet his *extemporaneous*, or rather his *unwritten* sermons or lectures were represented as admirable for beauty of style, for clearness of conception, and for adaptation to the occasion.

Says Dr. Baird, in a letter written several years ago: "I have no hesitation in saying, that Adolphe Monod is the most finished orator I have heard on the Continent. Modest, humble, simple in his appearance and dress, possessing a voice which is music itself, his powerful mind, and vivid but chaste imagination, made their influence felt on the soul of every hearer in a way that is indescribable. The nearest approach to giving a true idea of it would be to say, that his eloquence is of the nature of a *charm* which steals over one, and yet is so subtle that it is not possible to say in what consists its elemental force. It is an eloquence the very opposite of that of the late Dr. Chalmers, which was like a torrent that carries everything away. I have often heard Ravignan, the great Jesuit preacher, in France; and Bautain, by far the best preacher, in my opinion, in the Roman Catholic Church, that I have heard; but they were much inferior to Adolphe Monod. If the late Professor Vinet, of Lausanne," he adds, "was the *Pascal* of the French Protestants in these days (as he certainly was), Dr. Adolphe Monod was their *Bossuet*. But Drs. Vinet and Monod were incomparably superior to Pascal and Bossuet as expounders of evangelical truth, which is, after all, the highest glory of the Christian teacher."

It is well known that the late Abbé Lacordaire, the Dominican.

who was by far the most popular of the Romish priests in France, in his day, remarked to his friends, after hearing him : " We are all children, in comparison with this man." Beside a strong and vivid intellect, what the French call *onction* was the characteristic of Monod's preaching. He was ineffably impressed, himself, with the truth he preached, and the earnestness of his soul thrilled every tone and every gesture.

But great as were Dr. Monod's talents, and fascinating as was his eloquence, these qualities were rivalled by his unfeigned piety, his profound humility, his cordial friendship, his simple and truly Christian manners, the purity of his conversation, and the uniform cheerfulness of his life.

Dr. Monod is said to have left written productions from which several volumes might be formed, that would be equal in beauty of style, in beauty of thought, in force of logic, and vastly superior in true instruction, to anything which Bossuet, Fénélon, Flechiere, or Bourdaloue—the so-called "greats" of the Roman Catholic Church in France—ever wrote. He had published several things of great merit. His Introduction to the French edition of Dr. Hodge's "Commentary on Romans," his "*Lucille*," his "*Femme*" (Woman), his "Controversy with a Romish Priest," at Lyons, his "Lecture on the Delivery of Sermons," etc., are pronounced by a high authority "*perfect* GEMS."*

The accompanying beautiful and striking portrait of Dr. Monod is the only one ever presented to the American public. It has been engraved with great care from one published in Paris some years since, and which is pronounced by those acquainted with Dr. Monod, an admirable likeness.

* Rev. Robert Baird, D.D., to whom indebtedness is acknowledged for many of the above particulars.

DISCOURSE I.

THE MISSION OF WOMAN.

"And the Lord God said, It is not good that man should be alone: I will make an helpmeet for him."—GENESIS, ii. 18.

MY DEAR SISTERS:

If I address myself to you to-day, the other part of this audience, accustomed to observe its name at the head of our discourses, has no reason to be jealous. We are speaking for man when we address woman and endeavor to sanctify her influence. Yes, her *influence*. In refusing to her *authority*, which emanates from the strong over the weak—a necessity in the nature of things—the Creator has assigned to her *influence*, which generally emanates from the weak over the strong; an influence freely accepted, but accepted on the condition that it should not be manifest.

I hesitate not to say it : the mightiest influence which exists upon the earth, both for good and for evil, is concealed in the hand of woman. History declares it with me, although the *historian* does not always say it—perhaps because he is ignorant of this secret power, or because he keeps it secret to profit by the self-admiration either of one sex or the other. Let us study the past. Nothing more truly distinguishes the savage state from the civilized, the east from the west, paganism from Christianity, antiquity from the middle ages, the middle ages from modern times, than the condition of woman. Who knows not, for example, that the single word polygamy or monogamy determines the manners and destinies of a people? Let us observe what is going on around us. Woman will be found everywhere in the world, as the poet represents Agrippina in the Senate—

"Behind a veil, invisible and present."

As by a woman Satan entered into the innocent race, so shall we generally trace to woman the calamities and crimes which desolate humanity—the hatreds, the revenges, the trials, the suicides, the duels, the murders, and the wars. And as by a woman our Saviour came into the fallen race, so shall we equally trace to woman the thoughts and the works which elevate and bring peace to humanity—the tender devotions, the generous sacrifices, the holy aspirations, the religious institutions, and the public charities. Is it not for this reason that art and poetry, in all ages, have personified the moral powers by *women ;* and that the Holy Spirit himself, in the Proverbs, has delineated under the traits of two women the two opposite tendencies which divide the world ? *

Imparting to this terrible influence of woman a salutary direction, by studying with her the mission which she has received from God, we shall serve the highest interests of the human race.

By your mission, women who hear me, I understand here the *distinctive* mission of your sex. It has a general one which it shares with ours : to glorify in his representation on the earth the God who created us in his image, and who, seeing this image effaced by sin, has reproduced it in his Son. From this point of view, as "there is neither Jew nor Greek, neither bond nor free," so is there also "neither male nor female ; for we are all one in Christ Jesus." But, included in this common mission, which should be the first object of your ambition as well as of

---

* Compare Prov. vii. and viii. ; and ix. 1-12, with ix. 13-18.

ours, there is for you a special mission, adapted to your peculiar endowments. Depend not upon the world to teach you this mission ; it has never known it ; it is not able to comprehend it ; for it has ever reduced the question which concerns you to the meagre proportions of its own self-interest, or your vanity. It remains, then, that we refer it to the word of God ; to that word which, mainly occupied, as it shows itself to be, with " the one thing needful," resolves, in passing, all the great problems of humanity ; and, uniting example to precept, judges wisely concerning all things, because it judges spiritually.

I open to the first pages of the first book, so well named Genesis, because it reveals the secret of all existences in their wonderful origin, and throws out to us, as if spontaneously, the highest philosophy in primitive acts, recounted with the simplicity of primitive times. There, immediately after those few words, in which God sums up the general mission of humanity, "Let us make man in our image," do we discover another, in which he sums up in like manner the special mission of *woman*, before creating her in her turn : " It is not good that man should be alone ; I will make him an helpmeet for him." This applies to every woman, not simply to the one who is married ; for Eve is not only the wife of the first man, she is also the first woman : and, the representative of all her sex, as Adam is of ours, she presents in herself, as in a sort of miniature, a type of her sex.

Let us start out with this thought which presides at your very birth ; and let us take, as our guide in developing it, the inspired oracles of the old and new economy. We shall not be in danger of going astray in a path where God himself has marched before us. And well is it that your own heart will achieve the demonstration, and oblige you to say, while listening to the claims of God's word upon you ; yes, this is truly what I ought to be : this is truly what I ought to do.

" It is not good that man should be alone." Loaded with the gifts of God, he still wants something, of which he is himself ignorant, or of which he knows nothing except by a vague presentiment;—a helper "like to himself;" without which life is to him but a solitude, **and Eden** a desert. Endowed with a nature too communicative to **be self-sufficient, he** demands a partnership, a support, a complement, **and only** half lives while he lives alone. **Made to think, to talk, to love, his thought is** in search of *another* thought, **to stimulate it and to reveal it unto** itself; **his word dies away in sadness on the air, or awakens a** mere echo which does **violence to it, rather than** responds to it; **and his love knows not where to** fasten itself, and, **falling back upon himself, threatens to become a** devouring **self-love. His** whole being, in fine, aspires to another self,—but that other self **does not exist : "for Adam there was not found** a helpmeet." **The visible creatures which surround him are too far** *below* him; the invisible Being who **has given him life, too far** *above* him, to unite their condition **to his.** *Then,* God formed **woman, and the** great problem was solved. Behold here, what **Adam demanded;** that other self which is himself, **and at the same time** *not* **himself.** Woman is a companion whom **God has given to man to charm** his existence, and **to double it** by sharing it **with another. Her** vocation by birth is a vocation **of charity.**

To this vocation corresponds the *place* which God has assigned to woman. **It is not an inferior** place : woman **is not only a** helper for **man, but a helper "like to himself."*** She ought, then, to march along as **his equal, and it is only in this condition that** she can bring to him the assistance which he **requires. But it is,** nevertheless, **a** secondary and dependent place : for woman was formed **after man, made for man, in short,** taken from man. This last characteristic **speaks volumes to man.** Taken from him, "she is bone **of his bone and** flesh **of** his flesh," and so closely united **to him, that he** cannot depreciate her without depreciating **himself. But at the** same time, taken from him,

---

she owes to him the life which she breathes, and the name which she bears. By what right,—I ought to say with what *heart*,—can she dispute with him the first rank? Her position by birth is a position of humility. A vocation of charity in respect to man, in a position of humility next to man :—*This* is the mission of woman. As to the rest, that vocation and that position, revealed by the same acts, resulting from the same principle, are so inseparable in the formation of woman, that we may include them in the general idea of renunciation, bearing in turn upon self-will and self-glory.

This commentary upon Moses, I have taken from Saint Paul, recalling to the Corinthians the condition of woman, in order to justify his prohibition to her of praying or prophesying with the head uncovered. This subject does not require him to enlarge upon woman's vocation of charity : he merely indicates it in saying " the woman was created for the man."

But observe in what terms he explains her position of humility : " But I would have you know, that the head of every man is Christ ; and the head of the woman is the man ; and the head of Christ is God. The man is the image and glory of God : but the woman is the glory of the man. Neither was the man created for the woman ; but the woman for the man." Is not this the doctrine, which I just found in Genesis? But this doctrine the Apostle enforces with a rigor which would be out of place in any other mouth ; and for the general idea of dependence at which I pause, *he* substitutes the more precise one of subordination. He concludes from thence that woman ought, " because of the angels " who contemplate what is passing upon the earth, and particularly in the church, " to bear upon her head a mark of the authority" under which she is placed. Man, whose birth formed a part of that great work of creation which inspired the angelic songs of joy, being the image and glory of God, owes it to God to appear with the head lifted up to the view of the whole universe. But woman, whose formation is an event of the second scheme, and, so to speak, of a family character, being the glory of the man, owes it to him to remain hidden in a comparatively narrow inclosure as a modest spouse in her own home.

The intention of the Apostle is the more marked as the instructions which he gives here are intended for woman in rare cases. For it is only as an exception that a woman can be called to pray or prophesy before men. The order which God has established for a certain end he is free to modify so as the better to gain that end. We sometimes see that in promoting the good of man, a woman is called to depart from the way prescribed to her ; it may be to prophecy, as the women of Corinth, as the four daughters of Philip, the deacon, or as the mother of King Lemuel. It may be as Deborah, to judge a people, or even to preside over a mighty expedition. In such cases woman must obey, and she shall be blessed in her obedience : "Blessed above women shall Jael be, blessed shall she be above women in the tent." But then, as ever, aside from what is essential to the extraordinary ministry with which she is clothed, she should remain a woman, according to St. Paul, and, all inspired as she is to caution the man, should remember that she is "the glory of the man," and should withdraw herself from the eyes of the world.

Such being the order of creation, it remains to inquire if the primitive mission of woman was changed by the fall of our race, which disturbed so deeply the work of God. Satan commenced by beguiling the woman, after which he employed her to beguile man ; a doubly skillful move, by which he was most sure to succeed with her, because she is weaker than man, and close to man, and because she has greater power over him than he has over her. But has this sweet empire been given to her, that she may domineer over the conscience of man, become a snare to him rather than a support, and return to him for the life which she received from him, sin and death ? God punished her for her abandoned charity, by that supreme suffering without which she could not henceforth continue the race of man ; and for her unacknowledged humility, by abasing still lower her condition.

"Thy desires shall be unto thy husband, and he shall rule over thee." Woman is compelled to look to her husband for all that she desires—here is her increased dependence ; and to live under his authority—here is her dependence converted into submission.

Think not, meanwhile, that she ceases to be an "help-meet" unto him. Alas! when was this tender aid more needed? Such is the mercy of God, that the moment in which He humbles woman, is also the moment in which He confers upon her a ministry greater and more humane than ever. In order to elevate and reëstablish between the two sexes the disturbed equilibrium, it is by a virgin that He will one day give to man the longed-for Restorer, who shall destroy the works of the devil ; and the first name under which He announced his Son to the world is that of the "seed" of the woman : "And I will put enmity between thee and the woman, and between thy seed and her seed ; it shall bruise thy head, and thou shalt bruise his heel." Thus, the relations are not essentially changed by the fall ; the vocation of woman is still one of charity, and her position that of humility. Only everything has taken a more serious character ; the charity has become more spiritual, exercised in a more profound humility. Ashamed of herself, and anxious to reëstablish herself, woman lives henceforth but to repair the wrong which she had done to man in heaping upon him, with the consolation which can sweeten the present bitterness of sin, the warnings which may prevent its eternal bitterness.

Another commentary borrowed from St. Paul : "I will that women adorn themselves in modest apparel, with shamefaced-ness and sobriety ; not with broidered hair, or gold, or pearls, or costly array ; But (which becometh women professing godli-ness) with good works. Let the woman learn in silence, with all subjection. But I suffer not a woman to teach, nor to usurp authority over the man, but to be in silence ; For Adam was first formed, then Eve. And Adam was not deceived, but the woman being deceived was in the transgression. Notwithstand ing she shall be saved in childbearing, if they continue in faith and charity, and holiness with sobriety." Woman, says the Apostle here, was second in birth and first in sin—double reason why she should continue in an attitude of modesty, silence, and submission. Behold here, in no equivocal terms, the place of humility that we have already assigned to woman. But the Apostle would have her make it a place of honor by Christian beneficence. There is a chaste adorning which admirably befits her—that of good works;—*good works*, these are the tresses, the gems, the jewels, the adornings which give her beauty in the eyes of God and man. Nor is this all. Woman shall procure salvation for man, at the same time that she obtains it for herself, by the childbearing of the promised seed. This salvation a woman shall give to the world, in the fullness of time, by giving birth to the Saviour; but the woman, whoever she may be, will also give it to him in her way, who teaches him to know and love the Saviour. Here again is this mission of charity which we have assigned to woman, and which imposes upon her the obligation, we say rather which confers upon her the privilege, of consecrating herself with redoubled tenderness, not only to the consolation of suffering man, but also to the salvation of sinful man, whose attention she shall turn to Jesus Christ.

Woman is then, according to Scripture, which is to say according to God, since the creation, and more especially since the fall, a *companion* given to man to labor for his good, and above all for his spiritual good, in an attitude at once modest and submissive.

Thus Scripture instructs us; and nature teaches the same lessons. The task assigned by God to each half of the race discovers itself in their dispositions, reveals itself in their instincts. Consult, now, yourselves, and tell me why you were so created, if not for the mission which we have recognized as yours by the Word of God.

Your place, we have said, is a place of dependence and humility. Upon this point St. Paul hesitates not to appeal to the instinctive convictions of his readers, when, after forbidding a woman to pray or prophecy with her head uncovered, he adds : " Judge in yourselves ; is it comely that a woman pray unto God uncovered ? Doth not even nature itself teach you, that if a man have long hair it is a shame unto him ? But if a woman have long hair, it is a glory to her ; for her hair is given her for a covering ?" These principles appear so incontestable to the Apostle, that they cannot be denied, except by an unworthy spirit of chicanery which ought not to be entertained. " But if any man seem to be contentious, we have no such custom, neither the churches of God." Evidently, the long or short hair characterizes here a general and profound distinction between man and woman.

When man goeth forth from his house and gives himself to his labor until the evening, he chooses outward activity for his task, public life for his domain, and the world for his theatre. What do I say ? he presents himself in the sight of the angels, and places himself in affinity with the entire universe. He cannot carry too far the name and the image of that God whom he has a mission to represent, not only upon the earth, but before the whole creation. To resist the feeling which calls him to go forth, in order to shut himself up within the narrow circle of the domestic hearth, this would be on his part weakness, forgetfulness of himself, infidelity to his mission ; nothing more remains but to put a spindle into his hands and a distaff at his feet.

But it is altogether different with woman : the heart is her theatre ; the domestic life her sphere ; the in-door activity her work ; and the long hair with which the Apostle is pleased to see her covered, is an emblem of an entire existence hidden and silent, in the bosom of which she accomplishes most faithfully, and most honorably, the primary obligations of her sex. " Woman," says a great writer of the age, " is a flower which emits not its perfume except in the shade." To retire from notice, to remain quiet, to devote herself to her dependents, to keep the house, to govern her family, *this* is her modest ambition

2

If the wise man paints for us " a woman, noisy, and turbulent, appearing in the streets, whose feet abide not in the house," you will recall the woman to whom this applies.

Indeed, is not the humble sphere which we assign to woman, the one for which her whole being is predisposed and designed beforehand ? That more delicate conformation, but more frail ; that more rapid pulsation of her heart ; that keener nervous sensibility ; that exquisiteness of her organs, and even the delicacy of her features ; all contribute to make her, according to the expression of Peter, " a weaker vessel," and render her constitutionally unfit for stern and unyielding cares, for affairs of state, for the labors of the cabinet, for all that yields renown in the world.

And do not her intellectual powers hold her equally distinct ? It is sometimes asked whether they are equal to those of man. They are neither equal nor unequal, they are different, having been wisely adapted to a different end. For the work reserved to man, woman has faculties inferior to those of man, or rather she is not adapted to it. I speak here of the rule, not of the exceptions. That there may be among women some minds fitted for cares confined primarily to the other sex ; or that there may be for an ordinary woman some situations belonging to man, which she is obliged to fill in default of his doing it, I readily grant, provided these exceptions are clearly indicated by God, or demanded by the interests of humanity. After all, in the mission of woman, humility is but the means, charity is the end, to which all must be subordinated ; and why should not God, who has made exceptions of this nature in sacred history, also make them in general history ? Be that as it may, I leave the exceptions to God, and to the individual conscience ; and, jealous of discussing irritating, personal, or even disputed questions, I confine myself here to the rule.

Now, as a rule, that comprehensive glance into politics and science which embraces the world, that bold flight of metaphysics and of the lofty poetry which, transcending its limits, ventures into the void of thought and imagination, this is not the business of woman. *Language* even, above all ours (let us not sacrifice this useful remark to the fear of provoking a light smile), language, that simple philosophy of the people, often more profound than that of the schools, this sieve of the common reason, which, of all the bold expressions of the individual mind, allows only those to pass which respond to the good sense of all, proves this. It does not permit a woman to make herself notorious. It will not apply to her the word "man" accompanied by a feminine termination, except as an expression of ridicule or blame. The epithets taken from public life honor man, but dishonor woman in different degrees. To cite only those examples, which the delicacy of this place authorizes, endeavor to say, a " woman of science," a " great woman," a " woman of affairs," a " woman of state :" in like manner talk of a "*domestic* woman !"

But, on the contrary, while she acts within a narrow circle— narrow in extent, but vast in influence—where we exhort woman, with the Scriptures, to limit her action, she has faculties superior to those of man, or rather which belong to her alone There she finds her compensation, while she shows herself mis tress of the domain, and calls into use those secret resources which I should call *admirable*, were it not that a more tender feeling inspires me towards her and God who endowed her with them : that practical insight which we might say is all the more unerring because quick ; that glance which seems to prefer to be more brief that it may be more clear ; that art of penetrating into hearts by, I know not what subtle road, to us unknown and impracticable ; that incessant omnipresence of mind and body at all points at once ; that vigilance as exact as unperceived ; those numerous and complicated expedients of the domestic adminis- tration, always at hand ; access always open to every appeal ; and that perpetual audience given to all the world ; that freedom of action and of thought in the midst of bitter pains and accu- mulated embarrassments ; that elasticity shall I say ? or that indefatigable weakness ; that exquisite delicacy of feeling ; that tact so studied, if it were not instinctive ; that fidelity of perfection in little things ; that adroit industry to accomplish what she will with her fingers ; that charming grace with which she animates the sick, cheers the drooping, awakens the sleeping conscience, opens the heart long closed ; and, in fine, all the many things which we know not how to discern or to accomplish without borrowing her hands or her eyes.

But after all, to what advantage is the statement of these facts, when we can appeal to an inward sentiment, planted by the Creator in the depths of your soul, and which has preceded all personal reflections, all the announcements of others, and even the testimony of the Book of God ? That chastity, that modesty, to which a woman never ceases to pretend, even after she has ceased to keep it—what is this but the proof engraven upon your heart, and transferred irresistibly to your countenance, that order, repose, honor, is found for you in an attitude of dependence and reservedness ? Dependence and reserve ; the right of which never appears more inalienable than in certain delicate occasions, when the same nature is making a cruel play in efforts of one part against the other, without either obtaining a victory. What woman, conscious of this dependence, has not wished, at least sometimes, the arm of a man for support, and for a shelter the name of a man ? But what woman also, in the feeling of this reserve, keeps not her wish within her own bosom, waiting till she is sought—waiting if need be till death, hastened perhaps by the inward fire with which she would rather be consumed than let it outwardly be known ?

This invariable order of marriage, which assigns the initiative to man, and the appearance of which you will not allow, is not a refinement of civilization, nor even a scrupulousness of the gospel : it is a law imposed by woman, upon all times, without excepting the most barbarous, and upon all nations, without excepting the most savage. I exaggerate. I have a vague remembrance of having read, in I know not what account of a distant voyage, that a people was discovered among whom woman takes the first step. Only, it is a country where she is degraded to the rank of the brute, and men are cannibals.

If nature is in harmony with revelation as to the *place* which becomes your sex— one of humility—it is equally so as to the *task* belonging to it—one of charity. Here again, here above all, that which is within the *Book* is confirmed by that which is within the *heart* of woman. For what is your natural inclination, if it is not *to love*? I forget not, in speaking in this way, that your sex is no more exempt than ours from the egotism which reigns in fallen humanity. But try to recollect yourself, and to withdraw into the depths of your being; penetrate beyond the ravages which sin has made there, even to that primitive ground (allow me the expression), which came forth from the hands of God, and tell me if love is not its essence and base. "More superficial than man in everything else;" a Christian thinker has said, "woman is more profound in love." We are familiar with that touching word of a woman. "Love is only an episode in the life of man, it is an entire history in the life of woman."* She might have said yet more : it is her whole being. Your origin itself, as Moses narrates it, sufficiently indicates this. That of man, formed from inanimate dust, has something more supernatural, more striking, more magnificent about it ; that of woman, taken from the throbbing flesh of sleeping man, seems more intimate, more loving, more tender.

But, as regards love, it is less the *degree* than the *character* that is important. Love is the depth of your being, but what love? Think, and you will find it to be that which most predisposes you to the vocation of benevolence assigned you by the Scriptures. There are two kinds of love : the love which receives, and the love which gives ; the first delights itself in the feeling which it inspires, and the sacrifices which it obtains The second satisfies itself in the sentiment which it approves, and in the sacrifices it accomplishes. These two kinds of love

* Madame De Staël.

hardly exist separate, and woman knows them both. But do I presume too much of her heart in thinking that with her the *second* predominates ; and that her device, borrowed from the unselfish love of which our Saviour has given us an example, is this : "It is more blessed to give than to receive ?" To be loved, I know it well, my sisters, is the joy of your heart; alas ! a joy perhaps refused : but to love, to devote yourselves out of love, is the need of your soul, it is the law even of your exist ence, and a law which no one should hinder you from obeying Man also knows how to love and must love ; it is in love, that St. Paul sums up all the obligations that married life imposes upon him : "Husbands love your wives," as he sums up those of woman in submission: "Wives submit yourselves unto your own husbands." But we are now occupied, not with the faculty of the obligation, but with the inclination.

Now love, it must be acknowledged, is less spontaneous, less disinterested in man than in woman. It is less spontaneous. Man often needs to conquer himself before he can love ; woman only needs to listen and to follow her inward impulse. This is the reason, perhaps, why Scripture, which frequently commands the husband to love, refrains from enforcing it upon the wife, as if she were competent, from her nature to supply it. But above all, it is more *disinterested*. Man loves woman more for himself than for her ; woman loves man less for herself than for him. Man, because he is not sufficient unto himself, loves her whom God has given to him : woman, because she feels herself impelled to love him whom God has given to her. If solitude depresses man, it is because life has no charm apart from an "helpmeet ;" if woman dreads to live alone, it is because life is without an aim, unless she can be an "helpmeet" to some one. We might say of her, if I may be permitted this reference for the sake of the serious spirit in which I hazard it, We love her because she first loved us.

Moreover, what is the sentiment which has become among all nations and languages of the earth, the type of a love at once pure, living and profound ? It is woman's love, maternal love ; maternal love, which exhausts life without exhausting itself, and which, after suffering everything, labors by day, and watches by night, considering itself sufficiently repaid with a caress or a smile ; maternal love, celebrated as well by moralists as by poets, but whose praises, we believe, may be included in this one : that paternal love, itself, gives it the preëminence. What do I say ? This same love is that of which God made choice, when he sought among all human affections an emblem for the love which he himself bears to his people. " But Zion said, the Lord hath forsaken me, and my Lord hath forgotten me." We might expect to see our Father in Heaven replying to this doubt which offends him, by making an appeal to the love of a father for his child. But no, to a mother's love he appeals ; and to this mother he gives the name of *woman*, as if to give honor to the treasure of riches deposited in the heart of woman, found in the heart of the mother : " Can a woman forget her sucking child, that she should not have compassion on the son of her womb ? yea, they may forget, yet will I not forget thee."

But if such is the heart of woman, how can we fail to recognize a soil prepared expressly for this vocation of charity, which the Scriptures assign to you close to man ? Love not only inspires woman with a desire to furnish this career of devotion, but it also gives her the *courage* for it. *Courage*, that is the word. Yes, at the risk of seeming to advance a paradox ; I was about to say there is a kind of courage, and that which is the most necessary to do good, which impels your sex much farther than ours. I speak not of active courage ; here man excels you, and ought to excel. You yield to him without regret the merit of an intrepidity which would ill become your sex : and a man of spirit has dared to say, and that without violating the truth, that " women affect fear as men do courage." I speak of passive courage, which is more constantly required than any other in the daily and humble practice of good works, and of which woman furnishes the most beautiful examples. Man knows best how to *do*—woman, best how to *endure*. Man is more *enterprising*, woman more *patient*; man more *bold*, woman more *strong*. Would you be convinced of it? Behold her in that sorrow of sorrows reserved to her sex, at the cost of which is human life; see her and compare her with man, in solitude, in sickness, in poverty, in widowhood, in oppression, in secret martyrdom. I say designedly *secret* martyrdom; for in public martyrdom, man maintains himself in the rank of honor by the grandeur of the theatre; but, when it comes to that martyrdom cautiously and cruelly hidden in the subterranean cells of the inquisition, be assured the advantage is on the side of woman. God knew all this, when he portioned out life so that woman should have more of sufferings and less of pleasure than man; at least if we do not place in the first rank the pleasure of doing good. This pleasure woman enjoys even in suffering, and attaches herself, by suffering, to him for whom she suffers.

To a being thus formed, who dare dispute her vocation of self-sacrifice?—a vocation which her heart revealed to her ages before a line of Scripture was given to the world! Tell me not that Scripture alone holds woman to the special obligation imposed upon her to labor for man's spiritual good, by a holy charity which seeks God and eternity for him before everything else. Admirable to behold! nature has provided for it: not, it is true, sufficiently to make up for the teachings of revelation, but enough to make up for their deficiency, enough to make them perceived. For who does not know that woman's keener sensibility, her more open heart, her more sensitive conscience, her less logical mind, her finer and more delicate temperament, render her more accessible to piety, while, at the same time, her occupations being less abstruse, less continuous, less absorbing, than ours, leave her more leisure for prayer and freedom for the service of God? Who knows not also that the first conditions of success in the spiritual mission which everything contributes to mark out for her, are found less in activity, in word, in direct action, which man almost entirely appropriates to himself, than in that penetrating influence of example, of silence, of self-forgetfulness, which is peculiar to the woman who is truly a woman ?

Yes, we declare it boldly, if Scripture is not right, if woman was not made for a mission of charity in humility, nature has missed its aim ; for woman has been called to one work and prepared for another.

Yet understand us aright : I have not entered this place to flatter woman, but to sanctify her. In saying that nature has prepared you for the duty which Scripture imposes upon you, I have not meant to say that you are, in your natural state, capable of fulfilling it. By one of those strange contradictions which the fall has introduced into our race, troubling the work of creation without destroying it, woman is at the same time prepared and *unprepared* for her vocation : prepared, inasmuch as she possesses peculiar qualities which wondrously adapt themselves to it : unprepared, inasmuch as she has other qualities which interfere with it. " It is the enemy who has done this." In the same heart where the hand of God deposited the precious germs of a life conformed to the mission of woman, Satan has secretly sowed those noxious germs which choke, or neutralize, the first. He has done more. He has sought with his infernal skill, to corrupt these healthful germs in your heart, and to gather from good seed evil fruit.

Yes, these precious resources with which the Creator has endowed you to accomplish your work, the tempter knows how to convert into obstacles to this same work. Under his mysterious and formidable influence, we see this activity degenerate into restlessness ; this vigilance into curiosity ; this tact into artifice ; this penetration into temerity ; this promptness into unsteadiness ; this gracefulness into coquetry ; this taste into studied eloquence ; this versatility into caprice ; this aptness into presumption ; this influence into intrigue ; this power into domination ; this sensitiveness into irritability ; this power of loving into jealousy ; this necessity of being useful, into a passion to please.

The two principal tendencies which we have recognized in woman, humility and charity, have been perverted. The same mental peculiarity which assigns to her the narrow circle of home as her sphere, inclines her to take small views of things, and to centre her attention upon a single point, with a strength proportioned to the narrowness of the field which she embraces; and, little accustomed to doubt either of things or of herself, impatient of contradiction for want of believing more than she can understand, she enters insensibly upon a way of haughtiness by a road which ought to lead to humility. And then this same necessity of the heart which impels her to love and to self-devotement, exposes her to the danger of self-seeking, even in self-forgetfulness, and of carrying this renunciation to extremes—hardly willing that good should be done unless she can have a hand in it; jealous of the man she would help and please without rivalry; envious of the woman who also aspires to help and please; jealous, envious—note it well—from very strength of love, but a love transformed into passion and self-will in the dread laboratory of the tempter! Then woman, whom we cheerfully believe superior to man in spiritual things, if the essence of holiness is love, and the essence of love sacrifice, applies to evil noble instincts, which might enable her to excel in goodness, and delivers herself up to sin with an *abandon*, at the same time energetic and heedless, such as man hardly understands; carrying to a greater extent than he, vain glory, egotism, avarice, intemperance, anger, hatred, cruelty, love of the world, and forgetfulness of God, as if she would justify the old adage, "the greater the height the greater the fall." The heart of woman is the richest treasure upon earth; but if it is not *God's* treasure, it becomes the treasure of the devil; and one might be tempted sometimes to think that instead of having been given by God to man to be an "helpmeet" to him, the devil formed her, saying, it is not good that man should be alone; I will make a *snare* for him.

Accuse me not of slandering woman. I no more calumniate

her now than I flattered her a moment since. I spoke then, and speak still, according to the Bible. The Scriptures, which delineate with so much complacency the graces of woman and her humble virtues, present her faults and wanderings with a vividness unusual to them, and which they seem to reserve for this subject alone. St. Paul knows no worse scourge for the church than these women whom he describes in his first Epistle to Timothy. "For of this sort are they which creep into houses, and lead captive silly women laden with sins, led away with divers lusts, ever learning, and never able to come to the knowledge of the truth." In the same book of Proverbs, which closes with a sublime description of the virtuous woman, Solomon overwhelms with the strokes of his bitter and almost satirical eloquence, not only the abandoned woman, whose murderous work no one has described with a more holy horror (ye young, ponder his maxims!) but every woman unfaithful to the mission which she has received of God. The foolish woman, "who plucketh down her house with her hands;" the brawling woman whose companionship is more grievous than "to dwell in the corner of the house-top, or in a desert land;" the vicious woman, "who is as rottenness in the bones of her husband;" the odious woman who is "one of the four things which disquiet the earth;" the fair woman without discretion, whose beauty is as "a jewel in a swine's snout;" the contentious woman, "this continual dropping in a very rainy day; whosoever hideth her hideth the wind, and the ointment of his right hand which betrayeth itself." This same Solomon, in old age, gathering up the remembrances of his whole life, confesses that he had vainly sought a woman after his own heart. "And I find more bitter than death the woman whose heart is snares and nets, and her hands as bands; whoso pleaseth God shall escape from her, but the sinner shall be taken by her. Behold this have I found, saith the preacher, counting one by one to find out the account, which yet my soul seeketh, but I find not; one man among a thousand have I found, but a woman among all those have I not found.'

These astonishing declarations the Bible confirms and completes by its narratives, which are so many lessons. After explaining by Eve the entrance of sin into the world, it explains to us by Adah and Zillah, Lamech the first polygamist and blasphemer; by the daughters of men ensnaring the sons of God, the corruption of the earth and the deluge; by Hagar, the faith, the charity, and peace of Abraham for a time disturbed; by the women of the house of Laban, the faithfulness of Jacob for long time concealed; by Judith and Bashemath, the profane indifference of Esau; by the revenge of an adulterous wife, the injustice of Potiphar; by the daughters of Moab, the most terrible plagues of Israel in the desert, and by the daughters of Canaan, her wickedness and idolatry after the conquest; by Delilah, the shameful humiliation of Samson; by the companion of the Levite of Ephraim, a whole tribe cut off; by Bathsheba, David ceasing to be David; by strange women, Solomon serving other gods, and gathering from fall after fall the warnings which he would at a later period give to the world; by Jezebel, wicked Ahab, perjurer and murderer; by Athaliah, the kings of Judah following in the way of the kings of Israel; by Herodias, Herod beheading John the Baptist in spite of himself; by the Jewish women, Paul and Barnabas persecuted and driven from Antioch; by the prophetic women of the Apocalypse, the corruption of the whole earth. Holy liberty of the Scriptures which declare equally the good and evil, not to exalt human nature nor to humiliate it, but to give glory to God who creates the good and repairs the evil! This heart of woman, so ardent but so passionate, so tender but so jealous, so delicate but so susceptible, so impulsive but so hasty, so sensitive but so irritable, so strong but so weak, so good but so bad, must be subdued and transformed, in order that the sap of life which inundates it, may return to its legitimate course, diffusing itself wholly in the flowers of humility and the fruits of charity!

Subdued and *transformed* : but by whom? Ah! from whom could you expect this grace but from the Son of God, who, not content with having, through the organ of his inspired servants, restored your place and revealed your mission, has come Himself to show you the ideal of it in His life, and to open for you the way to it by His cross? Jesus living, perfect type of the gentle virtues as of the strong, is an example for woman as for man; and Jesus crucified, sole victim who expiates sin, is the only source of this holy love which, varying merely in the application, frees from sin both man and woman. But, between man and woman, if Jesus could sooner find access on the one side than on the other, would it not be on the part of woman? He, who is love; He, who "came not to be ministered unto, but to minister;" He, who satisfied himself only in privation and sacrifice; He, in fine, who took upon Him our nature in order to ascribe the highest charity in the most profound humility?

Am I mistaken, my sisters (it is for you to say), am I mistaken in thinking that there is nothing upon earth more in sympathy with Jesus Christ than the heart of woman? Superfluous question! Ah, no, I am not deceived, or your heart would deny all its instincts! The Christian faith, so truly founded in the depths of humanity that it is not wonderful only because common, adapts itself so marvellously to all the needs of your moral being, that you cannot be truly woman except upon condition of receiving the Gospel. The Christian woman is not only the best of women, but at the same time most truly a woman. O, you, then, who would accomplish the humble and benevolent mission of your sex—*beneath the cross, or never!*

Indeed, my dear sisters, the first aid which man has a right to expect from you is spiritual aid. It is little to be indebted to you for the consolation of this life of a day, if he owes not to you, so far as it is in your power, the possession of eternal life. Not only that true charity, which subordinates time to eternity, demands it of you, but justice itself, as we have shown from the Scriptures. Your sex has an original wrong to repair towards ours, and a spiritual wrong. That with which we reproach you in the fall where we have followed you, if we feel not bound to restrict our reproaches to ourselves, is not that death which you have introduced into the world, neither that embittered life which your sympathy even cannot always alleviate—it is a much greater evil, the only real and absolute evil—*Sin*, which the first man was doubtless inexcusable in committing, but which he was beguiled to commit by woman.

Imagine Eve kneeling with Adam beside the corpse of one son murdered by the other, whom the divine curse drives far out upon the wild and solitary earth. In sight of the visible and present fruits of sin, and with the thoughts of its invisible and future results, if the tender look of Adam said not to Eve, Give me back the favor of my God! give me back my peace with myself! give me back the days of Eden, and my sweet innocence, and my holy love for the Saviour and for thee!— doubt not that SHE said all this to herself! To her, it seemed very little to heap upon him the consolations of earth, if she could not bring to him those of Heaven; and, unable to repair the wrong she had done him, she urges, she implores him to turn his weeping eyes to the Deliverer promised to repair all, to reëstablish all, and to open to the fallen but reconciled race, a second Eden more beautiful than that to which the sword of the cherubims henceforth forbade entrance. If such are the sentiments of Eve, let her be blessed, although she be Eve! With this heart, Eve approximates Mary; and in the woman who ruined the world by sin, I discover already the woman who will save it by giving to it the Saviour.

Well, now, this that she would do, do yourselves. Though no one of you has been an Eve to man, yet be each of you a Mary to him, and give him a Saviour! This, this is your task! But, if you respond not to it, refusing to pass your life in the exercise of beneficence, you shall fail of your calling; and, after having been saluted of man by the name of "good woman," "deaconess," or "sister of charity," you shall be accounted of God, "as sounding brass and a tinkling cymbal!" But, how can you give the Saviour to others, if you do not possess Him in your own heart ? Women who hear me, yet again—*beneath the cross, or never !*

We say nothing of those holy women of the Old Testament, who died in faith before the coming of the Saviour, " not having received the promises, but having seen them afar off and embraced them :" neither of the pious Sarah nor of the modest Rebekah, nor of the tender Rachel, nor of the heroic Deborah, nor of the humble Ruth, nor of the sweet wife of Elkanah, nor of the prudent Abigail, nor of the intrepid Rizpah, nor of the retiring Shunamite. We confine ourselves to the women of the New Testament.

Beneath the cross, Mary, more touching now than at the cradle, offering herself without a murmur to the sword which pierces her soul, associates herself with the sacrifice of her son by a love more sublime than any other after that of the adorable Son, and presents to us a type of the Christian woman, who knows not how to aid and to love but in keeping her eyes fixed upon " Jesus and him crucified." Beneath the cross, Anna the prophetess, type of the faithful woman, gives glory first, in this same temple, where " she served God day and night with fastings and prayers," to Him whom the aged Simon had confessed by the Spirit, and in spite of her fourscore and four years, renews the energy and activity of youth " to speak of Him unto all them that looked for redemption in Jerusalem." Beneath the cross, Mary of Bethany, type of the contemplative woman, eager for the one thing needful and jealous of that good part, sits now at the feet of Jesus and feeds in silence upon the word of life, and at another time, in the same silence, anoints those blessed feet with pure spikenard of great price, and wipes them with the hairs of her head, as if she could not find a token sufficiently tender of her respect and love. Beneath the cross, Martha, her sister, type of the active woman, sometimes lavishes her unwearied attentions upon a brother whom she loved, sometimes busies herself for the Saviour whom she adored, serving him in every day life, invoking His aid in bitter suffering, and blessing Him in the joy of deliverance. Beneath the cross, the Canaanitish mother, type of the persevering woman, surpassing in faith and light those apostles whom she wearies with her cries, triumphs over the silence, refusal, disdain even, by which the Lord himself seems to contend against her invincible prayer, and, wrests from him at last, with the cure so much desired, the most brilliant homage that any child of Adam ever obtained : " O woman, great is thy faith ! be it unto thee as thou wilt." Beneath the cross, Mary Magdalene, freed from seven devils, type of the grateful woman, surpassing these same apostles in love and courage, after them at Calvary and before them at the sepulchre, is also chosen from among them all, the first to behold her Lord as He comes forth from the tomb, and charged to carry the good news of His resurrection to those who would announce it to the world. Beneath the cross, Dorcas " full of good works and alms deeds," type of the charitable woman, after a life consecrated to the relief of the poor and of the widows of Joppa, in her death shows what she was to the church by the void she left in it, and by the tears she caused to flow ; and, in the same spirit, Phebe, the deaconess of Cenchrea, " a succorer of many," and in particular of the Apostle Paul, gives birth in all succeeding times by her example to a multitude of deaconesses, clothed or not—it little signifies—with this official title before men. Beneath the cross, Priscilla, type of the servant of Jesus Christ, shares with Aquilla, her husband, many of those perils incurred to preserve to the church of the Gentiles their great missionary, or engages in those conversations by which the faith of the eloquent Apollos was enlightened and strengthened ; and, in the same spirit, Lydia hazards her life by opening her house to the apostles, which, transformed at once into a church, becomes the centre of evangelical charity in Philippi and Macedonia.

What more shall I say ? Shall I speak of Julia, and Lois, and Enodias, and Sintyche, and Mary, and Persis, and Salome, and Tryphena, and Tryphosa, and of the many women of the

Gospel, and of so many others who have followed in their steps, the Perpetuas, the Monicas, the Mary Calamys, and the Elizabeth Frys? Beneath the cross, with the Bible in hand—this Bible to which no human creature owes more than she, both in respect to the world and to Christ—beneath the cross—it is *there* that I love to see woman! Restored to God, to man, to herself, so worthy in her submission, so noble in her humility, so strong in her gentleness, gathering all the gifts she has received to consecrate them to the service of humanity with an ardor which we hardly know how to exhibit except in passion, she obliges us to confess that she who effaced our primitive holiness, is also she who now offers of it on this apostate earth, the brightest image.

O you who so well read our hearts, bear with me, because for a moment I have read yours. I have said enough, perhaps too much. You accept this mission at the hand of Jesus; you burn to fulfill it beneath the cross of Jesus. Come then, that passing from the principle to the application, I may show you how it can be accomplished in every condition ; and how woman can always —daughter, wife, or mother—be unto man an "helpmeet." You have considered the *mission* of woman, contemplate her *life;* this will be the subject of a second discourse.

I ought to close here to-day; but I am unwilling to leave this place without inquiring of the men who listen to me, how they regard the mission of woman, as I have exhibited it. Many, perhaps, have hardly been able to suppress a smile of incredulity, at hearing me assign to woman a sphere of action so humble and at the same time so elevated, since it calls her to apply, as one has said, "so great principles to so small duties." This smile may be explained by two opposite reasons : one places woman above the task to which I invite her, the other below it.

There are epochs and nations before which I might feel obliged to oppose the first of these impressions, and to defend against man the dignity of woman. This duty would be necessary, not only with the Pagans, both ancient and modern, but with many an elevated spirit, with many an eminent moralist nourished in the bosom of Christianity. To cite but one example, Kant, whom no contemporaneous philosopher has surpassed in the depth and energy of the moral sense, Kant, in his little book on "The Sentiment of the Beautiful," reserves to man the *noble virtues*, and leaves to woman only the *beautiful* virtues : by which he understands an agreeable, spontaneous virtue, exerted without effort. "Speak not to woman, says he, of duty, of obligation. Expect not from her sacrifices, nor generous victories over herself. You propose, for example, to give up part of your fortune to save a friend. Do not inform your wife of your purpose. Why check her lively gossip, and burden her bosom with a secret too weighty for it ?" What sayest thou to this, Christian woman ? One is ready to ask himself if the cautions of Kant with regard to woman, are much less humiliating to her than the abjectness in which paganism holds her ; and to combat language so stern and so haughty, it is sufficient to recall to man in default of what he owes to woman, what he owes to himself from whom she has been taken, and to God who has taken her from him.

Yet, in the full light of Christianity, in France, and in the ideas of the day, the danger of excess is on the other side. No more is claimed for woman against my doctrine, than has been done these sixty years past ; but it is claimed, not in the name of a worn-out gallantry, but in the name of systems and the prejudices of the day. One complains that I abase and sacrifice her, in assigning her a place so humble, instead of putting her on a level with man, and a path so self-denying, instead of exhorting her to live for herself. No, no : I promote, on the contrary, her true glory and best interests, because I oblige her to conform to the law of her creation, the first condition of all order and all repose for the creature. I no more degrade and sacrifice woman, in inviting her to live for charity in humility towards man, whose glory she is, than I abase and sacrifice man, who is the glory of God, in inviting him to "glorify God in his body and spirit which are his ;" no more than I abase and sacrifice the planet, in inviting it to continue in the modest path of its orbit, sole guaranty of its safety and harmony.

There is one who abases and sacrifices woman : it is this same world, sometimes frivolous, sometimes bold, which treacherously takes up her defence against me. You abase and sacrifice her whenever you entice her, to satisfy your egotism and glorify your theories, from the path which God has marked out for her, and in which we would keep her. You have abased and sacrificed her of late, in placing her upon the pedestal and man at her feet, in your romances, in your saloons, in your plays, because instead of the mission to aid and glorify man, you have substituted that of weakening and effeminating him. You abase and sacrifice her to-day, in seeking for another emancipation than that which she has received of the Gospel, in claiming for her the rights of man ; since for the mission which she can and ought to fulfill, you substitute one in which she cannot succeed, and to which she ought not to pretend. What idea then have you of woman, if you believe her willing to exchange the humble glory of accomplishing the mission which belongs to her, for the mortifying vanity of failing in that of another—satisfied with being an incomplete man, while she might be a complete woman ; and of losing her natural and legitimate influence in the sterile pursuits of an influence factitious and usurped? Nothing more remains to her than to regret the nature which God has given her, and to indulge this regret by begging without shame from our sex the name, the dress, and the gait of man. Doubt it not, I have the heart of woman on my side ; and if any one has smiled at hearing me exhibit her mission according to God, it is not she, I answer for her. What woman worthy of her name, has ever smiled when one has appealed to her spirit of renunciation and of sacrifice ? It is bread for her hunger, it is water for her thirst. What do I say? the woman worthy of her name ! Worthy or unworthy, every woman starts at these words of sympathy ; the heart of the worthy leaps for joy, and the unworthy is moved with bitterness. You even, who turn away from the way which I trace for you, confess it ; you think me right in the depths of your soul ; and in spite of all your words, you respect her while you murmur at her, if she follows my commands rather than yours, and you scorn her while flattering her, if she follows yours rather than mine.

Be that as it may, the greater part of those who hear me, I say it boldly, not content with admitting the principles which I have attempted to develop, appreciate and admire them. Let them learn then from this example to what a degree Scripture is true. For indeed, what have I done but interrogate it before you ? I confess, when I began to meditate upon the mission of woman, I was far from having upon this subject, so little studied, the precise and strong views which I entertain to-day. I had resolved to open the Bible, to listen to it, and to allow myself to be guided by it ; and I have been confounded at finding there, instead of some thoughts scattered throughout forty books and nineteen centuries, an entire doctrine, developing itself from book to book and from age to age, passing from the hand of prophet to apostle, as a work planned by one workman and transmitted by him to another to complete ; a doctrine, whose mission, plenitude, clearness, simplicity, brilliant in the midst of an ignorance profound and universal, excited in me a surprise which grew with meditation. For all this revealed itself to me by degrees ; the place assigned to woman in Scripture, limited at the first glance, continually enlarged itself before me. We must seek for woman in Scripture ; but once found, she appears there clothed with a ministry as beneficent as glorious. Her position there instructed me : I learned that such as she is in this book, she ought to be in life, great, but hidden. I say it boldly : of all religions and all systems, Scripture alone has known and understood woman. Alone, between the two opposite tendencies of the Southern and Germanic races, of antiquity and the middle ages, the one making her the slave of man, the other the arbiter of his destinies, it has spared her at the same time, "this excess of honor and this indignity." Alone in fine, by one of those combinations of truth in which the world only sees strange contradictions, it has at once restored to her her place and held her in silence, giving to her a work as much more noble as it is more humble, as much more loving as it is self-sacrificing.

Understand then, O man, the treasure which you possess in Scripture, and question it that you may gather from it the light which it spreads upon even those subjects which it does not seem to have intended to illuminate. Interrogate it, men of thought ; know if it does not retain concealed within its fertile recesses, waiting until your haughty pride shall abase itself to demand them of it, new revelations upon the plans of the Creator and the destinies of the creature, and the final solution of some of those problems which are the eternal despair of philosophy. Interrogate it, men of science ; know if our old earth, which has been obliged to open its bosom most profoundly to the most conscientious investigations, to show itself in perfect agreement with this biblical cosmogony to which one had opposed it with so much assurance, has not still some other secret to say to the genius of a Cuvier in favor of the inspiration of a Moses. Interrogate it, men of letters ; know if these sublime thoughts of poetry, the paintings so natural, the narrations so animated, the demonstrations so simple and so strong, that our greatest writers glory in imitating, without flattering themselves of ever equalling them, have not some salutary, some powerful regeneration in reserve for the ready, but premature, greedy, impure, still-born literature of our day. Interrogate it yourselves, men of state ; know if this divine constitution which has served as a model to modern legislation and created European civilization, holds not hidden within its unopened folds some yet unknown perfection for our proud age, and if it could not teach, for example, our magistracy, renowned in all the world, that the least that it can do for this Gospel which has founded all freedom, is to allow it to be itself free.

But, if Scripture has so many lessons upon subjects which hardly seem to occupy it, what will it not have to say upon *that* subject which is to it, and which ought to be also to each of us, the one thing needful? Oh! I beg you, interrogate it upon salvation. Interrogate it concerning sin and pardon, life and death, good and evil, heaven and hell. Woe to you, if your ears are too sensitive to hear this language! Yes, interrogate it upon heaven and hell; and you will find the only place where woman can accomplish her mission, is also the only one where you can yourselves find grace, peace and life. Beneath the cross, beneath the cross, all together, one in mind, one in heart! Beneath the cross to live, beneath the cross to die, beneath the cross to meet the judgment of the great day—happy in then recognizing in him who is our judge, him who has been our Saviour!

DISCOURSE II.

THE LIFE OF WOMAN.

"And the Lord God said: It is not good that the man should be alone: I will make him a helpmeet for him."—GENESIS ii. 18.

My dear Sisters:

My first discourse left you, I hope, convinced that your mission, according to the Bible, as well as according to nature, is one of charity in humility towards man ; and resolved to accomplish this mission in Jesus Christ who alone can prepare you for it. Are we then agreed as to principles ? Let us to-day pass to the application. Let us trace the mission of woman, in the *life* of woman : that is to say, let us see how this common mission can be realized by each of you (the Christian faith being taken for granted), according to the particular condition assigned of God.

I say, according to the condition in which God has placed you, and I insist upon this point to prevent a dangerous illusion. On hearing me exhibit the duties of woman in a position different from yours, you are tempted, perhaps, to whisper : Ah! if I were thus placed, with what devotion would I give myself to the work of loving and helping! Believe me, my sister, you may not only accomplish, with self-devotion, your mission as a woman in your present position, but you will acknowledge it to be the situation of all others, in which you can best accomplish it. Else why has God assigned it—He, "who makes all things work

47

together for the good of those that love Him?" You answer sadly, perhaps, that it is less God who has assigned you your place than your own will, and a will badly controlled. It may be, I admit (although I distrust the heart of woman in accusing her conscience); that you have come where you are, by a way which you cannot recall without regret or without repentance. Still, your place, as it is fixed to-day, is the one in which God wishes you to-day to be; and the best one possible for you, if you accept it at His hand, in a spirit of faith and submission. With Jesus Christ there is no more a condition without resources, than a soul without hope. Such is the power of the Gospel, that it reacts upon the whole course of life, and constrains a regretted past to take its place among those "all things," that work together for the good of them who love God. It is not position, but disposition, that is of importance with God, and the surest mark of a well regulated mind, is to accept our present position, as chosen by God, to promote our spiritual development. I take, therefore, your moral physiognomy just as it is, as the daguerreotype would take your natural physiognomy. The man to whom you ought to be an "helpmeet" is a husband, a son, a father, or a man, simply as man, apart from any individual relation. Your attitude towards him may either be that of equality, of superiority, of inferiority, or of independence; it matters little to the end which I propose. The only point of importance is, that you possess a true woman's heart; I would say a heart desirous of life not for yourself but for others; first, unquestionably for the Lord, according to the general mission you share with us, and next for man, agreeably to the special mission which occupies us, in these discourses.

Accordingly, the Scripture, content with exhibiting the works of holy women, whom it offers as models to their sex, does not trouble itself to explain their social or domestic condition, obliging us often to surmise it for ourselves. That Eunice was both wife and mother, that she might give to the Apostle of the Gentiles the most useful of his co-laborers; that Priscilla, as we may suppose, was wife but not mother, that she might follow her husband from place to place, and assist him in the service of the Gospel ; that Phœbe might not have been either wife or mother, so that she might remain free to carry from church to church her devotion, and her activity ; that concerning Dorcas the same thing may have been true,—this, with Scripture, was of secondary moment ; it is sufficient that in them all there was a faithful heart. The same heart which rendered a Dorcas faithful in the position of Dorcas, would have made her equally faithful in the position of Phœbe, of Priscilla, or of Eunice ; and the same heart which would render you unfaithful to your mission in your present position, would make you equally unfaithful in any other. But "although I thus speak, I am persuaded better things of you," my beloved sisters ; and it is in this firm confidence that I would inquire with you, how you can be for man, each in her place, an "helpmeet."

I penetrate at once to the heart of my subject, and take woman in her normal position, the one in which she was found as she came forth from the hands of God, that for which she was formed, that in which she can best accomplish her peculiar work, by a loving devotion in an humble equality—*marriage*. Married woman, that which woman is called to be for man, you are called to be for *one* man. God said, speaking of your husband : "It is not good that this man should be alone ; I will make an helpmeet for him :" and it is you whom He has given to him. If He did not guide you by His own hand to him, as Eve to Adam, He has done still better ; He has pronounced upon your union by the voice of His servants, a word of blessing, which gives it a holy character—what do I say ?—which makes of it a visible emblem of the invisible union of the Lord with His Church. Scripture alone would dare risk such a comparison, and only a Christian heart can comprehend it. But to what a height it elevates marriage with him who understands it ! And with what authority it clothes this double precept, which sums up so tenderly the obligations of the husband ; "Husbands, love

3

your wives, as **Christ also loved the** Church :" and so humbly those of women ; "Therefore, as the Church is subject unto Christ, so let the wives be to their own husbands in everything."

Perhaps, alas ! this word of blessing scarcely touched your heart when it was pronounced, the Lord having been the last consulted in the gift of your hand. But to-day, it regains its divine virtue, reanimated and renewed, as it were, by your faith, according to the power that we have recognized in the Gospel, to react even upon the past : and, provided you carry to-day into your married life the heart of a Christian woman, you may believe yourself truly chosen of God for your husband, and he for you, as was Eve for Adam, and Adam for Eve. As for him, I know not with what fidelity he fulfills his part of the obligation ; let him fulfill it or not, fulfill yours ; for to God we must all give account, not to man, and "each shall bear his own burden." Your mission, then, is no other than the general mission of woman, applied, and as it were concentrated, in your intercourse with your husband, and, if I dare so speak, carried to its highest perfection, by the closest and most individual of all relations. This position of humility, and this vocation of charity, which comprise the mission of woman, concentrate, gather up, upon one object : *then* shall you be what the married woman ought to be to her husband, a " helpmeet."

Freely and cheerfully assume towards your husband a humble, dependent, and submissive position. Is there here a spirit giddy enough to find in these words, food for the inexhaustible raillery with which this subject inspires the world ? Let it be understood, that I speak seriously for serious women, holily for holy women, and that I do not consider myself exempt from the duty of enforcing upon them the pure doctrine of God, because of puerile fear of exposing them to the ridicule of those who would seek in the church the curtains of the theatre, and who would judge this word, which must judge them at the last day. Yes, my sisters, whatever the sentiment or usages of society may be upon this subject, openly and frankly assume

towards your husbands a humble, dependent, submissive position. It is not *I* who demand it of you, it is God who commands you. "Wives," writes Paul to the Ephesians, "submit
yourselves unto your own husbands as unto the Lord ;" "for the
husband is the head of the wife, even as Christ is the head of
the church." That which he had said of man in relation to
woman, speaking to the Corinthians, "The man is the head of
the woman," he says here of the husband in relation to his
wife : it is the same doctrine, but this doctrine specially applied,
"Therefore as the church is subject unto Christ, so let the wife
see that she reverence her husband." St. Paul not only considers this submission one of the obligations of the married
woman, it is the chief obligation, including every other. Sometimes he names it alone, as here : sometimes he gives it the first
place, and subordinates to it all the rest. St. Peter expresses
the same thing : "Likewise ye wives, be in subjection to your
own husbands, that, if any obey not the word, they also may,
without the word, be won by the conversation of their wives ;
while they behold your chaste conversation coupled with fear."
"Whose adorning let it not be that outward adorning of plait-
ing the hair, and of wearing of gold, or of putting on of apparel. But let it be the hidden man of the heart, in that which
is not corruptible, even the ornament of a meek and quiet spirit,
which is in the sight of God of great price. For after this
manner in the old time, the holy women also, who trusted in
God adorned themselves, being in subjection unto their husbands ; even as Sara obeyed Abraham, calling him Lord : whose
daughters ye are, as long as ye do well, and are not afraid with
any amazement."

Doubt it not, the harmony and felicity of domestic life depend upon each one's holding this position. More than one
household which promised well, has been disturbed by confound-
ing duties which Scripture has carefully distinguished. We cannot with impunity depart from the divine arrangement. The
trouble which others give themselves to usurp the first rank,

give yourself to avoid this usurpation, **under** whatever skillful precautions, under whatever **tender** appearances it may disguise itself. Let **your husband be, next to God, the centre of** your existence ; **with your own name, sweetly lose in him your** own glory, and **your own will. Lose sight of yourself,** abide in silence, **avoid even the appearance of arrogance or** arbitrariness. Let it be your ambition to promote his praise, or rather to be yourself his praise, not by an outward *éclat* which depends not upon you either to give or to withhold, but by a conversation so irreproachable that all husbands may propose you for an example to their wives. Realize, in short, in its full meaning, this beautiful saying of Solomon, " A virtuous woman is a crown to her husband."

Modesty is not inaction. The Scriptures give you a place so humble, only that it may confide to you a work all the more beneficent. This special humility which it recommends to you in relation to your husband, is a pledge of the special charity with which you will devote yourself to his happiness. This home in which the Apostle would see you quietly remaining, he wishes you to make by your affection, by your presence, by your good government, by the care you bestow upon your children, a sanctuary of order, peace, and happiness, in which your husband may find, after the cares of business, his sweetest repose and favorite recreation. Let him so truly find it such, that he will not think of seeking elsewhere than with you, the satisfaction which he needs to dissipate his fatigues, to alleviate his pain, to calm his agitated spirits and to restore their elasticity. Let him find there, for I refuse you no way of being useful, let him find there, hidden in the bosom of home, wise counsels, salutary inspirations, which will follow him silently into public life, and which contribute their part in controlling the words of his lips, and the deeds of his hands, by motives superior to the passions and impulses of men at large. Let him find there, in short, all that can make him happy within, together with all that can render him useful without, so that, as he crosses the threshold of his door, to engage again in his noble labors, he shall utter to himself with gratitude towards you, and to God, who gave you to him, the touching words of Solomon, " Houses and riches are the inheritance of fathers, and a prudent wife is from the Lord." Happy if you can hear those words from his lips ! But no, that is not necessary : your conscience will tell you what he thinks. It will say to you, that when with gratitude he recalls to his remembrance all the good things he has received from God—fortune, health, family—the *first* and the *last* of his earthly treasures, that which he fears most to lose, is YOU.

Yet, let not your devotion be idolatry. Love and be loved in God. The most intimate of all relations ought to be also the most holy. The Gospel would never have seen in marriage a type of Christ and the church, if it had not anticipated there a sanctifying influence, exerted by each of the pair upon the other. For what knowest thou, O wife ! whether thou shalt save thy husband ? These serious words denote the grand obligation of marriage; that which the Apostle calls, for reasons given in my first discourse, the special obligation of woman. This loving, this penetrating, I had almost said irresistible influence, which God has placed in your hands, woe to you, if you know how to turn it to everything but its true use, the glory of God, and the salvation of your husband ! Are you happy in being united to a true disciple of Jesus Christ ? Hardly need I urge you, so sweet is the duty, to be to him a constant edification, never a snare. A faithful wife, sustaining the heart and strengthening the hands of a faithful husband for the conflicts of life, is a " helpmeet " in all her glory.

But I will suppose your husband, if not a stranger to the faith, at least floating between it and the unbelief of the natural heart—disturbed by the cares of business, carried away by the temptations of public life, and influenced by those of a skeptical and fault-finding spirit. To preserve him from so many snares, to gain him forever to the faith, he needs, perhaps, only to see it in action so near him, that he cannot overlook the reality of the facts, nor suspect the sincerity of the feeling. Do you not recognize this as your special vocation? Who but you will furnish him with this "demonstration of the spirit and of power," practical, winning, incontestable, which alone can make day within his soul? It is precisely for this kind of persuasion that you have been prepared by God, and no one else can supply your place.

Woman has not a mission as man, to preach the Saviour, and to reveal Him : she does even more ; she gives birth to Him by virtue of the Holy Spirit. She gives Him, all living, all complete. Instead of declaring Him by thought and word, she communicates Him by act, by sentiment, and, if we may so speak, by inspiration. She is not to preach the Gospel to her husband, but to insinuate it into him in her actions and her slightest words, in the pure and limpid depths of her being, in all the course of domestic life, making it all pervading, without *seeming* to place it anywhere. If we rely upon you for this precious influence, Christian woman, if we see in you the most efficient auxiliaries to our preaching, we only follow the example of St. Peter, whose thought I do but this moment develop. He recommends, as we have seen, "that wives be submissive to their own husbands," but why ? " that if any obey not the Word, they may also, without the Word, be won by the conversation of their wives, while they behold (literally, while they watch) your chaste conversation, coupled with fear." How is it possible to exalt higher the spiritual influence of the Christian woman ? She supplies the place of the Divine Word to her husband, when her conversation, watched by means of the conjugal intimacy, reveals to him the hidden power with which the Gospel operates in her heart. A man must be truly blind, truly hardened, not to yield at last to the daily spectacle of living and true piety which he beholds in his wife, one of which he gathers fruit so sweet that one is ready to ask, which has the most to gain from it, either he for the present life, or she for the life to come ?

However it may be, woman, be faithful, and await the fidelity of God. You envy the woman who hears her husband saying to himself, "a prudent wife is from the Lord." But what passes, think you, in the heart of that other woman, who some day involuntarily concealed, sees her husband fall upon his knees, exclaiming : "My God! I bless thee for having given me a faithful wife, who has led me to thyself!" Perhaps this testimony will be refused you upon earth ; but how many men render it at the tomb of a wife, whom henceforth they seek in a better world ! How many men at the last day, when every veil is raised, will say to their Judge, in the most profound sense of the word : It is good for me that I was not alone !

Would you see all that I have said, all that might be said upon this subject, summed up in a few lines? Read the description of a virtuous woman, guiding her son in the choice of a wife. If the general tone, or some detached features of this picture, seem to you to contrast with the Christian woman as painted in the Gospel, forget not that it is taken from the Old Testament, in which the splendor of visible things serves as an emblem of invisible, spiritual beauty. "Who can find a virtuous woman ? for her price is far above rubies. The heart of her husband doth safely trust in her, so that he shall have no need of spoil. She will do him good, and not evil, all the days of her life. She seeketh wool and flax, and worketh willingly with her hands. She is like the merchant's ships ; she bringeth her food from afar. She riseth, also, while it is yet night, and giveth meat to her household, and a portion to her maidens. She considereth a field, and buyeth it : with the fruit of her hands she planteth a vineyard. She girdeth her loins with strength, and strengtheneth her arms. She perceiveth that her merchandise is good : her candle goeth not out by night. She layeth her hands to the spindles, and her hands hold the distaff She stretcheth out her hand to the poor ; yea, she reacheth forth her hand to the needy. She is not afraid of the snow for her household ; for all her household are clothed with scarlet

She maketh herself coverings of tapestry ; her clothing is silk and purple. Her husband is known in the gates, where he sitteth among the elders of the land. She maketh fine linen, and selleth it, and delivereth girdles unto the merchant. Strength and honor are her clothing, and she shall rejoice in time to come. She openeth her mouth with wisdom, and in her tongue is the law of kindness. Her children rise up, and call her blessed ; her husband also, and he praiseth her. Many daughters have done virtuously, but thou excellest them all. Favor is deceitful, and beauty vain ; but a woman that feareth the Lord, she shall be praised !"

Behold a woman without humility, who, instead of being the glory of her husband, only seeks in her union with him the means of glorifying herself ; who loves to eclipse him, by whom she should desire to be eclipsed, and who finds less pleasure in his smile of approbation than in the flattery of strangers ; a woman without charity, who abandons to mercenary hands the first interests of her house, and of her children ; who even sets an example to her husband to seek his pleasures away from home ; who contradicts him with bitterness, and roughly magnifies her wrongs, supposed or real ; restless and slovenly at home, gracious and kind as soon as she crosses the threshold of her door ; a woman without piety, ready to say of her husband, as Cain of Abel, "Am I his keeper ?" or only using her influence to turn him from the Saviour, like the wife of Jehoram, whose fatal influence the Holy Spirit points out in a few words : "Jehoram walketh in the way of the kings of Israel, like as did the house of Ahab : for he had the daughter of Ahab to wife"—a woman, in short, who compels her husband to groan in secret over the day when he was blind enough to seek her hand, until he shall measure before the tribunal of God, the whole extent of the evil she has done him for eternity !

O, ye who recognize in this picture some features of your own image, what shall I say to you ? Change your course !—become the woman acceptable to God—acceptable to the heart of man !

Change you may, for to this is needful neither youth, nor beauty, nor superior mind : it is only needful that you become a CHRISTIAN woman !

But since, at this day, woman enters not as Eve, at birth, into marriage, let us take her at that point of her development where she commences to prepare herself for her future work, and address ourselves to the young girl. Understand well, my young sister, what determines the character of your condition and its privileges. The race to be run is yet all before you ; and while those who have preceded you cannot look back without seeing much to deplore, to repair, to efface if it were possible, let nothing prevent you from reserving for your mission as woman, under the blessing of God, all that you have of time, resources, life. Under the blessing of God, I have said ; for, without Him, what are our most sincere resolutions, and, above all, the resolutions of a young girl ? Nowhere is the spirit more willing, nowhere is the flesh more weak. The wind plays not more capriciously with the dust, than the tempter with the projects of fidelity which you form for the future. Alas ! how many women at your age, formed theirs, whose actual life responds so little to your ideal—still less to theirs ! Far be it from me, my dear daughter, to discourage your generous promises ; I would only that you carry them to the foot of the cross, and shelter your weakness under the strength of the Omnipotent God. Then, I will deliver myself without fear, to the pleasure of contemplating in you the living type of hope ; of hope, this incomparable grace of youth, exalted all the more in the young girl, by her greater influence, and by her hidden destiny. For, who ever thought of personifying hope, otherwise than under the traits of a young girl ?

In this uncertain expectation, it is asked, if the young girl should prepare herself for the general mission of humanity, or for the special mission of the wife. Authors who have treated the subject of the education of girls, are divided upon this point. We say, relying upon Scripture, either answer is incomplete

Yes, without doubt, the young daughter should be prepared for
the general mission of humanity, which is to glorify God, who
created us in His image ; but this preparation is not sufficient ;
for, independently of the general mission which she shares with
man, woman has yet a special mission, which is the subject of
these discourses. Yes, the young girl must be prepared for the
special mission of the wife, which is to be an "helpmeet" to one
man in particular, since, according to the ordinary course of
things, she will be married. But this preparation should not be
exclusive ; for every woman is not called to marriage, and a
special education in this sense is in danger of missing its aim.
Here is the secret of reconciling all. Together with the general
mission of humanity, and the special mission of the wife, there is
for woman a third mission, special as to the first, general as to
the second, peculiar to woman, and common to all women—that
which I have explained from the Scriptures, which Moses reveals
in calling woman an "helpmeet" to man, and Paul, in calling
her "the glory of man." I would prepare the young girl for
this mission, without losing sight either of the supreme necessity
of glorifying God, or the natural eventuality of marriage. She
will then be prepared for both, by the intermediate preparation
which we claim, if she is what she ought to be.

Let young girls look carefully to the spirit of this preparation,
and let their mothers look to it for them. Since a woman's
highest excellence, next to the fear of God, is in the humble virtues of domestic life, the first care of a daughter, after that given
to her soul, should be to cultivate these inward and hidden virtues. I hardly need say to her, abstain from all that has the
appearance of evil ; carefully avoid pictures, plays, readings,
which can bring the slightest stain upon the purity of your
heart. But it will be less superfluous perhaps to say to her :
Mistrust the maxims of an egotistical and sensual age, which,
seeking in a young girl merely an agreeable plaything to divert
the melancholy which devours it, decks her in haste with brilliant
charms, instead of adorning her by slow degress with useful

graces. A vain brilliancy, a precocious development, knowledge badly directed, the memory burdened without regard to the intellect, gifts of imagination placed in the first rank ; this is the tinsel which the education of the day prefers for our daughters, to the pure gold of an instruction, solid, beneficent, precious in the sight of God and man. This tinsel, I firmly believe, my young sisters, is meant by the world for itself, whereas there should be pure gold for you and for your house.

I do not exclude you from any serious study, because I would not deny you any legitimate mode of influence. Give yourself without scruple to the culture of the imagination, of literature, of art, which, in developing an essential and too much neglected side of the human mind, will be an aid to the beneficial influence you wish to exercise, by adding to your capacity to please. Only put everything in its right place, and arrange your subjects of study according to the demands of your mission. Above all, be yourselves, be women, and never sacrifice to the false tastes of man the distinctive occupations of your sex. Tell me not of a young girl, who can win the applauses of all, at a concert, but who knows not how to hold a needle, or to make herself useful at home ! Lastly, I may include all my exhortations in one : let the heart be well governed, and let it control the life. By the Word of God and prayer, nourish within you this humility, this charity, which are the peculiar graces of woman, and the first conditions of her mission. The world itself could teach you, in default of the gospel and your own conscience, that if humility and charity were banished from the earth, they ought to find a last refuge in the heart of a young girl. As for me, if I love to see woman beneath the cross, with Bible in hand, a young girl, above all, I love to contemplate in this attitude, preparing herself for a future career known only to God, but which can be faithfully accomplished, whatever it may be, only beneath the cross, with Bible in hand.

One word more, for you and your families, but a word without development, upon a matter as grave as it is delicate. Let it be understood, that deciding resolutely to marry only in the Lord, you will give your hand to none but a moral, religious man, capable of entering with you into the Christian idea of marriage. By this entirely passive resolution, not only ill-assorted unions might be prevented, but also a happy reaction would be exerted upon the manners and principles of society, and men would find in modest girls the most efficient "helpmeets," to say nothing of the most powerful reformers.

Yet you need not await this most uncertain event, to be a "helpmeet" unto man. You can be such now, believing that the accomplishment of your present task is the best guaranty for that of the future. Your actual position demands, it is true, a peculiar reserve. With one, it is the humble equality of the wife, with another, the respectful inferiority of the daughter who has hardly passed the period of childhood : but this reserve permits, it even encourages, a kind of useful activity proper to your age. True humility prompts true charity ; and the flowers which hide beneath the grass their delicate colors, are those which emit the most fragrant perfume. How many ways there are for you to do good, without going beyond the domestic circle ! You have a school, a parish ready for you, in the young children of the family, whose education already you share with their mother. Contrary to the common law of prophets, you are called to exercise your humble ministry "in your own country, and your own house." Do you realize all you can be to this young brother, over whom your advantage of some years gives you a kind of influence of your own, whose confidence in you is all the more free, because unrestrained by deference ? Like that loving sister, who watches beside the floating cradle confided to the Nile, when prudence permits not a mother to reveal herself : who, on account of her youth is employed without exciting suspicion, to give to Moses a faithful mother for nurse at the moment when God gives him an unfaithful princess for a mother, and who then disappears from the scene, content with having helped a brother forward into the world, whose name, one day, must eclipse her own—has God placed you beside your brother, to give him such help as he can find nowhere else, and which he would be least suspected of receiving. Beside him, yesterday, you taught him to read, or to-day, you inspire him with un-quenchable ardor in his fatiguing studies ; and to-morrow, you counsel him in his choice of a profession, or in that of a wife.

But those for whom you can do most, are those to whom, next to God, you owe all. Who can supply to the father and mother that daughter's place, who, timid and silent with strangers, is at home full of that sweetness and fire, which, at this age, are the marvellous combinations of nature ? Who will supply to them her light and caressing hands, her prompt and subtle spirit, her tender and submissive affection, her firm and simple piety, to lighten the burden of years, to soothe their pains, to dissipate their anxieties, to anticipate their wishes, to gladden their hearts, to comfort their souls, as if she longed to give back to them the life she received from them ? This young daughter that you see hiding herself behind her mother, blushing at the attention she attracts in spite of herself, do you not know, that she is more than the ornament of the house ? She is its joy, its life, its pillar, or if you prefer a term borrowed from Scripture, she is its corner stone ; " that our daughters may be as corner-stones, polished after the similitude of a palace." Coming from the Scripture, so exact even in its boldest poetry, you under-stand what is meant by this corner stone. Alas ! you will know *some day*, perhaps, the profound truth of this image, as you see the void made in the house by the removal of this loved child ! You will understand, then, what were her love, her devotion, her piety to those who shall surround her, and shed tears over her loss. But no, you will not realize it ; her family alone will understand it—let us retire—sympathy itself may be intrusive—let us not intermeddle with the secret of their grief, we, who have never penetrated into that of their joy !

This is not all. There are good works for which I permit the young daughter to leave the domestic sanctuary, and, if need be,

to lay aside the reserve even, which her age prescribes to her
Would you instruct the ignorant, relieve the poor, exhort the
sick, visit the widow and the fatherless? Go, my daughter ;
go, without hesitation, and may the Lord go with you ! I love
to see the young girl, who is ever ready to assist her mother in
the labors of housekeeping, to offer her arm to her aged father,
or to read the Bible with her brothers and sisters, turn from this
charity within to charity without, and bestow upon the unhappy,
attentions which they receive with double gratitude, surprised
to see her reserve for such uses, graces which so many others
think themselves permitted to devote to the world and its pleasures. Permitted ! it may be, if we wish it ; but, permitted or
not, a life of pleasure seems to you, without doubt, less desirable,
less conformed to the mission of woman, than that which I have
proposed to you. Or, indeed, do you recognize rather the
"helpmeet" in that other young girl, who prefers the shameful
horrors of a daughter of Herodias, to the modest glory of a
Rebecca ; who loves better to be the idol of saloons than the
treasure of the family, who finds more delight in loading herself,
at great expense, with rare ornaments, than to be herself as God
made her, the ornament of her home ; who consumes herself in
fruitless efforts to attract the notice of men, and to outstrip her
companions, I might say her rivals (accuse me not of exaggeration) ; who abandons herself to vanities, and casts into the
void this plenteous sap of life which has been given her for a
day, and which to-morrow she will seek, and no longer find.
Poor child, willing to bury herself all alive in the cold joys of
the present life ! Sad victim, day after day, night after night,
sacrificed to the folly of the world, by the vanity of her own
heart ! Some morning, at break of day, two young ladies suddenly meet in the silent street. One hastens from the ball to
her bed, that she may snatch some tardy repose after her pleasures ; the other, to the death-bed of one who calls for her in all
haste, unable to depart in peace, he says, without the presence
of his good angel ! Young ladies, choose !

We have contemplated woman before marriage, let us contemplate her now after marriage, intrusted with that precious fruit which Scripture calls "a heritage from the Lord :" let us turn to the wife now become a mother. Towards this son, whom God has given you, Christian mother, you occupy a position not of inferiority, as the daughter, nor of equality as the wife ; but of *superiority*, and that, too, a superiority which does not exclude the renunciation peculiar to the mission of woman. It is not good that the child should be alone, and God, who has given him to you, has given to him, at the same time, in you, a "helpmeet." Even the tender cares which his physical development claims, are dear to your heart. Anxious, by nourishing him from your own life, to prolong the pride of communicating to him being, you will not, without a necessity thrice demonstrated, deprive him of the treasures with which nature has enriched you, through him, and for him, nor deprive yourself of the holy pleasure of being an undisputed mother. Yet, a graver interest preoccupies me at this time ; the aid which you owe before all others to this little one, is education, the birth-giving of the soul, which follows by right that of the body, and which no one should dispute with you.

That ineffable joy with which you welcome your son, what is it but the natural joy of Eve, who called her first-born Cain, that is to say, "acquisition," because "she had gotten a man from the Lord ?" Or, indeed, is it the more noble joy signified by Christ, in these words, whose striking truth so often has made you start : "A woman, when she is in travail, hath sorrow, because her hour is come ; but as soon as she is delivered of the child, she remembereth no more the anguish, for joy that a man is born into the world." Maternity is a ministry, and the first condition of a faithful ministry is disinterestedness. Say not, here is my son, born to me, born of me, and for me ; but say, here is a man born into the world, for the good of the world. "What manner of child shall this be ?" demand earth, heaven, and hell, bending, as if suspended, in boundless expectation over the cradle of this frail creature, whose life has just disengaged itself from yours! The response—I say it not forgetting the divine operation, which is exerted through human instrumentality—the response depends, before everything else, upon the training; and the training depends, before everything else, upon the mother.

It has been often remarked, that the decisive moment in education is the point of departure. In the earliest years is implanted that strong bias which gives shape to the entire life. But the first years belong to the mother. Paganism took them from her; but Jesus Christ restored them to her. Grudge her not these beginnings. If they are too important for strangers, they are also too delicate and too exacting for a father. Aptness, freedom of mind, time, patience, are wanting to us. But all this, God has given to the mother. No one else so clearly discerns the nature of her son, the strength and weakness of his character, the allowance to be made for his temperament, the degree of severity and indulgence suited to his disposition, and the precautions needed to make him plastic without spoiling him. No other one possesses so truly the art of awakening his curiosity, of stimulating his ardor, of gaining his attention, of keeping his eyes open, and of initiating him by degrees in the practical knowledge of things, which, more living than that of books, has also a larger part in the development of the life. No other has a hand gentle, and at the same time *strong* enough, to give to the rising plant its early bias—a hand at once too strong to be resisted, and too tender to awaken a wish to resist it—and which controls all his future growth.

The greatest moral power in the world is that exercised by a mother over her child. Demand not from her a systematic account of it. She acts from inspiration, more than from calculation, and perhaps never says to herself what I say to you. God is with her in her work, and here is the secret. She appears to you perhaps, to guess at it; but let her alone. She understands it better than you, and will accomplish more by guessing, than you by your reasonings and calculations. Rely upon God, and the maternal instinct. "As a general rule, to which at least I have hardly seen exceptions," says a contemporaneous writer, " superior men, are all the children of their mother." * Contemplate that man, strong in heart, with intrepid voice, whose indomitable courage in turn braves the wrath of a prince and controls the popular wave, and whose determined will, equally invincible by obstacles and fatigue, seems anxious to justify the proud maxim : " Man can do what he will." You give, perhaps, the honor of his energy to nature. But learn that there appeared in his childhood a spirit so irresolute, a character so vacillating, that every one said : " He will never be a man." A *woman* has made him a *man !* and this woman is the same who brought him into the world. She alone has never despaired concerning him. Sustained by love, guided by instinct, she has discovered beneath his weakness, hidden virtues, which she labored tenderly, humbly, slowly to develop. She has formed him to perseverance, by combats wisely graduated, in which her faithful sympathy has wished to share in everything, but the honor of victory.

She has revealed him to himself, she has restored him to society. Then, when this son, upon his death-bed, recalls the good permitted him to accomplish for his people and generation, *to his mother*, next to God, he gives the glory ; and the last name upon his lips, in his delirium, is the same, which he attempted to pronounce fifty years before, in the lispings of his infantile days !

I may be permitted to add, without overlooking the value of our instruction, that maternal education is rendered doubly necessary by the tendency of our public instruction. We often hear the complaint that with precious resources, which it places at the disposal of all classes, it presents, to say the least, grievous deficiencies, it may be for the heart, about which it concerns itself too little, it may be also for the mind, with which it shows itself too exclusively occupied. It not only nourishes self love

* Michelet.

by an immoderate use of the principle of emulation, and does nothing to inculcate a holy respect for duty, but that which it does with so much skill, labor and sacrifice for the culture of the mind itself, is at least incomplete. The faculties which depend upon memory are sharpened by perpetual exercise, whilst those that depend upon reflection, even more important than the first, remain comparatively without employment. By too entirely occupying every moment of the pupil, by absorbing too much his ardor in a laborious preparation, we take from his mind the leisure, the elasticity, the activity, requisite to assimilate to itself what it receives. We accustom him to content himself with borrowed knowledge, into which his personality does not enter. Then the development of thought and character ceases, or a wrong direction is given to it. The flower of originality, as charming as vigorous, which nature refuses to no one, falls before yielding its fruit. We might say that a low equality has come upon all minds, and the man disappears in the child, because the child disappears in the scholar. For an evil so grave, I know no remedy but the counterpoise of family life, and domestic education, which alone can penetrate into the windings of the individual mind, and give it its proper direction. But I depend on the mother to save this family life, so threatened to-day by common life ; and this domestic education, I rely upon her to undertake. Urge her not to send away her child : let him remain a long while with her. When the time arrives for him to enter into contact with public life, she may be allowed still to interpose to maintain the rights of the heart, of the person, of the mind ; that is to say, of the *man*. Are you jealous of the too feminine influence she exercises ? Know that this influence, formidable if alone, is an indispensable complement of ours. Man has not all that is necessary to form the mind of man, because this mind has a feminine element. I so name this tender, penetrating, instinctive faculty, which seizes, or shall I say *divines* the truth, in opposition to that calm reason which gives an account of things, and to that strong will which gives an account of itself. In this sense it can be said with truth, "no man of genius was ever exempt from a feminine development." Hesitate not: place public instruction under the safeguard of the family, but the family presided over by the mother: it is the surest means of securing advantages to your son, as well as of saving him from perils.

Let us never forget in education, as in life, that "one thing is needful;" this one thing needful, is the result of the mother's success. Too often, alas! in the holy work of guiding her son to the Saviour, she has no one with her ; happy indeed, if all the world is not against her. But if alone, let her take courage ; it is here above all that God is with her, and He is sufficient for her. Are we speaking of a young child? This son beloved, but loved in the Lord, with whom she humbles herself each day at the feet of the Saviour, whom she teaches him to seek in his earliest thoughts, and name in his earliest words— she holds in a measure his soul in her hands. Alone in the world, she knows the ways by which to go in depositing the fruitful germs of salutary truth, instilled with so much love, implanted so profoundly, linked so strongly to the natural instincts (here learn the empire of her own image !) that neither storms without, nor storms within, shall be able to uproot them. Believe me, nothing is more irresistible to man, nor at once more indestructible in man, than these early impressions left by a pious mother, and shielded by the vague and simple charm of youthful remembrances. A son will twice doubt the mind of his father before he doubts once the heart of his mother.

Or, are we speaking of the age, when, no longer a child, and not yet a man, a son escapes insensibly from the watchful care of his mother, inspiring her with new solicitude? By a faithful use of her past influence, she has gained the confidence of this son, and this confidence to-day is an assurance for the future. In those tender disclosures which she has made a habit with him, and a need to him, she reads his heart to its depths ; and a heart to whose depths we read, is almost always one of which we are master

Passion speaks, perhaps ; he is about to yield : but he must tell his mother—impossible ; or he must conceal it from her—more impossible still ; and the temptation is overcome. At length the time arrives for the last embrace, prelude of a separation, perhaps, eternal . . . Christian mother, what dost thou fear ? Prepared during so many years upon the humble stocks of the family, *launch, since God wills it,* launch thy vessel upon the uncertain sea ! Let thy weeping eye follow it, even to the most distant limits of the horizon, and then, when thou shalt see it tossing upon the farthest wave, ready to disappear—disappearing—disappeared— offer thy prayer, committing thy treasure to Him who holds the winds and the waves in His hands, and who loves—more than *thou* lovest ! Thou hast been faithful from the beginning ; *He* will be faithful unto the end. Go on ; He will not forget the promise, which seems to have been given expressly for thee. "Train up a child in the way he should go, and when he is old, he will not depart from it."

Happy foresight, justifying a still happier experience. If it is true, that the greater part of distinguished men are the sons of their mothers, it is, above all, true of religious men. Scripture history, the history of the church, and contemporaneous history, agree in attesting it : we say rather in leaving it to be discovered ; for it is necessary to seek for the mother to discover her, behind this son whose name eclipses her own in the memory of man. But this is all a Christian mothers asks. If she has saved her son, she has accomplished her mission as a woman ; and if she has saved him without revealing herself, she has doubly accomplished it. Listen to the Bible. What is the object of the short preface placed at the head of the life of Samuel, if it is not to explain this holy man of God, this giant in prayer, this first link in the chain of prophets, this great reformer of the state and of religion, by the faith, the vow, the fidelity, and the songs of Anna, his mother ? How this recital atones for the brevity with which the Bible elsewhere explains in a similar manner, a Moses, a David, a Timothy ! and how it gives us the key to the apparent minuteness with which it names, in passing, the mothers of the kings of Judah! Open the annals of the church. Who hears the name of Augustine, that living light, twice almost extinguished, but delivered in turn from lust and heresy, to glorify God before the most distant posterity, without recognizing with him in this double deliverance, next to God, the hand of the loving, humble, patient Monica? But learn that Chrysostom, Basil the Great, Gregory of Nazianzen, and many others who have followed in their steps, each had their Monica, of whom we forget to inform ourselves, ungrateful as we are, even while tasting with delight the fruit of that which she sowed.

But we need not extend our glance so far : look around you. Study the ways of God, and you will find that the greater part of the servants of Jesus Christ, in whom our generation glories, are indebted to a mother for the first gleams of their piety. Not long since, in a pastoral conference, where were assembled one hundred and twenty American pastors, united in a common faith, each one was invited to relate the human cause to which he attributed, under the divine blessing, the change of his heart. Do you know many gave the honor to their mother? Out of one hundred and twenty, more than one hundred!

At another time, a mother equally faithful, seems not to have succeeded as well ; her son has wandered far from the path which she traced out for him. A mother, after all, mother though she be, is not God. But the greater the wandering of this prodigal son, the more we admire the maternal power to which he closes his ear, without being able to free his conscience, and which may (what do we know?) triumph at last over his resistance, long after the voice and prayers of his mother have become silent in death. Disregard the piety of a mother—that is possible, but *forget* it—never, no, never! A good man was hastening towards a church where religious service for sailors was being held. Opposite the church, at the door of an inn, he saw seated an aged sailor, with a rude and decided air, who, with folded arms, and a cigar in his mouth, looked with indifference, or else with disdain, upon those of his comrades who repaired to public worship. "My friend," said the stranger, approaching him, "come with us into the church." "No," answered the sailor roughly. His manner would have given this response to the stranger, who added, with mildness, "you appear to have seen hard times. Have you still a mother?" The sailor, raising his head, fixed his eyes upon the stranger, and remained silent. "Ah! well, my friend! if your good mother was here, what counsel, think you, would *she* give?" Wiping away, with the back of his hand, a tear which he vainly attempted to hide, the old man arose, and, with a choking voice, said, "I will go."

Mothers, mothers, understand your power! Feel your responsibility! Happy the child who has a good mother! Happy *your* son, if he has a good mother!

But, understand me; I waste not this name upon every one, who simply loves her child. A loving mother is one thing, and there are such even among the heathen; a good mother, according to God, is quite another thing. In our day, alas! the history of some men's relations with their mother is soon told. All this intellectual, moral, spiritual development is to them unknown. From her bosom, the poor child, (if it is not under the roof of a salaried mother) drops into mercenary hands, within the paternal mansion, until its age permits it to go forth from home to college, from college to the higher institutions, from the higher institutions to the army; and, returning from the army, if he returns at all, what will this mother, to whom he was almost always a stranger, be to him now, *but* a stranger? —stranger to his future course—stranger to his marriage— stranger to the education of his children. Oh, mother, who still hast a son to rear, awake! And thou, mother, who hast *thus* reared one, repent!

Yes, repent, but despair not. The word despair is not Christian. The eleventh-hour laborer may not only be admitted, he may even be favored. You can become a "helpmeet" to your

son, and educing, by the grace of God, good from evil, experience
the truth which contains in it the germ, the whole Gospel,
"When I am weak, then am I strong." One work completed,
another commences. Too late for that of education, another
remains to you, for which it is never too late, since weight of
years imposes it upon you. You reign no longer by authority
over children, who have become men ; but you can exercise
over them, a dominion of love and respect, which their maturity
will honor. Last link between past and future generations, frail
and precious vestige of that which has been, and which will be
no more, vigilant depository of the family traditions—you form
a venerable centre, around which group themselves, with silent
anxiety, many families whom your departure will soon disperse.
In your presence, the depths of their hearts are stirred by many
thoughts, many interests, many passions perhaps ; but all is
restrained by the common feeling which you inspire, and each
vies with the other in efforts and sacrifices to maintain the peace
of your last days. Your experience, your white hairs, your past
services, your present infirmities, a vague fear of not finding you
in your place to-morrow, gain for you every heart. Noble and
useful position which God has prepared for you ! Words of
power, received as the experience of life, as the warnings of
death, almost as the inspirations of heaven ! Happy the mother,
who faithfully completes a career faithfully begun ! But happy
the mother, also, who longs with a holy jealousy, to finish well
that which she began badly ; who knows how to turn to the
good of her children her own unfaithfulness. "The aged women
likewise, that they be in behavior as becometh holiness, not false
accusers, not given to much wine, teachers of good things, that
they may teach the young women to be sober, to love their
husbands, to love their children, to be discreet, chaste, keepers
at home ; good, that the Word of God be not blasphemed."
The secret of this beneficent influence, is in the inward life.
"The widow who liveth in pleasure, is dead while she liveth ;
but she that is a widow, indeed, and desolate, trusteth in

God, and continueth in supplications and prayers night and day."

If I mistake not, my dear sisters, before this picture which I have drawn of the Christian wife and mother, the heart of one woman sinks within her, and a silent tear moistens her eye. This woman, perhaps from circumstances, perhaps from choice, perhaps from a generous sacrifice, or from religious fidelity, has become neither wife nor mother. Understand it well; it is but a holy jealousy that troubles her this moment. Exclusively pre-occupied with the sublime mission of her sex, she would accept without difficulty, all of the incompleteness, according to opinion, according to the heart, and to the law of Providence, which her position offers. But having no one to whom to devote herself, she is compelled to restrain within her own bosom the thirst for sacrifice which consumes her, without profiting any one; to this she cannot consent. My sister, my noble sister, shall the deli-cacy of my subject close my lips? It signifies not that it is delicate, provided I accomplish my mission of the ministry of Jesus Christ, in aiding you to accomplish yours as a woman. You are, I love to tell you, in a complete illusion. Your position, viewed in the light of God, and the interest of your mission, is a privileged one, if you can so regard it. Believe the Apostle, writing to the Corinthians: "There is difference, also, between a wife and a virgin. The unmarried woman cared for the things of the Lord, that she may be holy both in body and in spirit; but she that is married careth for the things of the world how she may please her husband. And this I speak for your own profit; not that I may cast a snare upon you, but for that which is comely, and that ye may attend upon the Lord with-out distraction. But if any man think that he behaveth himself uncomely towards his virgin, if she pass the flower of her age, and need so require, let him do what he will, he sinneth not; let them marry. Nevertheless, he that standeth steadfast in his heart, having no necessity, but hath power over his own will, and hath so decreed in his heart that he will keep his virgin:

doeth well. So then, he that giveth her in marriage doeth well, but he that giveth her not in marriage, doeth better." Strange words, it must be confessed, and which it has been easy to misconstrue to the profit of erroneous views of celibacy, established at a favorite time in the church. Without doubt, the language of Paul must be explained by the particular circumstances of the time in which he wrote ; but we may boldly declare that he would never have expressed himself in this manner, if he had considered your position as of inferior importance to that of the wife, in the service of the Lord, and in the accomplishment of your mission. He chose himself an analogous position, not only to prove to the churches his disinterestedness, and to relieve them of the burden of his support, but to give himself "unto the Word and prayer," with greater freedom ; freedom of time, of action, of mind, and, in short, of heart.

These reasons are worth as much to you as to the apostles, and the last has a special value for woman : it is this, above all, which I desire to make you understand. There is in the heart of woman, a power of loving, to which man cannot attain. In the natural position, which is conjugal life, this power expands and satisfies itself in the family, upon a husband and children. In single life, it finds light by another road, and throws itself into one or the other of these two ways. In the first place, it turns within, and concentrates itself in selfishness ; from whence springs an egotism without measure or scruple. Probably in this class of single women we find the most humiliating examples of self-love, of curiosity, of idleness, of avarice, of worldliness, and altogether of petty existence, miserably consumed in trifling pleasures Or, in the other case, it turns without, diffusing itself in love to God, and to our neighbor, and impels woman to devote herself to the good of humanity, as a wife or mother lives for her family. Then, by an apparent contradiction, charity gains at the same time in breadth and depth ; in breadth, because it extends beyond the domestic circle, in depth because it assumes the ardor of a necessity, and the enthusiasm of personal feeling, saying nothing of a tinge of sweet melancholy, which well becomes it, and which also, in its way, stimulates it. In this way holy and Christian women are found ; or, as I might say, the daughters of holiness and charity, among whom we must seek for the most accomplished models of Christian benevolence ; who, weary of earth, impatient of heaven, by the simplicity of their zeal, by the purity of their renunciation, by the abundance of their good works, seem perpetually occupied in filling an immense void which God has made in their hearts for the good of humanity. Their ranks are open to you ; enter them, following in the footsteps of the many women who have chosen this position in order to be more useful to the world. Enter them, and give yourself no repose until you have learnt to see in your isolation a merciful privilege.

God has prepared before you, according to the Apostle, a path of good works : to walk in it you only need a heart truly consecrated, not with that selfish devotion which seeks self even in sacrifice, but with that disinterested devotion, which sacrifices, if necessary, even itself. "Open thine eyes, and thou shalt be satisfied with bread." Look first around you, and see if your family relations do not offer you the opportunities you desire. We find sometimes very near us, the thing which we seek at the ends of the earth. In default of a father and mother who have left you, you have perhaps a young brother at the outset of life, to whom you can be a friend and mother ; or a sister, it may be, ready to sink under the envied burden of a family, if she finds not in you that complement of strength, of time, of health, of light, which God has so plainly given her in you. Your heart demands a family. Well now, here is one. It is not yours ; I know it is not all that you desire ; but it is that which God has chosen for you, my sister, providing, at the same time, for the good of others, by your charitable labors, and for your own by your self-renunciation. No, when I demand of the whole earth, a type of the charity, most useful, most pure, most Christian, I find nowhere those conditions better fulfilled than in the good aunt, who, with a marvellous forgetfulness of herself, accepts the fatigues and the cares of maternity, without its ineffable compensations : mother, more than mother perhaps, when it is a question of serving and supporting ; putting herself out of sight, when it is one of reaping and enjoying ; sad, but with a heavenly sadness which translates itself into love and devotion.

What if an engagement of family binds you ; extend your view ; seek a family in all who need you, in relieving the unfortunate, in founding or sustaining charitable institutions, in aiding a faithful minister in his labors, in all the good works for which God seems expressly to have reserved your liberty. Or, embrace if you can, a still wider field : embrace the world, if you will provided it is in love. Renew in your person, the holy office of deaconness ; prepare yourself for it, if necessary, in these schools which a vigilant and ingenious charity opens to-day to pious females ; go, another Phebe, carry your services now to Rome, now to Cenchrea, sometimes in a hospital, sometimes in a family, sometimes in a church, wherever they shall be claimed, even if it be in behalf of some heathen nation, shut up under other skies. In fine, fulfill so well your mission, that at the hour of death, each of you will congratulate herself upon the happy isolation which permitted so much devotion ; so fulfill it, that in the affectionate regrets which follow to the tomb your mortal remains, none shall discover whether you were wife, or mother, sister or aunt, parent or stranger, because they see it not in your sacrifices !

If, instead of taking the difference of natural positions as the central point of my development, I had taken that of social positions, I could equally have shown you woman, finding by turn in a condition of equality, of superiority, or of inferiority, special resources for accomplishing the mission of her sex. The subject must be left to your personal reflections. Yet there is a class of women, that I cannot permit to leave this place, without some words of encouragement, because I believe they need them, and have a right to them.

Christian woman, whom God has placed in the humble rank of *servants*, the levelling spirit of this age, which disturbs all inferior conditions, has not, I hope, so carried you away that you cannot accept the trials of yours ;—I say more, that you cannot appreciate its compensations and advantages. But perhaps you say to yourself : this beautiful mission of woman is for all the world except me ! What can a poor servant do, who lives by dependence upon others ? Listen to my answer. You can accomplish the mission of your sex—I say not *in spite* of this dependence,—but even *by its help*. Many women have forced things to create for themselves a way of obedience, thus deceiving themselves in substituting *their* wisdom for that of God. But their error resulted from a profound instinct of woman, to which, in you, God has taken care to give satisfaction in choosing for you the lowest place. This is the place, which our Saviour prepared ; " Who took upon Him the form of a servant," and " Who came "—I love to repeat it—" to minister, and not to be ministered unto." Was it an obstacle to his work ? Was it not its support, its condition, its life ? It will be all that for you, believe it well, if you enter into the Spirit of your Master.

Hardly could I name one who contributes more to the order, the prosperity, the happiness of a house, than the truly Christian servant ; above all to day, when the treasure is so rare, alas ! and so imperfectly appreciated when found. This holy woman, " obedient to her master with fear and trembling, in singleness of heart as unto Christ ; not with eye-service as men pleasers, but as the servants of Christ, doing the will of God from the heart ;" anxious to please them, unwilling to oppose their wishes, espousing their interests, and faithful even in trifles ; at home accommodating herself to their infirmities, and concealing them when abroad—good and noble woman— with the veil of her charity ; elevating, in fine, her condition to the height of her sentiments—free by faith, a servant by love— what a gift of God for a family ! Appreciate this blessing.

you who have received it, without waiting for God to reveal its value to you, by removing her from you and filling her place with one of those servants, so numerous, full of the world, and of themselves; ill at ease, and, as in a prison, when at home—in constant conspiracy with those without, like a traitor in a besieged place, scarcely restrained by a vigilance more fatiguing to exercise than to submit to; as careful of her person in public as she is negligent of it in private; spreading through the town domestic secrets; curious, gossiping, crabbed, and, in fine, caring but for her own interests, and awaiting only an offer of the slightest advantage to break a yoke which is painful to bear.

Thus we see her in the present life—but in *another*? Ah! beware of thinking the spiritual mission of woman is denied you. In the humble sphere assigned you, you can do more than many others for the service of the Gospel, provided you are willing to serve it as a woman, gently, silently, endeavoring before all else, " to adorn the doctrine of God your Saviour" in all things, by a conversation without reproach. Besides, influence ascends more than it descends: many a one resists that of his superiors, against which he is on his guard, and yields to that of his subordinates, of which he is all the while unconscious. Hence the power of the enfranchised in Rome. Hence, in Proverbs, the influence of the wise servant who ruleth over a son that causeth shame, and who shall have his part of the inheritance among his brethren. Spiritual influence follows the one law of all influences, which gain in power as they are most concealed : being that which is most humbling to the natural pride. Go on, your spiritual opportunity is great, and in proportion to it, your responsibility. I tell you that there is a retreat into which you alone can penetrate; there is a conversion which God has reserved for you, and which no one can accomplish better than you; there is a proud heart which yields neither to a mother, wife, nor daughter, but which will be constrained to lay down its arms before the obscure fidelity of a servant;   he "last" here being " first."

When Peter, escaping from prison, knocked at the door of the house where the disciples were assembled, Rhoda, the servant, was permitted to run before him, and announce the news of his deliverance. It is a beautiful privilege to open the door to an apostle; and still more beautiful to open it, when the Lord knocks; He enters willingly by these private doors, which you only can unclose to Him. But the children, above all, the children, this hope of the future, do you consider the influence which God has given you over their minds? How often has it been remarked that children, instead of following the example of their parents, more readily form their accents, their language, their habits, from servants; it may be, because of more frequent intercourse, or less apparent efforts, and which least provoke resistance. The heart of man is thus made. This power, it only remains that you use for the interests of the Gospel. You dispute with the faithful mother the spiritual development of this child which you carry in your arms, or which you lead to walk: over the ordinary mother you have an advantage!

With works such as these to do, are you jealous of still greater works reserved for others? Then, finally, the greatness comes from God: and it depends upon Him to change the little things which you have accomplished into great ones, even in the eyes of the world. When it became necessary to put the powerful and vain-glorious Naaman in communication with the prophet, who would at the same time both heal him of his leprosy, and reveal to him the true and living God, a little Israelitish maiden is employed, whom the soldiers of the Syrian captain had taken prisoner, and whom he had given to his wife for a slave. Poor child! she hardly imagined when she struggled in the arms of her savage conquerors, that she would yet be a great blessing to the Syrian, and that the time would come when she would be cited as an oracle in the court of the king: "Thus and thus said the maid that is of the land of Israel." Was not this circumstance narrated for your encouragement?

Do you remember how Illyricum received the Gospel in the first age of the church? By a Christian woman, who was there sold as a slave. I say all this not to excite your vanity, or to be a snare to you, but to awaken in you a holy jealousy, to lead you to appreciate the position in which God has placed you. Yes, my dear sisters, conform yourselves to His views; not a word of complaint or regret; no ambitious dreams of change, but a fidelity full of joy, to your peculiar mission, and a heart which envies one nothing but a more active charity and a more profound humility!

Woman, in fine, whoever thou art, and wherever thou art, take to thy heart this word, "I will make for him an helpmeet," and determine, without more delay, to justify the definition which God has given of thee.

Useless woman, who groanest under the thought that thou hast, even to this day, burdened the earth, as a tree without fruit; that thou mightest be taken away from it, without leaving any greater void than is made in the water by the sword which we plunge into it and quickly withdraw from it; thou, who hast hitherto lived without knowing from whence thou camest, or whither thou goest, here is discovered the vague object after which thou longest without knowing it. Here is a work for thee, to which, living, thou mayest consecrate thyself, and dying, will be able to say, "I have finished the work which Thou gavest me to do." Enter to-day, even, according to thy position—whose apparent difficulties are real resources—upon this life, at once so humble and so glorious, so full of meaning, and so devoted, for which God destined thee in the day when he said, "I will make an helpmeet for him," and which Christ restored to thee when He gave Himself for us, "that He might redeem us from all iniquity, and purify unto Himself a peculiar people, zealous of good works."

Worldly woman, who hast consumed thy most beautiful years in cares, innocent, I grant, but frivolous and unworthy of thee, infatuating and infatuated, using for the interests of thy pride, a power which God has confided to thee for his glory and the good of his people, here, in place of this brilliant existence, but brilliant as a meteor, resounding, but resounding as an empty vessel, here is a life glorious and full, in which, in a word, thou wilt find, in finding thyself, the satisfaction which thou hast vainly (is it not true?) demanded of the world. Take off thine heart from vanity, and give it to charity! Believe me, leave this artificial life, which supplants and abridges the real; reserve for thy home the labors of the day and the repose of the night; count as lost the day in which thou hast not done some good; enjoy, in short, the happiness of being a *woman*—and thou wilt know that if made to be to man a " helpmeet," it is better to be useful to him, than to be flattered by him; to serve him, than to fascinate him!

Isolated woman, from whom God, who renders not an account of his doings, has taken away with the husband of thy youth, the attraction, the aim, the life of thy life—and thou, also, widow of a living man, forsaken wife, whom the husband of thy youth, after a short joy given and received, has overwhelmed with grief by his coldness, if not by his unfaithfulness; tender plant, torn from the earth, that it may be transplanted into a better soil, but which has been cast upon the road-side, abandoned to the scorching fire of the sun; thou, whom the Lord has chosen as a type of the most ineffable griefs, take courage—thy consolation is found! If the sweetness of being loved has been taken from thee, allow not thyself to be despoiled of the privilege of loving, of loving first, loving last, loving always, of loving notwithstanding all. Follow in the steps of Jesus, who was despised as thou art, but was never cold and unjust as one is with thee. Be still unto him who has wronged thee, a " helpmeet." Drink without a murmur the cup which his cruel hand offers thee each day; oppose his ingratitude only with an increased submission and devotion. Be silent, humble thyself. Go on; this heart which thou seekest will be restored to thee, conquered by thy love! But should it persist even to the last in its injustice, shonld it—O horrible thought!—finish its murderous work by raising some day against thee a threatening hand, yield, still blessing him—accomplish even to the end thy mission as a woman, rely upon God whom thou lovest, and who loves thee in order to make thee a partaker of His glory through his cross!

And thou, whom I hesitate to name, fallen woman, charity will not permit me to leave thee without a response—without a response, for I hear thy heart interrogating me. Fallen woman, —"let no one trouble this woman!" a sinner who repents is a spectacle, if not worthy of *you*, yet worthy of *angels!* As for me, if I could despise her tears and disdain her repentance, I could not believe myself a disciple of Him who said to the penitent sinner; "Thy faith hath saved thee—go in peace!" My sister, my poor sister, yes, this is also for thee! Believe not thyself alone excluded from this appeal, and beware of despairing of thyself. Thy heart burns within thee to accomplish this mission of woman, to become to man what God made thee, a "helpmeet." Thou canst—yes, thou canst; none can better than thou, if none feels a deeper thirst for grace! Knowest thou that many of the holy women who shine in the first ranks among the benefactresses of humanity upon the earth, and among the redeemed of the Lord in heaven—a Rahab, a Mary Magdalene, a penitent sinner, commenced as thou hast? Well, then, finish as they did! Humblest among the humble, the most charitable of the charitable, remember the past, only for the good of the future. Permit none to recall the past, except to admire in thy change both the divine compassion, and the vocation of woman! And upon thy guilty head, all covered to my eyes by the blood of Jesus Christ, let the blessing of the Father, and the Son, and the Holy Ghost, descend with mine!

But we, my brethren, witnesses of this new baptism of woman, have we gathered naught from it but a vain spectacle? It concerns our interests, our dearest interests; but also our *conscience.* If woman owes to man the aid of a "helpmeet," does man owe

nothing to her? If woman has her influence over us, have we
no influence over her? This duty of acknowledgment, of
reciprocity, how have we fulfilled it? We said, in our first
discourse, that sin came to us by woman: alas! have we not
returned it to her, returned it with usury! If woman has dis-
regarded her mission, who has taught her to disregard it? If
woman has been idolized, who has placed her upon the shameful
pedestal? If woman has been degraded in paganism, in poli-
gamy, in licentiousness, who has degraded her? In fine, if one
should give you this problem to resolve, which of the two has
done to the other the greatest wrong—man to woman, or woman
to man? what would be your answer?—Question sad as difficult! in the room of which I would propose to you, on the contrary, another: Which of the two will henceforth do the other
the most good? Do you see her who, in meditation before God,
is seeking to know henceforth how she can be to us a "helpmeet?"
Let us meditate, for her sake, upon the same problem at the feet of
the same Saviour! Most truly are the principles the same, the
applications alone vary. Humility, charity—if we abandon them
to woman, ah! what will remain to us ourselves? Humility,
charity—was the man Christ Jesus anything else? With a god-
ly jealousy, one of the other, let the humility and charity of the
woman aid the man; let the humility and charity of the man aid
the woman, looking forward to the time when, beneath purer
heavens and upon a regenerated earth, the humility and charity
of the elect of God, in whom all earthly difference shall be forgotten, shall glorify from age to age this Saviour God, doubly
our Father, having created us in a day of love and saved us in a
day of grace!

DISCOURSE III.

THE LOVER OF MONEY.

"Take heed and beware of Covetousness."
LUKE, xii. 15.

In the warning which the Lord gives to his disciples in our
text, there is something deep and solemn which claims no ordinary attention. We feel that it is his desire to put them upon
their guard against certain illusions full of peril. What are
these illusions? We believe the three principal to be, deception
as to the nature of covetousness; deception as to God's judgment concerning it; and, finally, deception as to the empire
which it holds among men. A plan of meditation is thus furnished for the present occasion; and we shall endeavor to show
what covetousness is, how great is its criminality, and how generally it prevails.

I. COVETOUSNESS.—We are deceived in regard to the nature
of Covetousness; and the fault is to be attributed less to ourselves, than to our language which does not perfectly agree with
that of Scripture. It is usual to call a man covetous who, loving
money for its own sake, thinks only of amassing it, without
making it the means of enjoyment to others, or even to himself.
Is it astonishing, then, if, being habituated from infancy, to this
mode of speaking, we should regard it as the language also of
the Scripture, and if we should believe involuntarily that the
Scripture condemns in the covetous man only that which the

world itself reproves as parsimony ? I say *involuntarily*; nevertheless we have a secret motive for understanding it thus. For
this kind of covetousness being fortunately somewhat rare, and
not easily charged upon most of us, we regard the language of
Scripture as not meant for us, and have the satisfaction of being
able to say : I am not the man. But be upon your guard ;
you are placing your reliance upon a word, and upon a word ill
understood. The covetous man of our language is one person,
and the covetous man of the Bible is another. Far from confining this appellation to the sordid *hoarder*, the Bible scarcely
mentions him. In Holy Writ you will not find a single description of him ; he appears only in apocryphal writings, upon the
pages of profane authors ; and it is here alone that you must
look for him. Doubtless, the Almighty foresaw that human
reason would do justice to a sin so grave, a folly, at least, so
crying. This kind of covetousness is a scandal, a madness, a
disease. The world has suffered too much from its effects to
tolerate it ; and, accordingly, those polluted by it are treated
more severely than libertines or reprobates.

The covetousness against which our Lord warns us, is quite
another thing. Judge concerning it, either by the circumstance
which furnished to him an occasion to give this warning, or by
the parable wherein he cites an example of it. A certain man
had just said to our Lord : "Master, speak to my brother, that
he divide the inheritance with me." What mark of covetousness could there be in this request, if the name of covetousness
were given only to a sordid parsimony ? And again, where
would there be the covetousness of the rich man of the parable,
whom our Lord represents as thus speaking to himself : " I will
pull down my barns, and build greater ; and there will I bestow
all my fruits and my goods ; and I will say to my soul, Soul,
thou has much goods laid up for many years ; take thine ease,
eat, drink, and be merry ?" This is not the language of excessive
meanness, but rather that of selfish prodigality. Thus the Lord,
applying this parable to his disciples, warns them, not against

parsimony, but against the cares of life and the thirst for riches.

In order to discover the Lord's true meaning of covetousness, it is only necessary to recur to the original text; a precaution which the interpreters of the Scriptures cannot too carefully observe, and which is often more profitable than much research. There are three words in the Bible which in our versions are rendered by the words *Covetous* or *Covetousness*. The first signifies *a man greedy of gain*, and not very scrupulous in general, as to the means of getting it. The second signifies properly *a man who always desires to have more;* and this is the word employed in our text. The last signifies simply *a lover of money.* Thus when in our translation of the Bible we read, " And the Pharisees also who were covetous derided him :" (Luke xvi. 14), " A bishop must not be covetous :" (1 Tim. iii. 3.), " Let your conversation be without covetousness :" (Heb. xiii. 5.), we read in the original, " And the Pharisees who were *lovers of money* derided him :" " A bishop must not be *a lover of money :*" " Let your conversation be without the *love of money.*" So again, in that hideous picture which St. Paul has drawn of the last days (2 Tim. iii. 2–4), the following traits, " Lovers of their own selves," " *covetous,*" " lovers of pleasures more than lovers of God," answer to different Greek words which signify literally friends of self, *friends of money,* friends of pleasures, more than friends of God. See, then, how the Bible itself enlightens us as to what is meant by covetous. A covetous man is a friend of money ; covetousness is the love of money. Everything is now explained in our text. This man who wished Jesus to compel his brother to divide with him the inheritance, was a covetous man, a lover of money ; or he would not have interrupted the " words of Eternal life " which were issuing from the Saviour's mouth, in order to promote his petty interests. The rich man of the parable was a covetous man ; or he would have been less desirous of heaping up worldly goods for himself, than of being rich in God. The disciples, in their turn, might have sinned through covetousness, through the love of money, if they had abandoned themselves to anxiety, or if they had sought their treasure here below.

It is scarcely necessary to add, that the lover of money, such as the Bible speaks of, is a man who loves money to excess, as the lover of pleasure is a man whom the love of pleasure engrosses. Money has a real value, which the wise man cannot misunderstand. Such is the condition of human society, that money is to it the key of all enjoyments, and of all advantages. Money is a condensed world. He who is the possessor of money, holds in his coffers all that his eyes can desire ; lands, houses, food, and drink, the means of diverting as well as of instructing himself, and even the power of securing the favor of his fellow men. This law is in nature, and we are so much the less able to find fault with it, as it has for its authority the word of God. "Wisdom is good with an inheritance (or as good as an inheritance) ; for wisdom is a defence, and money is a defence." (Eccl. vii. 11, 12.) "A feast is made for laughter, and wine maketh merry ; but money answereth all things."—(x. 19.) It answers not only our comfort, but also our imperious wants, our sacred obligations. To desire it is a thing as innocent as the act of breathing ; but, from a legitimate attachment for it, to an extreme attachment, the passage is short and slippery.

In observing the irresistible power with which money draws everything to itself, we are inclined to yield to the temptation to pursue it as the chief good, and whatever love the heart may possess for the world, is concentrated and hidden in the love of money. We begin by loving it for the advantages which it procures, and then learn insensibly to love it for itself, or, if you choose, for the unforeseen uses to which we fancy it may be applied at some future time, which we shall, perhaps, never see. We may avoid certain extremes, and escape the charge of covetousness, but, at the same time we may be none the less governed by a thirst for riches ; for thereupon the heart may be fixed. Covetousness is communicated like a contagious dis

ease ; men nourish it, and, even without speaking, their very
looks seem to say : "Taste, and see how good *money* is." Thus,
by degrees, is formed and developed a love of money which
goes beyond all bounds, which subjects piety, instead of suffering
itself to be governed thereby, and which makes of him who
possesses it, according to an expression of our Lord, "A servant
of mammon."

This love of money takes different forms, and changes its
name before men, without being in any wise changed before
God, who regards the heart. One loves money for the sake of
keeping it ; this is the miser, properly called ; the covetous man,
according to the world. He knows, perhaps, how to avoid
certain appearances, in order to escape this shameful title ; but
we are sure that to separate him from his treasures, would be to
tear from him a part of his being, and he would willingly say of
money what God has said of the blood : "Money is life." Covetous persons of this character are not so rare as we imagine, but
they conceal with skill, and often the secret of their parsimony
is known only after their death. Another loves money for the
sake of spending it ; this is a *prodigal covetous man.* For one
may be at the same time covetous and prodigal ; not, certainly,
in accordance with our idiom, but in accordance with the Bible.
The prodigal must necessarily be the lover of money, because
it is more needful to him than to others. These two dispositions, far from excluding one another, mutually encourage ; prodigality keeping the love of money always in exercise, and the
love of money providing prodigality with its daily bread. Thus,
a historian, well acquainted with human nature, described a
great criminal by these two traits : "Covetous of the goods of
others, and prodigal of his own." A third loves money for the
sake of acquiring it ; this is the *ambitiously covetous man.* It is not
the desire of hoarding that governs him ; it is not even that of
spending ; but the pleasure of his eyes, and the pride of his
heart is to see streams of gold flowing from his hands.

Of these three forms of cupidity, parsimonious cupidity is more especially the vice of old age, prodigal cupidity is that of youth, and ambitious cupidity is that of mature age. In other respects, covetousness is found in all conditions of life. A rich man, who makes his happiness depend upon his fortune, and who desires constantly to add thereto, "less rich on account of what he possesses than poor on account of what he has not," is the lover of money ; is a covetous man. But a poor man is not the less so, if he cannot be contented in the condition in which God has placed him, and if his heart runs after fortune as the chief good. In point of fact, these two men are the same ; and we can easily believe that if one of them should succeed the other in position, he would succeed him also in sentiment. In a single word, covetousness is cupidity under all possible forms, and in all situations ; it is selfishness applied to money.

If covetousness, as we have been accustomed to understand it, is not uncommon, all will agree that covetousness such as we have just seen it defined by the Bible, is much more so. But is it then so culpable? And whence then comes this so earnest exhortation : "Take heed, and beware of covetousness?"

II. The Criminality of Covetousness.—We deceive ourselves as to God's judgment concerning covetousness. We believe ourselves free, after all, to enrich ourselves as much as we can, and to do afterwards as we wish with our wealth. Thereupon, we give ourselves up to covetousness. We would not give ourselves up to intemperance, or to robbery. But covetousness seems to be regarded as a sin of quite a different character. While the former vices are shameful and shocking to the feelings ; while they are attended by disorders that disturb the repose of society, and the peace of families, covetousness seems to be a sort of prudence and attention to one's duties. It dreads noise and scandal ; it is generally creditable in its appearance, estimable even according to the world, which cheerfully gives to it the names of generous ambition, useful industry, or praiseworthy economy. I will grant to it more than

this ; the covetous man may have religious habits, may give an
example of respect for religion, and for the Word of God.
"The love of money," says a Christian thinker, "is almost the
only vice to which a person may yield himself, and still preserve
the appearance of piety. But do you know what will be the
consequence of this sin ? Listen, then. There is every reason
to believe that of all sins, it is the very one that will destroy the
greatest number of persons who profess to serve the Lord."
For, as Jesus Christ said to the Pharisees : "That which is
highly esteemed among men, is an abomination in the sight of
God."—(Luke xvi. 15.) Reflect seriously upon these words.
They refer directly to our subject. Jesus Christ had just explained, by the parable of the unfaithful steward, the use which
a pious man ought to make of riches ; he had closed by declaring, that no one can love God, if he is carried away by the love
of money. "And the Pharisees, also, who were covetous," and
who were, nevertheless, regarded as models of devotion, "heard
all these things, and they derided him." Then it was that the
Saviour gave them this solemn warning : "Ye are they which
justify yourselves before men ; but God knoweth your hearts ;
for that which is highly esteemed among men, is an abomination
in the sight of God."

Thus, whatever may be the opinion of the world, the virtue
and piety of the lover of money are, according to Jesus Christ,
only an abomination in the sight of God. And why ? Because
God knows the heart. Under these creditable appearances,
under this religious cloak, he discovers in the heart of the covetous man an abyss of iniquity. What, in fact, is the love of
money, except a dethronement of God, and a setting up of
Mammon in His place ? The covetous man loves Mammon, as he
ought to love God, "with all his heart, with all his soul, with
all his mind, and with all his strength." He does more · he
confides in Mammon, instead of relying upon the Almighty.
While the true disciple of Jesus Christ "trusts not in uncertain
riches, but in the living of God, who giveth us richly all things

to enjoy," the covetous man esteems himself happy in his gains;
" he has made gold his hope," and said to the fine gold, " Thou
art my confidence."   It is for this that the Holy Spirit calls the
covetous man, " an idolator" (Eph. v. 5), and covetousness,
" idolatry."—(Col. iii. 5.)   Thus, our Lord declares the love of
money absolutely incompatible with the love of God.   " No man
can serve two masters," said He upon more than one occasion,
" for either he will hate the one, and love the other ; or else he
will hold to the one, and despise the other.   Ye cannot serve
God and Mammon."

This incompatibility is so true, that it is betrayed by the excuses of the lover of money ; he can justify his covetousness only
by giving it to be understood that he has renounced the faith.
" My fortune is my own ; I am at liberty to do with it as I please."
Your fortune your own ! you can do with it as you please !
Have you then renounced the Master who redeemed you ?
Does not all that you possess belong to Jesus Christ ?   Do not
you yourself belong to him ?   If neither your body, nor your
mind belong to yourself (1 Cor. vi. 19–20); if for the sake of
Christ you ought to abandon your father and your mother, your
wife, and your children, and even your own life (Luke, xiv. 26); is
your money so sacred that it alone must be excepted from this
universal sacrifice ?   Your fortune your own !   At liberty to do
with it as you please !   And why may not another say: My mind
is my own ; I am at liberty to apply it to thoughts which may
pervert it, or to causes which may corrupt it ?   Or a third say :
My body is my own, and I am at liberty to yield my " members
servants to uncleanliness and to iniquity unto iniquity."   No !
says the Apostle, for " your bodies are the members of Christ"
(1 Cor. vi. 15); and I say in imitation of him : No ! for your fortune is the treasure of Christ.   He is its true possessor ; you are
only his steward, and you are bound to use it only in his service.
He who does otherwise is unfaithful, according to the judgment
of our Saviour (Luke xvi. 12) ; quite as unfaithful as the
steward of the parable, who wasted the goods committed to his

care. Your fortune your own ! At liberty to do with it as you please ! Take care. There is but one way in which you can legalize this pretension, and that is to break with Jesus Christ. It does not rest with you to make the conditions of your alliance with him ; he has made them, and you will find them written in St. Luke, xiv. 33 : "So likewise, whosoever he be of you that forsaketh not all that he hath, he cannot be my disciple." Under no circumstances can you serve God and Mammon. The love of money is a separation of the heart from the Saviour, an idolatry, an abomination in the sight of God.

As is the tree, so is the fruit. You have just witnessed the love of money in the heart ; now observe the works which it produces. "The love of money," says the Holy Spirit, "is the root of all evil."—(1 Tim. vi. 10.) If we were to treat this subject in its whole extent, we should have material for a book, instead of a discourse ; let us confine ourselves to what covetousness has done, at all times, against the advancement of the kingdom of God in the world.

I open the Old Testament, and amid that multitude of crimes by which men have thwarted, as much as they could, the plans of God for the salvation of the nations, I find many, and they of the blackest character, due only to the love of money. What drove Balaam to harden himself against the warnings of the Lord, against the cries of his own conscience, against the naked sword of the angel, against the miraculous voice of a stupid beast, and to try, by turns, impious enchantments and infamous seductions in order to shut up to the chosen people the road to the promised land ? The love of money. What induced Achan to conceal the accursed spoils, to disobey the command of God, to brave His threats, and to cause His wrath to fall upon the victorious armies of Israel ? The love of money. What induced Gehazi to scandalize the newly-born faith of Naaman, to render useless the disinterestedness of a holy prophet, and to cause him to be suspected, perhaps of hypocrisy ? The love of money. What made in Israel those prevaricating magistrates, those iniquitous judges, those lying prophets who conducted the people of God only to lead them astray, and to "destroy the way of his paths ?" The love of money.

Let us pass to the New Testament ; we shall then see the evil growing and assuming a more odious character. Scarcely had Jesus commenced his work, than covetousness lifted itself up against him ; it everywhere intruded upon his path ; it disputed every step that he took. It misunderstood and forsook him, in the person of the rich young man ; it excited his holy anger in the person of the sellers in the temple; it hated him ; it railed at him; it persecuted him in the person of the Pharisees ; and, in the person of Judas it tithed the fruit of his charity for the poor ; it begrudged the honor destined to his burial ; it betrayed him, it delivered him up, it sold him. Oh, prophetic crime, which casts a sad light upon the future of the Church of Jesus Christ ! This same crime of him, who for thirty pieces of silver sold the blood of the Son of God, is the very crime which will show itself most active in depriving men of the ineffable benefit of this shed blood ; for it will oppose equally the salvation of the individual, the fidelity of the church, and the conversion of the world.

In regard to the salvation of the individual. A man cannot turn towards the Lord, but covetousness seems to waylay him in order to thwart his purpose, and he is thus beset from the moment that he receives his first religious impressions, to the most advanced period of his faith. Is he simply an invited guest to the great feast ? Covetousness persuades two invited persons in three to excuse themselves by saying : "I have bought a piece of ground," or "I have bought five yoke of oxen."—(Luke xiv. 18, 19.) Has he listened to the truth and received the good seed into his heart ? Covetousness cultivates thorns beside it ; soon "the cares of this world, and the deceitfulness of riches" threaten "to choke the word, and he becometh unfruitful."—(Matt. xiii. 22.) Has he made some progress in the ways of piety ? Covetousness does not yet despair of turning him aside and of adding him to the number of those who, possessed by the love of money, " have erred from the faith."—(1 Tim. vi. 10.) Happy if, "taking the whole armor of God," he is "able to withstand in the evil day, and having done all, to stand." Happy, if he does not imitate those imprudent travellers whom Bunyan describes as leaving, at the invitation of Demas, the road to the holy city to visit a silver-mine in the hill called Lucre." Now whether," says Bunyan, "they fell into the pit by looking over the brink thereof, or whether they went down to dig, or whether they were smothered in the bottom by the damps that commonly arise, of these things I am not certain ; but this I observed, that they were never seen again in the way."

The love of money does not oppose itself less to the fidelity of the church. Ah ! who does not know the history of the Christian church ? Who does not know the sad influence that covetousness has exercised upon its development, upon its organization, upon its discipline, upon its very doctrines ? Who does not know that, trampling under foot the maxim of its founder— "freely ye have received, freely give "—the church has made so much traffic of the truth of God, of His promises and of His threats, of paradise and of hell, of holiness and of sin, that its name has become in the language of the world the type of venality ?

But there would be so much to say in regard to the evil which the love of money has done in the church, that we will speak only of the good which it has been the means of preventing. The church was planted in the world for the good of the world. Depositories of eternal life, Christians ought to communicate it all around them, and even to the ends of the earth ; the church was born to be a missionary to the human race. This, she understood at her birth ; and that angel of the Apocalypse, that flew through the midst of the heaven bearing the everlasting Gospel, is a true image of the ardor with which the first disciples labored to gain new kingdoms for Jesus Christ. But why has this ardor abated from century to century? Why has such a glorious conquest been arrested? Why has it gone backward, and finally limited itself to so small a portion of the globe? Why have those very nations in the midst of which God first lit up the olden faith, been compelled to acknowledge, for nearly three centuries, their indebtedness to pagan people? Alas! and why should that holy cause, in behalf of which all Christianity ought to be engaged, why should it now find among us so many hostile, or, at least, so many indifferent hearts? One of the fathers of the church, St. Cyprien, replies to these interrogatories, and you shall judge, whether or not, what he wrote in the third century of the Christian era applies to ours. "Every one," said the holy martyr, groaning, "every one devotes himself to increasing his worldly substance; and forgetting what the faithful did during the times of the Apostles, and what should always be done, Christians cherish an insatiable desire of augmenting their fortune." Where, then, could be found that entire devotion to the salvation of men, which can alone establish missions, and those generous sacrifices which can sustain them? And thus the work became abandoned, or at least neglected; and *what* a work, oh, my God! The world was perishing of hunger, hunger for the word of God. The compassion of God was moved. The message of grace was ready. The church was charged to bear it through every land, and not to rest so long as there should remain upon the earth a single nation, family, or man, to whom the glad tidings had not been carried. The church, for a time, was faithful; but the spirit of the age returned and paralyzed its activity. Is the evil now less pressing? No. But the church has other cares; like the world, it is occupied in buying, in selling, and in getting gain. Its devotion to Mammon will not allow it to be faithful to the Lord.

The covetousness of the church engenders still another evil. Not contented with preventing the church from evangelizing the world, it scandalizes the world through the church. Judge in

regard to this, my brethren. Let the man of the world give his
heart to money, which is the key of the world ; it is precisely
what must be expected : **but you**, Christians, believing the Gospel, have, without doubt, adopted its spirit : it is in heaven that
you lay up your treasure. And seeking first the kingdom of
God, and his righteousness, everything **else** touches you feebly in
comparison with the one thing needful. **Oh ! if the detachment**
from earth, taught by your maxims, had exhibited itself **in your
lives !** Would not your example **have excited among** men
a holy emulation similar to that with **which the** faith of the
martyrs formerly inspired the pagans ? And would not the
world, in seeing **you make a sacrifice of its** vanities, have confessed that **God is truly among you ?** But what is the real state
of things ? The world has heard you *conversing* like Christians,
and seen you *acting* like itself. It has seen you quite as much
attached to money as others, quite as eager to acquire it, **quite
as slow in detaching yourselves from it.** And what do you wish
the world to think, I do not mean of yourselves, that would be
an unimportant matter, but of the Gospel ? Has not, then, that
Gospel, with all its precepts and all its promises, no more **power**
to detach your hearts from worldly things, than the lessons of
philosophy ? Faith, grace, regeneration, all are suspected of impo-
tency ; " the salt has lost its savor." So true is it that the
love of money makes war against the works of Christ, as it has
made war against Christ himself : seducing the individual, cor-
rupting the church, and scandalizing the world.

Now behold what damnation **God has in store** for the covetous
man. Its visitation upon him commences even during the present life. He punishes himself, indeed, by his iniquity itself : **no
one can be more** miserable than a covetous man. Solomon
exhibits the lover of money as unable to satisfy himself therewith, his cares increasing with his fortune, **every one enjoying**
his good, except himself, sleep flying **from his eyes, and** " all his
days eating darkness, and having sorrow and wrath with his
sickness."—(Eccles. v 10–17.) Saint Paul, in his turn, has

shown the covetous man as "pierced through with many sorrows" (1 Tim. vi. 10) ; and our Lord tells us in the simple but expressive words which follow our text : " A man's life consisteth not in the abundance of the things which he possesseth." And if anything is wanting to this punishment which the lover of money, with his own hands, inflicts upon himself, divine justice makes up the deficiency. The mercenary Balaam having failed of a recompense, perished by the edge of the sword. The covetous Achan, troubled by the Almighty, for having troubled His people, was stoned to death with all his family, and even the treasures that had tempted him were destroyed. The faithless Gehazi carried into his own house the leprosy of Naaman as well as his presents, and thus transmitted to his posterity the double heritage of a fortune and a scourge. And Judas, the perfidious Judas, devoured by remorse, alas ! but not touched with repentance, casts his money into the temple, gives himself to two deaths at once, carries upon his mutilated body the seal of divine vengeance, and goes " to his own place."

To what place ? What is the eternal portion of the covetous man ? You think that covetousness is only one of those infirmities that God tolerates among his children ; but you must learn from God himself that it is one of those sins that exclude the offender from his kingdom. You would charge us with exaggeration and injustice if we were to place the covetous man in the same rank with the drunkard and the extortioner : but learn that God associates the covetous man, I mean the covetous man of the Bible, the lover of money, God, I say, associates him with the drunkard, with the extortioner, and with even greater criminals.

Open the Scriptures, and examine those frightful lists of the most detestable sins ; you will find scarcely one in which the covetous man has been forgotten. We see covetousness enumerated among the sins which characterize the apostasy foretold of the last times : " For men shall be lovers of their own selves, covetous, boasters, proud, blasphemers, disobedient to parents, unthankful, unholy, without natural affection, truce-breakers, false accusers, incontinent, fierce, despisers of those that are good, traitors, heady, high-minded, lovers of pleasure more than lovers of God ; having a form of godliness, but denying the power thereof."—(2 Tim. iii. 2-5.) When Saint Jude, describing the false teachers who seduced the church, assembles in a single verse the three most culpable that ever lived upon the earth, the covetous Balaam figures between the murderer Cain and the rebel Korah.—(Jude 11.) When Saint Paul collects in a hideous picture the vices that prevailed among the heathen, covetousness is named among the first.—(Rom. i. 29.) The covetous man is an offender that should not be tolerated in the church, and with whom the faithful should hold no intercourse, however great may be his professions of piety. " If any man that is called a brother, be a fornicator, or covetous, or an idolater, or a railer, or a drunkard, or an extortioner ; with such a one, no not to eat." —(1 Cor. v. 11.) Finally the covetous man appears upon that shameful catalogue, wherein the Holy Spirit designates to the Church Universal those who are farthest removed from God and from his kingdom. " Know ye not that the unrighteous shall not inherit the kingdom of God ? Be not deceived ; neither fornicators, nor idolaters, nor adulterers, nor effeminate, nor abusers of themselves with mankind, nor thieves, nor covetous, nor drunkards, nor revilers, nor extortioners, shall inherit the kingdom of God."—(1 Cor. vi. 9-10.)

Behold, now, the covetous man, the lover of money, who passes, perhaps, in the world for a moral man, for a religious man, behold him advancing in the centre of the most infamous company that ever existed, giving his right hand to the drunkard, and his left to the thief, with the adulterer (not to repeat names still more odious) with the adulterer before him, and the extortioner behind him ! Is he journeying on towards the kingdom of God ? No, he is marching towards the place of the thief and the drunkard ; towards the place of the extortioner and the adulterer ; towards the place of the traitor Judas ; towards the place of Satan and his angels. Let the covetous

5

man cease from blinding himself, at least let him know what
he is doing and where he is going. Let him not flatter himself
that the door is open to him, if he dies such as he is ; it will
open to him only when it shall open to the drunkard and the
adulterer, whose hands.knock thereat simultaneously with his
own !

And if your soul were to be demanded this very night !—O
Lord, preserve us from covetousness ! Are we in danger of falling into it ? Would we have lived in it ? Would we live in it
still ? Enlighten me, O Lord, and let me not be of the number
of those insensates "who flatter themselves in their own eyes,
until their iniquity be found to be hateful."

III. The Prevalence of Covetousness.—We are deceived
in regard to the empire which covetousness holds among men.
There is, perhaps, no sin more ignored by those who give themselves up to it than covetousness. "No one confesses the sin of
covetousness," said a pious bishop, who had long officiated at the
confessional. The drunkard or the adulterer cannot conceal his
infractions of the law of God ; the proud man, even, or the
vindictive can perceive and condemn the passions which govern
him ; but the covetous man scarcely ever knows himself. The
object desired by the drunkard and the adulterer being bad in
itself, they are treated as open enemies. It is not so with the
love of money. Money is good in itself ; money is necessary for
the preservation of life ; money is useful even in doing good.
Beyond this, what ready excuses have you for acquiring it?
Well, we refer you to your conscience ; but, let it be understood,
to a conscience fair and enlightened. We wish simply to pro-
pound to you a few questions, upon which we leave to you the
care of examining yourselves before God. They will bear upon
three points : the means which you employ in order to acquire
money, the ardor with which you seek it, and the use which you
make of it.

Are the means which you employ to gain money always honest?

Do not be offended by this question ; I do not speak of those means that lead to the galleys or to the prison ; but as exempt from crime, are yours always legitimate in the sight of men, and especially before God ? Is there no one among you who lends money at an interest which the laws of the country, as well as charity, forbid ? In your business transactions are there no secrets which you would blush to see revealed ? Is fraud absolutely unknown in your affairs ? Have you no false weights, no false measures, no false samples, no false charges of expense, nothing, in short, that is false ? Is falsehood banished from your transactions ? Have you never promised what you could not perform, nor deceived a buyer as to the quality of your merchandise, or as to its value, or as to the place whence it came ? Do you never demand for what you sell an excessive price, and one which the chances of commerce cannot justify ? Do you never abuse the position or the ignorance of those with whom you have to do, in order to impose upon them onerous conditions, and such as you yourself would not accept ? Has the love of gain never prompted you to retain some office or receive some commission which your conscience disapproved ? Have you never risked the property of others in hazardous speculations ? Have you never enjoyed the fruit of wrongs committed by others, or refused to restore what you justly owed, but what the law could not compel you to pay ? Have you never resorted to harsh means in collecting what was due to yourself, forgetful of that touching recommendation of God to Moses : "If thou at all take thy neighbor's raiment to pledge, thou shalt deliver it unto him by that the sun goeth down : for that is his covering only, it is his raiment for the skin ; wherein shall he sleep ?" Do you never, in order to increase your fortune or to preserve it, engage in divisions, family quarrels, lawsuits, which would not have been found to be unavoidable if you had remembered this passage of Scripture : "There is utterly a fault among you, because ye go to law one with another. Why do ye not rather take wrong ?" Finally, if you are entirely innocent of all these bad practices, is there not one of them to which you would not have resorted if you had not been restrained by the terrors of the law or by the fear of opinion? Examine your hearts. I do not pretend to judge you; I wish simply to aid you in judging yourselves, before your own consciences and before God.

I admit that your wealth may have been fairly acquired. Honesty does not preclude covetousness. Here, for instance, is a man who becomes rich by the cultivation of his fields; what revenue could be more honest? Here is another who becomes so, by receiving his share of the paternal heritage; and what, again, could be more legitimate? Jesus Christ does not, on this account, tax them the less with covetousness, because they both seek money with such ardor that the things of God are not visible in them. Do you feel, also, my dear hearer, this supreme ardor for the acquisition of money! To make your fortune, if you are poor, or to increase it if you are rich; is this the thought that governs your life? Is it this alone that can explain your tastes and your distastes, what you do, and what you leave undone? Do you find time for the exercise of a lucrative profession, while you find none for praying to God, and for reading the Bible? If you should find it necessary to labor on the Sabbath, in order to preserve your revenues, what would you do? And in case you have already decided this question in favor of God's service, do you carry into His house a heart that walketh after gain, and which says, as said those Jews of Amos, "When will the new moon be gone, that we may sell corn, and the Sabbath, that we may set forth wheat?"

If you could make choice between two careers, the one brilliant, but strewed with temptations, the other safe for your soul, but modest; what would you do? Think seriously; what would you do? In reading that exclamation of our Lord: "How hardly shall they that have riches enter into the kingdom of God!" have you trembled that you were rich, or blessed God that you were not? Even at this moment, what are your feelings in listening to my words? Do you say in your heart:

these are very good maxims for the pulpit, but impossible to be observed in real life? Do you say that provided you could make a fortune, you would willingly run the risk, and that he who preaches against the love of money, thinks in the bottom of his soul as you do? Are your strongest emotions, your liveliest joys, your most bitter regrets, to be ascribed to the favors and the frowns of fortune? Does a trifling gain, a slight loss, affect you more than the satisfaction that follows a good work, or than the unhappiness that results from sin? Do you sigh inwardly for an inheritance? a delicate thought which one fears to examine? In choosing a wife, are you more anxious to know what she has than what she is? In fine, are you most desirous of being a Christian eminent for piety, or of being a man full of riches? And if you were now to begin to serve the Lord, as you have been serving Mammon, and to serve Mammon as you have been serving the Lord, which of them would gain by the change? Examine your heart. I do not wish to judge you; I desire simply to aid you in examining yourselves.

In the meantime, I admit again, no one observes in you an extreme ardor in the pursuit of fortune; but what use do you make of money? I do not ask whether you spend it, but whether you spend it usefully. For my object is to aid you in discovering, not whether you are a miser, but whether you are a lover of money; and you might be a great lover of money, even while squandering it for your personal advantage. The wicked rich man who suffered Lazarus to die of hunger at his door, "fared sumptuously every day;" and the hand of prodigality, open through vanity or selfishness, is also as tightly closed as that of parsimony to the appeals of charity.

Do you give? The Gospel principle, in regard to alms and pecuniary contributions, is admirably shown by St. Paul, when exhorting the Christians of Corinth to aid those of Judea: "That now at this time your abundance may be a supply for their want, that their abundance also may be a supply for your want; that there may be equality: as it is written, He that hath gathered much had nothing over ; and he that had gathered little had no lack." An obligatory and absolute equality is not alluded to here ; the Apostles never preached this ; even the Church at Jerusalem did not practise it ; and you must look into systems entirely foreign to Christianity, if you seek this beautiful chimera, which has been falsely attributed to the Gospel. But, in distributing unequally the advantages of fortune, God has shown that He intended that the superfluity of some should supply the deficiency of others ; and by this law of fraternal love, he determined to provide for the wants of the latter while exercising the charity of the former.

And now, my brethren, have you entered into the spirit of this law, and do you honor it by your example, or do you think yourselves permitted to trample it under foot as did the wicked rich man ? Do you give to the poor ? Do you provide for your own kindred, as the Lord has especially commanded you in saying : " If any provides not for his own, he has denied the faith, and is worse than an infidel ?" Do you give to those charitable institutions which are multiplying in our churches, and which procure for those whom they assist the bread which nourishes the soul as well as that which nourishes the body ? Do you give to those religious associations which characterize our age, and which propagate in the world the knowledge of God and of His word ?

If you give, *how* do you give ? Do you give spontaneously, and from an inclination that causes you to seek opportunities for so doing ? or is it only in mere imitation of others, or because you are urgently solicited, or overcome by shame ? Do you give in secret, and do you experience a special pleasure in those good works that are witnessed by God alone ? It is written : " God loves the cheerful giver." Do you give cheerfully ? Is he who collects for charitable objects welcomed at your house ? Is your door one of those at which he enters with pleasure, or is it one of those at which he knocks only after having won a victory over himself ? Do you encourage him by your reception, or do you begin by telling him that the times are bad, that your affairs are not in a very prosperous condition, and that the demands upon you are very numerous? Poor collector! His task may have been an enviable one in the church of Jerusalem; but rendered what it is by such as yourself, would you take his place?

But especially, *how much* do you give? Is your liberality—speaking in the words of Saint Paul—made ready "as a matter of bounty, and not as of covetousness?" Yes, as of covetousness; the word employed by Saint Paul in this place (2 Cor. ix. 5), is the same as that of which the Lord makes use in our text. The gift is of covetousness, when it is reduced as much as it can be honestly, and when the desire of giving is less exhibited than that of retaining. Do you give in a way that may serve as an example to others, or do you content yourself with giving as much as those who give but very little? If every one were to give in the same proportion with yourself, would the prosperity of the institutions for which you contribute be secured, or would their existence be placed in peril? Do you give systematically? Does the reign of God, and do charitable interests occupy a place by themselves in your account-book, or do you devote to them only what happens to be in your hand, as you would in the case of little unforeseen expenses? Do you give more, do you even give as much for charitable purposes as for superfluities? and could you maintain the luxury of your dwelling, or that of your table, with the sacrifices which you present to the Almighty? Have you, in order to be able to give, worked with your own hands, according to the exhortation of the apostle? Have you, for this purpose, triumphed over a single inclination, sacrificed to a single taste, renounced a single pleasure?

But I will spare you; I will not push my questions as far as I could, or as far, perhaps, as I ought. For what, in fine, would you think of me if I were to ask you whether you would give your whole fortune if God were to demand the sacrifice? And this sacrifice was, nevertheless, demanded of the rich young man spoken of in the Gospel, who, not being willing to make this sacrifice, could not be a disciple of Jesus Christ ; and if he continued to be unwilling to make it, he is at this moment with the wicked rich man in hell. Jesus Christ, it is true, does not impose this obligation upon all, but the disposition is required of all ; and he who would not do what the young rich man refused to do, cannot be a true Christian. What do you say to all this ? Consider, examine. I do not pretend to judge you ; I wish simply to aid you in judging yourselves.

But, if I ought not to judge an individual, I cannot shut my eyes to the condition of society. I look around me ; I reflect upon what is taking place at the present moment in this country, in this city, and I am constrained to answer yes, to each of the three classes of questions which I have just propounded to you.

Yes, bad means are often employed in the acquirement of riches. If I were obliged to prove this from your personal experience, I would here point you to slavery, that curse of pagan nations, that shame to Christian people ; slavery, whose object seems none other than to exhibit in a single action all the crimes and misery that the love of money can produce ; slavery, that national sin, against which public opinion begins to clamor, but which we have practised for centuries, which we still retain in spite of generous examples, and which finds defenders even in our legislative assemblies.

But it is needless to go so far for arguments ; we have them all around us. The usurer, who deserves not to be named among Christians, is not unknown either among our poor, or among our rich, or in our towns, or in our fields ; and those who engage in this business, know that it is criminal, since they take care to leave no written traces of their dark transactions. Frauds, and falsehoods, great or small (a distinction which the Lord my Master has not taught me how to make); frauds and falsehoods, I say, abound in business matters. This fact is proverbial ; it is confessed, it is justified, and commerce has a code of morals of its own, which agrees but ill with that of Jesus

Christ. There are, however, faithful men, who desire, at any price, to keep their conscience pure; but the smallness of their number, their embarrassments, the temptation which they experience, either to withdraw from a competition which their delicacy renders unequal, or to continue a career which the world does not condemn, attest more conclusively the greatness of the evil. It is a very easy matter, at the present day, to count these upright, clean-handed merchants, who, controlled by conscience, even when not compelled by law, think, in adverse times, of increasing their own fortunes only after having repaired the losses of others; but it is not a very rare thing to see persons risking in rash enterprises, a borrowed capital, getting out of difficulty in case of accident, by declaring themselves bankrupt, and then beginning anew, with no damage to themselves except of conscience.

Distrust is felt everywhere; bad faith is always counted upon; we weigh after the seller has weighed; we beat down the price of everything, and this bad habit which shows itself in the most honest people in spite of themselves, gives a fair exhibition of the morality of commerce. Even the public health is jeopardized by it, and poisonous substances find their way into the bread which nourishes us, and into the liquors which we drink. Jealous of one another, overseers and workmen seem associated together only for the sake of mutual injury. Not long since we saw the latter combining unjustly to compel manufacturers to raise their wages. But we see, every day, manufacturers taking advantage of the necessities of the poor, and obliging them to undergo labor so excessive as to destroy mind, soul, and body. We see young children (oh, that the representatives of the nation, who have revealed to us the depth of the wound, might find an efficacious remedy!), we see young children working in our factories from six o'clock in the morning until ten o'clock at night with scarcely time to eat and sleep, deprived of schools, without religious instruction, and induced by a brutish fatigue to resort to more brutish means of excitement. We see them,

5*

sometimes (shall we say it?) more abandoned than the very slaves of our colonies, for the simple and frightful reason that more care is taken of what is bought than of what is hired. We are told in reply to this, that the manufacturer is forced to conform to the general custom, if he would not shut his workshop. This may be so ; I do not pretend to judge ; but what is then our condition, if the individual can be absolved only at the expense of society? Ah, how few fortunes, great or small, wherein sin has not had a hand ! and how generally does the manner in which money is acquired, justify the name given to it by our Lord : "the Mammon of unrighteousness !"

Once more fortune is pursued with insatiable ardor. This ardor has always existed, but during our day, it has a peculiar character ; it is a passion for sudden riches. Everything is ventured, in order to obtain everything ; the chance of falling into absolute poverty will be taken, rather than forego the opportunity of securing fortune ; and that honest mean which the pious Agur placed above everything in his humble prayer : "Give me neither poverty nor riches ; feed me with food convenient for me," is what the present age seems to shun with the greatest care.

Cast your eyes about you. Every one is covetous, every one is eager to enrich himself, even in a single day. Commerce is covetous : competition is without bounds ; rapid fortunes, unheard-of successes, sudden falls, speculations without end, hazards, lotteries, excitements for gaming under all forms ; such is the new mode of satisfying the old thirst for gold. Industry is covetous : those admirable inventions which are continually succeeding one another, aim less at the progress of art than at the making of money ; produced by the hope of gain, they hasten towards gain ; in their headlong march, imprudence is inevitable, and accidents multiply ; but this is of no consequence, and cupidity drives the impatient wheels over the scattered ruins, and the ghastly dead ; the earth soon drinks up what little blood is shed, but the money will remain. Ambition is

covetous ; that solicitation for office, which crowds all the
avenues to authority, aims less than formerly at honor, and more
at money ; and the venality of office is revealed even in the
praiseworthy but humiliating precautions which are considered
as necessary to be taken against it. The struggle of parties is
covetous : if the levelling spirit of some often conceals a desire
of building up and enriching themselves, is the love of order in
others always so pure that it never covers the desire of preserv-
ing their own advantages? and if many of the friends of equality
are such in regard, above all, to propriety, are there not many
conservative men who are such in regard, above all, to their own
fortunes? Legislation is covetous : in it, money is the chief corner stone ; money choses the arbiters of our social and political
destinies ; it does more, it choses the managers of our churches;
and, judging by appearances, one would believe that the rich
enter most easily the kingdom of heaven. Marriage is covetous : the union of man and woman is ordinarily a secondary
matter ; it is two *fortunes* that are pleasing to one another, that
woo one another, that win one another, and are married to one
another ; and the most intimate of all associations degenerates
into a calculation, and is transformed into a contract. Literature is covetous : that desire of perfection, that persevering
labor, that earnest study, that conscientious worship of the beautiful, of the good and the true, which formerly characterized our
great writers, are sought in vain among their successors ; impatient of producing, and more impatient of acquiring, the
literature of the present day spends its strength in unfinished,
defective, extravagant works, alas ! perhaps immoral and impious, but which cater for the tastes of the multitude, and pour
into the hands of their authors streams of gold unaccompanied
by glory.

What shall I say yet? What if we were to search into the
part which the love of money has in those numberless errors
that, by turns, toss the human mind, and in those senseless
systems that topple, one upon the other, after having been

sustained a few years by the appeal to material interest? the
part which it has in those crimes that sully the pages of all our
public journals ; in the murders, the poisonings, the suicides, the
law-suits, the divorces, the hatreds, the revenges, and in all the
fruits of sin which we harvest abundantly in a field sown with
infidelity ?

A covetous use is, in fine, made of the goods of fortune. Not
that they are not spent ; let them, indeed, be ever so much
spent, they are, with few exceptions, spent for self-gratification,
not sacrificed to charity. I will cite but a single proof of this,
the condition of our religious and benevolent societies. The
Lord has, in our day, inspired his followers with the happy idea
of propagating the Gospel by means of association, that powerful instrument of our age. He has raised up faithful servants
who have given their time, their strength, and their money, to
organize and maintain institutions devoted to the good of mankind and the glory of God. When they have urged the
churches to engage in their pious works, what has happened ?
Help has been obtained, and the work of the Lord has not been
stopped ; it has been productive of good, much good, and, after
God, we bless the authors of these sacrifices in which God
delights. But are the contributions liberal ? are they sufficient ?
Do we give, generally, as we could, as we ought to give ? Do
we even approach it ? No, my brethren, no ! Our societies
vegetate rather than live. One proposes to publish an edition
of the Bible for the aged, but the enterprise must be delayed
until sufficient funds are specially gathered together for it.
Another begins its work with a deficit, the first year, of fifteen
thousand francs ; and the following year, with a deficit of thirty
thousand francs. A third has five missionaries ready for the
people of Southern Africa, who are anxiously awaiting them ;
but the sum of 25,000 francs is needed to fit them out, and
during the last five months all France has been ransacked without finding more than half of the required sum. Poor Bech-
uanas ! we will give you missionaries, but on condition that you

pay for them ! You must give the half of your wretched income, the only good that you possess in the world, the fruit of a whole year's economy ! Ah ! that you may be ignorant at least of our covetousness, and not judge by us of that Gospel which we preach to you !

Again, everything is embarrassed, mean, uncertain in our societies ; and thus it will be, so long as the plan of our liberalities shall not have undergone a complete revision, a radical reform. Money is not wanting, but it takes a wrong direction. Instead of flowing abundantly in the channels of charity, watering the garden of the Lord, it is emptied into the gulf of Parsimony, or swallowed up in the thirsty sands of Prodigality. Making allowance for the necessities of life, for habits, social comforts, provision for the future, the establishment of children, etc., would there not be, with prudence, abundant resources for every good work, provided that some would retrench expenses which they know to be foolish, and which they dare not defend ; and that others would have the courage to lay a bold hand upon those useless treasures that they are, day by day, accumulating ? And what, oh, my God ! if we were to do as did the disciples of a crucified Master, if we were to impose upon ourselves true sacrifices, if we were less mindful of our case, of our tastes, of our welfare, of what we deem necessary, but which is, in fact, superfluous ? What, if we were to enter into the spirit of those beautiful words of David : " Neither will I offer burnt offerings unto the Lord my God of that which cost me nothing ?"

My brethren, I do not wish, nor is it in my power, to tax you. But compare what you give with what was given by the primitive Christians : I do not mean at Jerusalem, but in the other churches. " We do you to wit of the grace of God bestowed on the churches of Macedonia," wrote St. Paul to the Corinthians (the grace of God bestowed ; do you feel the force of this expression ?) ; how that, in a great trial of affliction, the abundance of their joy, and their deep poverty, abounded unto the riches of their liberality. " For to their power I bear record, yea, and beyond their power, they were willing of themselves ; praying with us with much entreaty, that we would receive the gift, and take upon us the fellowship of the ministering to the saints." **Ah, my brethren, when shall we** exchange places with them ? **When shall the time come, when you will** press us to receive, and we shall be obliged to moderate your zeal ? **Compare** what you give with what **is given, at** the present **day, by,** whom ? the richest nations of **the globe ? the** English ? **the Americans ? no,** but by liberated negroes. **The** five hundred thousand negroes of Jamaica, slaves but yesterday, have recently, in the course of a **single year, given for religious** and benevolent purposes, from twelve to fifteen hundred **thousand francs ; a sum enormous, in consideration of their poverty, a sum double, triple, quadruple,** quintuple, perhaps, that given during the **same time, and for** similar objects by all the united Protestants of France. **Finally, compare what** you give with what the law of Moses obliged **the Jews to give for** the support of religion, **and for charitable purposes. The tenth** part of their revenues was for **the Levites, and the fortieth part** superadded for the priests. Besides this, **the Jews were** obliged to give the produce of their fruit trees during four years, the first fruits of all **their** harvests, the sixtieth part **of their crops, the fruits of the earth during the year of jubilee, which returned every** seven years, and the debts contracted in the **interval** between one jubilee and another. **Add to all this, personal** taxes, multitudinous sacrifices and oblations, with frequent **jour**neys to Jerusalem, and we shall find that God imposed upon his **people a** tribute that exceeded the third of their revenues. Who **would dare to propose to us** such sacrifices ?

But should love, under the new economy, do less than *law* did under the old ? **If God,** treating us with the confidence of **a** father, is contented to say to us : " Thou shalt love the Lord thy God with all thy heart, and thy neighbor as thyself," and at the same time allow us to apply this perfect rule, shall we abuse this confidence by spending what we owe to God and to our neighbor ? We do not assume to tax you, I repeat it, when God has not done it ; what we could wish, what God wishes, is that charity should tax itself, " each one as God hath prospered him."—(1 Cor. xvi. 2.) But that charity is stifled by the love of money. Such a one enjoys those pleasures which force a relative, a brother, I will not say a father or a mother, to struggle against the privations and the fatigue of poverty. Such a rich man spends less in a whole year for the support of charitable institutions, than he lavishes in a single day for the maintenance of his house. Such a fashionable woman will find scarcely five or ten francs for the advancement of the kingdom of God, while she will find five hundred or a thousand to throw away upon an evening party. Such a cultivator, full of wealth, will draw from his coffers a few francs for the evangelization of the world, or of France, and spend a few thousand for the construction of a more commodious and more elegant mansion. Oh, my friends, bear with the freedom of my words. I make no personal application of them, and I beg that no one will apply them except to himself. But I speak of things which every one knows, which every one sees, and if I hold my peace the very stones will cry out. Oh, what covetousness is in the world ! What covetousness is in the church ! What covetousness in the noisy city ! What covetousness in the quiet fields !

But I return, my dear hearer ; I am not now dealing with society, but with you, with you alone. Place your hand upon your heart. Forget the poor sinner who is addressing you. Suppose that Jesus Christ, your Lord and your God, were himself to come to you, and, with that tender love that pierces the heart, that divine unction that moves it to its very centre, should say : " My friend " (it was thus that he addressed Judas), " My friend, *art thou one of my friends,* or *art thou a friend of money?*" If you feel that the truth condemns you, do not forsake the light ! Pluck not out the arrow that has penetrated your soul ! You are living in sin, in sin that is destroying you ! You must abandon it, whatever it may cost, *you must* abandon it !

If the Lord says to you : "Take heed and beware of covetousness," he warns you also to save yourself from covetousness. And how will you do it ? I will tell you very briefly, for time urges us ; besides a few words will suffice, if you are sincere ; and if you are not, all the instructions in the world will profit you nothing.

To save yourself from covetousness ! Ah ! it is the vork of God alone. But God can do it. God has done it for others. Lovers of money and those enslaved to the worst sins have been transformed into free men. Witness Zaccheus, that tax-gatherer, "that man that is a sinner," enriched by wrongs committed upon his neighbor ; not only was he completely changed, but he was changed in a single day. Take him for a model. Zaccheus did two things. First, he became a disciple of Jesus Christ; secondly, he disposed of his fortune, according to the direction of Jesus Christ. Do ye likewise. Give to the Lord, this day, your heart and your hand.

It is in the heart that we must begin. The love of money is in the heart. But what must be done to drive it out ? Form an energetic resolution to combat and stifle it ? Such indeed is the advice of the moralists of this age ; and thus they have never been able to accomplish anything, and thus Seneca gave an example of covetousness, while thundering against it in his eloquent pages.

The Gospel employs quite another method : it opens our heart to another love, to the love of the Saviour. There is in the heart of man a thirst which the love of money will always fail to satisfy, so long as it is not quenched by the love of Christ. Give your heart to Jesus Christ ; this is not so difficult ; for in order to love him, it is only necessary to contemplate him. You have read the Gospel, but you have not given attention to it ; return to it, and, upon your bended knee, implore the Holy Spirit to aid you in comprehending and feeling the Divine word. See him, that holy, just, and innocent One, without spot, separate from sinners, exalted above the heavens ; see him coming down to earth "to seek and to save that which was lost," to seek even *you*, to save even *you*. See him, "who was rich,"—and with *what riches* !—" for your sake becoming poor," and with *what poverty !* See him living upon the earth—him your Lord and your God— living as you yourselves would not wish to live, nourished by charity's hand, not even a penny wherewith to pay the tribute demanded of him, nor a place whereon to lay his head. See him sold for that miserable money which you prefer to all things, deliv- ered into the hands of wicked men, condemned as a criminal, insult- ed, crowned with thorns, crucified between two malefactors, and for whom ? For you, yes, for you who have, until this very moment, loved the thirty pieces of Judas more than the blood of your Saviour, but who wish henceforth to love the blood of your Saviour more than the thirty pieces of Judas. See and believe, and fall at His feet, crying with the Apostle Peter, "Thou art the Christ, the Son of the living God." Then, doubt it not, the shameful chains with which you have been bound by Mammon, will fall from you of themselves.

How would you still call fortune the chief good, and poverty insupportable ? Your Saviour became poor that you might have eternal riches. How would you still be anxious for your life, or for your family ? He has said unto you, "I will not leave thee, nor forsake thee." How could you be unable to suffer the deprivation of your goods ? You have in heaven treasures better and enduring. How refuse the sacrifice of your fortune to the Lord ? It belongs to Him, and He has confided it to you, He who first gave himself for you, and who is himself alone your riches, your gold and your silver. Ah ! it is only necessary to be a Christian, in order to be the most disinterested of men ; and if there are so few uncontrolled by the love of money, it is because there are so few true Christians even among true Christians.

Such is the first step, *heartfelt faith ;* behold now the second, *liberality of the hands,* which springs from this faith, and which, in turn, nourishes it. Zaccheus had no sooner known the Lord than he presented himself before him, saying : "Behold, Lord, the half of my goods I give to the poor, and if I have taken anything from any man by false accusation, I restore him fourfold." Imitate him, like him, give with method ; like him, establish a rule, broad and generous. What each one ought to give, or the manner in which he ought to give it, is with him to settle with the Lord ; the Gospel has not prescribed in such matters, it has been left with your charity. Justify this confidence. Raise yourself above cold custom, and make your account not with men but with Jesus Christ. Be not satisfied with the exclamation : "That is well done." Be filled with the thought that your fortune belongs to Him more than to you, and that you are appointed to administer it in His name. Remember the words of Christ : "It is more blessed to give than to receive ;" and give like a man who feels that even giving is a favor which God has accorded to him. Congratulate yourself upon living in a time when occasions for giving profitably are increasing. Blessed is he who can at the same time respond to the appeal of the age, to the appeal of mankind, to the appeal of the Lord, and to the appeal of his own heart, but of a heart animated by charity !

For you who are rich, this is a happiness exceeding all others. Learn then to enjoy your fortune. Understand why God has given it to you. Spend it for his glory as long as you live ; and forget not in your last will Him to whom you owe your temporal and eternal inheritance. Of what use are your riches, if you make them not the means of doing good, if you are not "rich in good works, ready to distribute, willing to communicate ?" Then alone will you be happy in being rich, and the world happy in that you are so. Then this prosperity which has destroyed so many others, will be for you a means of making "your calling and election sure." Then in parting with your earthly treasures, you will remember with joy that you have sown in the field of the Lord, where you will reap many fold ; and, like the charitable man of whom we read, you may cause to be written upon your tomb : " What I kept, I lost ; what I gave away, I retained."

And you to whom the Lord has given what was desired by the wise Agur, complain not that you cannot give what you could wish, but rather give what you can. " For if there be first a willing mind, it is accepted according to that a man hath, and not according to that he hath not." Try hard, and you will find that you can do more, much more than you imagine. An ingenious charity will enrich you in the Lord ; impracticable sacrifices will become easy ; necessary expenses will seem to you superfluous ; and if the rich have the advantage of offering more abundant gifts, you will have the advantage of exercising more self-denial in yours.

And finally, to you, whom the Lord has placed in the same situation in which He lived while upon the earth, to you should Christian liberality be forbidden ? No, my brethren, no. Take the example of the poor widow. Have you nothing to give ? She had no more than you, but a sacrificing spirit enabled her to discover in her profound poverty, an offering which excited the admiration of the Lord. Do you say that what you might be able to give would be too little to be of any service ? Were the two mites of the widow lost ? Have they not been more serviceable, yes, literally, more serviceable than the rich offerings that fell with hers into the treasury of the temple ? These two mites have been multiplied from age to age, by the faith that offered them and by the blessing of the Lord who accepted them, and who determined that His Gospel should perpetuate their remembrance. These two mites have, from century to century, provoked sacrifices on the part of a multitude of poor Christians, who would have never known that they had anything to give, if they had not been taught by the poor widow, and who, by reason of their number, give, as has often been calculated, more than the rich. These two mites have already drawn into the treasury of the church sums immensely great, and their work is not yet done ; they will continue to act " wheresoever this Gospel shall be preached throughout the whole world ;" and if you, yourselves, decide this day to imitate the widow's charity, it will be a new fruit of her humble offering. Why should there be no fruit of yours ? Be faithful only, and wait upon Him who increased the oil of the widow of Sarepta, and multiplied the mites of the widow of Jerusalem !

Lord Jesus ! Thou hast come to us, to-day, saying : "Take heed and beware of the love of money." And we come to Thee saying : Save us from the love of money ! Beat off, destroy this serpent that enfolds us ! Faith, liberality, everything comes from thee ! Bestow these upon us, so that, washed in thy blood and baptized in thy spirit, we may henceforth consecrate to thy service all that we have and all that we are ; glad to offer thee a thousand fortunes and a thousand lives if we had them, and still regretting that we had not more to offer, in return for that ineffable gift whence flow our happiness and our eternal wealth !

DISCOURSE IV.

THE CONFLICT OF CHRIST WITH SATAN.

"And Jesus, being full of the Holy Ghost, returned from Jordan, and was led in the Spirit into the wilderness, being forty days tempted of the devil. And in those days he did eat nothing: and when they were ended, he afterward hungered. And the devil said unto him, If thou be the Son of God, command this stone that it be made bread. And Jesus answered him, saying, It is written, that man shall not live by bread alone, but by every word of God. And the devil, taking him up into an high mountain, shewed unto him all the kingdoms of the world in a moment of time. And the devil said unto him, All this power will I give thee, and the glory of them: for that is delivered unto me; and to whomsoever I will, I give it. If thou, therefore, wilt worship me, all shall be thine. And Jesus answered and said unto him, Get thee behind me, Satan: for it is written, thou shalt worship the Lord thy God, and him only shalt thou serve. And he brought him to Jerusalem, and set him on a pinnacle of the temple, and said unto him, If thou be the Son of God, cast thyself down from thence: for it is written, He shall give his angels charge over thee, to keep thee: and in their hands they shall bear thee up, lest at any time thou dash thy foot against a stone. And Jesus answering said unto him, It is said, Thou shalt not tempt the Lord thy God. And when the devil had ended all the temptation, he departed from him for a season."—LUKE, iv. 1–13.

MY CHRISTIAN FRIENDS:

The aspect of Scripture truth oftentimes varies, according as we regard it with the eyes of human wisdom, or with those of faith: and nowhere is that difference more striking than in the page which we have just read. For my own part, I remember a time when I never met this passage without a kind of shame for my own understanding, and I might almost say for the word of God: whereas now I turn to it again and again, as to a favorite passage, where my soul finds food both grateful and abundant

117

This is so because the narrative is as full of wholesome instructions for the little child who simply trusts to God's testimony, as it is of mysteries for the philosopher who assumes to judge the Scriptures, instead of consenting to be judged by them.

There is mystery in the personal existence of the devil, and in the influence which he exerts upon us. His influence is so clearly asserted in the Scriptures that we cannot deny it without doing them violence. But as to its origin, its nature, its extent —on all these points we are left in almost total ignorance. There is mystery in the power granted to the devil to lay his infamous snares for the Son of God himself. We can understand how he tempts us, for by sin we have become subject to his sway ; but how can we conceive of his being permitted to tempt "The Lord of lords, the Holy of holies," him "in whom he hath nothing ?" There is mystery in the nature of the temptation to which Jesus Christ was subjected. "He was tempted," and yet "without sin :" these two facts are expressly affirmed in the Scriptures : but seek to take a step further, and you are hedged in on every side. How can we explain a struggle against temptation, when there is no inward propensity to sin ? Yet, how can we reconcile an inward propensity to do wrong, with unspotted holiness ? If it were impossible for Jesus to fall, where is the glory of his triumph ? If it were possible, what becomes of his divine nature ? There is mystery, finally, in the manner in which the scene here described took place. Its basis is assuredly a real fact ; everything proves it, the tone of the narrative, the locality assigned to the event, the character of the book : and yet the text, considered both as a whole and in its various details, shows no less certainly that the fact was beyond the limit of human experience. How can we solve this apparent contradiction ?—this conflict, of which earth was the theatre, while the actors were taken from heaven and from hell ? Where did it occur ? Was it in the visible or the invisible world ?—or was it on some dark boundary territory, in its nature partaking of both ?—Mysteries on mysteries !

These obscurities I do not even attempt to solve. I examine my text simply from that practical point of view which a child could apprehend as well as we, and, perhaps, better. Guided by these words of the Lord—"I have given you an example, that ye should do as I have done,"—let us seek the instructions which he here gives as the rule of our life. Now, in this terrible conflict of the Son of God with the spirit of darkness, we distinguish three principal things : *the conflict itself, the victory,* and *the weapons.* Each of these three will in turn afford us instruction. By the conflict which he endured, Jesus teaches us to expect a conflict also. By the victory which he won, Jesus teaches us that we in like manner may conquer. And by the weapons which he employed, Jesus teaches us how we make certain our triumph. The subject is so vast, that I have thought proper to devote three separate discourses to its consideration. We will restrict ourselves, on this occasion, to the CONFLICT which our Lord maintained in the wilderness.

This conflict should reconcile us to that which we ourselves are compelled to maintain. It is the outward expression of the struggles of our own souls. • From you who are the children of God, and who are experienced in the Christian life, I fear no contradiction in saying that its temptations confound you, and at times even threaten to prove your ruin. Upon entering the ways of the Lord, it seems to us that the devil should be kept at a distance, where it is impossible for him to annoy us. When we feel his assaults, a secret terror creeps upon us, as if the Lord were leaving us altogether. Our anxiety increases if the temptation be prolonged and rendered more fierce, especially if it happens in moments of communion with God, and, so far as we can see, answers no good purpose. In such a case, we may be driven well-nigh to a state of despair. Now, the conflict of Jesus corresponds to all this.

Jesus is tempted.—The struggle you are undergoing, He underwent before you. What do I say ? Your trial hardly deserves to be mentioned when compared with His. Temptations are manifold; they are not equal, nor is the temptation equally strong in the case of different individuals. In order, then, rightly to appreciate the nature of a temptation, we should ascertain, not only what it is in itself, but also to him who is called to endure it.

Must we, then, in the first place, consider the temptation in *itself*? Among all you have borne, you will find none to compare with that which Jesus had to endure, as related in my text. Think of it, and endeavor in imagination to put yourselves in the position of our Lord—separated from the society of men; cast out alone into the midst of a desert; surrounded by wild beasts; deprived of all food; with the devil at his side incessantly attempting to ensnare him; and all this lasting forty days and forty nights.* This situation, in which you dare not even imagine yourselves, was that of your Saviour.

But we proceed. The true standard of temptation lies not in its external conditions, but in the internal sensibilities of him whom it visits. The cold, slimy touch of a serpent is one thing to the rough skin of a herdsman, and quite another to the delicate sensitiveness of a young child. The tempter's attacks are not the same when directed against a sinner like you or me, as when directed against the "Saint of saints." If we account it a terrible thing to contend with the spirit of darkness, what must it have been to the Son of God? To us, conceived and born in iniquity, fully subject to "the prince of this world," his assaults—his onset and the blows which he aims at us—are in keeping with the natural order of things. But for "the only begotten and well beloved Son" to be exposed to them—is not this fearfully contrary to the nature of things? and must not His whole divine Being have risen up against that conflict with unspeakable horror? However this may be, He has actually been in conflict with the tempter.

---

* It appears from the account of the evangelists, that the Lord was tempted during forty days, and that after this space, the devil directed against him a final effort, which alone is detailed to us in its full particulars.

Children of God, behold this only begotten and well beloved Son, wrestling, as you now are, with the eternal enemy of God and His people! Suppose yourselves to have been living in Judea, eighteen centuries ago, and to have been informed that the promised Messiah was somewhere on the face of the earth. Where would you have sought him? I know not; but you would surely have sought Him anywhere rather than where He really was; not in the carpenter's humble abode; not among those whom John baptized, on the banks of the Jordan; above all, not in the *wilderness*, fighting with the devil. And yet there you would have found Him, and you would have searched elsewhere in vain for forty days and forty nights. But had you there at last discovered Him, would not the sight of *His* temptations have explained to you the inexplicable mystery of your own? Ah! I acknowledge it at last. The conflict before which I recoil, and under which I had well-nigh sunk, is the common lot of humanity—a lot so unavoidable, that it must needs be waged, even when humanity was united to divinity itself! Then let temptation come, let it come in its most bitter, its most prostrating form, nothing shall either surprise or terrify me! Jesus we must seek in the wilderness; Jacob at the brook of Jabbok; Moses at Massah, and at Meribah; Daniel in the lion's den; John in his exile; Chrysostom in his disgrace; John Huss at the Council of Constance; Luther at the Diet of Worms!

Jesus "was tempted"—and *in what?* The Holy Spirit answers "in *all points.*" Yes, verily, "in all points;" follow Him by the light of my text, and you will see Him tempted at all times, in all places, in all ways.

1. *At all times.*—This is but "the beginning of sorrows"—a beginning which the sequel will complete. "The temptation" being "ended" for this time, "the devil departs from Him, but only for a season." He will return to the charge—do not doubt it—he will return to it throughout the whole of Christ's career; he will renew it especially when it shall reach the great, the decisive hour. After having once wounded his heel in the

6

wilderness, he will inflict a second wound at Golgotha, in order that Jesus, who has begun to tread upon this serpent in his solitude, may finally crush his head on the cross. Thus, at the two extremes of the ministry of the Son of God, do we find two great temptations, the most terrible of all, opening and shutting the series of all those which assailed Him in succession for three and a half years. The first a temptation of covetousness—the rejection of all earth's promises; the second, a temptation of suffering—all the rage of hell, and even the wrath of heaven to be endured. We, too, shall find on our way this double temptation of the desert and the cross, and, generally, in the same order. At the beginning of the Christian course, we are called upon to overcome earthly desires by self-denial; at a later period, and especially in the last struggle, to subdue by patience the pains of the body and the anguish of the mind. "If any man will come after me, *let him deny himself*, and take up *his cross.*"

2. *In all places.*—Here we need not wander from our text. We here find Jesus tempted in the wilderness, tempted on the mountain, tempted in the holy city. There are men who have buried themselves in deserts, hoping thus to avoid temptation—strange delusion! Did they, then, forget that it was in a desert that the Lord was tempted? You may have escaped the company of your fellow-men, but how will you escape Satan, and your own heart? These two foes, the outward and the inward, banded together against you, will follow you wherever you go. In the wilderness, on the mountain, in the holy city—that is to say, in solitude, in the world, in the church—*everywhere*, you will have to meet temptation. Our business is not to flee, but to fight: not to exchange the temptations of one form of life for those of another—temptations so much the more dangerous in such a case because of our own selecting,—but stoutly to contend against the temptations of that particular position in which it has pleased God to place us.

Finally, and this is my **principal** remark—*in all ways.* Here, once more, I appeal to my text. The devil stops only after having "ended *all* the temptation." Of all the temptations to which Jesus was subjected, that of the desert is the most characteristic and complete. We see here the enemy collecting his whole energies, exhausting in turn all his resources, all his means. It is more than *a* temptation, it is *the* temptation ; it is a system, and, so to speak, an entire course of temptations. For the devil acts according to a plan, which we should know, and which the Holy Ghost reveals to us : "the lust of the *flesh*, the lust of the *eyes*, and the pride of *life*."* He adhered to that plan with Eve, who yielded to temptation when she saw, first, that the fruit "was good for *food*," then "that it was pleasant to the *eyes*," and lastly, that it was "to be desired to *make one wise*." He adopted it, especially with Jesus, whom he tempted first by the wants of the flesh ; secondly, by the exhibition of earthly pomp; lastly, by the pride of a wonderful miracle. His intention in this place will appear very clearly if, instead of simply looking at the temptation as such, you penetrate into its spirit. Satan endeavors to make the Lord succumb, in the first place, by a spirit of distrust towards God ; then, by a spirit of unfaithfulness to God ; lastly, by a spirit of rash confidence in God. He appeals in succession to want of faith, to forgetfulness of faith, to abuse of faith. How skillfully is all this contrived, nicely arranged, and prosecuted to the end!

Still farther, everything is an instrument in the tempter's hands. When his own resources fail, he employs those that are used against him, and turns into weapons for his own purpose, the very means of resistance. Jesus has just heard a voice proclaiming him as the Son of God ; the devil endeavors to seduce him by that glorious title. Jesus has been clothed by the Holy Ghost with superhuman dignity ; the devil endeavors to make

---

* 1 John, ii. 16. The order in which the Apostle names the three great principles of human covetousness cannot have been taken at random, especially as that order occurs in Eve's temptation, and in that of our Lord (as recorded by St. Luke). It seems that the three temptations were here arranged according to their degree of subtlety. The first was a temptation of the flesh ; the second, of the eyes ; the third, of the spirit.

him abuse his power.   Jesus fasts ; the devil seeks to push him
to extremities by hunger.   In order the better to succeed, the
traitor "is transformed into an angel of light ;" he acts the
saint, he consents to make use of holy things ; the holy temple,
the holy city, and even the holy word of God, are made available by his perfidious hands.

Observe, especially, the use he makes of the name Messiah,
which Jesus bears.   Upon it he constructs the whole temptation.
Jesus may exhibit himself as the Messiah, provided his Messiah-
ship be not such as the holy prophets have described, but according to the conceptions of the carnal-minded Jews.   In this he
expected the better to succeed, from the circumstance that he
was addressing a Jew, and a Jew interested in answering the
expectations of his countrymen.   The Messiah is endued with
supernatural power : Satan desires him to use it, not according
to the sense of the prophets, that he may save the souls of men,
but according to the sense of the carnal Jews, in satisfying his
carnal desires and theirs—"If thou be the Son of God, command this stone to be made bread."   The Messiah must inherit
all the kingdoms of the world :—be it so.   Satan desires that
he receive them, not, as the prophets have foretold, from the
Father's hand, and as the reward of his sacrifice ; but as the
carnal Jews expected, without a struggle, and from the hand of
the prince of this world—"If thou wilt worship me, all shall
be thine."   In fine, to the Messiah attach glorious promises of
aid and of deliverance.   Satan wills that he should make use
of these, not, in the acceptation of the prophets, that he may
accomplish his work of mercy in spite of all obstacles, in spite
of Satan himself ; but, as the carnal Jews anticipated to forward
his own glory together with that of his people—"If thou be the
Son of God, cast thyself down from hence."   Such are the wiles
of this fallen spirit ; such are the coils of this serpent !   So true
is it that he spared no effort to procure the downfall of Jesus,
had it been possible for him to fall.

O you, then, who are besieged, and, as it were, overwhelmed

with temptations, cease from your complainings ! When all things conspire against you ; when your endeavors, your precautions, your supports, your very prayers become a snare to you ; when you feel comfortless, weak, abandoned of men, separated from God, ready to die of anguish—cast one look, one single look, at Jesus in the wilderness ! Believe it ; one moment spent with Him during those forty painful days, would have left you recollections capable of strengthening you forever against the doubts which the overwhelming force of temptation suggests, and against the murmurs which it forces from your lips. If you supply, by faith, that interview, you will feel your courage rise. What can happen to you which has not happened to Jesus ? What, indeed, can you meet with but what is far below the trials He had to suffer ? No, no, children of God, your Father has not forgotten you ! He but deals with you as He has dealt with His only-begotten and well-beloved Son. In this are ye " conformed to the image of his Son, that he might be the first-born among many brethren." " We have not an high-priest which cannot be touched with the feeling of our infirmities ; but was in all points tempted like as we are, yet without sin. Let us, therefore, come boldly unto the throne of grace, that we may obtain mercy, and find grace to help in time of need."

Jesus is tempted—and *when ? after* what ? and *before* what ?

After His baptism, after His fervent prayer, after the heavens have opened above His head, after the Holy Spirit has descended on Him, after the voice from heaven has been heard : " This is my beloved Son, in whom I am well pleased ;" after all this, and even, according to Mark, " immediately" after. It is this moment of glory and of spiritual blessing which is selected for the temptation. Selected by Satan, because then the Son of God excites to the highest degree His anger and His jealousy ; but, at the same time, selected by God, because his Son is then better fortified against all the assaults of the enemy. When, therefore, you are a prey to temptation, do not suppose that you have been forsaken of God. If Satan gathers all his forces against you, it is, perhaps, because signal graces are making you the object for his blows, whilst, at the same time, they prepare you to repulse them.

We said that temptation is the common lot of humanity : let us add that extraordinary temptations constitute the privilege of the best. God keeps such trials in store for those heroes of the faith, whom no impediment arrests, and no difficulty confounds : for a Moses, a Samuel, a Jeremiah, a poor woman from Canaan, a centurion of Capernaum, a Peter, a Paul. Nor is this all. He reserves them not only for the strongest, but, farther, for the period of their greatest strength. God has spared them during the early season of their spiritual career, when they could only lean upon the conscious piety of first-love ; just as a humane ordinance of Moses exempted for one year every newly-married man from the service of war, in order that he might "remain at home and cheer up his wife which he had taken." But, when once this power of feeling has been replaced by another power, more constant and firm—that of the faith, which knows how "to hope against hope," then comes the season of fatigue and of war ; then the Lord calls His children to severer contests, which keep alike and develop their holy courage. You have just been baptized with a fresh baptism of the Holy Ghost; you have just poured out your whole heart before God in a humble, fervent prayer ; you have just seen heaven opened, in some sort, over you, and heard the voice of the Almighty, " bearing witness with your spirit that are a child of God :" you believe that, for this time at least, you are beyond the attacks of the evil one. Be not deceived. This is the very moment when you should expect him, and place double watch around your heart : watch, then, and pray. But also remember, that this is the moment in which God has been careful to strengthen you beforehand ; therefore, take courage. It was when Paul had been "caught up to the third heaven," that there was "given to him a thorn in the flesh, a messenger of Satan to buffet him."

And *before* what was Jesus tempted? Before, immediately before the beginning of His ministry ; on the eve of entering upon a career wholly devoted to the glory of God, to the salvation of men, to the holiest work that ever was known. As long as Jesus remains at Nazareth concealed in humble life in the workshop of Joseph, we do not hear that the devil went to seek Him ; but He no sooner commences His public duties, He no sooner devotes himself to the mission which He has received from His heavenly Father, than He is arrested at the very outset. Be not, then, astonished at seeing temptation either approach or increase when you are engaged in some good work, some pious undertaking, some enterprise approved of God and man.

You especially, young servants of the Lord, who are preparing to exercise in His church the ministry of the Word,* do not think that anything extraordinary has happened to you, if the time you spend in this holy preparation should be for your soul a time of uncommon trial. As long as you lived under the shelter of the paternal roof in happy obscurity, the faith you imbibed there was as a second nature increasing with your years, and seemed to you so deeply rooted that no storm could ever shake it. But now, deprived of a father's watchful guidance, and of the tender counsels of a faithful mother, called upon to face an unbelieving, a profane world—a world that tolerates everything but what is holy and true—now, having learned enough in the science of divine things to raise more than one perplexing question, yet not enough to solve the questions raised, you are terror-stricken by thoughts of a skeptical nature creeping into your heart.

My young friend, be not troubled ; this is the common history of all those who have trodden the path before you ; it is the history even of the holiest and most faithful. "The enemy hath done this ;" and he does it because he sees you so profitably

---

* These three Discourses were preached before the Theological Students at Montauban

occupied. He might, perhaps, consent to leave you more at ease, if you yourself would consent to bury the talent which you have received from the Lord ; for, then, by causing you to fall, he would be injuring you only. But now it is your future ministry he hopes to frustrate ; it is a whole people he hopes to deprive of the Word of life, if he succeeds in robbing you of "your most holy faith." It is this that renders him so vigilant and so active. The work of the Holy Spirit and that of the devil are closely connected ; the first provokes the second ; and in the invisible world, heaven is nigh unto hell. The Holy Ghost conducts Jesus into the wilderness where He is tempted by the devil ; and Satan, when about to tempt Job, appears "in the heavenly places," in the midst of "the sons of God." Forewarned as you are by the example of the Lord himself, fearlessly await the evil one. "Resist the devil, and he will flee from you." Does he render you indifferent in the perusal of the Bible ? Pursue your meditations with increased eagerness. Does he discourage you in prayer ? Pray with more ardor, with more perseverance. Does he turn you away from the simplicity of the faith ? Endeavor to grow in the disposition of a little child, as well as in the learning of a theologian. As soon as the enemy sees that you turn his attacks to your own advantage, he will become weary, and desist rather than benefit you so much. At any rate, he can undertake nothing against you which the temptation of Jesus Christ should not have caused you to anticipate. The doctors of the synagogue themselves can here instruct you. One of their apocryphal books, Ecclesiasticus, begins its second chapter thus : "My son, if thou come to serve the Lord, prepare thy soul for temptation."

Finally, Jesus is tempted—and *why?* The complete answer to this question touches upon those mysteries which we do not pretend to investigate. But the Scriptures tell us everywhere that our Lord's temptation was necessary. "It behoved him," the Apostle expressly says, "to be made like in all things unto his brethren, that He might be a merciful and faithful high priest in all things pertaining to God, to make reconciliation for the sins of the people. For in that He himself hath suffered, being tempted, He is able to succor them that are tempted." It was, no doubt, necessary likewise, to justify, by the victory of Jesus Christ, the condemnation of man, overcome in the same conflict ; to fill the measure of the Messiah's expiatory sufferings ; to begin to exhibit in him, before the face of heaven, of earth, of hell, that the Son of God was manifested, "that He might destroy the works of the devil ;" perhaps, for aught we know, to reveal Him completely to himself, to make Him "perfect through trial," and to carry Him forward, "conquering and to conquer." Whatever the reason may be, it was necessary that Jesus should be tempted ; that is enough. The temptation was no mere accident in His life ; it was useful, essential to it ; it entered into the plan of our redemption. All the images under which the prophets had described the coming Messiah, looked to a strife between himself and the spirit of darkness—a strife, of which the narrative supplied by the text is but the prelude. Having come to establish a kingdom, but to establish it upon the ruins of a usurper, the Messiah—that true Joshua—could obtain His dominion only by conquest ; He could receive "the inheritance of the nations" only by wresting it from "the prince of this world." The Jews had understood it thus themselves, and it was an article in their belief that the Messiah should be tempted by Satan at the very outset of his career. Our text, in its turn, acknowledges in the temptation this kind of necessity. Everything is foreseen, arranged, willed by God. Jesus "is led," or, as Mark has it, "driven by the spirit" into the wilderness, where He is tempted by the devil.* Matthew expresses himself in terms still more positive : "He was led up of the spirit into the wilderness, to be tempted of the devil." The devil tempts Him, and then departs from Him, "having ended all the temptation ;" as having played his part, for we know that whilst

---

* Mark i. 12 ; the expression of the Evangelist has peculiar energy, it signifies *cast*, *thrown*.

tempting Jesus, as well as whilst crucifying Him, he could only do whatsoever "the hand and the counsel of God determined before to be done."

Let us learn from this, my dear friends, that the trials of which we complain are useful to us also, essential to perfect our holiness, and to fit us for the work which God hath given us to do in the world. "God," says James, "tempteth no man," because he never drives us to sin; but he may bring us into temptation, as he did in the case of his Son, in order to "prove us, and to know what is in our heart." If we resist temptation, we come forth from it stronger and more devoted, purified as gold in the fire. But if we yield, then, no doubt, we bear the punishment of our cowardice; although, even then, if repentance lifts us up again, we have, at least, learned to know our own weakness, and to seek our strength only in the Lord.

It is by this incessant battle while proceeding from victory to victory—or, alas! instead of constant victories alternate victories and defeats—that the wholesome exercise, of our faith acquires its development. The tempest prostrates and uproots the tree slightly rooted in the soil; but, if it shakes the one whose grasp is firm, it is only for the purpose of driving deeper and deeper down those thousand hidden arms by which it penetrates and clings firmly to the earth. "Tribulation," the Apostle writes, "worketh patience, patience experience, and experience hope." * What is here said of tribulation, that species of temptation most frequently dwelt upon in the Word of God, is also true of all other forms. And hence the Apostle James,

* Rom. v. 3, 4. In order to understand distinctly these deep truths, we must bear in mind that *experience* here means, the test which tribulation makes of our faith, and the tested (or tried) character it imparts to it. *Hope*, likewise, does not signify an expectation more or less uncertain, but the firm assurance of those good things to come which we as yet possess only by faith (Rom. viii. 22, 24). When we are afflicted, we are exercised to patience; when we have suffered with patience we know on trial our faith to be genuine; and when our faith has thus been tried, we have a firm and glorious assurance in the grace of the Lord.

in the energetic and paradoxical language so peculiar to him, exhorts us " to count it all joy when we fall into divers tempta tions ; and calls " blessed," *not* the man who is not tempted, but him who " *endureth temptation*," that is to say, who undergoes it without yielding to it ; for, " when he is tried," viz : when he has resisted in seasons of trial, " he shall receive the crown of life, which the Lord has promised to them that love him."

If Jesus needed his temptation, we need ours also. Satan's work is necessary to complete that of the Holy Spirit ; and in this world nothing comes to perfection except it has been helped on by the devil. In order to enlighten Job's faith, to strengthen his heart and perfect his joy, the cruel display of Satan's malice was necessary. The perfidious detractors who cast Daniel into the lion's den were necessary to him, in order that he might know during the peaceful night which he spent amidst those terrible animals, all the power, and all the faithfulness of his God. Paul needed that " thorn in his flesh," that " messenger of Satan sent to buffet him," that he might be kept humble, and not " exalted above measure through the abundance of his revelations ;" that he might feel the power of that word which comforted him, and which will comfort the saints to the end of time—" When I am weak, then am I strong." Peter needed that court of the high priest, to show him his own weakness ; so that after the confession and the forgiveness of his sin, he might reappear in the eyes of the church worthier than ever of the distinction which the Lord had bestowed upon him, and which he continued to him notwithstanding his fall. Chrysostom needed the anger of his master ; Augustine, the perils of his youth ; Luther, the mortal conflicts of his soul ; Calvin, his weak health and his implacable enemies.

And you, my dear brother, whom Satan seems to have selected as the object of his most powerful attacks ; you upon whose downfall his whole pride appears bent ; you who are driven to the last extremity, and ready to succomb ; you who join in the

Messiah's cry of anguish in the Psalms : " I am come into deep waters, where the floods overflow me. . . . my throat is dried ; mine eyes fail while I wait for my God "—be assured, all this was necessary for you ; it was the very thing you required to teach you to serve God, to confound the great adversary, and to fill you with "joy unspeakable, and full of glory !" You are a child of God, his beloved, his privileged child ; and, in very truth, if we could rise above the flesh, and judge according to the word of God, we should be more inclined to envy than to pity you. " Cast not away, therefore, your confidence, which hath great recompense of reward ;" but rather resist, hold fast unto the end, give glory to God, and abound in thanksgiving !

Young servants of God, if temptation is necessary for all, it is doubly so for you. This fight which you are beginning to carry on against the opposition of the world, and especially against the natural unbelief of your own hearts, should not surprise you. It is the narrow path through which you must proceed, in order to reach a firmer faith ; in order to learn, as your Saviour did, by the anguish of temptation, to sympathize one day with the infirmities of others, and to succor those that are tempted. Listen to what was said on this subject by a great master in the school of Christian experience—a hero who fought valiantly against the powers of the world and of hell. Luther, writing to a young theologian, makes him observe, in the 119th Psalm, three principal means by which the inspired writer strengthens himself in the divine life—prayer, meditation on the Scriptures, and temptation ; and hear how he expresses himself on the last of these three points :

" Temptation is the touchstone which will make you not only know and understand, but feel, how correct the Word of God is, how true, how sweet, how lovely, how powerful, how consoling, how wise above all other wisdom. Without temptation there are no good preachers, but only mere babblers, who know not themselves of what they speak, nor why ; as says Paul to Timothy, ' desiring to be teachers of the law, understanding neither what they say, nor whereof they affirm.' This is why you see David in our psalm often complaining of all sorts of enemies, oppressors, rebellious and obstinate spirits, whom he must endure, because he carries everywhere with him the Word of God. For as soon as you begin to give your witness to the Word of God, the devil will endeavor to tempt you, that you may become a good divine, and that through the trials by which he visits you, you may learn to explore and to love this Word of life. I am under the greatest obligations to the Papists myself, who, with the aid of all the din of Satan, have so ill-treated me, and driven me to such an extremity of anguish, that they have succeeded in making of me a tolerable theologian, which I never could have been but for their assistance ; and as for what, on the other hand, they have gained from me, I willingly yield to them the honors, the victories, and the triumphs, which make up the whole object of their desires."

Lord Jesus ! we would no more complain of temptation. We have this day found thee in the wilderness ; thither we will not refuse to follow thee. We have glanced at what thou hast suffered, being tempted, and the sight has affected us to the very depth of our hearts. Thou didst endure temptation in order to be like unto us ; shall we not consent to suffer that we also may be like unto thee? We distrust ourselves, Lord, and, as thou didst teach us, we say : " Lead us not into temptation !" But if into temptation we must be led, then, we confidently add, as thou hast further taught us : " Deliver us from the Evil One !" It is enough for us to remember that we have in thee " a merciful and faithful high priest, who, because he has himself suffered, being tempted, can also succor those who are tempted." How sweet is this thought to us, O Lord ! Thus, whatever be our temptations, thou hast known them before us, thou hast beforehand overcome them for us ! Therefore it is, Oh, our compassionate Saviour ! that we pour out our hearts in thy presence with a holy freedom ; and were it possible for us to be tried as thou wert thyself tried, still would we " come boldly unto the throne of grace, that we might obtain mercy, and find grace to help in time of need." It is not at *us* that thine enemy and ours levels his blows ; *thee,* THEE alone, he attacks in us : Thou, therefore, must defend us ! Triumph over him in us ! And since thou hast been tempted like as we are, make us conquerors like unto thy-self ! Amen.

DISCOURSE V.

THE VICTORY OF CHRIST OVER SATAN.

" And Jesus, being full of the Holy Ghost, returned from Jordan, and was led by the Spirit into the wilderness, being forty days tempted of the devil," etc.—Luke iv. 1-13.

MY DEAR CHRISTIAN FRIENDS :

The conflict of Jesus has reconciled us to that which we must endure : His victory will be a pledge that we too shall conquer in turn.

That which makes us feeble to resist temptation, is our uncertainty as to the issue of the strife. Nothing would be impossible to us, were we assured of victory ; but doubt, bitter doubt, destroys our courage. You are tempted by a spirit of sloth ; you wish you could become " fervent in spirit," and " instant in prayer ;" but you doubt whether you can overcome your spiritual indolence—and, in spite of yourself, you continue to creep slowly along the path in which God invites you to run. You are tempted by a spirit of discontent : under the weight of a heavy and prolonged affliction, you wish you could abound in thanksgiving ; but you doubt whether you will be able to overcome the grief which oppresses you—and your life continues to be spent in fruitless and ungrateful complainings. You are tempted by a spirit of unbelief ; you wish you could rely upon God's word with an unshaken confidence ; you well know that from this source must come your peace, your strength, your satisfaction ; but you doubt whether you will be able to eradicate a sluggishness of faith which has been fostered by temperament, by education, by example, by habit—and you go on wretchedly vacillating between the truth of God and the cavils of the natural heart. You are tempted by a spirit of lust; while abstaining from such excesses as would dishonor your Christian profession, "you make provision for the flesh, to fulfil the lust thereof," and you feel weighed down under a humiliating yoke which is burdensome to bear; but you doubt whether you can address yourself to a life of self-sacrificing devotion—and you go on indulging in a pleasurable and enervating indolence.

Oh! you, who recognize yourselves in this sad picture, come and learn from the history of my text, that you can conquer every temptation. Jesus, like you, has been tempted; and while the first Adam yielded in Eden, the second Adam has gained a universal conquest in the wilderness. His victory is complete. After forty days of unceasing attacks, after a final and desperate assault, the adversary sees himself at last compelled to raise the siege, ashamed and convinced of his weakness, and Jesus has acquired the right to say: "The prince of this world has nothing in me." Not one of "the fiery darts of the wicked" could find an open way to His heart. It is written: "He was in all points tempted like as we are, yet without sin;" no sin before nor with the temptation; no sin after the temptation, nor proceeding from it. In him we have "an high priest who is holy, harmless, undefiled, separate from sinners." Well, if Jesus has thus conquered, you too may conquer.

Here, as before, we must begin by setting aside the mysterious part of our subject, and the questions more curious than useful to which it has given rise. Between the temptation of Jesus and our temptation, the analogy is not complete; for, as children of a corrupt race, we harbor within us lusts which Jesus never knew. Although He took upon himself the infirmities which sin had introduced into our nature, far be it from us to suppose that He shared in the slightest measure the sinful tendency itself. We may distinguish three kinds of temptations: that of Jesus, that

of Adam, and our own ; the first was without sin, both before
and after the trial ; the second without sin before the trial, but
not after ; the third accompanied by sin before, as well as after,
according to the declaration of St. James in that passage of his
epistle : " Every man is tempted, when he is drawn away of his
own lust, and enticed ; then when lust hath conceived, it bringeth
forth sin." Hence, upon the moral character of temptation, and
the degree of holiness to which we can attain during this life,
have arisen those questions which have more than once agitated
the church, but which we think it neither necessary nor possible
satisfactorily to solve. However this may be, I here confine
myself to the application which concerns us in our actual condition, and I leave the subject on that practical ground chosen by
the Apostle James in the words just quoted. Our business is to
prevent lust from conceiving, and from bringing forth sin ; we
can always do this. Of all the temptations you encounter on
your way, there is not one which you cannot overcome, as Jesus
overcame his, and as Adam might have overcome his also. Thus,
you who are tempted by a spirit of sloth, can " have life, and
have it more abundantly." You who are tried by a spirit of
discontent, can " rejoice evermore," and sing aloud " with the
voice of thanksgiving." You who are tempted by a spirit of
unbelief, can " continue in the faith, stablished, strengthened,
and settled ;" and you who are tried by a spirit of sensuality,
can " keep under your body, bring it into subjection, and mor-
tify its deeds through the spirit." You *can* do it : for, what you
are called upon to do, Jesus has already done.

Perhaps you will answer : Jesus was the Son of God ; His victory proves nothing as to us. If such an objection were valid
here, it would be equally so elsewhere. Then would it be vain
to set forth the pattern of Jesus before men ; then would the
Holy Spirit have said in vain : " Christ has left us an example,
that we should follow His steps." But this objection comes from
a source which accounts for many other errors, both of doctrine
and of practice ; which is, that we ignore, or, at all events, lose

sight of the human nature of our Lord, which it is quite as necessary to be kept in mind as His divinity. Yes, Jesus was the Son of God, but He was also the Son of man ; and as it was in His human nature that He was tempted, in His human nature likewise He overcame temptation. In thus speaking, we by no means leave out of sight the divine nature of the Lord in the narrative of the text. We do not forget that Jesus had been, immediately before the temptation, declared to be the Son of God, filled with the Holy Spirit, and thereby strengthened for the conflict which awaited Him. I would only have you observe, my dear friends, that during the conflict itself the narrative of the Evangelists shows us in Jesus the Son of Man alone, while the Son of God disappears. And yet I mistake—the Son of God does show himself, but only in the words of Satan. The devil reminds Jesus of that title, for the purpose of tempting Him now by doubt, then through presumption, and then again through ambition : but Jesus does not make use of it as a means of defence. Had He wished to display His divine power, He might have prayed—as He himself declared in that other struggle which marked the close of his career—" to His Father, who would have given Him more than twelve legions of angels." What do I say ? He needed no angel ; one word from His lips, and Satan would have been overthrown like the messengers from the Sanhedrim in the garden of Gethsemane. But He does nothing of the kind ; He confines His energy to man's sphere of action. He wrestles against Satan with man's infirmities, and with the means which man has at his disposal. He endures hunger, and allows himself to be approached, parleyed with, and tempted like a man. Like a man, He stands through confidence in God, and triumphs by the power of God.* Above all, like a man, He quotes the Scriptures, which were written by men for men. As we see Him on another occasion in His anguish supported by an angel—Him " whom the angels of God worship "—so we here

---

* Ephes. vi. 10, and following verses. In this passage St. Paul seems to allude to our Lord's conflict.

see Him resting upon Moses, Lord and master of Moses as He
is ! Wondrous source of astonishment and of admiration ! What
need had He to turn over as we do the books of His servant, in
order to find answers to the seductions of the evil one ? Might
He not have drawn them from His own resources ? Is He not
the only begotten Son who is in the bosom of the Father," who
is in heaven, and who " speaketh from heaven ?" Yes, but it
was necessary that here He should speak from earth, to be an
example for those who are " of the earth." This remark is so
true, that, not satisfied with appealing only to the Scriptures,
He selects from the Scriptures only those passages which apply
indiscriminately to all believers. As for the numerous testimonies concerning the Messiah exclusively, and which guarantee to
Him the victory, He alludes to none of them—so resolved is He
to draw merely from the common treasury of the whole church.
The more extraordinary this circumstance, the more manifest is
its intention. Against a temptation common to man, Jesus
gains by human resources a human victory, to teach human
beings that they may overcome even as He overcame.

Still farther : not only did Jesus conquer in humanity, but *for*
humanity. Engaged in the contest of the wilderness as the
Saviour and representative of man, it is in the name and on the
behalf of man that he gains a victory, the fruits of which will
be gathered by all who believe in his name. Had he not conquered for us, how could his triumph strengthen us against the
tribulations of the world ? " In the world ye shall have tribulation : but be of good cheer, I have overcome the world. He
alone could "bind the strong man ;" but the strong man once
bound, he does not enter alone "the strong man's house, and
spoil his goods ;" we also enter after him. Satan is *already*
defeated, before he attacks us ; and his power is so much the
less against us, as he finds Him present in us by whom he was
vanquished in the wilderness. The victory is made so sure unto
us in Jesus, that the Scriptures represent us as having already
obtained it : " Ye are strong, and the word of God abideth in

you, and ye have overcome the wicked one." In Jesus all is accomplished ; "we are more than conquerors through him that loved us :" nothing more is left for us except to join in his triumph, and in order to join in it we have only to believe on his name : "Whosoever is born of God overcometh the world ; and this is the victory that overcometh the world, even our faith." "That roaring lion who walketh about, seeking whom he may devour," is, no doubt, formidable : but he has vainly tried his strength against "the lion of the tribe of Judah, the root of David, who hath prevailed,"* and to whom the spirit of prophecy thus speaketh : "From the prey, my son, thou art gone up ; he stooped down, he couched as a lion, and as a terrible lion ; who shall rouse him up ?"† He alone is invincible, and it is he who fights for us : "For thus hath the Lord spoken unto me : Like as the lion and the young lion roaring on his prey, when a multitude of shepherds is called forth against him, he will not be afraid of their voice nor abase himself for their number, so shall the Lord of hosts come down to fight for Mount Zion, and for the hill thereof."‡ Fear not : "greater is he that is in you, than he that is in the world."§

Let us then rest assured that the victory of Jesus guarantees our own, and that we shall find in him efficient aid, since he himself has met and overcome temptation. Such is the idea of the Holy Spirit in those two passages from the Epistle to the Hebrews which we have already cited : "Because he himself has suffered, being tempted, he is able to succor them that are tempted ;" and again : "As he was in all points tempted like as we are, yet without sin, let us therefore come boldly unto the throne of grace, that we may obtain mercy, and find grace to help in time of need."

* Rev. v. 5.   † Gen. xlix. 9.   ‡ Isaiah, xxxi. 4.
§ 1 John iv. 4. Compare with this passage 2 Kings vi. 16: "Fear not, for they that be with us are more than they that be with them ;" and 2 Chron. xxxii. 7: "Be not afraid nor dismayed for the king of Assyria, nor for all the multitude that is with him ; for one more powerful than all that are with him is with us."

I might stop here : this doctrine is sufficiently established, especially as supported by the narrative before us : but the soul that is "weary and heavy laden" is not so readily assured : it wants new encouragements, which I have no disposition to refuse. In the presence of temptation, it is tormented by two things : its own weakness, and the strength of the temptation. If we examine ourselves, we find that we are unable to resist even the most ordinary temptation ; and if we consider the temptation, we see that it is strong enough to overwhelm us, even when we are strongest. But let us once more draw nigh unto Jesus tempted in the wilderness : his victory will help to reassure us in both these respects.

You are *weak*, my dear brother ; so weak, so languishing, so destitute, so cast down both in body and in mind, that you find yourself unable to overcome the least temptation. Such, indeed, would be the case, if you were left to triumph in your own strength. But do you suppose that it was in his own strength that your Lord triumphed in the desert? You conceive of him, perhaps, as a stranger to all your weakness—calm, unmovable. But this portrait is the work of your imagination, not of the Scriptures. They show the Messiah to us as "a man of sorrows, and acquainted with grief." They say nothing, it is true, about the state of his mind during the struggle in the desert ; and it does not become us to supply what they have left unsaid, nor to state how far his forty days' fast must have exhausted his strength or impaired his courage. But the Scriptures exhibit the Saviour elsewhere under the weight of sufferings which you have never known—in Gethsemane, "exceeding sorrowful, even unto death, falling on his face, and praying in agony, while his sweat was as it were great drops of blood falling to the ground." They exhibit him on the cross crying to his God : "My God, my God, why hast thou forsaken me?" Where, then, does he find his strength? In God. The aim of the whole temptation is to separate him from God : first, let him provide for his own wants independently of the providence of God ; then, let him receive the ownership of the nations, but not as the gift of God ; finally, let him display his divine glory without the command of God. But solely upon God does Jesus rely : it is not in his own strength that he wrestles and conquers ; but in the strength of his Father.

Receive instruction, then, my dear friends. / If you are less strong than Jesus, your God is not less strong than the God of Jesus. Let this rock be your rock, and His strength shall be your strength. For Jesus, for Adam, for yourselves, the question here is not a question of strength ; it is one of *faith*. As your own strength could not deliver you *without* faith, so neither can your own weakness injure you *with* faith. Nay, if advantage be taken of it, this weakness may be of service to you ; and a sense of it driving you, it may be, to seek God's help, you will experience the truth of this word : "When I am weak, then am I strong." Strange paradox ! sublime truth ! Instead of stopping to discuss it, believe it, live upon it. You are, my dear brother, poor and languishing, downcast in body and in mind, incapable of overcoming the least temptation ! This is well, you are in the very condition which will enable you to triumph. Now it is, that conscious of all the illusions of pride, and absolutely despairing of yourself, you will seek to " be strong in the Lord, and in the power of His might ;" now it is that you will " take unto you the whole armor of God, that you may be able to stand against the wiles of the devil." Cling to God, as the branch does to the vine ; in Him you will find "grace to help in time of need." *In time of need*, note well this expression ; it is for the moment of need that His strength is promised you. You would like to enjoy it beforehand, to reassure yourself against the terrors of the future, by a complacent consideration of your spiritual supplies. But such are not the Lord's ways ; He does not give you to-day what you require for to-morrow ; but He will certainly supply to-day for to-day, and to-morrow for to-morrow. The man whose hand was withered, and to whom Jesus said : " Stretch out thine hand," would never have done so, if he had waited to receive beforehand the strength requisite for that act ; but at the Lord's word he stretches out his hand, and lo, it is healed—" only believe, and thou shalt see the glory of God !"

The temptation, you say again, is *strong*, terrible, overwhelming ! But was that of Jesus less so? Compare it with that of Adam. The Scriptures themselves suggest the parallel, for it is not without design that one of those temptations has been placed at the beginning of the Old Testament, and the other at the opening of the New ; opposing here as everywhere, "the second Adam" to "the first." Adam is tempted in Eden,* Jesus, in the wilderness ; Adam, amidst the abundance of all things ; Jesus, in want and in hunger. Adam is tempted once and falls, Jesus is tempted three times, we should say rather He is tempted for forty days, and He resists. And what a temptation ! How subtle, how perfidious—mixing so adroitly truth and falsehood, good and evil, that it seems impossible to separate them ! Verily, this is the masterpiece of the spirit of darkness. It is true, as we have already stated, that we cannot exactly balance the Lord's temptation either with Adam's or our own ; but we know at least, that He had to undergo a conflict, by a mystery which we do not attempt to penetrate, a terrible conflict, of which the anguish of Golgotha and Gethsemane can give us some idea. But what signifies the strength of the temptation ? It is enough that it was the Holy Ghost who led Jesus into the wilderness to be tempted there. God, who allows the trial, is also He who measures it ; and He will have taken care, you may be sure, to strengthen His Son for the combat according to His need. He will do the same, my dear friends, for you ; and this is why no temptation, present or to come, should appear to you irresistible. For, recollect this, although it is the devil who tempts, and not God, it is God who measures the temptation, and not the devil ; and He measures it either according to the

* *Eden* signifies " a place of delights."

strength which you have, or according to that which He has in store for you.

This consolatory truth is shown to us in the clearest light by the history of Job. Was Satan ever allowed greater liberty against a poor servant of God? Nevertheless, he still is fastened to his chain, which God lengthens or shortens at His pleasure, but which Satan never can outgo ; and the Holy Spirit makes us perceive it on this occasion, that we may know the devil is never without his bonds, although we do not always see them. Satan can undertake nothing against Job without first having obtained God's permission ; "Put forth thine hand now, and touch all that he hath." Then, when God grants him the permission, God makes reservations in favor of His servant. First, Job's person is reserved : "Behold, all that he hath is in thy power, only upon himself put not forth thine hand." At a later period, when this first temptation has fortified Job for a harder trial, God once more, entreated by Satan, abandons to him the person of his servant, but on this occasion he reserves his life : "Behold, he is in thine hand, but save his life."* If Job had fallen under the first surprise of this new attack, if he had yielded to despair, he would have justified the enemy's insolent prediction : "He will curse thee to thy face." But now he has leisure to recollect himself, to listen to Elihu, to humble himself before God ; and notwithstanding a few imprudent words which the excess of his bitterness forces from his lips, he remains firm, he drives back the adversary in confusion, and, recovering God's favor in a double measure, he is referred to as a model of patience in the New Testament.† Be comforted, then, my dear

---

* Job ii. 4. Notice the gradation which Satan introduces in the temptations he successively presents to Job ; the loss of his fortune, the loss of his family, the loss of his health, and, if he had obtained leave, the loss of his life. A certain pride of feeling would, perhaps, have induced us to reverse this order ; but "the old serpent" knows this matter better than we do, and the dexterity of the course he follows is warranted by God's own authority in this surprising narration.

† James v. 11. We can scarcely refrain from surprise in seeing Job proposed by St. James as a pattern of patience. How are we to reconcile this testimony with those many bitter complaints to which Job gives expression in the third chapter of his history? God

friends, by the thought that the devil can never tempt you but by the leave of your heavenly Father, and never beyond the extent which he permits.* Without this permit, or beyond those limits, he can do nothing against you. Never, then, say that your trials exceed your strength; such an accusation, apparently aimed at the devil, would be directed against God himself.

If the proof which I have just given you from history does not seem sufficient, if you demand a formal declaration from the Lord's own hand, here is one; but after that be satisfied, and doubt no more. It is written: "There hath no temptation befallen you but such as is common to man." So much for the past; now for the future: "And God is faithful, who will not suffer you to be tempted above that ye are able, but will with the temptation also make a way to escape, that ye may be able to bear it." What more do you want? Recall the past: "There hath no temptation taken you but such as is common to man;" that is to say, connected with human nature, and consequently surmountable by it—I say by human nature, not such as it was in Jesus, nor even such as it was in Adam, but such as it

---

is more merciful in his judgments than we are in ours. God measures the patience of his saints not simply by the degree of their submission, but by that degree combined with the extent of their sufferings; just as a man may evince more physical strength while dragging painfully a considerable weight, than another man would by carrying easily a light burden. Above all, God looks to the heart; and the heart is revealed but very imperfectly through those external manifestations which alone are perceptible by man. A man who utters bitter complaints may have more inward submission to God's will, than another who is better able to moderate the expression of his feelings. This last remark is confirmed by a deep study of Job's complaints. Even in the boldness which characterizes them, and which we cannot entirely justify, we perceive a liberty and familiarity with God, which indicates an unshaken confidence in Him, and which honors and pleases Him more than the blameless moderation of many. Job's heart is revealed to us by that of Jeremiah in the following Scripture, which will prove offensive, perhaps, to more than one reader, but which is, I know infinitely precious as viewed by God: "Righteous are thou, O Lord, when I plead with thee; yet let me talk with thee [or, *reason the case*] of thy judgments."

* The same doctrine is found in Luke xxii. 31, 32: "Simon, Simon, behold, Satan hath desired to have you, that he may sift you as wheat; but I have prayed for *thee*, that thy faith fail not."

7

is in yourself. If Adam before his fall, and Jesus in the wilderness, endured any temptation beyond your strength, it is enough that you have certainly been spared them. Much more, God pledges himself to you for the future, and does so in the name of his own faithfulness : " God is *faithful*, who will not suffer you to be tempted above that ye are able" (he does not say, above what Jesus was able, nor even above what Adam was able—he says above what *you* are able); " but will with the temptation also make a way to escape, that ye may be able to bear it." After this, my dear brother, if you tell me : " Here is a temptation which I cannot overcome, it is stronger than I am," I must choose, you see, between your assertion and God's word ; for the first affirms what the second declares to be impossible. No, whatever the appearances may be, as long as God is God, and the Bible is his word, we can never have to endure a temptation which it is impossible for us to surmount.

The lesson which we have just learned from the victory of Jesus in the wilderness, is taught us in many other places of the Scriptures, and implied everywhere : we are never *compelled* to yield to temptation. Having before me a great variety of texts, I quote merely a few relating or alluding to our subject.

Some of the clearest are to be found in that very 91st psalm which Satan so imprudently placed in our hands, and which we should not have dreamed of but for the unworthy abuse he makes of it against our Master. This psalm is full of promises of victory ; but consider especially the words which immediately follow those which Satan calls to his support: " Thou shalt tread upon the lion and adder ; the young lion and the dragon shalt thou trample under feet." Why didst thou not finish the quotation, cruel enemy of our souls ? Does that verse have nothing to do with thee ? The lion and the serpent, those two images twice associated in so short a passage, may well represent all the enemies we have to encounter ; but they refer more particularly to the leader who directs and inspires them, and whom the Scripture likewise calls elsewhere, sometimes a lion, sometimes a serpent. That lion, we shall tread upon ; that serpent we shall trample under foot.

This assurance is still further given us by the words of the Apostle, where Satan is distinctly named : " The God of peace shall bruise Satan under your feet shortly." In this passage, Paul alludes to the first prophecy: " It " (the seed of the woman), " shall bruise thy head ;" and he shows what we learn in like manner from an attentive study of the prophecy itself, that the victory is there promised not only to the Messiah, but also to the whole family of believers. The same doctrine may be found in James, who no doubt had in view the temptation of Jesus in the wilderness when he wrote : " Resist the devil, and he will flee from you ; draw nigh to God, and he will draw nigh to you." But nothing can be compared with the fullness of the promises which the Holy Spirit has given us in John :   " For this purpose the Son of God was manifested, that he might destroy the works of the devil. Whosoever is born of God doth not commit sin, for his seed remaineth in him ; and he cannot sin, because he is born of God. In this the children of God are manifest, and the children of the devil." This is not the place to enlarge upon the sense of this difficult passage ; * but every one must acknowledge that it at least means that the child of God possesses in himself a secret virtue, by which he can subdue the enemy, and that he is never irresistibly constrained to yield to him the victory.

It will not do to urge against me your experience : I know too well that every one of our days is marked by some fall ; but for this we only are to blame. It will not do to urge even the experience of the most faithful among the Lord's servants, among his saints, his prophets, and his apostles. I do not forget, that, unblamable as their lives may be, when compared with

---

* The expression " cannot sin," explained by these *to commit sin*, is employed here to designate, not " a brother overtaken in a fault," but a heart *enslaved to sin*.

ours ; justified as they may be in saying to us : "Brethren, be followers together of us," yet they had also cause to say : "In many things we offend all ;" but what then ? is it through a fatal and imperative *necessity* ? Ah ! the holier they are, the more will such a thought inspire them with indignation and horror. Go and tell a Noah, that he could not have avoided becoming intoxicated in his tent ; a Jacob, that he could have obtained the promised blessing only by a lie ; a Moses, that he could not have glorified God at Meribah ; a David, that he could not have resisted the charms of Bathsheba ; an Elijah, that he could not have overcome the discouragement of his soul ; a Hezekiah, that he could not have subdued a movement of vanity; a Job, that he could not have restrained his rash complaints ; a Zacharias, that he could not have believed the words of the angel ; a Peter, that he could not have confessed his Master in the court of the high-priest : and you will see them all smite upon their breast, and lift up their eyes towards heaven, saying : "O Lord, righteousness belongeth unto thee, but unto us confusion of face !" Every time we fall, it is through our own fault ; it is because we have not faithfully used the means, always sufficient, with which God has furnished us to enable us to stand. Whatever may happen, "let God be true, but every man a liar." Let his faithfulness never be suspected. "Let no man say when he is tempted : I am tempted of God ; for God cannot be tempted of evil, neither tempteth he any man." My brother, my dear brother, "Lift up the hands which hang down, and the feeble knees." Wrestle with courage, with good cheer. You say : Oh ! if I were sure to overcome ! Well, you can always overcome in Jesus ; we are not fatalists, we are Christians. Do not make up your mind to any fall. Live not, knowingly and willingly, on terms with any sin. "Be not overcome of evil, but overcome evil with good."

Learn moreover of Jesus, the conqueror in the wilderness, what may be the results of one single victory. In our Lord's history, the temptation is one of those critical epochs, which decide a whole life, just as a battle, lost or gained, may decide a whole campaign. Thus circumstanced, the victory of Jesus not only keeps Satan away for a season ; it abates his confidence, and he will return to new conflicts weakened by the presentiment of a new defeat. There are also for *you* such decisive days ; nay, perhaps this very day is one of them : feel its value, its importance. If you fight valiantly, if you obtain a complete victory, you may discourage the enemy forever. If, on the contrary, you give way, and leave the issue undecided, you will embolden him, and be constantly a prey to his attacks. Only one moment of weakness, think you, one single moment more . . . but *that* moment is the one selected by the tempter for a last trial, and in it you are about to ruin his hopes forever, or to give them fresh vigor. Courage, then ! Stand firm ! Give not back a single step ! Falter not, for a moment ! Dispel every illusion of the enemy ! Prove to him that with you he loses both his time and his trouble ! And by the reception which you give him, compel him to recognize in the *disciple*, the MASTER who overcame him in the wilderness !

It costs something, indeed, to conquer . . . . . No human undertaking requires so much resolution as the fight of faith ; and it is the secret sense of the mighty effort you have to make over yourself, which keeps you in a state of indecision. Yes, but think of the joy of triumph ! Think of the joy of Job when delivered from trial, and sanctified by trial ! Think of the joy of the three young men after they came out of the furnace, or of Daniel when he left the lions' den ! Think, especially, of the joy of Jesus returning from victory : "Look unto Jesus, the author and finisher of our faith, who, for the joy that was set before him, endured the cross, despising the shame, and is set down at the right hand of the throne of God." What will not your own joy be, when you have overcome that very temptation which has hitherto seemed to you insurmountable ; a joy so much the greater, because, by your victory, you will strengthen your brethren," as Jesus has strengthened you by his victory ! Amen.

DISCOURSE VI.

THE WEAPON IN CHRIST'S CONFLICT.*

"And Jesus, being full of the Holy Ghost, returned from Jordan, and was led by the Spirit into the wilderness, being forty days tempted of the devil," etc.

LUKE, iv. 1-13.

MY DEAR CHRISTIAN FRIENDS,

ADMONISHED by the conflict of Jesus, of the combat which awaits us, assured from his victory that we too can overcome, it remains for us to examine the weapons by which He has conquered, and by which we too can conquer in our turn.

Before entering upon the subject, it would have been pleasing to dwell upon the preparation of Jesus for the conflict. It would have taught us what is requisite in order to be in a position of defence against the attacks of the tempter ; and this is half the victory. But our theme expands with its study, and this discourse would be too long : we must confine ourselves to a statement of the main ideas.

Let us, at the outset, cast aside a slavish imitation which substitutes the letter for the spirit. In order to be conformed to the example of Jesus in preparing for his victory, we have no need to go to the desert to get rid of temptation. In order to be conformed to the example of Jesus in fasting forty days, we have no need, every year, to bind ourselves down to a forty days'

---

* Dr. Monod acknowledges, in a foot note to this sermon, his indebtedness in some of its paragraphs, to the sermon of Krummacher, on this same subject, found in this volume.—TRANSL.

abstinence. By acting thus, we should expose ourselves to temptation,—not guard against it. Here we should bear in mind a principle of which the imitator of Christ should never lose sight—*to imitate is not to copy.*

Jesus was " filled with the Holy Ghost," when he was " baptized, and praying." This was the secret of his strength Let us " pray without ceasing," that we may be " filled with the Holy Ghost ;" for he who is " full of the Holy Ghost," is also " full of wisdom, of faith and of power."

Jesus has just been proclaimed by God " his beloved Son, in whom he is well pleased." This character, while it designates him as we have seen, for the tempter's attacks, strengthens him also against them, because it permits him to apply to God as to a " Father who hears him always." We need that " the Spirit should bear witness with our spirit, that we are the children of God," his well beloved children. We shall thereby be the more exposed to the assaults of the enemy ; but also the better able to resist him : " Whosoever is born of God overcometh the world."

Jesus is " led by the Spirit " to meet the temptation, and he does not encounter it of his own accord : hence his confidence. Where God is the guide, God is likewise the defence. Let us not court danger. Peter paid dearly for having set at defiance all warnings, and forced his way into the temptation which, he had been told, would overcome him.* Let us do all we can in order that the trial may be spared us. If this cannot be, then we shall meet it with the freedom which springs from a good conscience, and with the strength which accompanies humility.

Finally, Jesus fasts before and during the temptation. This fasting which the devil makes use of against Jesus, gives at the same time new strength to Jesus against the devil. Our Saviour fasts, whilst praying, and in order that he might pray. His

* John xviii. 15, 16. When Jesus enters into the court of the high priest, John follows him, " because he was known of the high priest ;" but Peter remains outside. John leaves the court on purpose, and speaks to the door-keeper that Peter may be admitted

abstinence is explained to us by that of Moses, who, on two
occasions, " fell down before the Lord forty days and forty nights,
without eating bread or drinking water." An example which
has been abused elsewhere, but which we have too much neglected. The use to which both Jesus and his Apostles apply fasting,
shows us in that exercise, a means sometimes necessary to wrestle
successfully against temptation : "This kind (of spirit) can
come forth by nothing but by prayer and fasting." Besides,
abstinence from food is connected with an abstinence more general, and always in season, which consists in subduing the flesh
and its propensities : " I keep under my body, and bring it into
subjection." "Make not provision for the flesh, to fulfill the
lusts thereof." Satan has his footing in the flesh : when the
flesh is bridled, he loses his hold and is powerless.

Jesus being thus prepared, let us follow him to the enemy,
and see by what weapons he obtains the victory.

The *weapons* of Jesus ?—say we rather *the weapon*, for he has
but one ; it is the *Word of God*. Three times tempted, three
times he repels the temptation by a simple quotation from the
Scriptures, without explanation or comment. " *It is written,"*—
this one expression tells upon the tempter like a tremendous
discharge upon an assaulting battalion. " It is written,"—the
devil withdraws for the first time. " It is written,"—the devil
withdraws for the second time. " It is written,"—the devil gives
up the contest. God's word is the weapon which Satan most
dreads—a weapon before which he has never been able to do
aught but succumb. Most justly does Paul call it " the sword
of the Spirit ;"* and John describes it, in the Revelation, as
" a sharp, two-edged sword, proceeding out of the mouth of the
Son of man." With that " sword of the Spirit" in our hands,
our cause becomes that of the Holy Spirit himself, and we shall

---

* Rev. 1. 16; ii. 16; xix. 15–21; Heb. iv. 12. " The word of God is quick and powerful, and sharper than any two-edged sword, piercing even to the dividing asunder of soul
and spirit, and of the joints and marrow, and is a discerner of the thoughts and intents
of the heart."

be as superior in strength to our adversary, as is the Spirit of God to the spirit of darkness. Without it, on the contrary, left to ourselves, we shall be as much below him as is man's nature below that of angels. Adam fell, only because he allowed this sword to drop. Jesus triumphs, because no one can wrest it from his hand. But why is it that the Son of God, instead of meeting the enemy with some new sword brought from the heavens whence he came, took up only our own weapon, from that very earth where Adam had, with such cowardice, left it? This is for our example. From what that weapon accomplished in his hand, we must learn what it can do in ours. Let us, then, take it up in our turn ; or rather, let us receive it from him, re-sharpened, as it were, by his victory, and we shall have nothing to fear. To all the adversary's attacks let us oppose a simple "*it is written,*" and we shall render vain his every endeavor.

The devil would entangle you again in the snares of the world. He proceeds with consummate skill in this attempt. Insinuating himself into your company, he represents to you that it is scarcely compatible with charity that you should keep yourself so distant from the society of men ; that a better way to win them over to the Gospel, would be to frequent their social meetings, thus showing them that your religion is not that of anchorites ; lastly, that too many precautions do not become him who would grow strong in Christian virtue, and that there is no glory in a triumph obtained without peril. Thus speaks the tempter. If you only resist by your own understanding, you will be the more easily convinced, in proportion as your natural heart is but too much inclined to his suggestions. But if you take up God's Word, if you answer in faith : It is written, "Be not conformed to this world"—this one quotation puts everything in its true place ; the adversary is unmasked, and his malice confounded.

The devil would make you disbelieve that Christian faith is the only way to salvation. He takes you to some large square in a great city, and pointing out to you the multitudes passing to and fro without intermission, he says : Can you really think that all these are on the road to perdition? Neither your understanding nor your heart can respond to such a doctrine. And yet, for the most part, these people do not believe in Jesus Christ ; at least, their faith is not yours, not that of those like you. Is it true, then, that the only path to life everlasting is the little track in which you go? Are not your ideas on this subject narrow and unworthy of God ? Thus argues the tempter. If you resist him only with your own wisdom, you will not hold out long against him ; you will return from the fight uncertain, trembling, and spiritless. But if, taking up the Word of God, you unhesitatingly reply : It is written, "I am the way, the truth, and the life ; no man cometh unto the Father, but by me"— the spell is destroyed, " the snare is broken, and you are escaped" out of the hand of the perfidious fowler.

Once more, the devil wishes to take away from a faithful minister of Jesus Christ, all the vitality of his preaching. He recommends him not to be so inflexible, not to cry out "heresy" for such trifles, not to make heaven so inaccessible and salvation so difficult, and not to throw gloom over the goodness of grace by imaginations of a devil and a hell. This new course, by gaining him the good-will of all his hearers, will enable him to bring them more surely to the faith, and turn to a more profitable account the precious gifts which heaven has bestowed upon him. Thus advises the tempter. If you consult nothing but your own light to refute him, you must needs fall into the snare ; so skillful is he to make good appear evil and evil good— to make light seem darkness and darkness light ! But if you rest upon God's word, if you answer with assurance : It is written, " If any man preach any other Gospel unto you than that ye have received, let him be accursed"—the "strong man" has found a "stronger" than himself, and he has only to quit with consternation the field of battle.

Oh ! if we did but know what the Word of God can effect

even in our own hands ! If we knew the terror with which it inspires our formidable adversary, at the very time when he affects to laugh at it in our presence, that he may induce us to give it up ! If after having heard him, on the theatre of temptation, scoffing at the word of God, we could (allow me the expression) follow him behind the scenes, and hear him confess to his accomplices that he is lost if he cannot succeed in wresting from our hands this irresistible weapon !—If we did but know all this, and if, like the valiant Eleazar, "we could keep hold of our sword till our hand clave unto it"—oh, then we should be invincible, yea, *invincible !*

But, in order that the Word of God may have in our hands the power it possessed in those of Jesus, it must be for us what it was for Him. I know of nothing in the whole history of humanity, nor even in the field of divine revelation, that proves more clearly than my text the inspiration of the Scriptures. What ! the Son of God, " He who was in the bosom of the Father," and who could so easily draw His resources from himself, preferring to borrow them from a book which He finds in our hands, and to derive His strength whence Joshua, Samuel, David, derived theirs ? What ! Jesus Christ, the Lord of heaven and earth, calling to his aid, in that solemn moment, Moses, His servant ? He who " speaks from heaven," fortifying himself against the temptations of hell, by the word of him who " spake from earth ?" Ah, how can we explain that astonishing mystery, or rather that wonderful reversing of the order of things, if for Jesus the words of Moses were not " the words of God, rather than those of men ?" if he were not fully aware that " holy men of God spoke as they were moved by the Holy Spirit ?" I do not forget, my dear friends (and here I address myself more particularly to the young ministers of the Word) I do not forget the objections which have been raised against the inspiration of the Scriptures, nor the real obscurities with which that inspiration is surrounded ; if they sometimes trouble your hearts, they have troubled mine also. But, at such times, in

order to revive my faith, I have had only to glance at Jesus
glorifying the Scriptures in the wilderness ; and I have seen that
for all who rely upon Him, the most embarrassing of problems is
transformed into a historical fact, palpable and clear. Jesus,
no doubt, was aware of the difficulties connected with the inspiration of the Scriptures ; and the part of Scripture which He
quotes, the Old Testament, is that which presents the greatest
of these difficulties. Did this prevent Him from appealing to its
testimony with unreserved confidence ? Let that which was sufficient for Him, suffice for you. Fear not that the rock which
sustained the Lord in the hour of His temptation and distress,
will give way because you lean too entirely upon it. Whence
comes your perplexity about inspiration ? Is it from the varia-
tions of the different manuscripts ? These were unavoidable,
without a perpetual miracle ; and, in the days of Jesus, there
were already various readings for the Old Testament, which He
here quotes three times. Is it from the little discrepancies of
the sacred writers, when they describe the same event, such,
for instance, as we find in Luke and Matthew, in the very history which constitutes my text ? Discrepancies quite equal to
these exist amongst the books of the Old Testament ; for instance,
between the Kings and the Chronicles. Is it from the degrees
of inspiration ? Are you afraid lest there should be less inspiration in the historical, than the prophetic books ? Jesus uni-
formly quotes the Scripture as an authority which " cannot be
broken ;" and in the passages we are now considering, His quotations were all taken from an historical book—Deuteronomy.
Finally, do you hesitate about the theory you should adopt
respecting inspiration ?—what its mode or its extent, what it
leaves to man's agency, whether it directs the mind of the
sacred author or his pen ? and other questions of a similar nature.
Here again, take example by Jesus. He enters upon no explanation concerning all these speculative points. But when the
practical question is at issue, when that question is the confidence with which you may quote the Scriptures, all the Scrip-

tures, and even a single word of the Scriptures*—then it is impossible to be more clear, more firm, more positive than was He. Go and do likewise. Quote the Scriptures as Jesus quoted them, and hold respecting inspiration whatever theory you will. Jesus takes a higher position than that occupied by our theological systems, one more free from earthly influences ; let us follow Him to those heights where we breathe an atmosphere that is luminous and pure, and where the vapors with which the world obscures the truth of heaven, will settle beneath our feet.†

Ah ! when the devil attempts again to insinuate into your mind some one of those scholastic subtleties which he has always in store against the inspiration of the Scriptures, content yourselves with referring him to Jesus : "Why didst thou not say all this to my Master, when, in the wilderness, He repelled thee by that Word which now seems to thee so weak and so uncertain? Go, carry to Him thy quibbles, and when they have shaken Him, *then* may they shake me also !"

Jesus had no other weapon against Satan than the Word of God ; but how does He handle this weapon? Let us study each of the three quotations which He borrows in succession from the Scriptures. Thus, as by His example we have learned the power of God's word, so, by His example, shall we also learn the use we ought to make of it.

After forty days and forty nights spent in the wilderness, Jesus is conscious of hunger, from which He does not appear to have suffered during the course of His fast, everything here being supernatural. Then it is that the devil draws near, and begins his attacks. We have already had occasion, in another

---

* John x. 35. The quotations of Jesus prove only the inspiration of the *Old* Testament. The inspiration of the New Testament has its peculiar proofs, and rests equally, though in another manner, upon Christ's authority. Besides, except the Jews, no men receiving the inspiration of the Old Testament, have rejected that of the New.

† "Eat in peace the bread of Scripture, without troubling thyself about the particle of sand which may have been mixed with it by the millstone."—*Bengel's advice to a young divine.*

place, to contemplate the three temptations in the wilderness, from what may be called their external side, that is to say, in relation to the objects to which they refer : "the lust of the flesh, the lust of the eyes, and the pride of life." Here we consider their inward character, I mean the feelings through which the devil hoped to cause the Lord to yield, and which properly constitute the spirit of the temptation. Viewed thus, the first temptation is one of distrust ; the second, one of unfaithfulness ; the third, one of presumption.

The devil begins thus : "If thou be the Son of God, command this stone that it be made bread." The moment was well chosen, and the temptation subtle. The tempter would have Jesus employ, for his own personal advantage, the divine virtue with which He is invested as the Messiah, admitting Him to be the Messiah, which, at the same time, he would, perhaps, induce Him to doubt. It was as if he had said to Him : "Employ the means at your disposal to supply your wants, instead of depending upon God whom you call your Father, but who appears to have forgotten you." Had Jesus yielded to this proposition, concealing as it does so mischievous a design under appearances so benevolent, He would have forsaken God's ways by having questioned God's assistance ; He would have used this power just as Satan had used his for His own private satisfaction ; and so the work of redemption would have been destroyed at its very beginning. Hence He refutes the enemy without hesitation, by meeting him simply with this plain answer from the Scriptures ;* "Man shall not live by bread alone, but by every word of God." This quotation may, perhaps, seem to you strange, and hardly suited to the occasion ; you will think so no longer when you have ascertained its meaning.

It is taken from Deuteronomy, and from the history of the people of Israel in the wilderness. Observe that the two other

---

* Jesus, who refuses here to make use of His Divine power, in order to provide for His own *necessities*, employs it elsewhere to procure *superfluities* for others.—John ii. 1-11.

answers of Christ to the tempter are borrowed from the same history and the same book. Whence comes it that Jesus, with the whole field of Scripture open before him, entrenches himself against the attack of the enemy in this particular place, as in an impregnable fortress? It is because He perceives a secret parallel between himself, the Son of God, preparing to lay the foundation of His kingdom by forty days' fast and temptation in the wilderness of Judea, and *Israel*, that other son of God, qualified for the conquest of Canaan by forty years' privations and trials in the great desert of Arabia. Israel, who is presented to us as a type of the New Testament church, is also the type of Jesus, the head of that church, in whom it is complete : therefore, Jesus instructs and strengthens Himself by what is written for Israel. Admirable connection of the Scriptures ! Wonderful unity of spirit in both Testaments !

"And He humbled thee," says Moses to the people of Israel, and suffered thee to hunger, and fed thee with manna which thou knowest not, neither did thy fathers know, that He might make thee know that man doth not live by bread only, but by every word that proceedeth out of the mouth of God," or as our text has it, "by every word of God." Bread is the usual means by which God provides for man's subsistence, but not the *only* one He has at His disposal ; for the secret of the nutritive virtue resides, not in the bread, but in the command of God, from which alone proceeds every power and every blessing. If bread becomes assimilated to the substance of our body, it is because that word said from the beginning : "I have given you every herb bearing seed, which is upon the face of all the earth, . . . to you it shall be for meat ;" and if, instead of pronouncing that blessing upon wheat, the same word had pronounced it upon stone or wood, wood or stone would nourish us as well as wheat does now ; nor would the sight be more astonishing, than that of the word sweetening the springs of Marah, or of the rock supplying Israel with water in his thirst. Without God's word, bread itself could nourish no one, and we should eat it, without being satisfied ; but that word can, independently of bread, feed whom it pleases, and as it pleases. God proved this abundantly in the people who were with Moses, by nourishing them forty years with manna, which ceased to fall from the day they set their foot upon cultivated ground. Nay, the word of God can support the body of man without bread, without manna, without visible means of any kind. On two occasions, Moses lived forty days on Mount Sinai, "without eating bread or drinking water." Elijah journeyed also for forty days, towards the same mountain, and across the same wilderness, without food or drink. Jesus, in His turn, led by His Father's will into a desert where everything was wanting, was there so marvelously sustained during His forty days' fast, that He did not even suffer hunger. He relied to the end upon Him who led Him into the wilderness, to be supported in the wilderness. As for the choice of means, He cheerfully resigns it to His Father's wisdom, having learned from Moses that "man shall not live by bread alone, but by every word of God." Scarcely had this Scripture, taken in its intimate and deepest sense, been quoted, than it overthrows the whole effort of the enemy, and annihilates his first attack. My dear, friend, whenever the tempter induces you to call in question God's assistance, because ordinary means are wanting, answer as Jesus did : "Man shall not live by bread alone, but by every word of God."

You have hitherto earned with some exertion your own bread and that of your family : but suddenly employment fails, or your health give way, or your usual resources vanish. This is an opportunity which the devil will not neglect to improve. He will not dare to propose to you to deceive, or to steal ; but he will say : "Has God, thy Father, no other banquet for thee but those stones and those thorns amidst which he allows thee to vegetate ? Well, since he forsakes thee, help thyself ; be not afraid of wandering a little from the beaten track, and of providing for thy wants by some of those means about which you are too scrupulous. Speculate, try the dazzling chances of the gam-

ing-table ; be less exact respecting the choice of thy acquaint-
ances ; flatter without scruple those whose protection may be
necessary to thee ; command this stone that it may be made
bread." Let your answer be, "Man shall not live by bread
alone, but by every word of God !" "The God whom I serve
can deliver me," and He will deliver me ; but if not, I will not
turn aside from His paths ; and should I die of hunger, I will
" abstain from every appearance of evil ! "

Your soul's sustenance gives rise to similar temptations, which
you must repulse in the same spirit. You find yourselves confined in a spiritual desert, shut up in an abode where your heart
" faints for the courts of the Lord," and for the communion of
his people ; you are bound to a situation, engaged in a society,
where everything is directed against your " growth in grace ;"
for you, the way of sanctification is hedged up with temptations
and impediments. But it is God who prepared this desert for
you ; it is He who selected this position ; you cannot leave it
without violating your imperative duty. This family to which
you are bound, is that of your natural relations, whom God has
commanded you to take care of, under the alternative of " denying the faith, and being worse than an infidel." In moments like
these, the devil will say, Is it not time to provide for the welfare
of thy soul ? Put an end, at any cost, to that state of things
which renders the Christian life impossible for thee ; command
this stone that it be made bread. Let your answer be, " Man
shall not live by bread alone, but by the word of God !" The
blessing comes from God, and it is restricted to no human circumstances, I am where my Father wills me to be ; that is enough.
He who, at his will, " turneth the wilderness into a standing water,
and dry ground into water springs," is also he who can turn the
most terrible temptations into precious means of grace ! He will
keep me in all my ways, except in that of disobedience !

You are a minister of God. Under the manifest direction of
the Lord, you have been appointed over a church where remarkable blessings have unceasingly confirmed your calling. But

the church is poor, you are so yourself, and as you begin the year, you know not how you will be able to meet the expenses which each of the three hundred and sixty-five days of which it is composed will bring with it. Dear brother, you are truly in a wilderness, but in a wilderness to which God has led you, as if by the hand. The devil then says, "The God whom thou servest so faithfully, is forsaking thee. For so many years that thou hast put up thy request to Him for thee and for thine, what has He done to relieve thy becoming solicitude ? Why delayest thou ? Give up so wretched a situation, seek some other sphere of duty which may supply thee with "thy bread and thy water, thy wool and thy flax, thine oil and thy drink ;" "Command this stone that it be made bread." Let your answer be, "Man shall not live by bread alone, but by the word of God." God, faithful to those who are faithful, has resources ready at hand for all my wants : wherever he has sent me, he has never left me to want : as long as I am convinced that the place I now occupy is of his own appointing, I shall remain "and quietly wait for his salvation."

Answer thus, my friend, and God will be your support. Not a few of your brethren have been visited as you are ; they have waited for the Lord ; and now that God has "shown unto them the salvation" promised "to him that ordereth his conversation aright," they would not exchange for all the gold in the world, the lessons they have derived from their distress.

The first temptation has been overcome—overcome by God's word—the devil has recourse to another. "And the devil, taking Him up into a high mountain, showed unto Him all the kingdoms of the world in a moment of time."

And the devil said unto Him, "All this power will I give thee, and the glory of them ; for that is delivered unto me, and to whomsoever I will I give it ; if thou, therefore, wilt worship me, all shall be thine." How did this mysterious scene take place ? We are ignorant. I have already said that I come to this narrative as a child ; and without endeavoring to penetrate, "the

hidden things which are for the Lord our God," I go straight
to "those revealed things which are for us, and for our children." There is much to be learned here concerning the wiles
of the adversary, and the means we should employ in order to
escape them.

What must we think of this boast of Satan : "That is delivered unto me, and to whomsoever I will I give it ?" It is com-
pounded of truth and falsehood, like all the insinuations of the
adversary ; for if they had the character of truth alone, the
very object of "the father of lies" would be defeated ; if the
stamp was exclusively that of falsehood, his designs would be
too apparent. It is too true that Satan exercises in this world
a prodigious empire which he holds from sin, and which he dedi-
cates to the service of sin. He usurped it in Eden, where, not
satisfied with possessing himself of the spirit of man—that king
of the earth—we see him taking the place of the King of heaven
himself, as the object of man's obedience. We need only cast
our eyes around us, to perceive the fatal power which the enemy
has acquired over us ; history, politics, science, art, literature,
everything connected with glory and beauty, bears too striking
a witness to the sad fact. For this reason, Satan is called in
the Scriptures "the prince of the world," such is his power
over it, and even (oh, shame !) "the god of this world ;" so
much is he adored in it. But this power of Satan, such as it is,
"has been delivered unto him," and this he is obliged himself
to confess. Having then been delivered to him, it is not absolute ; he exercises it under the control of God, who makes it
subserve the final accomplishment of His own purposes ; and if
Satan is the prince of this world, God alone is "its Sovereign,
ruling in the kingdom of men, and giving it to whosoever He
will."

Further, having been delivered to him, it is not eternal ; it
will be taken from him when sin, on which alone it rests, shall
have been abolished, and it is to abolish it that the Messiah came ;
"He appeared to destroy the works of the devil," and to build

upon the ruins of his empire a new kingdom "which shall never be dissolved." That which Satan dares to claim here, that which he pretends to make over to the Son of God, really, then, belongs to that Son to whom the Father has promised "the heathen for his inheritance, and the uttermost parts of the earth for his possession."

However this may be, Satan offers to Jesus what he can give, and perhaps what he cannot give. He causes to pass before his eyes "all the kingdoms of the world and their glory ;" the pride of power, the *éclat* of riches, the splendor of luxury, the vanity of honors, the intoxication of pleasures, and all those earthly pomps which excite so violently man's desires ; then he tells Him : "All shall be thine," on the one condition, "that thou wilt worship me." The spirit of the second temptation consisted in inducing the Son, instead of waiting for and conquering the inheritance promised by the Father, to receive it at once and without a conflict from the hands of Satan, by rendering him the homage due to God alone. This temptation has something in it more revolting than the first ; the condition to which the empire of the world is attached, is nothing short of a compact with the devil. Thus, Jesus no sooner hears the impious proposal, than He lays aside for a moment the calmness which characterized His resistance ; and, for the first time calling Satan by his name, He repels him with a holy indignation : "Get thee behind me, Satan ; for it is written thou shalt worship the Lord thy God, and Him only shalt thou serve."* This quotation arrests immediately the enemy's efforts, and sends him back a second time defeated.

Here things are so clear, Satan's proposition so detestable, and the reply of Jesus so simple, that any explanation would be superfluous. Not so, however, with the application of the subject. However detestable the temptation may be, God's children are all exposed to it ; and however plain the answer, it is im-

---

* These words are borrowed from Deut. vi. 13, but according to the Septuagint version, which gives the thought of Moses, without confining itself to his very words.

portant that we should know always where to find it. There is not one among us to whom an alliance with Satan has not more than once been offered. I thus designate a tacit agreement, by which a man engages to serve the God of this world, in order to secure the world's favor ; an agreement by which a Christian, perhaps, consents to do homage to Satan for the purpose of making sure in his impatience "of the glory which comes from men," instead of following by faith "the glory which is from God only." Let us give a few examples borrowed from the experience of youth.

The most common form under which Satan proposes to us his odious alliance is the lust of riches. A moral, pious young man has just entered upon business. The hope of making a brilliant fortune takes possession of his mind ; how is this hope to be realized ? Among other means some suggest themselves, which generally obtain in the world, but which are sinful : lies, deceit, injury to neighbors, lawsuits, family divisions, neglect of God's service, sabbath-breaking.

What is this but the devil saying : "If thou wilt worship me, all shall be thine ?" Alas ! and how few fortunes have been made without some concessions to Satan :—Answer him, my young brother, "Get thee behind me, Satan ; for it is written, Thou shalt worship the Lord thy God, and Him only shalt thou serve." Let Satan keep all his advantages, since he puts upon them such a price. Do not beg from the devil the deceitful semblance of a glory, the reality of which God will bestow upon you, if you are faithful. Besides, even here below, the blessing comes from God : "Godliness has the promise of the life that now is, and of that which is to come."

Sometimes Satan's alliance is concealed under a project of marriage. A young lady is treading faithfully in the paths of the Lord. By her fervent, and yet modest piety, she is an example to her companions, an honor to the church, a blessing to the world. Her hand is sought by a young man having every advantage—fortune, intelligence, rank—he is amiable, and, perhaps, beloved, but a stranger to piety, to whom she cannot be united without endangering her faith. This again is Satan saying, "If thou wilt worship me, all shall be thine." "See what a prospect opens before thee : what honor, what happiness, what love! wouldst thou be deprived of all this? and for what? for the sad pleasure of leading an austere and gloomy life? Keep thy faith, thou mayest only conceal it in thy heart, and be of the world whilst thou art in the world." How can artless youth resist a manœuvre of the enemy so cunningly devised? By this simple word : "Get thee behind me, Satan ; for it is written, Thou shalt worship the Lord thy God, and Him only shalt thou serve." Yes, my young sister, answer him thus, and your victory is secure. "The grace of the Lord is sufficient for you." Go and lay down quietly at the foot of his cross all the dreams of happiness which your poor heart has entertained, and you will find in the love of God enough to repay, with interest, your greatest sacrifices.

The sanctuary is no shelter against the offers of an alliance with Satan. A young minister, enriched with the choicest of God's gifts, enters into the service of the church. He can aspire to the glory of the world, to the applause of man, to the most lucrative or influential offices ; but to obtain these he must either preach the doctrines of the age, or accommodate truth to its fastidiousness, or join in the frivolity of its pleasures, or make common cause with it against God's children. This again, is Satan saying, "If thou wilt worship me, all shall be thine." How many young ministers perhaps yield to this temptation ! How many a Demas has forsaken his brethren, "having loved this present world !" How many have believed on Jesus, yet "do not confess him, because they love the praise of men more than the praise of God !" Oh, my young friends, be faithful, be unmovable ! answer "Get thee behind me, Satan : for it is written, Thou shalt worship the Lord thy God, and Him only shalt thou serve." If you seek to please men, you will not be the servants of Christ. Confess Jesus Christ for your God, his word for your rule, and his people for your people, and "when the chief shepherd shall appear, ye shall receive from his hands a crown of glory that fadeth not away."

Twice overcome, Satan makes a last attempt, for which we may presume that he will collect all his stratagems, all his resources. "He brought him to Jerusalem, and set him on a pinnacle of the temple, and said unto him, If thou be the Son of God, cast thyself down; for it is written, He shall give his angels charge over thee, to keep thee, and in their hands they shall bear thee, lest at any time thou dash thy foot against a stone."

In order to understand well the spirit of this temptation, we must oppose it to the first, with which it forms an evident contrast. The tempter had endeavored in vain to make Jesus doubt his Father; this means, the first which he generally employs, and which succeeded but too well with Eve, had failed before the firm faith of Jesus in God's assistance. Then the tempter conceives the hope of seducing him, by that very confidence, although a perversion of that confidence.

He disguises himself as an angel of light; he surrounds himself with holy things; he conducts Jesus to the holy city, places him upon the pinnacle of the holy temple, and encourages him by the holy word of God, to throw himself fearlessly down, that he may give to the multitude, by the miracle of the promised protection, a striking proof of what he really is. Yes, but was the hazardous act proposed by Satan to Jesus, necessary? was it according to God's will? did it present the conditions required to make the promise of the ninety-first psalm applicable? Had Jesus yielded to the suggestions of the tempter, He would have presumptuously claimed his Father's fidelity; He would have used God's word more as an amusement than as a support; He would have created the danger for the frivolous satisfaction of obtaining the deliverance; and that deliverance failing, He would have risked the glory of God as much by his blind and presumptuous confidence, as he would have served him by humble and obedient faith. Therefore He answers without hesitating, to his treacherous adviser : " It is said, Thou shalt not tempt the Lord thy God."

What is " tempting God ?" Why would Jesus have " tempted God," by throwing himself down from the pinnacle of the temple ? " To tempt," or to *try* God,* is, as the natural meaning of the words indicates, to put God upon trial, and thus to test his faithfulness ; while faith simply trusts to God, and relies upon his fidelity as upon an immovable rock. Faith speaks thus : " God has said, and will He not perform it ?" The only pledge He asks of His promise, is the promise itself. He who tempts God, speaks altogether another language : Can God do it ? Will He do it ? Then, in his anxiety to solve his doubt, he takes upon himself to prescribe to God certain conditions, which he must see accomplished before he can rest upon his promise. The Israelites tempted the Lord at Rephidim, by asking water to drink, and asking in such a spirit, that they would judge, from the reception given to their request, " whether the Lord was amongst them or no." They tempted him again at Kibrath Hattaavah, by demanding a new species of nourishment, and by saying : " Behold, He smote the rock, and the waters gushed out, and the streams overflowed ; can He give bread also : can He provide flesh for his people ?"

Under forms less gross, the same spirit reappears in the Christian church. The new disciples who opposed the Apostles in the council of Jerusalem, tempted God, by seeking to impose upon the converted Gentiles a yoke which they themselves had not been able to wear ; whereby they seemed to impose upon God the necessity of an extraordinary outpouring of His grace, such as they had no right to expect. This conduct is the more reprehensible because, when the Lord is thus provoked, if it please Him to refuse the conditions which men have thus dared to pre-

---

* " Your fathers have tempted me and proved me ; they have also seen my works." The word *to prove*, which signifies properly *to try*, explains the word *to tempt* which precedes. The idea of the verse is this : As your fathers put my power to the proof, I made it known to them by displaying it against them.—See besides Is. vii. 12 ; Acts v. 9.

scribe, either His character or His word will seem to be at fault : false confidence borders upon distrust, and presumption upon unbelief ; their principle and their results are similar. Jesus, in His turn, would have tempted God, if He had thrown himself down from the pinnacle of the temple ; for having neither command nor necessity to impel him to so strange an act, he could not say : God will keep me ; but at most, Will God keep me ? will He conduct me safe to the ground ? Let me try.

Had He said this but once, he would have been defeated ; but His refusal, His quotation from the Scriptures, "Thou shalt not tempt the Lord thy God," disconcerts the adversary's plan, and puts him to flight for the third and last time. Dear brethren, Satan can tempt us also to tempt God. Examples abound ; the difficulty is only in the selection.

"Silver and gold belong to the Lord of hosts." For an undertaking formed for the glory of God, and conducted according to His Spirit, we may expect from Him the needful resources. He will not put our faith to shame : and certainly, without that faith, the noblest works of Christian piety and charity would have been stopped at their commencement. Francke, Cotolingo, Mary Calame, for instance, would have failed in their respective missions. "But beware, under pretence of confidence in God, of rushing inconsiderately into the first path which opens before you. Here, too, you will have to guard against the suggestions of Satan. He will prompt you, sometimes, to mistake for an inspiration from God a design which, notwithstanding its plausible appearance, tends less to His glory than to your own ; sometimes to incur, even in the execution of a plan approved by God, which are neither commanded by necessity, nor consistent with evangelical simplicity ; sometimes to anticipate impatiently the time of God, and thus to disturb that slow and sure progress by which He delights to insure the success of the cause, whilst He brings into exercise the submission of the instrument. What dost thou fear, the tempter will say, O man of little faith ? Go on in the name of the Lord. Give, promise,

8

purchase, build, do whatsoever thy hand findeth to do. If thou art a child of God, trust thy Father, "cast thyself down." Listen to Him, and you will find yourself insensibly bound by obligations which you cannot meet. Then the Gospel will be compromised in the eyes of the world ; which will say, when it beholds your unfinished projects : This man began to build, and was not able to finish ; "and you yourself may be annoyed by pecuniary difficulties which will break your heart, if they do not shake your faith." Avoid so great an evil, by walking carefully with God, by tempering the liberty of Christ with the prudence of Christ, by forsaking the trodden path only to answer a mani fest vocation, or to obey a sure direction of the Spirit : this is the secret of prayer. In all other circumstances, "thou shalt not tempt the Lord thy God :" let this be your answer, and this the ground of your peace.

Fathers and mothers, you are about to supply me with my second example : Lend me an attentive ear. I will suppose the time to have come for your son or your daughter to leave the paternal roof and turn to account the resources of public instruction, either to complete their studies, or to form their mind and character. What principles will guide you in the selection, so serious and so difficult, of that second family to whom you are about to intrust your child ? If you think above all of "the one thing needful," you will experience the truth of this promise : "Seek first the kingdom of God and His righteous-ness, and all these things shall be added unto you." But if, too anxious for the glory which comes from men, you seek, before everything else, for your son the means of distinguishing himself in the world, and for your daughter the means of pleasing the world ; if you place them for years in a circle where the name of Christ is neither honored, loved, nor perhaps even known : nay, if you surrender that confiding spirit and inflexible intellect to the influence of a proselytism, blind, obstinate, and whose very scruples your own recklessness seems to have tried to over-come, what will you have done but tempt God ? The voice that then whispers : " Are not the advantages of a brilliant education worth some sacrifices ?   Besides, cannot God preserve thy child from the contagion of error, or the seduction of example ? Cannot you win him over to piety, except by a kind of Bible-persecution ?"—whence comes that voice but from him to whom Jesus said : " Thou shalt not tempt the Lord thy God ?"   Alas ! how many parents I might name, who now weep bitterly their sin and folly in relying upon God to deliver their children from dangers into which they had plunged them without His per-mission !   Another time, the tempter will induce you to frequent questionable company, because God can guard you from all evil ; or to dissipate your inner life by frivolous, if not corrupt read-ing, because God can preserve you from the influence of the poison ; or to listen to divines who preach dangerous innovations, because God can close your heart against the seduction of their discourses.   These are so many varieties of His advice to Jesus : " Cast thyself down." It is written : " Thou shalt not tempt the Lord thy God."   When exposed to any danger by the will of God, be firm and immovable ; but never create perils for your-selves ; never try God, never engage His glory for naught ; and if placed on the pinnacle of the temple, do not cast yourselves down, but descend quietly and humbly by the stairs of the edifice.

But there is in this last temptation, one feature which deserves our particular attention ; it is the use which Satan makes of the Scriptures.   He sees that by them Jesus has twice repulsed him ; he forms the audacious project of turning against his conqueror that sword of the Spirit of which he has just experienced the irresistible power.   Wonderful dexterity of the tempter, who finds instruments in everything, and who, arming himself against us with our own resources, endeavors to make us weak through our strength, as God makes us strong through our weakness. " Cast thyself down from hence ; for it is written, He shall give His angels charge over thee, to keep thee ; and in their hands they shall bear thee up, lest at any time thou dash thy foot against a stone." Wherein consists the perfidy of this quotation? Some answer, that Satan maliciously mutilates the passage which he adduces ; the Psalmist had said : "He shall give His angels charge over thee, to keep thee in *all thy ways ;*" and these last words, which the tempter suppresses, show that we can reckon upon the promised assistance, only as long as we remain in the path of our calling.

This remark seems to me subtle ; it would seem also that if it were well founded, Jesus would have answered by reëstablishing in its integrity the mutilated text. The assistance guaranteed in the 91st Psalm has its fixed conditions—conditions from which Jesus would have wandered, had He cast himself down from the pinnacle of the temple. God intends to strengthen against danger those of His children who are unavoidably exposed to it, not those who rush into it by choice and with necessity. But as this restriction is not found in the expressions of the Psalmist, how will Jesus prove that it was in the mind of the Holy Ghost? Will He do so by appealing to reason or to natural feeling? No, He will do it by an appeal to the Scriptures themselves. Jesus does not answer : "The meaning thou givest to this passage cannot be the true one, because it is too far fetched." He answers : "This meaning cannot be the true one, because it is contrary to another Scripture." This intention of the Lord is still more evident in Matthew's narrative, which adds to that of Luke the word *again*, very significant in this place : "It is written *again*, thou shalt not tempt the Lord thy God." We must combine these two testimonies which complete and explain one another ; and Jesus has no right to rely upon the intervention of angels, except on condition of not tempting God.

This is very instructive. There are in the Bible, written not by philosophers for philosophers, but by simple men for simple men, passages which need elucidation, and which, when not well understood, can supply the tempter with arms against us ; the elucidation must be sought, not from human wisdom, but from the Scriptures speaking in another place. Besides, if we allow human wisdom to qualify the Scripture, where shall we stop? We shall soon see one rejecting the doctrine of the devil's personality, as opposed to his reason; another discarding that of the eternity of punishments, as wounding his feelings; a third, hiding that of the atonement under glosses which destroy it; and there will remain no divine authority. Scripture can be qualified only by Scripture; and to an "it is written," the only solid objection we can oppose, is, "it is written again."

Satan beholds a Christian applying himself diligently to the work of his salvation, praying without ceasing, meditating on the Scriptures night and day, and watching to avoid the pollution of the world. He has vainly attempted to turn him from prayer, to make him doubt God's words, to inspire him with the love of this present world. He then takes up his Bible—you have just seen that he has one—and begins speaking to him after this fashion: "Why, friend, what burden is this you are laying upon yourself? Must you serve God till you are quite out of breath? A glance at you is enough to disgust any one with religion. I will teach you a way both easier and more orthodox; for, after all, your sanctification is the work of God, not your own. Be not so strict. Follow the inclination of your heart, and leave God to do the work; It is written: "It is God which worketh in you both to will and to do of His good pleasure." Ah! yes, follow the inclination of your heart, and I can readily believe that the devil will be less anxious about you. Ah, my brother, answer that "holy Satan," as Luther somewhere calls him: It is written again, "Work out your own salvation with fear and trembling." "Strive to enter at the strait gate."

Satan proposes to abate the activity of a minister of the Gospel, whose powerful preaching is making a breach in "the gates of hell." He has vainly endeavored to stop him in his work by discouragement, by vain glory, by the hatred of the world. He then has recourse to Scripture, and says: "Man of God, why are you at so much pains about the spiritual food

which you should give to your people? Can you not say things
holy, true, and wholesome, without thus wasting your strength
over your Bible and your books? Go more simply to work.
Trust to the fluency of speech God has given you; surrender
yourself up to the Holy Spirit, and say what he puts into your
heart. Thus you will honor the Lord more, to say nothing of
the extra time which you will gain for his service. It is written,
' It shall be given you in that same hour what ye shall speak ;
for it is not ye that speak, but the spirit of your Father which
speaketh in you.'" This, my friends, is a snare nicely adjusted
to your natural indolence. If you fall into it, you will have
reason to fear lest your preaching should be struck with imbe-
cility, as has been the case with so many of God's servants, who,
under specious pretences, dispense with troublesome work, in
order to indulge in spontaneous effusions which costs no effort.
But here is your deliverance. Answer: It is also written,
" Give attendance to reading, to exhortation, to doctrine. Neglect not the gift that is in thee; take heed unto thyself and
unto the doctrine ; for in so doing thou shalt both save thyself
and them that hear thee."

And so for all the rest of the scriptural temptations of Satan.
Be upon your guard against all the devil's interpretations, and
refuse them simply by the Scripture itself. What one passage
omits, will be told you in another ; as if the Bible judged him
alone worthy to penetrate its inmost sense, who endeavors to
bring together and reconcile its various teachings. If it is
written, "man is justified by faith without the works of the
law," it is again, " Faith without works is dead." If it is written, " Neither be ye called masters, for one is your Master, even
Christ ;" it is written again, " Obey them that have the rule
over you, and submit yourselves." If it is written, " Your
Father knoweth what things ye have need of, before ye ask
him ;" it is written again, " Ask, and ye shall receive ; seek,
and ye shall find ; knock, and it shall be opened unto you."
If it is written, " I am persuaded that no creature shall be able

to separate us from the love of God, which is in Christ Jesus our Lord ;" it is written again, " Happy is the man that feareth always." If it is written, " To the pure all things are pure ;" it is written again, " Abstain from all appearance of evil."

By the example of Jesus refuting the threefold attack of the tempter, you have just learned, my dear brethren, the use you should make of the Scriptures against temptation. But to follow this example, you must know the Scriptures as Jesus knew them. Do not be astonished that I speak of the knowledge which Christ had of the Scriptures : for we cannot repeat it too often, though he was the Son of God, he was likewise the Son of man, and it is *as* the Son of man that he overcame in the wilderness. How familiar must the Bible have been to him who could quote from it with so much precision, who could adapt it so exactly to the infinite variety of human temptations ! Jesus is as familiar with the Scriptures as we are with a city which we have known from our infancy, have crossed and recrossed from end to end, and of which each street, each square, and each house is engraven on our memory. Thus ought you to know the Scriptures. You cannot hope to fight effectively against the enemy with a mere smattering of the Word of God.

The more precise you are in the use you make of it, the stronger you will be. For the special temptation which assails you, there may be a special declaration of the Holy Spirit—a declaration for which no other would be a complete substitute : you must discover it. The Scriptures must be for you an arsenal, so well explored that you can immediately lay your hand upon the weapon which you require for your defence ; or a dispensary, so well ordered that you can find immediately the precise remedy for your disease. You cannot constantly have your Bible before your eyes ; you must carry it about in your heart, if you desire that it should never fail you. But in order to that, what a study of the Scriptures—what constant reading —what deep meditation ! Well, this is only what God has himself prescribed to us : " Blessed is the man whose delight is in the law of the Lord, and in his law doth he meditate day and night !"

"This book of the law shall not depart out of thy mouth, but thou shalt meditate therein day and night." This is only doing what those holy men did whose example we are called upon to follow. "Oh, how I love thy law ! it is my meditation all the day. . . . . Mine eyes prevent the night-watches, that I may meditate in thy Word. . . . At midnight I will rise to give thanks unto thee, because of thy righteous judgments." This is only copying the example given us by our forefathers, even in the days of the wilderness and of martyrdom ; those old witnesses, respecting whom it has been said that if the Bible should ever be lost, the combined recollections of a few among them would have sufficed to write it out again from the beginning to the end. What then, O my God, is the state into which we have fallen ! What ignorance of the Scriptures among our people ! What ignorance of the Scriptures among our pastors ! Lord restore to us the former days !

But farther, that mere knowledge of the Scriptures by which we may remember them from one end to the other, is not what it is most important we should imitate in the conduct of Jesus. If he triumphs through the Scriptures, it is because he apprehends their meaning and their spirit ; not because he knows the words which they contain. The Bible contains the precepts of the kingdom of God, but those precepts are clothed in an earthly form ; and he alone penetrates it, who is able to disengage the heavenly maxims from the human covering which surrounds them. This is what Jesus does in my text : he goes deeper than the surface of the volume, he sounds " the thoughts and intents " of what " is written." I need no other proof of this than the first of his three quotations, " Man shall not live by bread alone, but by every word of God." You must grant that if you had been tempted like the Lord, you never have thought of defending yourself with this passage; and that it might have often passed and repassed under your eyes, without sug-

gesting to you the thought which Jesus found therein. You
would have found there the wonderful fact of the manna
granted to the Israelites instead of bread ; a pledge of hope for
any nation placed in similar circumstances, if those circumstances should ever be renewed ; an encouraging proof of God's
love for his creatures, and of his faithfulness towards his people;
but there your interpretation would have stopped, limited by
the history and the miracle. How much more penetrating is
that of Jesus ! He goes to the very foundation, he arrives at
the very intent of the Holy Spirit ; and deeper than the
miracle, beneath the history, beneath all that is transitory, he
discovers this general and permanent principle : *All virtue
resides in the word of God, which is not restricted to the means it
usually employs.*

At that depth, Israel's temptation and that of Jesus meet
together, if I may so speak, under ground, and at the root ; so
that the word of Moses, interpreted by Jesus Christ, applies as
well to the second as to the first ; I may say yet more, it applies
equally to the temptations of God's children in all ages.

And yet in this application of the words of Moses, extended
and varied as it is, there is nothing either forced or arbitrary ;
not even either allegory or double meaning ; nothing but the profound meaning of the Holy Spirit, hidden in the profound language of the Scriptures, the true substance in the true form.
Such, my dear friends, is the interpretation of Jesus Christ ; spiritual and substantial ; alike accessible to the learned and to the
simple ; alike attractive to the understanding and wholesome to
the soul. Compared with it, how superficial and cold is our
common method of interpretation, even when it is the most
learned and the most conscientious !

No wonder : for the one is encumbered by the things of earth,
while the other rises to the everlasting thoughts of heaven. How
beautiful a book would the Bible be—and, alas ! how *new* a
book to us—if studied in this spirit ! The Bible—if I may be
allowed the expression—*is heaven-spoken* ; but we must separate

Q*

heaven from the word which invests it, while it reveals it ; and
this is what Jesus Christ teaches us to do. It is an interpretation, moreover, which no commentary can supply for us ; we
must seek it upon our knees, saying to God : " Open thou mine
eyes, that I may behold wondrous things out of thy law !" Then
we shall receive God's witness within ourselves ; then what
is written in the heart will agree so well with what is written in
the *book*, that we shall recognize in both the work of the same
Spirit. The Bible, we said, just now, *is heaven-spoken ;* the Bible
thus listened to, *would be heaven seen, felt, lived !*

We have reached, dear brethren, the end of our proposed
task. For three Sundays I have spoken to you of the temptation of Jesus in the wilderness ; this is not too much for so vast,
so instructive a subject. As for me, I shall remember with peculiar feelings the three weeks during which I have steadily contemplated the struggle my Saviour underwent, the victory He
obtained, and the weapon by which He conquered. I have
found in this contemplation something particularly solemn and
salutary ; and I hope, through God's faithfulness, that it will not
be without a blessing either to me or to yourselves. Return
often to the wilderness. Whenever the number and the strength
of the temptations to which you are exposed, seem ready to
overwhelm you, remember that Jesus was tempted in all things
like as you are. Whenever you have any doubts about the
possibility of resistance, remember that Jesus bruised Satan
under His feet, and has promised to bruise him under yours also.
Finally, whenever you are uncertain respecting the means
which you should employ in order to overcome, remember that
Jesus repelled all the blows of the adversary, and forced him
at last to retreat, with the sword of the Spirit alone.
And you, my future fellow-laborers, I cannot dismiss this subject, without addressing to you a special exhortation which I
recommend to your most serious attention. The temptation of
Jesus is placed between the end of His personal preparation, and

the beginning of His public life. There is in your course, a corresponding moment : it is the interval which separates the conclusion of your studies from the commencement of your ministry.* Be careful of this interval ; it may decide your whole career. Consecrate it as a spiritual retreat ; spend it in the company of Jesus wrestling in the desert ; and when you enter the church, let men recognize in you the men who have just left the wilderness. The wilderness, and not the world ! If you are full of the recollections of the world, if you have just breathed the impure atmosphere of its vanities and pleasures, you are not fit for the service of Jesus Christ. The wilderness, and not Nazareth ! If you are governed by family affections ; if, in selecting a field of labor, your first consideration is a father or a mother, a wife or child, you are not fit for the service of Jesus Christ. The wilderness, and not the school ! If you are still covered with the dust of the academy ; if your faith, your knowledge, is only that of books, you are not fit for the service of Jesus Christ. Jesus Christ has need of ministers separated from the world, unfettered by creature engagements, and nourished by the teachings of the Holy Spirit. Either be men of the wilderness, or not be men of the church ! Amen.

---

* The reader is again reminded that these three discourses were preached particularly to the theological students at Montauban.

DISCOURSE VII.

THE OMNIPOTENCE OF FAITH.

Then Jesus went thence, and departed into the coasts of Tyre and Sidon. And behold a woman of Canaan came out of the same coasts, and cried unto him, saying : Have mercy on me, O Lord, thou Son of David, my daughter is grievously vexed with a devil. But he answered her not a word. And his disciples came and besought him, saying, send her away; for she crieth after us. But he answered and said, I am not sent but unto the lost sheep of the house of Israel. Then came she and worshipped him, saying, Lord help me. But he answered and said : It is not meet to take the children's bread, and cast it to dogs. And she answered and said : Truth, Lord, yet the dogs eat of the crumbs which fall from their master's table. Then Jesus answered and said unto her : O Woman, great is thy faith : be it unto thee even as thou wilt. And her daughter was made whole from that very hour.—MATTH. XV. 21-28.

THERE is a faith which makes man more mighty than God. But this assertion we would not dare to make, had not God himself authorized us, when he said to Jacob, "Thy name shall be called no more Jacob, but Israel ; for as a prince hast thou power with God, and with men, and hath prevailed." We find in our woman of Canaan an accomplished model of this faith ; and if she was not an Israelite by birth, she was truly one by sentiment. For what do we see in our text, but a struggle between the Lord and her, from which she comes forth "more than conqueror ?" Let us notice the successive phases of the combat ; we shall learn therefrom in a few words, more of the power of faith than the most perfect treatise could impart.

We will begin by observing the position of this woman, and the conduct of the Lord towards her.

Doubtless the woman of Canaan believed in Jesus Christ pre-

vious to the scene narrated in our text. But how did she attain
to such faith ? It is well to inquire ; for in her conversion may
be remarked that strength of soul which triumphs over all
obstacles, and such a commencement explains all that follows.
She was a Gentile, as her name indicates ; and had not acquired,
with other Gentiles who had been converted to the Lord, such
as Zaccheus, or the Centurion, the privilege of dwelling among
the Jews. Thus, living at a distance from the Lord, from his
disciples, and from all the privileges of Judea, she had become
acquainted with the word of God only through the medium of
Jewish prejudices, the fame occasioned by the Saviour's discourses, and the miracles which He had performed either for the
benefit of His own people or for the good of strangers. By such
insufficient means had she been led to faith ; and to *what* faith,
while a multitude of Jews were closing their eyes to the flood of
light with which the " Word of God made flesh " was inundating
them ! So true it is that salvation depends less upon the position than the disposition. The Abrahams, the Rahabs, the
Naamans believe, while the Caiaphases, the Judases, and the
Demases harden themselves or turn aside. And we, my dear
friends, are also of the number of those who have much light.
Are we also among those who have much faith ? Ah ! if any
of you complain of a want of resources, or of evidence sufficient
for belief, it will not be a Peter or a Paul alone who will rise up
at the last day to testify against you, but there will also appear
this woman of Canaan. You cannot believe, because you will
not ; and that will be your condemnation.

The conduct of the Lord in the case of the woman of Canaan,
is consistent with His manner of acting towards Gentiles in
general, and with the particular motives for His mercy in this
instance.

Jesus had come to the Gentiles, in the sense that His doctrine
and His reign were to extend to all the nations. But He had
come solely to the Jews, in the sense that His personal ministry
was to be exercised only within the limits of Judea. It was

reserved for His disciples to pass beyond these limits, and this
they were to do only after He should have left the earth. Hence
a double point of view, and, as it were, two distinct phases in
the Lord's conduct towards the people ; so distinct, indeed, as
to appear inconsistent, if His special mission is not kept continually in view. Faithful to His special mission, Jesus confined His
ministry to his own country, and commanded His disciples to do
the same, as long as He was with them. " These twelve Jesus
sent forth, and commanded them, saying, Go not into the way
of the Gentiles, and into any city of the Samaritans enter ye
not." Meanwhile, from time to time, He bestowed, in passing,
the gifts of His grace upon Gentiles who fell in his way, and
whom faith united to the people of God ; and thus He indicated
what He would do at some future day, and corrected mildly the
prejudices of His disciples, making them familiar, by degrees,
with the doctrine, so incredible to them, the calling of the Gentiles : " And I say unto you, that many shall come from the east
and west, and shall sit down with Abraham, and Isaac, and Jacob,
in the kingdom of heaven."

But are these considerations sufficient to explain the attitude
of the Lord in regard to the woman of Canaan ? Did He not
treat her with a severity, an apparent harshness which He exhibited neither towards the Centurion, nor towards Zaccheus, nor
towards any of those who had recourse to Him ? And does He
not seem, in her case, to have divested Himself of that gentleness and of that inexhaustible patience which formed the basis
of His character ? Ah ! observe more closely, observe especially
what St. James calls " the end of the Lord," and you will
judge otherwise. Jesus assumes this inflexible air only to make
His mercy more striking ; while at the same time the blessing
which He accorded to the woman of Canaan, was the more precious, and salutary, as it was more painfully bought and longer
expected. Let us not forget that He who speaks here, is not a
man, but the Lord. He reads the heart, nay, He operates
therein according to his good pleasure. Fear not that he will

tempt his poor servant beyond what can be borne ; while he tries him, he strengthens him, and will, in the end, give him "an issue" worthy of his fidelity. Besides, He knows with whom he has to do, and He has different ways for souls differently disposed. To the feeble He makes advances, and accommodates Himself to their infirmities ; the strong, it pleases Him to make to wait, to withdraw from, to provoke to holy combat, in order to exercise their courage, and, at the same time, to display before the eyes of men and angels the beautiful spectacle of their victory. Thus He strengthened the faith of the woman of Canaan, while he instructed His disciples so much the more, as he had, at first, appeared to adopt their prejudices. Doubt it not ; it is for choice souls, for beloved children, that He reserves these extraordinary trials. "What coldness in His language !" you say ; yes, but what love in His heart !

With this explanation, let us now see how the woman of Canaan struggles with the Lord, pursues Him, if we may be permitted to speak thus, from retreat to retreat, and finishes by obliging Him to say : "Be it unto thee even as thou wilt."

Jesus often sought retirement, and for different reasons. Sometimes it was for the sake of allowing His body repose ; sometimes from reasons of prudence, when desirous of avoiding the hatred of His enemies ; sometimes from humility, in order to escape the applause of the multitudes ; sometimes from the pious wish to apply himself to secret prayer. But, at this time, His reason for retirement was a special one, and closely connected with our narrative : He was approaching a country of the Gentiles, where His ministry must not be carried. Saint Mark represents Him as taking means to conceal himself : "And He entered into a house, and would have no man know it ; but," adds the Evangelist, "He could not be hid ;" and why ? Because the woman of Canaan would not permit Him.

This pious woman who ardently desired to see Jesus, this sorrowing mother, who expected her daughter to be healed only through the Lord's mercy, kept her ear continually open to

everything that she heard of Him. While He is yet at a great
distance, she receives eagerly the first noise of His approach,
and no sooner is He upon the frontier of her country, than she
leaves her beloved daughter, and flies to seek Him. But how
many obstacles does she encounter! Jesus is not advancing to
meet her; it is she who must go out to stop Him. She is not
sustained by a multitude bringing sick persons to the Lord; she
is going alone in search of Him. Nor has He called her to
Him, as He did others, saying: "Come unto me all ye that
labor and are heavy laden." He avoids her looks. She must
force His door; must pursue Him into a house where He had
entered expressly to be concealed, and where He is surrounded
by His disciples, by Jews filled with the pride and prejudices of
their nation, and, upon this occasion so much the more disposed
to drive away a poor Gentile, as the fidelity which they owed
to their Master seemed to make it a duty. Behold more than
enough to discourage an ordinary soul. The moment is not
auspicious; "I shall not be permitted to enter; my presence will
be unwelcome; I shall be badly received; self-respect ought to
restrain me." But the woman of Canaan did not make these
reflections, or did not dwell upon them. An ardent desire
inspired by maternal tenderness, sustained by an unshaken
confidence in the word and promises of the Lord, renders her
capable of surmounting everything. The occasion seems to her
propitious, the only one, perhaps: her daughter may die; Jesus
may return into Judea; to-morrow, perhaps, may be too late.
She sets out; she advances; she overcomes all difficulties. How?
the Gospel narrative does not tell us; but here she is at the
feet of the Saviour offering her petition: "Have mercy upon
me, O Lord, thou son of David, my daughter is grievously vexed
with a devil."

Now if the Lord was unable to conceal Himself, understand
that it was because He did not in reality wish to do it. He
could not escape the faith of the woman of Canaan, in the same
way that He could not grant anything to the incredulity of the

Nazarenes, concerning which Saint Mark says : " And He could then do no mighty work, save that He laid His hands upon a few sick folks, and healed them ; and He marvelled because of their unbelief." It is voluntarily, and without prejudice to His sovereign power, that the Lord is overcome, or rather that He suffers himself to be overcome, in the contest into which He enters with us ; whether He comes to us, and the blessings which He may bring be turned away by our unbelief, or whether He avoids us, and the blessing which He may refuse be torn from Him by our faith. It is He himself who has established this double rule, that unbelief should receive nothing, and that faith shall obtain all things.

Behold, then, the first victory of the woman of Canaan : she triumphs over the precautions of Jesus. And do you, my dear brethren, do you know, as she did, how to find the Saviour when He is concealed, and how to open a passage to Him upon those gloomy occasions, when obstacles of every kind accumulate upon your pathway ? Or would you be of those sluggards who, not satisfied with being arrested by real difficulties, and with "not ploughing by reason of the cold," yield to imaginations, and refuse to go out for fear of "the lion that is in the street." Go, learn what these words mean : "He that observeth the wind shall not sow ; and he that regardeth the clouds shall not reap."

Once in the presence of Jesus, the woman of Canaan is tranquil. He knows what efforts she has made in order to reach him. How can he send her away empty ? His tenderness is well known. A mother who prays for her daughter, ought to be particularly entitled to it ; especially when she asks to see that daughter delivered from a demon that afflicts her soul more than her body ; doubtless the deliverance will be effected. . . . Poor Canaanite ! the obstacles which thou hast overcome, are small in comparison with those which thou art destined to encounter : the former were only in the external circumstances that hindered thee from approaching Jesus ; now thou art about to meet with obstacles in Jesus himself. What wilt thou do when He upon whom thou hast relied for deliverance from trial, shall himself study to try thee? Jesus "answered her not a word." This woman who has forced herself upon him is a Gentile; He suffers her to cry to him without giving to her a reply.

This silence!—Ah, what contempt, what bitterness for this poor mother! If, with a denial to her prayer, she had received one word of consolation, one word of pity: but to be gazed upon in utter silence! A father solicited by a child, a master besought by a servant, even though he may not wish to gratify, will, at least, reply. The poorest reception that one can give to the prayers of the meanest of men is a word in reply. "Jesus answered the Centurion. He answered the nobleman of Capernaum. He aswered the leper. He answers when he grants; He answers even when he refuses. He answers all others; I am the only one to whom he answers nothing; the only one whom he suffers to cry without some token of compassion." Is this then the Messiah, who "with righteousness shall judge the poor;" who shall not break a bruised reed, nor quench the smoking flax, who says to the poor sinner: "Call upon Me in the day of trouble: I will deliver thee, and thou shalt glorify Me."

But if these doubts knock at the heart of the woman of Canaan, they find no entrance there. She walks by faith and not by sight. This silence surprises her, it is inexplicable to her, but it shakes not her faith. Jesus may have motives for this silence which she knows not. Perhaps he wishes to exercise her patience. Perhaps he wishes to give a lesson to his disciples. Perhaps he wishes something else. Whatever it may be, he is the Son of David, the promised Messiah, the Lord. Whatever it may be, "he is good to all, and his tender mercies are over all his works." The woman of Canaan relies upon his promises, as upon a rock which cannot fail her. Let Him do whatever may please Him, she is resolved never to doubt His word. He is silent, but it is only for a season. Far from being silent in her turn, she will cry "so much the more." She will constrain him to speak. She will give him no peace until she shall have obtained a reply.

This reply she finally obtains in an unexpected manner. The disciples coming between her and their Master, exclaim : "Send her away, for she crieth after us." Send her away; but how ? Shall it be by granting her urgent request, or by driving her off as a miserable Gentile ? Perhaps the disciples made use designedly of an equivocal expression : they dared not suggest to the Lord what He ought to do ; but in one way or another, either by granting or refusing what she wished, they desired to be rid of her. But the reason which they give, "for she crieth after us," lends a dark tone to the sentiment which dictated their intervention : it shows that what touched them most was the annoyance which the cries of this woman caused to Jesus and to themselves. So little did they understand the heart of their Master, that they believed Him to be weary of the prayers of the afflicted, as did those servants of Jairus who came to him saying : "Thy daughter is dead ; trouble not the Master." It was because they judged Jesus by themselves. Oh, unworthy sentiment ! to be less touched by the anguish and supplications of a mother who sees her daughter in the power of a demon, than by the trouble and embarrassment that she gives ! Let us beware, Christians ; even we, the servants of God, let us beware, and not hasten to cast a stone at the disciples. Has nothing similar ever happened to us ? When some one has spread before us the anguish of his heart, has spoken to us, perhaps, of his sins and of the salvation of his soul, has it never happened that we have listened with distraction, and been less touched by his sufferings than fatigued by the length of his story ? He has found us, perhaps, preoccupied with some unimportant care, some secondary interest, some pleasure, some repast that awaited us. Oh, selfish hearts, more troubled by a small contrariety of our own, than by the bitter grief of others !

But these reflections are ours ; the woman of Canaan did not

make them. Of what importance to her are the motives of the
disciples, or even their contempt, provided their impatience
break the silence of Jesus ?   It is not of them that she is thinking, it is of their Master. She has eyes and ears for him alone.
Now see, his mouth is opening—that mouth, one word from
which can heal her daughter, as it has healed so many sick, con-
soled so many afflicted, raised to life so many dead ; what more
does she need ?   It is enough that she has triumphed over his
silence, and constrained him to speak.

Recall, my dear friends, those gloomy times when the Lord
has tried you by His silence ; when He has suffered you to cry to
Him without giving any answer or any " token of good ; when
you have in vain said to Him : " Teach me thy paths, for Thou
art the God of my salvation ;" when you have sought, without
avail, in His Word for some light to your feet ; when, in fine,
you have found, notwithstanding all your efforts, only a God
without a voice and a heaven of brass. What have you done,
then ?   Have you, like the woman of Canaan, besieged the
throne of grace until you obtained a response ?

" Go in peace, thy faith hath made thee whole ; let it be unto
thee even as thou wilt : thy daughter is healed." These are the
words that the woman of Canaan expected from Jesus. But,
instead of them, what does He say to her, or rather, what does
He say to His disciples, for it is to them rather than to her that
He addresses His reply ?   " I am not sent but unto the lost
sheep of the house of Israel ;" or, according to a more literal
translation, " I am not sent but among the lost sheep of the
house of Israel."

We have seen that the mission of Jesus was, in one sense, to
the Jews alone, and, in another sense, to all nations. He was
sent only *among* the Jews, and His personal ministry was not to
extend beyond their borders ; but He was sent *for* all men, and
His salvation was, finally, to be made known throughout the
world ; a fact which He was making known by conferring
blessings upon a small number of Gentiles, who waited not

to receive them until the Gospel should have penetrated into their country. Had He said this to the woman of Canaan, she would have been relieved of her anxiety. But of these two phases of the question He showed her only that which could discourage her, and that, even, under the severest aspect. He had said unto His disciples, in sending them to preach the Gospel : "Go not into the way of the Gentiles, but go rather to the lost sheep of the house of Israel ;" but to her He said, in terms more absolute and more inflexible : "I am not sent, but among the lost sheep of the house of Israel."

If the silence of Jesus had appeared cruel to the woman of Canaan, these words must have appeared to her more cruel still. His silence had, at least, left her hope ; His words seem to take it from her. Jesus cannot grant to her what she asks, without, in some sort, departing from His mission. He is sent only among the Jews, and has nothing to do with the Gentiles. The very law of His ministry, and the principles of the kingdom which He has come to establish, exclude the woman of Canaan from His benefits. He is the Saviour, but of the Jews ; there is deliverance in Him, but it is not for her.

We, it is true, comparing our text with another, and discerning "the times and the seasons," can explain the reply of the Saviour in such a way as to leave, still, an open door to the Gentiles. But the woman of Canaan possessed not our light and our theology ; and the word of the Saviour, that word which she had so ardently desired, had decided against her. What could be done then, and what could be resorted to in such a trial ? If any other than Jesus had forbidden her to hope, she would have appealed to Jesus ; but from Jesus himself, to whom could she appeal ? The greater her confidence in Him, the greater is her reason for losing courage. It is He who turns against her, it is He who studies to torment her, it is He who constrains her, apparently, in despair of her cause, to cry out : "Mine affliction increaseth. Thou huntest me as a fierce lion ; and again thou showest thyself marvellous upon me." But, fear not for the woman of Canaan. If she has not our theology, she has what is better : she has a faith that we possess not, and this faith will enable her to triumph over the words of Jesus.

Remember David at Nob. He reaches the house of God, pressed by hunger, and finds no other bread than that which was consecrated to the Almighty. Concerning this bread it was written : "And it shall be Aaron's and his sons' ; and they shall eat it in the holy place : for it is most holy unto him of the offerings of the Lord made by fire by a perpetual statute." And the word of God permitted neither David nor his men to touch it. But David, by his faith, anticipates the liberty of Gospel times : this faith raises him above all that is written ; the Holy Spirit causes him to understand that the Levitical law is but a transient type ; he feels the approval of God, in acting against the letter of the commandment, and eats in peace the bread sacred to the priests. Our woman of Canaan is sustained by a similar feeling. Her faith anticipates the time set for the calling of the Gentiles, and places her beyond the reach of the words just uttered by the Lord. She knows not what to say in answer to these words, but she feels in the bottom of her soul something that outweighs them. It is in vain to tell her : This is not for thee. In vain, even, may the Lord himself tell it to her ; she will never believe herself excluded from grace. She feels that there is here something mysterious that will be explained to her, something apparently contradictory that will, in good season, be made clear to her ; everything is possible to the Lord, except to abandon a soul that waits upon Him. And she perseveres, and she stoops more humbly, and she prays more earnestly, and she approaches nearer to that Saviour who attempts to escape her, and she prostrates herself before Him and cries out : "Lord have mercy on me." Sent to me, or not, here Thou art, oh ! Saviour of the unfortunate ! Called, or not, here am I, a wretched mother ! Thou *must* hear me, Thou *must* cure my daughter, Thou must drive away this demon ; *I will not let Thee go*, until Thou hast delivered me !

My brethren, the word of God which was given to us for our eternal consolation, seems sometimes to turn itself against us— God permitting Satan to tempt us as he tempted Jesus in the desert. We find in this word conditions which do not seem to be fulfilled, signs of conversion which we do not seem to possess, promises to which we believe ourselves strangers, threats which fill us with dismay. In moments like these, there is peace for us only in that faith which here sustains the woman of Canaan. It is not a dogmatic deduction, it is not the anxious discussion of the meaning and limits of a condition or of a promise that can deliver us ; we must rise higher. We must go directly to the Saviour. We must have recourse to that witness which the Spirit of God renders to our spirit : Whatever may befall me, He is " my rock "—my heart hath told me to " seek thy face "— " I know whom I have believed "—" Thou art mine, and I am Thine."

The whole strength of the woman of Canaan is in that confidence with which the love of the Saviour inspires her. It is in the heart of Jesus that she seeks a secret protection both against His silence and His word. But what will become of her, if even this protection, if this last refuge should fail her, and if she should find in the heart of Jesus nothing but severity and disdain ? What did I say, O my Saviour ? Severity and disdain in Thee, the " meek and lowly in heart ?" Ah, never didst thou so much love her ! Thou triest her, because thou lovest her : but because thou art faithful, thou wilt not try her beyond her strength, that strength which thou measurest exactly, nay, which thou thyself givest to her ; for, by what strength can one struggle against the Lord, except by the strength that cometh from the Lord ?

But this faithful love of Jesus is, for a moment, concealed under appearances of severity and disdain ; and how can we describe what passes in the heart of the poor woman of Canaan, when her tender, her ardent prayer, " Lord help me," receives this reply : " It is not meet to take the children's bread, and to cast it to dogs?" You understand what He means: the children are the Jews; the dogs are the Gentiles, of whom this Canaanite is one. However cruel this expression may be in our language, it was still more so in that of the Jews; for dogs never appear in Holy Writ except under the most repulsive circumstances; to the Jew, and, in general, to all the nations of the East, the dog was an unclean animal, the type of profane and persecuting impiety, as the swine, with which he was associated, was the type of an inordinate and sensual impiety.

Truly, this temptation was greater than the others to which the woman of Canaan was subjected. Saint Mark felt it so strongly, that it is the only one of which he makes mention in his narrative, and, passing by the silence and the first reply of the Saviour, he stops only at the reproachful comparison made between the poor supplicant and the unclean dogs. Behold, then, Jesus adopting, over-acting, even, the contempt shown for the Gentiles in the language and prejudices of His people. Behold, not simply the spirit of the woman of Canaan troubled, but her heart wounded, bruised, overwhelmed; I say her heart, for it would be too little to say her self-love. Her confidence is responded to by coldness, her resignation by indifference, and her love by contempt. Ah! here she might have been overcome, if it had been possible to overcome her.

But she cannot be overcome, because she will not doubt. It is the Lord, let Him do what seemeth good in His sight; though He slay her, yet will she trust in Him. Far from suffering herself to be shaken, she is scarcely troubled. She triumphs over the contempt of Jesus. She preserves all her freedom of soul, and with a presence of mind that we should admire, if our attention was not absorbed by a spectacle far more beautiful, that of her faith, she arms herself against the Lord with the very weapon with which He has just pierced her: she "judges Him out of His own mouth." This humiliating comparison, which, in our opinion, would have been so revolting to her heart, she adopts without murmur, and from it draws a new argument to overcome the Lord's resistance; so much does she forget herself in her anxiety to save her daughter, and to gain the favor of Jesus. "Truly, Lord, I am satisfied with what Thou sayest, I am, in comparison with Thy people, only what a dog is in comparison with a child. But even then I am entitled to the portion of a dog. The dogs eat the crumbs which fall from their master's table; I ask for nothing more." "A single crumb of that bread with which Thou satisfiest the desires of Thy chosen people, a single word, a single look, and my daughter shall be healed!"

It is done, O Canaanite! The victory is thine; thy child is healed. "And Jesus answered and said unto her: O woman, great is thy faith; be it unto thee even as thou wilt." Now the tables are turned: it is man who triumphs, and the Lord who yields: it is the Creator of the heavens and of the earth who says to the poor sinful creature: "Thy will be done." Such is the power of faith. And what is it that has decided this astonishing victory? It is this simple expression of faith and humility: "The dogs eat the crumbs that fall from their master's table." These are the decisive words, as we find in the narrative given by Saint Mark, when the Saviour says: "For this saying, go thy way; the devil is gone out of thy daughter." For this saying! We have often admired the efficacy of the words of God; it is now time to admire the efficacy of the words of man. The words of the woman of Canaan open the heavens, triumph over the Lord, drive away the devil, and accomplish whatever she wishes. "As the Lord God of Israel liveth, before whom I stand," said Elijah, "there shall not be dew nor rain these years, but according to my word." It was because this word was the word of faith. Faith gives us some mysterious share in the omnipotence of God himself. If it is written: "With God, all things are possible," it is also written: "All things are possible to him that believeth." Fear not that pride may be engendered by this glorious power; it is exercised only in humility; it escapes when the heart is inflated; the woman of Canaan is all-powerful at the moment when she abases herself most profoundly. Oh, wonder of wonders ! Oh, wisdom incomprehensible ! **Mystery** unfathomable ! Light divine ! How happy are those meek ones whose expectation is in the Lord their God ! "They shall inherit the earth," they "shall judge angels," they "shall reign on the earth."

My brethren, when the heart of Jesus shall seem to fail you ; when your prayers even shall serve only to increase your trouble; when, in return for the most fervent supplications, and most tender confidence, you shall seem to find his ear closed, his heart inaccessible, and his hand repelling you, remember then, oh ! remember the words that saved the woman of Canaan ! Beware of entertaining the thought that the Saviour can abandon you. It is written : "For a small moment have I forsaken thee ; but with great mercies will I gather thee." Humble yourself beneath his powerful arm. Present to him that "broken and contrite heart," to which he hath made the promise ; and from the midst of your distress, and even while he is refusing you, lift up a new cry, a more earnest prayer which He cannot resist, and which shall draw from Him this reply : "For this saying, go thy way ; be it unto thee even as thou wilt."

Like combat, like victory. The more the woman of Canaan had suffered and resisted, the more precious to her was her deliverance, and the more comforted was her faith. Oh, with what eyes beheld she her daughter snatched from the dominion of the devil ! Then, how well did she understand that the Lord had much tried her because he had much loved her ! Must there not have been in the remembrance alone, of this touching and terrible scene, enough to fortify her until the end, against the griefs of life ? What this remembrance was for her, let her story be for you. The miracle of the Saviour was wrought for her, but it was recorded for you. If the Lord tries you, be assured that He loves you. If for you He has appointed special trials, be assured that in his heart He has kept for you a special place. A soul sorely bruised is a soul elect. Let the experience of the woman of Canaan instruct and strengthen you. Like her, give glory to the Lord, and never doubt His goodness. As long as you shall be able to say, from the bottom of your heart : Whatever may befall me the Lord is good, you will be invincible.

But the experience of the woman of Canaan will strengthen you, only if you share her faith. If her support had been derived only from the experience of those afflicted persons whom the Lord had delivered before her, she would never have remained firm against temptation. To the experience of his kindness towards them, she would have opposed the experience of his apparent severity towards herself, and she would have yielded. It always seems to us that the experience of others does not correspond exactly with our own. That which confirmed the woman of Canaan, that which made her conquer, was a resolution to rely upon the Lord and upon His word, whatever might be the consequence ; it was an unwillingness to see anything, to hear anything opposed to her faith. Thus was she rendered capable of resisting, not only this trial or that, but all the trials that might come upon her. It was when everything had been tried, exhausted, and when she had been found not only unvanquished, but invincible, it was then that the Lord said to her : "O woman, great is thy faith." Oh ! if she had lost courage before the close of the combat ! if she had abandoned her hope, when there was but one step more to take ! Perhaps you are at this very point. One more step—one more effort—one more prayer, and you will be saved. Do not say : It is a year, five years, ten years that I have been praying and the Lord has not answered me ; but say : The Lord cannot reject me. Do not say : I have such and such evidence that the Lord will not answer me ; but say : The Lord cannot refuse me. Arm yourselves, my brethren, with the faith of the woman of Canaan, with a faith that excites His admiration. Say to Him with Jacob : "I will not let thee go except thou bless me." Lord Jesus, who commandest faith, and who crownest it, thou art he also who givest it, and who, having given it, increasest it. "We believe, Lord, help thou our unbelief." Lord increase our faith ! Amen.

FRED. WILLIAM KRUMMACHER, D.D.

BIOGRAPHICAL NOTICE.*

FREDERICK WILLIAM KRUMMACHER was born on the 28th of January, 1797, at Meurs, near the Lower Rhine, Germany. His father was Dr. Frederick Adolph Krummacher, Professor of Theology, and afterwards General Superintendent and Court Preacher; and who died while pastor at Bremen. He was the author of the famous "Parables," and several other works.

Frederick William, the son, was converted in the year 1819, ordained as assistant minister in Frankfort on the Maine, and first settled as pastor at Ruhrort. His education was at Bernburg, and Halle, and Jena; and he attributes his conversion to some peculiarly rich Christian experiences with which he came in contact, in certain humble day-laborers, who had read and been enriched by the writings of Gerhard Tersteegen.

In the year 1823, he was called to Barmen, and afterwards to Elberfeld. In 1847, at the call of the king of Prussia, he took up his residence in Berlin (for three years past at Potsdam, near Berlin), as Court preacher, and pastor of the Court and Garrison Church; with some five thousand souls under his charge. He says "in the days in my youth I worked in a blooming vineyard" (referring to his first field of labor), "but now I am trying to reclaim a wide, sandy desert."

The published writings of Dr. Krummacher are very voluminous, some of which are quite a number of volumes of sermons, a Refutation of Rationalism, a System of Christian Doctrine, Last Days of Elisha, Elijah the Tishbite, The Martyr Lamb, and The Suffering Saviour. These last named works have been widely read by the

* The essential facts as to Dr. Krummacher's early life, official stations, etc., are derived from a letter from his own hand.

people of this country, and have rendered his name honored and beloved by thousands of pious souls among all classes, and in all parts of the land.

Dr. Krummacher is tall and full of proportions, light hair combed back sleekly over his ears, blue and expressive eyes, peering now, in the sere of "three score and ten," through a pair of gold spectacles, and of a heavy, lion-like voice. He is a man of undoubted piety, and, considering his antecedents, liberal in his views of religious toleration, has great influence with the king, and is, perhaps, the most eloquent of living divines. Some of his sermons are represented to be like earthquakes; while, at another time, one would think, from the exquisite beauty of his sentences, that his mind was a picture-gallery, or a garden of sweets, with meandering streams and endless forms of life and beauty.

Some of Krummacher's peculiarities are well brought out in a reminiscence of Dr. Abel Stevens. "When I told him the other night, at a tea-party, the number of some of the editions of his 'Elijah' among us, and that it was read in our log-cabins in California and Oregon, he seemed hardly to believe me, for the extent of the American press is scarcely known in Europe; and when I assured him that if he would come to New York, we could place him in sections of the city, where, for whole squares, he could read German 'signs,' and hear the children playing in German; and if he liked 'lager-bier,' drown himself in an ocean of it, he laughed as you might suppose a lion would, were it the habit of that noble creature to laugh at all,—his mighty voice ringing into the adjacent apartments. But suppose not that there was anything peculiarly humorous in my remarks, or uncommon in Krummacher's uproarious outbursts. It is the 'vocal style' of the man. What the watchman said of George Whitefield, can be said of this great German: 'He preaches like a lion.' He not only *preaches*, but *prays*, and makes speeches so, and even 'says grace' at the table in the same manner. He introduced our public dinner, the other day, with a 'grace' in German, which was roared out, as if addressed to an army half a mile off."

The following sermons on the Temptation of Christ, are considered among the ablest which he has published. They are generally printed as one discourse; but in their translation we have thought it best to keep up the divisions.

DISCOURSE VIII.

THE TEMPTATION OF CHRIST.*

" Then was Jesus led up of the Spirit into the wilderness, to be tempted of the devil. And when he had fasted forty days and forty nights, he was afterwards an hungered. And when the tempter came to him, he said, If thou be the Son of God, command that these stones be made bread. But he answered and said, It is written, Man shall not live by bread alone, but by every word that proceedeth out of the mouth of God. Then the devil taketh him up into the holy city, and setteth him on a pinnacle of the temple, and saith unto him, If thou be the Son of God, cast thyself down: for it is written, He shall give his angels charge concerning thee: and in their hands they shall bear thee up, lest at any time thou dash thy foot against a stone. Jesus said unto him, It is written again, thou shalt not tempt the Lord thy God. Again, the devil taketh him up into an exceeding high mountain, and sheweth him all the kingdoms of the world, and the glory of them; and saith unto him, All these things will I give thee, if thou wilt fall down and worship me. Then saith Jesus unto him, Get thee hence, Satan: for it is written, Thou shalt worship the Lord thy God, and Him only shalt thou serve. Then the devil leaveth Him, and behold, angels came and ministered unto Him."—MATT. iv. 1–11.

WE now find ourselves on one of those famous battle-fields, where laurels were won which to this day bloom on *our* brows, and triumphs achieved which make *us*, in Christ Jesus, conquerors before the fight, victors even in defeat.

Never has a struggle been carried on, more wonderful in its character, and more blessed in its results, than this, which approaches us so nearly, and is so closely interwoven with our most sacred interests. It is worth our while to linger here, and fasten our eyes upon its whole progress.

* The title of these sermons on the Temptation of Christ, in the original, is, *Satan's Tiefen The Depths of Satan.*—TRANS.

JESUS LED INTO THE WILDERNESS.—No sooner had Jesus been consecrated and anointed to the office of Mediator of the new covenant, by the water of Jordan, and the fire-baptism of the Spirit, without measure, than there descended upon Him from heaven an audible testimony, that He was the only-begotten of the Father, in whom He was well pleased. The sonship of our Lord, and His essential unity with the Father, seems, in the days of His flesh, to have been, even to Himself, more an object of faith than of sight and enjoyment. It is possible that, at moments at least, His Godhead might have been so obscured, or so concealed, that He could have been conscious of it only by naked faith in the naked word of the Father. It was not for His disciples only, but for His own sake also, that the Father ever and anon exclaimed from heaven, "This is my beloved Son," in order to strengthen His belief in Himself; which, as we have observed, sometimes—as, for instance, in the hour of desertion on the Cross—was nothing but a bare belief destitute of all sensible enjoyment.

Consecrated and divinely equipped for His priestly office, Jesus now hastens into the interior of the wilderness. The power by which he is impelled and guided, is, according to the gospel, the Holy Spirit. Was the Lord aware why the Spirit led Him into the wilderness? Perhaps partially only, and in general; the particular object, the Father might have concealed from Him. We too know, by experience, that the Holy Spirit is not always pleased to disclose to us, beforehand, the reason why He impels us hither or thither. He not unfrequently leaves us to pursue our course altogether in the dark. Inwardly we hear His call: "Arise, and go here or there, to such a place, into such a house, to this brother, into that connection, or whithersoever it may be." We ask, "Why? what have I to do there?" —but there comes no answer. Only the louder yet and more penetrating do we hear the call in our hearts, "Away, be gone; tarry not!" We inquire anew what this inward drawing and impulse may signify, but it remains a mystery; we must go forth

in the dark : and should we hesitate, at once there is the conscience in uproar, and a bitter taste of divine displeasure in the
soul. We must away—we *must;* and afterwards the *wherefore*
first reveals itself. There, Philip finds a treasurer who is waiting for his instruction, and here, Elijah a widow, of whose perfect regeneration he is to be the instrument ; here, a mourning
brother welcomes us, and says, " Ah, like an angel from the
Lord art thou come to me !" and there, in a different way, we
come to find why the Spirit has so called and urged us ; and not
till we have set out, does the sun rise on our way and all become
bright and clear. At other times, the Holy Spirit condescends
to reveal to us, in a slight degree, why He leads us this way or
that ; but the rest, nay the most important part of that which
is awaiting us, He reserves to Himself, and keeps it hidden from
our eyes. We may indeed say, " I must enter my closet to pray,
—this house, to render assistance,—that office, to be useful ;" but
what we may have to do in that closet, this house, and that
office, beside praying, assisting, and being useful,—that we are
here to wrestle with the Lord ; there to be crushed and broken ;
that here the flames of the purifying furnace are to assail us ;
there the " Mahanaim " (Gen. xxxii. 2), to meet us ; or whatever else it may be,—of all *that* not a syllable had been revealed
to us. With this, for wise reasons, we were to become acquainted
afterwards, in the way of experience.

It would appear that this latter was the case with the
Saviour. He went into the wilderness, half in the light, half in
the dark. He had, perhaps, only a certain general knowledge
of what was to befall Him : " I am to fast, to suffer, to deny
myself, and in the extremest depths of humiliation and poverty to
begin my priestly office." So much the Spirit had revealed to
Him ; but the severe, frightful temptations that awaited Him
were, according to the counsel of His Father, carefully hidden from His eyes. The unexpectedness of what was to befall,
was so to increase the difficulty of the struggle, that the triumph
should appear the more splendid and glorious.

THE FAST.—Jesus went into the wilderness to *fast*. So far
His foresight reached for the present ; yea, farther, even to anticipate the great object, the mysterious signification of this fasting. Did not, then, this fasting of Jesus come within the
particular plan of Him who led Him into the wilderness ? Certainly : that He should fast was the design of God, but only a
part of it. And do you ask now, For what reason was Jesus
obliged to fast, and why in such dreary solitude, and why was
his abstinence so painful, and protracted through forty days and
forty nights ? Know then, in the first place, that the fasting of
Jesus was of a different nature from that of Moses, for instance,
on the Mount, and of other saints. The fasting of our Lord was
more than a mere spiritual exercise, or preparation for his priest-
hood ; it was an actual sacrifice, a commencement of the priestly
office. The key not only to His temptation, but also to His
fasting, we find behind the barred portals of the lost paradise.
It is atonement for Adam's sin, payment of *his* debt, expiatory
passion. If the first Adam lived in the delightful fields of Paradise, we find the second Adam in a waste, howling wilderness.
If Adam, the man of the earth, dwelt amid the fragrant bowers,
and enjoyed the delicious fruits of Eden, the man from heaven is
shut up to hunger in a desert, surrounded only by stones and
unfruitful shrubs, where not one blade of corn was to be found
to appease the cravings of His nature. If our first parent was
blessed with the unutterable happiness of holding sensible communion with the Almighty and His holy angels, and was glad-
dened with the society of a spotless wife, Jesus is banished into
a dreary solitude, dwelling, as St. Luke expresses it, among wild
beasts, and beset with the old serpent, Satan, and his angels.
Horrible contrast, but so God determines. By fasting and privation in the gloomy and inhospitable desert, the Surety and
Substitute expiates, in the sinner's stead, for the unpardonable,
the desperate presumption with which Adam, in despite of God's
explicit warning and threatening, stretched forth his hand
towards the fruit of the forbidden tree. Yes, Jesus expiates it

for us, His people ; expiates it for His elect. We have nothing more to expiate, nothing for all eternity. But you, who have no interest in the eternal satisfaction of the Lamb, you only see in those circumstances in which Jesus finds himself in the wilderness, a faithful picture of your own coming fate. So will you be compelled to house forever in eternal deserts ; and when you hunger, stones will be crammed into your mouth for bread ; and when you thirst, you must swallow flames instead of water ; you must live as among ravenous beasts, filthy dogs, roaring lions, and hissing serpents ; and will be desolate amid multitudes of the damned : for in hell there is neither sympathy, nor friendship, nor interchange of love : there, hatred and selfishness prevail, and each is too much engrossed with his own agony and torments to commiserate the anguish of others. The duration of this sorrow is *eternity!* With this truth, methinks, one could burst rocks, and make mountains tremble ! And your hearts tremble not ! Alas ! here is more than stone and rock !

But there are also fast-days in the kingdom of God upon earth, bodily and spiritual fast-days of all kinds, both painful and delightsome. The most joyful are observed in the spring months of the new life, in the beginning of conversion, after the first assurances of God's mercy, after the heavenly bridegroom's first declaration of love, when God has just called his Son out of Egypt. Then there is no need of a command, "Renounce, deny thyself, abstain ;" all this comes of itself. With what haste, then, does the soul flit away as on swift wings from the broad pastures and pleasure grounds of this great world !

How can one continue to fill his belly with husks when he has tasted of the vineyards of the promised land, and drank of its rivers of milk and honey ? How can he listen with delight to the fiddles of the dancer or the songs of fleshly rioters, after that he has heard the melody of King David's harp ? How can he gaze with pleasure on theatrical farces and puppet-shows, after he has once seen the heavens open before him with all their glories ? Or, how can he loiter away time on bolsters of

ease and debauchery, when He, whom our soul loves, hangs
before our spiritual sight, bleeding on the accursed tree or
crowned with thorns? Ah! away then, quickly away, with the
shadows of your pitiful joys, and the glittering tinsel of your
vanities! We are enjoying a fast day.

It is often debated and asked, whether this or that enjoyment,
or pleasure, suits with the Christian profession? Cease asking,
and become a Christian—so will you learn what *is* consistent and
what is *not*—and how far the "may" and the "can" of a rege-
rate spirit—an heir of God and His kingdom—may stretch in
a given direction.

There are yet other fast days in a state of grace—fasts of a
painful sort—where the soul is not led out from the meadows of
the world into those of the Lamb—but from those of the Lamb
into the wilderness: and this is a bitter change. It was to us—
ah! how unspeakably delightful as we leaned on the bosom of
Jesus—such sweet, tender emotions and feelings--such a blissful
enjoyment, and affecting taste of the grace and nearness of Christ
as then filled our soul—it made us wish for nothing more than
just to die on the spot, and so pass away from the delightful
forecourt into the very interior of Paradise itself. The south
wind blew through our garden, so that the spices dropped, and
rich clusters of Canaan hung down to our very mouths, and a
delightful blessedness lay spread like the dew of morning upon
our soul, and we were royally quickened, and forgot all the sorrows of this world. But, ere we were aware, the fast-day is
announced, and the bridegroom is taken from us. The fountains
of milk and honey are sealed, and the soul, robbed of its sweet
draughts, sits poor, emotionless, and parched, on the sand. She
must hang her harp on the willows, and do no more, at the most,
than continue to sigh, with feverish tongue, for one little drop of
grace, as she sits on the baked earth.

These are fast-days of God's children in the wilderness.
Happy he whose feet are then set on the rock—who is not led
by his individual emotions and feelings, but by Christ and His

word. "His bread shall be given him, and his waters are sure."
Although he has it not sensibly, yet he has it in simple faith ;
and however the pleasing experiences may fail, yet his peace
remains unmoved. He lies at anchor by the rock of the sure
declarations of God, which stand forever ; and he knows that
though "the mountains may depart, and the hills be removed,"
yet the favor of God will never depart from him, nor the covenant of his peace be disturbed. Even such fasting in the wilderness, if God wills it, is good and wholesome. That very grace
which feeds and loves us to-day, suffers us on the morrow to
hunger and thirst, and hold fast-day. What more can we wish,
if it be *but* grace which leads us ? May it ever guide us
according to its good pleasure !

THE TEMPTATION—Jesus went into the wilderness to fast :
but in the plan of God, there was yet more than this contemplated. What says the Gospel ? "Then was Jesus led up of
the Spirit into the wilderness to be *tempted* of the devil." How
frightful this sounds ! The Holy Spirit leads out the Son of God
to meet the devil ! and for what ? In dry, unambiguous words,
there it stands : "*to be tempted of the devil.*" What a circumstance ! Yet, comfort yourselves with it, ye children of the
kingdom ; stay yourselves thereon, ye tempted souls. For
your consolation is it written. Let none of you imagine that
the roaring lion roams about in Israel loosed and unrestrained ;
and has free play, and can fall upon whomsoever he will, and
shoot his arrows at pleasure, and lay his snares unperceived, as
if the captain of the Lord's host knew not of it. Far otherwise.
Our Leader keeps him ever in His eyes, and holds him fast by
His strong words ; so that what the preacher says is true also
of the devil : "The race is not to the swift, nor the battle to
the strong." There is no fear that he will ever touch one concerning whom Jesus has said to him : "On this mine anointed
lay not thine hand." Around such an one this little word of
the Master erects a wall of fire, and a rampart over which no

fiery dart of the evil one can leap. And whomsoever the devil does assail, him he assails with the express permission of Jesus, consequently as a means for his salvation and blessing. Moreover, is there marked out by the royal sceptre a line prescribing how far he may proceed. At a certain little spot, is the injunction laid. "Thus far, and no farther."

What does the evil one wish? He has been led out, and openly exhibited, and Immanuel has worked a triumph out of him, through himself. Henceforth he belongs to those powers in Heaven, on Earth, and in Hell, with whom Christ does what He will. He uses him like Nebuchadnezzar, and Korah, and other reprobates, for the good of His seed, as rods, and as goads—as a means of discipline; and when he has used them enough—these awful, terrible scourges—then will He break them over His knee, and fling them away, and chain up the dragon in the abyss.

Rejoice, then, ye lambs of God, that the devil is nothing more than your great shepherd's dog, who must dance to his pipe, and howl at his voice, and must go and come as he bids. As often as the fiery darts whiz around you, think of this, my beloved; that it is the Lord and His Spirit that has led you into the wilderness and set you in the strife, and He himself is with you on the plain.

All temptations which assail the children of God, by divine permission, have but one object. They are designed to make evident, and bring to light, what lies hidden in the heart. Oftentimes it pleases the Lord to watch this development of secret things himself. He takes delight in His own works. When Father Abraham had made ready his little sacrifice on Mount Moriah, then the Lord called to him from heaven: "Now I know that thou fearest God, seeing thou hast not withheld thy son, thine only son from me." The Lord, indeed, knew this before; but He wished to observe this holy fear, which He had wrought in the heart of His servant, openly manifesting itself. It was to Him a feast of the eye. So must also many a dear child of God pass through gloom, and strife, and tribulation, because the Lord Jesus likes to hear His little child pray, and sigh, and continue doing so, and to see him walking trustfully by His side over the raging billows. This gives Him joy. This, however, we may not say directly to these dead souls; they would think we mocked them; for they themselves see in it nothing beautiful which could delight their Lord. But the Lord truly sees it, and He will see it.

Ofttimes the Lord suffers his little children to be tempted and brought into straits, in order that the hidden life within may be displayed, not so much to *himself*, as to their *brethren* and ourselves. So he shows to us an Abraham's faith; a Job's patience; a Moses's love; an Elijah's zeal; a Canaanitish woman's humility and fervor, in order that we may praise his power, which is so mighty in the weak children of men. But are we desponding, and disposed to think that such saints might all reach heaven, while with us it will be otherwise? Then he sets before our eyes, here a David, and there a Simon Peter—grapes which, in the press of trial, yielded not wine merely, but also bitter drops of sin from their hearts. Such a sight makes us pluck up courage, especially when we learn that Simon was nevertheless called a rock; and David a man after God's own heart.

And so has it often happened, that those men whose sanctity has shone out with peculiar splendor, and who have enjoyed extraordinary esteem in the world, have at last, under the buffetings of the tempest, been stripped and blasted and compelled to display their weakness and frailty, and miserable sinfulness. Yea, with all their bright sanctity, and glorious activity for God —to lose themselves like a little rivulet in the sand: they who were once such noble streams, that, compared with what they *were*, it would be difficult longer to recognize them. And this the Lord permits in order that all idolizing of mortal men may be prevented, grace preserved in its proper splendor, and the honor given to Him alone, to whom alone it is due.

As a rule, the object of those temptations to which we are exposed, is to bring before our view what is in us, and to *keep us properly humbled* in the dust. We mortals become pious far too lightly ; but Jesus seeks *sinners*. We are righteous all too soon ; but the Lord is after the *unrighteous*. We are swift to soar ; but Jesus wants to see us in the *depths*. Therefore does he suffer the devil, at times, to create a little stir in the sink of our corrupt hearts, in order that the vile odor may mount and strike our senses ; and the hideous viper-brood which nestled quiet and unseen at the bottom, may rise to the top, and sprawl about on the surface before our eyes. Therefore does he occasionally permit the evil one to scare up the swarm of rebellious thoughts and desires, which were lying dormant in the inner chamber of our souls, and set them in motion, in order that we may know all that the temple of God still harbors, and be constrained to forego all our boasting and pride. For this cause is it that he allows the accuser, now and then, to take us by surprise, and startle our slumbering passions as by the trump of doom.

Ah ! how astonished are we then to find that they are still there—these old hateful companions—whom, as we fondly hoped, we had long since swept away with the besom of our pious exercises, and so made our home perfectly clean. But now, alas ! it is quite otherwise. Then the dear bride sees all the fair cosmetics fade away from her cheek, and she becomes again as at first, an Ethiopian, black and without beauty, and renews her former repentance—but also loves again with her early love—for thus will the bridegroom have it. Now under the feet of the high-climbing saint, the topmost round in the ladder of sanctity suddenly gives way, and, alas ! he stands no more even on the lowest, but lies beneath, utterly prostrate, and is a poor wretch, such as, perhaps, he never was before. Now the proud peacock sees his brilliant train suddenly drop to the earth ; his glitter passes away like a mist ; the creature that boasted begins to sneak—becomes naked and bare, slinks ashamed into a corner, and comes, at last, to rejoice with all his heart that Another will bestow on him the wedding garment—that a cross stands on Golgotha, and that on the throne there sits a queen, who is called—*not* righteousness—but *grace—grace.*

DISCOURSE IX.

THE OBJECT AND AGENT IN THE TEMPTATION.

"Then was Jesus led up of the Spirit into the wilderness to be tempted of the devil," etc.—MATT. iv. 1-11.

WE have learned the chief cause why God employs the devil among His children. The question now is, why did God ordain that Jesus our Lord should be tempted. And here, at the outset, we protest most solemnly against that degrading view and teaching, which unshrinkingly asserts that Jesus was placed in the fiery ordeal in order that He, in battle and strife, struggling and praying, might overcome and slay those sins which He had carried in His own flesh—and in His own members. No, we can listen to nothing of this sort respecting our Saviour. That He appeared in the *form* of sinful flesh—this we know ; but yet only in *form*, not *in* sinful flesh *itself*—and though like us in all things, yet was there one point excepted—namely *sin*. God be praised that on this subject the divine word does not leave us in doubt. With the perfect sinlessness and purity of our Mediator, stands or falls the whole structure of our evangelic hopes. Had the white linen of His innocence been stained with the smallest particle of unholy desire and emotion—could any one but prove this—then might the church be shut—the Bible burned—confidence cast away—and despair only reign. For then would Jesus not be our Saviour—and His ransom not be available—and sufficient.

The temptations of Jesus were in their design far different from those which *we* are wont to experience. He endured them, not for Himself, but for us and in our stead. They were a part of His mediatorial sufferings. We saw Adam tempted by the serpent, and wantonly giving up the ship to the eddying vortex of his allurements. But the second Adam repairs the evil by exposing Himself to a still severer assault; breaking the lance of the foe—completely overcoming the accuser, and rendering to the Father a perfect obedience. Adam had by disobedience become the prey of Satan, and the second Adam drinks for him the curse, and descends from His throne of majesty into the society of evil spirits—into the very pool of hell.

Unexampled humiliation! The Almighty God touched by the murderous hands of Satan—the Sovereign of the universe hissed at on every side by the old serpent—the only Holy One beleaguered by the powers of darkness, and the Lord of hosts a football for accursed angels of hell—caught up by them—snatched away—carried off and tempted, and urged by them to the most shameful things! What a horrible position for the Son of God! more horrible and monstrous than we can conceive; for we by nature stand much nearer Satan who is our father. To us who carry his likeness, his blackness is not so hateful, not so repulsive, as it must be to Him who dwells in light, and is Himself nothing but light : Verily, no trivial suffering must it have been for Him to be compelled so to dwell among friends! But down into this very pool—this abyss—must the Son of God descend. So must the floods of Belial terrify Him, in order that payment may be made for the gigantic guilt which we have heaped up. And under such oppositions and hindrances must He alone— deserted of help—through battle and strife—execute the Father's will, in order that with His own brilliant, spotless obedience, He might cover the disobedience of Adam and his seed in the sight of God.

Another object of the temptations of Jesus was this : that He might become our sympathizing **High Priest**. This, indeed,

He could have been without actually tasting our temptations. But now we, weak mortals, can more firmly believe that He *is* so, and enjoy greater freedom in pouring out our hearts before Him, and in the dark **hour of** temptations bewail to Him our sore need.

When two persons meet who are **able** to recount similar necessities—and the same buffetings of Satan, oh, what mutual disclosures take place ! what trustful communicativeness—what tender sympathy is then manifest ! Then one soul gushes out and flows over into the other, and time steals rapidly on. But on the other hand, towards one who knows not our needs by experience, we are dumb, reserved, and take no pleasure in communicating, because we fear that he will be able neither to understand nor sympathize with us. So, indeed, would we have kept farther **away from our** Heavenly Friend, had He not become our companion in **tribulation.** But **now** the thought is exceedingly refreshing, that **He Himself, was** tempted in all points like as we are—and knows the bitterest anguish **of our soul from** His own experience. Now, even though no fellow-man understands us, ah ! still we know there is yet *one* Friend at hand, to whom we need but lisp a word of our affairs and concerns, and He at once comprehends all we feel. His experience reaches down into the thickest nights of the soul—into the most frightful depths of inward sufferings or conflicts. Under no juniper tree canst thou sit, which has not overshadowed Him ; no thorn can wound thee, from which his heart has not bled ; no fiery dart can hit thee, which has not been shot at His sacred head. He can indeed have compassion. Yes, only believe it, dear soul ; as often as thou liest in the furnace, over thee the eyes of the watchful Refiner melt in tears—and a great, holy, mother-heart, bleeds for thee in sympathy from heaven.

It was then out of pure compassion and love towards a sinful world, that God placed His Son in the fire of temptation.

We may now further ask, whether God had not some design in this thing also towards the tempter himself ? and this question

I am the more disposed to answer affirmatively, from the distinguished position which this prince of fallen angels occupies in
the realm of spirits. That satyr-form, with horns and hoofs,
under which the popular faith is wont to picture the devil, and
which has more of the elements of the ridiculous, and the coarse,
and the vulgar, than of the grand, and the awful, has little
truth in it. Incomparably deeper and richer in meaning and
reality, is that view which we find living in so many popular
traditions of a grey antiquity, which is wont everywhere to
associate with the devil, in some way, whatever is monstrous,
wild, fearful, and savagely formed in nature ; and which points
out to us in woody, mountainous, and rocky regions—now here,
and now there—a devil's stone, a devil's ladder, a devil's chapel,
or a devil's bridge. Let a person but peruse connectedly those
isolated and scattered traits, which the Scriptures have in many
places, half-cursorily sketched of this fallen morning star—this
firstling of creation, and in presence of this prince of hell, he
will hardly be able to avoid a certain degree of fear and amazement.

He is the Leviathan of whom the Lord says : "Wilt thou
play with him as with a bird ? Wilt thou bind him for thy
maidens ? Canst thou put a hook in his nose ? or bore his jaw
through with a thorn ?" He is the mighty one of whom it is
asserted : "None is so fierce that dare stir him up. Who can
discover the face of his garment ? or who can come to him with
his double bridle ? who can open the doors of his face ? His teeth
are terrible round about. His scales are his pride, shut up
together as with a close seal ; one is so near another that no
air can come between them. By his neesings a light doth shine,
and his eyes are like the eyelids of the morning. Out of his
mouth go burning lamps, and sparks of fire leap out. Out of
his nostrils goeth smoke, as out of a seething pot or caldron.
His breath kindleth coals, and a flame goeth out of his mouth.
In his neck remaineth strength, and sorrow is turned into joy
before him. His heart is as firm as a stone, yea, as hard as a

piece of the nether millstone. When he raiseth up himself the
mighty are afraid. The sword of him that layeth at him cannot
hold ; the spear, the dart, nor the habergeon. He esteemeth
iron as straw, and brass as rotten wood. Darts are counted as
stubble ; he laugheth at the shaking of a spear. Upon earth
there is not his like, who is made without fear. He beholdeth
all high things. He is a king over all the children of pride."
These are the features of that mighty spirit, who, viewed in his
original splendor, is no other and no less than the son of God,
such as the rationalists describe him.

This Satan—a ruin of indescribable grandeur—grand even in
desolation, and worthy of all wonder—still an object of honor
to the Master who created it—for where is there an understanding—where a policy—where a perseverance—an energy—and a
power like his ?—and these things which so excite our astonishment, are but the *remains* of his original grandeur—*this* SATAN,
I say, even *as* Satan, is portrayed in Scripture with a certain
air of majesty. Not only is he there called a lord—a power—
a prince—but he is also styled the "*god* of this world ;" and it
is not to be denied, that to him, as such, a certain degree of
respect is shown. Reflect a moment, how the Apostle Jude
says, that even " Michael, the archangel, when, contending with
the devil, he disputed about the body of Moses, durst not bring
against him a railing accusation, but said, ' The Lord rebuke
thee.'" In Job, also, we see Satan standing, with angels and
good spirits, near the throne of God, and the Lord holds conversation with him, and asks him whether he has known and
considered His servant Job ; and in reply to the crafty insinua-
tion of the accuser : "Doth Job fear God for naught ?" the
Lord gives him power over all his servant's possessions, and
permits him to plague and try Job, in order that he, the devil,
may learn how the power of God was mighty in Job's weakness.

What an extraordinary circumstance ! One might almost
say, that it was pleasing to the Almighty that even this prince

of darkness should acknowledge Him, and do Him honor.   And so it is ; for it is written : ".As I live, saith the Lord, every knee shall bow to me, and every tongue confess that He is Lord."

In like manner, also, was the devil to take a glance into the depths of God's atoning work, and preëminently, by means of the temptation, to learn to recognize the Paschal Lamb in His purity, and our surety in His all-sufficiency, in order that he, too, might know, that "Zion should be redeemed with judgment," and not with caprice, and that no well-grounded objection could be urged against the salvation of sinners.   If the craftiest and most sharp-sighted of all spirits is constrained to wonder at the wisdom of God, to admire His works, to be speechless at His counsels, and to praise His doings even against his will and pleasure,—surely this redounds not a little to the glory of the divine name.   One of the grandest and most solemn moments in the day of God's revelation and glory, will be that in which even Satan will be compelled publicly to acknowledge, that to the Lamb belongs all honor, and glory, and praise ; and when, if I may so speak, one god will tremblingly bow the knee to another.   This will be a doxology no less lofty and glorious than the hallelujahs of the heavenly hosts.

Observe now the TEMPTER's approach.

Forty days and nights had the Lord spent in the solitary wilderness fasting, and " He was an hungered."   Then came the tempter to Him visibly, yet disguised, and transformed into " an angel of light."   He came with a twofold design.   First, he wished to ascertain whether Jesus was actually the Son of God, or not ; and secondly, in case He were so, it was his purpose to put such a stumbling-block in His way, as that on it the whole work of His redemption might be forever wrecked.   To me it appears highly probable, and what has also been affirmed by others, that the devil yet stood in doubt respecting the person of Christ.   Thirty years had Jesus walked in deepest seclusion—a carpenter's son, who had learned His Father's handi-

craft, had earned His bread with the sweat of His brow working
in the shop, had lived plainly and honestly, and had done
nothing, and said nothing, which other men could not have said
or done.   No one dreamed that He could have been anything
more than a very amiable man ; and it is possible that even
Mary and Joseph themselves had lowered not a little in their
expectations concerning Him, as no more miracles occurred, and
the voices from heaven had ceased.   God veiled His Son to
such a degree that even the keen eyes of Satan could easily
have been deceived about this plain carpenter.   Yet they were
not altogether deceived.   Among men, however, not one supposed that this simple laborer at Joseph's bench could have
been the Messiah.

But Satan was shrewd enough not to concede too much to the
external appearance of poverty and meanness.   He might
possibly have surmised that this carpenter, notwithstanding his
humble guise, might nevertheless be the Lord himself.   He
discovered nothing incongruous in the Redeemer's beginning
his work in such a lowly station ; and many circumstances
seemed plainly to indicate that Jesus of Nazareth was the Son
of God.   Yet this was only a surmise.   He knew it not certainly.   And it was this certainty he desired in order to take
his measures wisely.   Had the devil been already assured that
Jesus was the real Messiah, there would have been in his conduct much that was inexplicable, as we shall see hereafter.
But now, the immediate object of his obtruding himself upon
Jesus, was to sift him thoroughly.

And very craftily did the wily spirit so insinuate his temptations, that in case Jesus were to prove himself the Messiah, his
redeeming work should at the outset receive a shock that would
for ever annihilate it.   His next design was to throw the Saviour
off the mediatorial track by a dexterous side-blow, and so, if
possible, strengthen for ever his own dominion over mankind.   In
order to carry out these purposes, he presents before Jesus the
appearance of a kind, well-meaning friend.   He professes to

desire nothing so earnestly as the carrying out of the work of redemption. He acts as if he only wished to point out a shorter way to this exalted end; and manages everything with all the cunning, finesse and artifice that might be expected of a being who, from the highest stage of wisdom and understanding, had sunk into the lowest abyss of wickedness.

Witness too, the aptness of the temptation. Armed with the utmost craft and malice, the tempter accosts Jesus. He hoped that the fearful solitude of the dry, barren wilderness, in which Jesus found himself, would facilitate his victory. The fact that Jesus hungered gained him an advantage for making his first attack. Thus does this murderer of souls always understand how to direct his weapons against *us*, at the right place, in the right time, and amidst befitting circumstances. When we are alone, apart from all society—when there are no human eyes to watch us, no dear brethren to awaken and warn us, no redeemed associates to strengthen and encourage us—when our thoughts wander as they list, then this strong man draws near, bends his bow, and seeks to inject his poison into the heart; and when we hunger or thirst—when there spring up in us desires for this or that object, for gold or bread, for rest or honor, ease or pleasure—when wishes mount high in the heart, even though in themselves they are not censurable, then is he right at hand —friendly and insinuating—proffering us one good advice after another—suggesting to us means upon means for gratifying our wishes:—and, however opposed to God these propositions may be in themselves, yet he understands how to adorn and color them, and how to bring them into such seeming harmony with the word of God, that we take them for the promptings of some good angel; when, after all, it was none else than Satan in an angel's form.

This unfathomable mystery of iniquity, art, and malice, in Satan, has never been so apparent as in just those temptations with which he assaulted the Saviour. Then Christ *could* be tempted? Yes, and not this merely—Paul says, "He was

tempted on all points like as we are." Luther translates it
" Everywhere." The hand of the dear good man might have
trembled, perhaps, at the thought of writing it "in all points."
Out of holy timidity and deep awe, he therefore rather chose to
write " Everywhere." Our Saviour appeared, as the Scripture
saith, "in the likeness of sinful flesh," *i. e.* in human nature
weakened by the fall. All the consequences of sin passed over
on Him, save sin itself. He was tempted, yet without sin. The
innocent impulses and weaknesses of our nature were also His
inheritance. He hungered and thirsted, He could become weary
and sleepy ; He could weep and rejoice, need rest and refreshment, etc. These infirmities and necessities, blameless in themselves, the tempter thought to use as handles on which to lay
hold, and lead away our Lord from his divinely appointed path.
He proposed to Him ways and means for satisfying these wants,
which were by no means God's ways or means. Had the
Saviour adopted these measures, yea, had he even cherished the
remotest desire to do so, then would Satan's monstrous design
have succeeded. The Lamb would have had a spot ; the Priest
a blemish ; the offering would have been unavailable ; the whole
plan of salvation forever broken up, and all of us immediately
consigned to hell. Oh, how much was there at stake in the wilderness ! What an incalculably weighty and momentous occurrence is the temptation of Jesus ! With what utmost ten-
sion of soul should we look for the further development and issue
of this event !

DISCOURSE X.

THE ONSET AND THE ARMS IN THE TEMPTATION.

"Then was Jesus *led up* of the Spirit into the wilderness to be tempted of the devil," etc.—MATT. iv. 4–11.

WE come now to the first onset.

The tempter had waited a favorable moment for his opening assault. Jesus was an hungered ; then slips he before Him, and says "If thou be the Son of God, command that these stones be made bread." This was the first attack, by which the tempter designed, partly to make sure regarding the person of Jesus, and partly, in case He were really the Lord from heaven, to annihilate at a stroke His whole sacrificial work. The Devil's aim was, if possible, first of all, to stain the pure soul of Christ with the sin of unbelief, as in Paradise he began his assault with —a "Yea, hath God said," in order to cause our first parents to stumble at God's command ; so also here. The "If thou be the Son of God," is at bottom nothing else than a "Yea, hath God said?" in disguise. It is an attempt to make the Lord doubt the testimony which He had received from the Father at His baptism.

Now, just observe, once for all, the monstrous, unexampled cunning of the tempter. In that single word, "If thou be the Son of God, command that these stones be made bread," he sets before our Saviour, not one, but countless snares and traps— each one more hidden and dangerous than the other. "Either, thought the devil, if He is the Son of God, He will now err in regard to His Sonship, and the witness of God, deeming it utterly improbable that God could suffer His child thus to starve and be put to shame amid the stones and fruitless thorns of a wilderness, and so will His soul be defiled with unbelief ; Or," thought the artful one, " He will cast off the veil before me, and in His eagerness to convince me of His Sonship by a miracle, will He act counter to the purpose of God, whose decree it is, that He should be poor, and suffer, and empty Himself of His glory, in order to expiate Adam's sin. But should I not succeed, imagined the devil again, in moving Him to forsake the path of poverty, and to step out of His humiliation in order to disclose His real dignity to me and others, yet, perhaps, the stress of hungering nature will urge Him to follow my proposal. He will deem it pardonable to employ the power which God has given Him, in rescuing Himself from starvation ; He will convert the stones into bread ; by self-help will He raise Himself superior to His sufferings,—and so put from His lips that cup of bitterness, without draining which no atonement is possible."

Such were the devil's thoughts. He hoped, that though Jesus might escape His first snare, He would yet be caught in the second or the third. And in fact, no plan could have been more adroitly devised and set. Without a miracle of preservation, the Holiest here would have fallen. The slighest trace of sin, had it existed in Jesus, would now have sprung forth to the light ; and shown itself. But no ! not the slightest particle of dust discolors the white linen of His innocence. He stands alone in the field—no one supports—no one protects Him. Nevertheless He breaks all the lances of the foe victoriously—the devil is beaten—Jesus triumphs.

The temptation to turn stones to bread, is one of the commonest in our every day life—something of it is experienced by all the children of God in one way or another. There are brethren among us—I mean brethren in the Lord—who are required to fast in these times. They have no work, no wages, and are driven to much anxiety for their daily bread. Brethren, ye sit among the stones and brambles of the wilderness, and are "an hungered." It would be a miracle if the tempter did not steal up to you also with an "Art thou indeed a child of God, that He should let you starve thus?" and then again with the suggestion—"Speak to those stones that they be made bread." Most strange would it be, if he did not also come to you with his varied proposals—such as, "Fawn and flatter that thou mayest obtain favor and employment"—or "deceive and lie that thou mayest make money; adopt this or that iniquitous trade, and save thyself from starvation;" or "throw thyself on the side of scoffers and enemies of the cross that they may support thee"— or "buy into a lottery that thou mayest share its good luck," or whatever other ways he may point out to you. All this means nothing else than—"Command that these stones be made bread." But, my brethren, let stones be stones,—and remain stones, and look for your bread to Him who has promised to give it you,— yea, who has promised to give you greater things than this. God—who has numbered the very hairs of your head—will let none of His little children be put to shame. Is it not far better to fast and starve in the name of God, than to see good days in the name of the devil? Your fastings will have an end, when they shall have worked out for your salvation that which God has decreed. Be of good cheer, then. Ye are wandering in the wilderness, in order to behold the faithfulness and the glory of God, which is more clearly seen in the wild and arid desert, than in the fat lands.

There are souls among us who obtain from their Christianity nothing but shame and contempt—and have but little joy or refreshment. It would be a wonder, dear friends, if Satan did not mix himself therein,—either to make you despise Christianity altogether, or to display to you in the world and its objects those pleasures which you find not in God. Brethren, it is the devil who thus counsels, and would fain induce you to convert the stones of your sufferings and joylessness into bread, in obedi-

ence to your own caprice, and without the will of Christ. But
methinks we would prefer to this—if it must be so—to spend
the few days of this life in the desert with Christ, or to lie in
the furnace, and then to share in his glory : while we gladly
leave the convict's farewell-meal, which the devil might have
prepared for us, to those who appear to take pleasure in the
prospect of burning and howling with their dark chief in the
lake of fire for ever and ever.

"The Lord rebuke thee, Satan," be our war cry, as often as
we hear this dragon crawling in our neighborhood. God be
praised, since the true Michael fought and overcame him, his
power over us is at an end. He may, indeed, buffet us with
blows, and try to trip us up also, so that we may even at times
come near reeling and falling ; but, ruin us—this can he never ;
and although he may lurk around our tent,—" this roaring lion,
seeking whom he may devour,"—yet has he a ring in his nose and
a chain about his neck. Our Prince and Captain holds him fast,
and marks the limits to which he may go. Only let us, on our
part, fence ourselves around with the wounds of Jesus. In this
fortress we are safe, and here we may joyfully sing :

> The Prince of this world
> May rage as he will,
> In naught shall he harm us,
> His doom he will seal.
> One word from our Jesus
> Can level him low,
> Can rescue his followers
> And prostrate their foe.

Behold now the WEAPON with which Jesus achieved his victory.
It was the word of God. One simple and believing "It is
written," and the devil is vanquished, his assault frustrated.

The Bible is the arsenal for God's warriors, the spiritual armory, whose walls are overlaid with shields and coat of mail,
and glisten and flash with swords and spears. Every one who

has at any time gained a spiritual victory, has armed himself
here for the strife. Whenever a spiritual Goliath has fallen to
the earth defeated, the smooth stones which shattered his
temples, were here selected. He who frequents this armory
will give the devil something to do. Satan dreads these weapons of the Divine word, and ever since the world began, has
he been considering how he might empty or close up this armory
of the Scriptures—spike this dangerous artillery—and shiver
these lances. What has this sly sophist not tried? What has
he not dug up, and brought to market, in order to involve the
word of God in suspicion and contempt, and rob it of the respect due to an unerring oracle? What accursed lies has he
not put in circulation, respecting the origin and authenticity of
the Bible, under the spacious title of *exposition*? There is not a
single book in the Scripture at which he has not shaken his head
—not a miracle which he has not wished to stamp as fable—not
a promise which he has not sought to invalidate or destroy.
And still he is ever busy, be it through his instruments and servants—or through false prophets—professors or other evil agents
—or be it in his own person by direct suggestion. He is still
ever busy in misleading us in reference to the infallibility of the
Divine word ; for this word is his destruction. But spit him in
the face—this accursed dog—and turn your back on him, when
he opens his mouth—for he is a murderer and a liar from the
beginning—yea, the father of lies.

But do you ask in what way God's word can render such remarkable service in temptations? I will tell you. Whenever
the devil would catch and mislead, his first and chief care is to
confuse our ideas. What is wrong he represents as right ; what
is human as divine ; what is evil as good. The truth he seeks to
turn into a lie, and a lie into the truth ; and when he has thus
betrayed and blinded us, we do his will, perhaps under the idea
that we are doing what is really good. But this nefarious
witchcraft of his can never succeed, if we abide faithfully by
God's word. This word will guard us from all error and

treachery. In the most unequivocal manner it declares to us what is right, and what is wrong; what is true, and what is false; and what in each particular instance we ought to do, or say, or think, according to the will of God.

A few illustrations will make this clear. The devil, for example, wishes to corrupt the work of the Gospel minister and weaken his preaching. He begins slily. He suggests to the preacher, that he should preach a little smoother; that he should make the way not quite so narrow, the gate not quite so strait; that by this means he would keep on good terms with the congregation; indeed, that many whom he now only irritates, would be thus more readily won to the truth; and so, with whatever plausible argument he can present, the deceiver labors to support his proposal. If now the preacher is left to his own reflection, and has no other shield than his own judgment, then is he already caught, and the fiend's proposal will seem reasonable; for the devil is more cunning than he. But if he plants himself by faith on God's word—if he can believingly retort: "It is written, 'Strait is the gate and narrow is the way which leadeth unto life;' again it is written, 'Cursed be he who preaches another Gospel than that has been preached;'" what will the devil do then? This bold stand upon God's word— this believing "It is written," is an artillery discharge which Satan cannot resist, and which compels him to retreat on the spot.

Another example. The devil would fain rob you of the belief, that Christianity is the only way to salvation. And how does he proceed? Very craftily—very warily. He leads you in the spirit up into a high mountain, and then from the summit he points out to you the millions of souls, who, in heathen and in Christian lands, are living without Christ; and then he begins his discourse: "Tell me," he says, "are all these to be indeed lost? Surely neither your reason, nor your hearts, will ever affirm this. Yet *they* do not believe in Jesus, at least, as you and your denomination do. Can, then, Christ be actually the only way? Can that, which you call the new birth, be the absolute condition of salvation? Would it not be the height of bigotry and narrowmindedness to think thus of man's eternal well-being?" So the devil now, if you are out upon the field, fortified by reason only, you surely will not escape this snare; you will yield to the devil's sophistry, and he will boast of having made the ground whereon you stand, rock beneath your feet with an easy effort. But, on the contrary, if you can grasp the weapons of God's word, if you can boldly confront the tempter with some saying of God, and declare to him in faith: "It is written, 'Verily, verily, except a man be born again he cannot see the kingdon of God;'" "It is written, 'I am the way, the truth, and the life, no man can come unto the Father but by me;'" "It is written, 'Few there be that go in thereat —few are chosen;'" if you can, I say, grasp such divine declarations believingly, then is the devil instantly beaten and his net torn. He will cease trying to convince you that Christ is not the only ground of salvation; or else he must hope to be able to discredit with you the very words on which you ground your defence.

Take another example still. The devil, say, would fain bring you back into the world. How does he go to work? He insinuates himself into your presence, and begins to remonstrate against your excluding yourself so entirely from society, and shunning the company of those of a different persuasion—a course, as he suggests, not at all in accordance with a Christian love of your neighbor. He would have you occasionally attend fashionable parties, in order to let your light shine, and prove to people that Christianity is far from making us austere monks and nuns, but that it rather renders men cheerful and social, so that you may in this way win them to the Gospel. Nay, he would go farther, and under the pretext of exercising yourself unto godliness, and so becoming strong, he would have you not withdraw from the world at all, inasmuch as it would cost no effort to remain holy, when there were no solicitations or provocations to sin ; but he would have you face evil in the eye, and say unto it, " I will have nothing to do with thee "—an exploit this, he would say, which would " be to the point." Thus does Satan argue, and this pleases the old Adam in us well. Now, if you trust your own wits in disputing with him, then rely upon it, you will be the loser—Satan will soon get the advantage, and hold the field. No doctor or professor knows how to argue like him. He can make the sheerest absurdities appear plausible and convincing. But if you can, on the other hand, firmly encounter him with a word of God ; if you can, for example, in this last instance, say to him, " It is written, 'Be not conformed to this world,'" then is he at once disabled, and you have struck the sword from his grasp.

Thus is the word of God, when it is laid hold of in faith, and skillfully handled, a mighty " sword of the Spirit," as the apostle calls it, whereby we can slay the old dragon. " Yes," as one has said, " the ten commandments, when they are fairly written in our hearts, and uttered against him boldly, are sufficient to drive him utterly away. They are like ten Samson-shouts, or like ten Michael-swords against the roaring lion."

Now, how did the Lord prevail ? Satan counselled Him to make bread of stones, and thus, by His own exertion, relieve himself from the pangs of hunger. This was a most insidious and taking proposal, as you have seen. There was, speaking after the manner of men, much to induce Jesus to comply with it ; and had He done so, you are aware that the whole work of atonement would have been frustrated. But He did not comply. He let the stones be stones, and hungered on. And what restrained Him from following the specious advice of the unknown stranger ? It was a word of God. His inward eye fell on the passage (Deut. viii. 3), and, seizing this by faith, He opposed it to the tempter. " It is written, 'Man shall not live by bread alone, but by every word that proceedeth out of the mouth of God.'" In this declaration He found motive sufficient to suffer hunger yet another forty days and forty nights—yea,

longer, if needs be, rather than anticipate the help of the Father
by any distrustful attempt at self-deliverance.   " The Father can
sustain me without bread ; He has led me into this wilderness—
I can trust in Him."   Such was his thought, and truly it proved
an impenetrable coat of mail around his breast.   Now must
Satan take heart, and devise other schemes.   All prospect of
inducing Him to self-deliverance, and to the throwing off of that
which He, as our surety, was obliged to endure, in expiation
of Adam's sin—had entirely vanished.   It is plain, Jesus believed
the divine word, that God could feed Him in extreme famine
without food—could refresh Him without drink, and by the
mere word of His mouth could nourish and support Him effectually.   Against this faith, as against an iron bulwark, all the
lances of the devil were necessarily shivered.

The words with which Jesus overcame the temptation are
recorded, as was said, in Deut. viii. 3.   Moses there, on the very
borders of the promised land, sets forth to the children of Israel,
according to the divine direction, how the Lord had led them
along in mercy and faithfulness for the space of forty years.
" He humbled thee," he says, " and suffered thee to hunger, and
fed thee with manna when thou knowest not, neither did thy
fathers know, that He might make thee know that man doth not
live by bread only, but by every word that proceedeth out of the
mouth of the Lord."   Yes, the Lord needs neither mills nor
ovens, to support His children ; He can rain bread on them out
of the clouds, as He did in the wilderness.   He can give His
children bread during the night, while they sleep.   So did He at
Cherith (1 Kings, xvii. 5), so at Zarephath to the widow (1
Kings, xvii. 10), and so in many other places.   For Him it is an
easy thing to do this.   And this outward material bread, which
He gives us—*this* is not that which nourishes us, and whereon
our life depends ; but that which properly nourishes, and
strengthens, and preserves us in every case, is His word, His
will, His blessing, and that hidden power which He adds to
the external means.   Because He wills that it nourish us, there-

fore does the bread we eat nourish us ; and, as soon as He ceases to will it, we may knead, and season, and bake as we may, it is all of no avail ; we waste away, and our strength decays in the midst of superfluities.

Since then, the nutritive power lies not in the bread, but in the will and word of God alone, it will readily be seen how with five loaves and two fishes, He could perfectly satisfy five thousand men ; how by means of a single barley-cake He could sustain Elijah forty days and forty nights ; yea, how He satisfies and preserves many a poor family now, who, besides a morsel of dry bread in the morning and in the evening, scarcely see any other food during the day. The Lord needs no bread at all for our sustenance, if He does not will it. His bare words, " let him live," is enough—and we live. Without bread, Moses was maintained at Sinai—Jesus in the wilderness—and many more. He needs but to speak, and the very air we breathe turns to milk and wine, and we eat the costliest dainties—we imbibe pure vigor and strength without opening our lips, without sitting at table, without reaching out our hand. This is what is meant by " Man shall not live by bread alone, but by every word that proceedeth out of the mouth of God." In times of persecution, thousands of God's children have experienced this in its most literal sense ; the believing poor continually experience it still ; it is as true as there is a God in heaven.

Therefore, let every sufferer among us lay hold of this truth, that it may protect him from fear and despair, and be his shield and breast-plate against the attacks and temptations of the wicked one. It has pleased our gracious God to bring many of His dear children into great distress. Everything now begins to fail—bread and fuel—work and wages, and, perhaps, even prospects and credit. They are truly in the wilderness among stones, and there is much of sighing by day and by night. Steal and cheat they will not—God will mercifully keep them from that. But the devil will gain much if but the thought finds room, " we are forsaken of God, and must now see how we can shift for ourselves." Great will be his success the moment we are betrayed into unbelieving anxiety and care as to " what we shall eat, or what we shall drink, or wherewithal we shall be clothed ;" or even should the thought occur, " God is intimating to us through our necessities, that we must help ourselves, either by some daring speculation and by gambling and fraud, or by some other unlawful methods." Then, indeed, I say, would the tempter have made a great advance. But, my afflicted brethren, concede to the arch-accuser no such triumph. Meet him with the weapon which your Master employed, and which has, from this fact, received a peculiar consecration, sanctity, and power ; and say in faith, " It is written, ' Man shall not live by bread alone, but by every word that proceedeth out of the mouth of God. '" This is the truth. Hold fast to this ; build thereon—and wait, only wait a little in the wilderness, and surely God will not desert you.

There are brethren among us, and I could call them by name, who have been in greater straits than yourselves. But they believed that word without misgiving—and, in this faith, they have resolutely and without ceremony shown the devil the door as often as he has approached with his accursed counsels, and they have hoped in the Lord. Now their mouth is filled with laughter. Not for mountains of gold and silver would they barter the experiences which they have gathered during their destitution in the wilderness. They have seen the glory of the Lord, and become living witnesses to the truth that " man does not live by bread alone, but by every word that proceedeth out of the mouth of God."

" If thou be the Son of God, command that these stones be made bread !" Thus spake the devil. He required Jesus to prove His sonship. But Jesus chose rather to leave this to His Heavenly Father. Oh, my brethren, would that ye even so might, in all cases, leave the proof of your sonship quietly to the Lord. He will make it known that you are His children ; not perhaps by letting you live in homes of plenty, but yet no less certainly, by maintaining you in the midst of the wilderness—causing you to sing among stones and juniper trees, and nourishing you, without bread, by the bare word which proceedeth out of His mouth.

Witness now, the SECOND ATTACK. The first attempt of the devil against Jesus failed. He could not yet know whether Jesus was the Son of God ; and, if He were, the temptation had not turned Him aside one finger's breadth from His media-torial course. Satan now prepares for a second assault. He taketh Jesus up into the holy city, and setteth Him on a pin-nacle of the temple. Shall we say only in a vision ? No, bodily, as the letter of the narrative constrains us to believe. In some supernatural way, Jesus was caught up, and trans-ported in a moment through the air into the holy city, and then, quick as lightning, buoyed up to the flat roof of a side-portico of the Temple overhanging the mountain. The same power which the Holy Spirit afterwards exerted on Philip, was here loaned to the Evil spirit by God. As an eagle with his prey, so did the prince of darkness soar away with the Lord of glory. It was an awful, frightful procedure—but the most awful things was Christ willing to experience and feel, and, to the most appalling things surrender himself, that He might drain to the dregs the cup of our curse, and leave not a farthing of our debt unpaid. He was willing to become the sport of the spirits of hell, in order that we, accursed ones, might be borne in the tender hands of the angels of God into Abraham's bosom. But was Jesus aware that it was the devil with whom He had to deal ? I think not ; by the divine decree was this fact still hid from Him, in order that the temptation might be the more severe—and, also, the triumph more meritorious and brilliant.

Jesus stands on the high Temple-roof—Satan at His side—and beneath their feet a dizzy abyss. Far below lies the city—and deeper yet, in the bottom of the valley, flows the brook Kedron—shrunk to a slender thread—and well-nigh imperceptible—Satan wears the aspect of a well-meaning friend, who heartily holds with Jesus, and who, in case He were the Son of God, prosecutes the same cause with Him, and is anxious for nothing so much as that the work of Redemption might be completed as speedily as possible. He points to the frightful depth below and says—"If thou be the Son of God, cast thyself down." It is possible he added yet more, and perchance to the following effect : "See, I would gladly know if thou art the Son of God. I only wait for assurance in order to bow my knees at once, and yield Thee homage—nor am I the only one, who is anxiously looking for the full disclosure of Thy person and dignity. Thou wilt become the king and commander of a great people as soon as Thou art pleased to display Thy royal majesty. Now, behold ; here is your opportunity. Leap from this height and land safely below. A miracle like this will astonish the world. It will leave no doubt of Thy majesty, and at once all knees will bend into the dust. Thou wilt be as a God—and not only others, but Thou Thyself also, wilt then assuredly know that Thou art the Messiah, and that God has not forsaken Thee, as Thy starving in the wilderness has appeared from the beginning to indicate." Something of this sort the devil might have added, and, in order to effect his object the more surely, he calls to mind the glorious promise of the 91st Psalm, which was given to Him pre-eminently : "He shall give His angels charge concerning thee, and they shall bear thee up in their hands, lest at any time thou dash thy foot against a stone." In fact, the plan was cunningly contrived and the temptation pressing. The tempter here truly assumed the aspect of a well-meaning angel, and his proposal seemed pious, and good and suitable.

Now, then, there stands the Lord upon the giddy height ; and what will He do ? One step forward—and He is exalted ; the angels bear Him gently to the bottom below ; the people break out into Hosannas ; and He becomes the admired—the wonderful—the worshipped ; but then, the work of reconciliation is eternally—eternally annihilated ; for the High Priest has left

the sacrificial path of poverty and self-denial ; the Mediator
has contravened the plan and counsel of God ; the Lamb carries
a blemish, and it is spotted with the sin of tempting God, and no
longer fit to be the Paschal offering.   Oh, fateful moment !—but
God be praised, Jesus sees through the satanic artifice.   He
knew indeed, that the angels would bear Him up.   But, should
He claim the power and faithfulness of God in self-chosen paths
of danger ?   No—no—on no account ; His holy soul shuddered
at the satanic proposal.   One Bible text was quoted to catch
and precipitate Him if possible ; another shall serve for a support—a shield and a lance : " It is written again, ' Thou shalt
not tempt the Lord thy God.' "   He utters it—and the devil is
beaten a second time.

And there are to us SPIRITUAL PRECIPICES.—In the holy city,
the spiritual Jerusalem, Satan still employs his most cunning arts,
and makes his most wicked proposals ; and his most brilliant
victories, of however short duration, are usually achieved by
these means in the same holy place.   There are still temptations and spiritual conditions occasioned by the devil's artifice,
which closely resemble this transporting of our Lord to the pinnacle of the Temple.   There are Spiritual precipices, I say.   The
best and happiest condition on earth is indisputably this, to cling
like a worm to the feet of Jesus—to dwell in craving poverty of
spirit, like Lazarus at the rich man's gate ; and with the Canaanitish woman to desire, like a dog, the crumbs which fall from
the Lord's table.   Then are we blessed ; then are we rich—then
safe.   But certainly this is to spoil the devil's game.   No wonder,
then, that the impostor is intent on nothing so much as to decoy,
by some means, the children of God out of this state of lowli-
ness and spiritual poverty; and he seeks to bring this to pass in
various ways.

Let me mention an instance or two.   Clothed in the form of
an angel of light, he accosts you and leads you into the holy
city ; that is, he spreads out before you all the gifts and graces,

the rights and privileges, of which you, as a member of the heavenly kingdom, have become partaker, so that you think, in fact, some good angel is affording you this blissful prospect. Then the tempter selects from these gifts one—perchance the gift of the Holy Spirit—and begins to unfold to you all that you possess in this gift : how the Holy Spirit sanctifies and enlightens you, how he guides you into all truth, how he searches out the deep things of the Godhead—leads and inspires you—speaks and bears witness in you ; and so in every other particular unfolds his work just as it is. Then the devil proceeds yet further —and endeavors next to convince you, that the Spirit must also be able to reveal to you something new,—something which the Bible contains only partially, or not at all. From this he goes on—and teaches you to take some thoughts of your own for the suggestions of the Spirit. He then advances another step, and pronounces you an inspired person—one, who no longer needs the outward light in the altar, because he has the inner light ; and alas, before you are aware, you are vanished away to the pinnacle of the tempter, and feel yourself exalted above God's word and testimony, the church, and the sermon. All these objects, together with the entire Jerusalem of the remaining believers, you see lying far below your feet ; and if, upon this giddy height, you do not grow dizzy—and finish by plunging headlong into the frightful abyss of insanity, you will owe your preservation to that almighty grace alone, which has saved you. Such were the diabolical snares into which our brethren at S—— fell, who would conform to no order, nor suffer themselves to be directed by God's word, but appealed, instead, to the Spirit, who, as they said, had taught them other and higher things. There may be among them some true children of God, who will yet return to right paths, but yet it must ever be regarded as a sad and awful perversion. God preserve us from such delusion ! Seize the words, my brethren. "It is written : 'But though we or an angel from heaven preach any other Gospel unto you, than that, which we have preached unto you, let him be accursed.'" "It is written : 'Thy word is a lamp unto my feet'"—such an "*it is written,*" spoken in faith, routs the devil.

When Satan is baffled in one attempt, he tries another, and ceases not, until every means has been exhausted. We have seen people of all descriptions, standing on dizzy temple-roofs, transported thither by various methods. One is elated by the pleasing fancy, that for him there is no more any mystery, and it seems as if he had been specially enlightened of God, and carried the key of David in his pocket. In the midst of his superabundant knowledge, the devil catches him, and according to his infernal exegesis, explains to him the clause, "Ye have an unction from the Holy One, and know all things." Another fancies himself to be the man who shall smite the earth with the sword of his mouth, and rule spirits with the sceptre of his words, and after whom none may speak. His gifts for teaching and preaching have, through the cunning of the devil, been turned into a gin and a snare. A third is inflated with the thought, that there is something peculiar in his relation to God, as if he were seated in the kingdom of God a couple of benches higher than the rest of us poor sinners ; and perhaps it was from some answers to prayers he had received, that the devil prepared for him the sweet intoxication. A fourth has a fixed idea that without him the kingdom of God could not exist—that he, apart from his fellows, is a pillar there—an apostle—the Elias of his day. In his case the blessings which God had bestowed upon his word and testimony, has been converted by the devil's art into a lime-twig whereby he has been caught. A fifth is deluded into the belief, that all his dreams and fancies are genuine divine visions and revelations ; and the poor man deems himself a seer—a prophet—a beholder of visions. To a sixth, the devil presents some magic mirror—and the poor man beholds himself therein, with a halo round his head ; or the devil sends him friends who laud, admire, and deify his meekness, patience, faith, and love ; and thus the deluded spirit is beguiled by degrees, into the notion that God must have set him up as an example of saintliness among men.

So these are precipices ; thus it is to be set on the pinnacle of the temple. And well would it be if it ended only here ; if these poor deluded men would stop with regarding themselves as apostles, saints, and martyrs. But let them only reach such a height, and they not seldom mount yet higher. It is not all who are brought from thence safely down a stairway to their true place again in the plain below. Many plunge themselves down from these giddy heights into the lowest depths of insanity. Unhappy instances of this sort have existed at all times—persons who have at last given themselves out to be God, or Christ himself, or the Holy Ghost ; and this too, in the very midst of the holy city.

Brethren abide in your refuge ; keep in the dust : above all, ye who are rich in gifts, and apt to teach—who are respected among your fellows, and speak publicly in assemblies—who lead the devotions of the church and whose light shines brightly in Zion. Among such, the devil readily finds a handle by which to lay hold, and spirit them away to lofty eminences. Gird around you for a breast-plate, the text : " Blessed are the poor in spirit, for theirs is the kingdom of Heaven." Set as a helmet on your head the truth : " Whosoever shall not receive the kingdom of God as a little child, he shall not enter therein." Take as a sword into your hand the word : " God resisteth the proud, but giveth grace unto the humble." And hold fast to the belief that the golden rose, Jesus, bloomed, not on lofty heights, but in lowly vales. And if the devil is seeking to urge you into presumptions and bewildering speculations upon unfathomable mysteries—if he is alluring you into vain refinements, whether it be regarding the Trinity or the idea of Eternity—or the two natures in Christ—or regarding any other unsearchable problem, then rally yourself and exclaim, " It is written, ' We know in part and prophesy in part ; but when that which is perfect is come, then that which is in part shall be done away.' " Tell him in the name of Jesus, that you desire to know no more than is needful for your salvation. So will you expel the Wicked One.

DISCOURSE XI.

THE DEMAND AND THE PROMISED REWARD.

"Then was Jesus led up of the Spirit into the wilderness to be tempted of the devil,"
etc., etc.—MATT. iv. 1-11.

THAT the devil gladly uses our heavenly sonship for the purpose of urging us the more easily to all sorts of ungodly steps,
is a well known fact. For instance, he may have learned that
there yet lurks in your members some bosom sin, which you have
not yet mastered. In this case he leads you into circumstances,
which not only excite your lust, but also give you the means
of gratifying it. There you stand on the verge of an abyss.
"Cast thyself down," whispers the devil. You attempt to
escape. "Stay, stay," he adds, again, "it is so pleasant below."
You resist. "Cast thyself down," he shouts yet louder. You
tremble at the danger, but nevertheless cannot break away.
You are charmed to the spot. "Cast thyself down," once more
cries Satan. "Thou art a child of God. Thou certainly wilt
be pardoned." He speaks, and if God do not hold you back,
you are gone. You are, say, of an irritable temperament, and
the inmates of your home thwart your plans and set all your
heart in a foam. You would gladly retaliate, but you know not
whether you dare do it. You are standing over an abyss.
"Cast thyself down," the devil cries. "Thou art a child of God,
and between God's children and the world there should be no
peace, but only a sword, and separation—gratify thy zeal." He

speaks, and ere he has uttered all, you are heaving with rage, and hot breath, and are heaping sin on sin.

Again you are fast in deep distress, and weary of life. Thereupon the devil at once places you on the roof of your house, or on some steep rock, or on the margin of some deep stream. Oh, God! what a frightful precipice you are standing on! "Cast thyself down," whispers the wicked one. You would gladly do it, but you shrink from taking the leap. "Why lingerest thou?" continues the tempter. "Cast thyself down. In the arms of death sleep is sweet, and all trouble is over." "Cast thyself down. Thou art in a state of grace, and grace abides, and yields not even though the mountains depart." "Cast thyself down, and hasten to thy home," says the serpent. Oh, horrible! You waver—you look below. Your desire is strong—the burden heavy—the will is there. And O great God! if now the hand of divine piety does not quickly interpose, the leap is taken.

Satan proposed to our Lord Jesus that He should convince the people of His divine Sonship, in a sacrilegious manner, that is, by a voluntary leap from the pinnacle of the temple. With like propositions does he also sneak up to believers, "Your Christian character is doubted," he insinuates. "People hesitate to reckon you among the children of God. Show them who you are." And now it is high time to seize the sword against the tempter, and to encounter him with the word, "The Lord knoweth them that are His," and with this to remain satisfied. Most precious souls even are, in such a case, often betrayed into monstrous errors; this one into shameful falsehood, by boasting of spiritual experiences which he never enjoyed; that one, into the wicked forcing of the Spirit, by trying to beget in himself such frames of mind as the Lord alone can give; another, into criminal dissimulation, by feigning an unction which at the moment is not granted him; another, into fatal perversions, by performing deeds in his own name, and then endeavoring to regard them as the work of God's Spirit, achieved through him.

And what abominations can be more heinous in the sight of God than these? How might the devil scornfully laugh when he has succeeded in plunging the children of God into such filth as this?

"Cast thyself down," said Satan, and he might have added by way of motive, that He could thereby accelerate the execution of the divine purposes. All too pleasing would it have been, could he but have awakened some impatience in the heart of Jesus at the tardy progress of His redemptive work. And oh, how gladly also would he now excite believers to like impatience! How eagerly does he spur them on to perfect rapidly their sanctification by self-imposed austerities, and mount with quick steps to higher degrees, and to loftier stages of personal glorification. And with what delight does he call to them in this regard: "Spring off, and choose the shortest way;" for the cunning cheat well knows that such advance is retrogression, because it is a turning aside from the throne of grace, and from the blood of the Lamb; and that in such self-chosen paths, no angels will bear us up in their hands, but that there our feet will stumble upon mere stones, and we shall fall into nothing but error, darkness, pride, and self-complacency. Are they witnesses and preachers. Oh, how does he rejoice when they begin to think the Lord delays too long to crown their efforts; and how gladly does he foster this impatience in their hearts; how readily does he call to them, "Cast thyself down from the pinnacle of the temple."

And what joy is his if they obey, and with their own wild-fire, attempt to force the conversion of their congregation. How does he exult, when they undertake, with carnal noise and bustle, to drive the people, by storm, as it were, into the kingdom of Heaven—and, because God does not do it, to gird, anoint, and arm themselves. Then does the devil hold high festival, for he knows that now, they will least of all succeed, since the Holy Spirit will never countenance such dark and selfish attempts. Those on the contrary, whom the Lord chooses to employ are broken tools, and they lie quietly in the hands of their God, and suffer themselves to be led, driven around, and governed by Jesus. And thus it is the work prospers; storming accomplishes nothing.

"If thou be the Son of God, cast thyself down." Thus said the devil to Jesus. In fact a severe proposal. But children of God, not to say the Son of God himself, may venture something yet greater. Peter could boldly step out from his boat and tread the foaming waves; and the three men in "Daniel" could enter the flames of the fiery furnace. There was no danger there. Our promises are large. Resting on them we can undertake great things; and that divine assurance which Satan quoted with pious look in order to tempt Jesus to take the leap, is far from being the most encouraging we have. Certain is it that the angels of God are charged to bear us up in their hands. They are associated with us as a body guard and sure protection, on whose guidance and watch we may joyfully count, in all those ways wherein God bids us go. Relying on this promise might the Lord have boldy plunged headlong. But he did not. Why not? He preferred at this time to choose the natural method, and to go down the stairway. Wherefore? Because the other way had not been commanded him by God. Scarcely had the Satanic proposal been made, when at once the divine command occurred to the soul of Jesus : "No," thought the spotless lamb, "for such self-chosen ways is the promise not given." And when Satan said, "It is written, the Lord will give his angels charge concerning thee," Jesus met the tempter with a like weapon drawn from the armory of God's word. He replies : "It is written again, 'Thou shalt not tempt the Lord thy God,'" and once more the devil is defeated.

What is it then to tempt God? It is, in the first place, to incur danger presumptuously in order that God may rescue us. To such unworthy steps would the devil gladly beguile us, and for this end has learned by heart the strongest promises of God, in order that he might take us unawares. Therefore, when any

11

word of God is proposed to us for the purpose of inducing us to some bold step, let us inquire, whether this word suits the occasion, and whether we have the right, under the circumstances, to draw comfort from it. Thus we shall ascertain who has suggested the word, and the devil will not so easily overreach us.

If one comes, for instance, and says : "Steer out into these surging breakers, and rescue thy brother from the waves, for it is written, 'When thou passest through the waters I will be with thee, and through the rivers, they shall not not overflow thee ;'" or if another calls out : "Rush into this burning house and snatch the screaming child from the flames, for God has said, 'When thou walkest through the fire thou shalt not be burned, neither shall the flame kindle upon thee.'" If there comes a whisper in thy heart, "Give this starving beggar thy last penny, for it is written, 'Inasmuch as ye have done it unto the least of these my brethren, ye have done it unto me ;'" then, my friend, in God's name, up with your anchor and out to sea. Do in every case as you are bid. A good angel speaks to you, and you may hope for help. But if one comes to you and says, "Come friend into this or that convivial circle, for it is written, 'The Lord preserveth the souls of his saints ;'" or if the advice is suggested, "Just go and venture once, give up thy work and keep holiday, for it is written, 'He giveth his beloved in his sleep ;'"* then be sure it is the crafty devil, with whom you have to do. Answer him back, "It is written again, 'Thou shalt not tempt the Lord thy God.'" Tell him, "He who runs presumptuously into danger will perish therein."

Fiendish snares like these, drawn even from the word of God itself, are still more numerous. Of this sort, also, is that accursed temptation, whereby we are induced to examine, whether this or that divine declaration is true ; and so to test the truth and faithfulness of God by our own standards. Thus, for example, he is said to have succeeded in a monstrous artifice with

---

* This is the Lutheran, and the correct version of Ps. cxxvii. 2.—TRANS.

three preachers. He called up to their minds (Matt. xviii. 20),
" When two or three are gathered together in my name, there
am I in the midst of them," and then that other word, " If two
of you shall agree on earth as touching anything that they
shall ask, it shall be done for them of my Father which is in
Heaven ;" and then he inquired " Can this be so ?"   Then alas !
the preachers thought, " We will prove it," and accordingly they
fixed an hour when they should meet and pray that the Lord
might personally appear to them. In this way they meant to
test whether he had spoken truly. And they met and began to
pray. " O Lord, manifest thyself." But the Lord appeared not.
Thereupon the devil shouted " Victory." The heinous wickedness was committed. Subsequently the Lord did, indeed, appear
to them, but it was in a far different mode from what they had
expected. He became to them as a moth and a maggot, and
henceforth there was neither blessing, nor light, nor peace, nor
joy to these men, even unto the end, but a spiritual apostasy and
declension set in, which could not be arrested. May the Lord
in mercy guard us from such attempts at proving Him! Let the
slightest whisper of the sort, which may stir within us, be a sure
token that danger is lurking near—and loud and earnestly as
we are able, let us cry " Satan, it is written ' Thou shalt not
tempt the Lord thy God.' "

One of the most common strokes of Satan is, by means of the
word of God itself, to infuse into us doubts respecting it. Extraordinary things are in this way experienced. For example, he
exhibits to us at a glance a multitude of insignificant circumstances in the Bible ; as, for instance, that Paul writes to
Timothy to bring him the cloak which he had left at Troas, and
many other things of the sort ; and while these are before
the mind, he maliciously asks : " And are *such* words too, inspired by the Spirit ?" And thereupon he quickly adds, " Then
is the whole Bible not inspired !" From this he proceeds to
inquire, " What is of the Spirit, and what not ?" and soon he
reaches the conclusion : " The Bible is an unsafe foundation."

And in fact, he now and then succeeds with such arts, for the moment at least, to shake the whole structure of the Bible about our heads, and everything appears to totter and reel, until we at last come to our recollection.

In order to make us suspect the word of God, he not unfrequently, with lightning speed, thrusts before our eyes this or that passage, just at the moment when some occurrence in life appears to falsify it. For instance, if you are lying in despair, suffering great necessities and bitter trials, and all help seems wanting, just then he reminds you of this sweet verse : "Like as a father pitieth his children, so the Lord pitieth them that fear Him." And thereupon with grinning mockery he asks : "Where, then, is your father ? and that pity, that boasted help, where does it linger ?" And what can delight the villain more than the exploit of defiling your soul with doubt, unbelief, and impatience ? If you have long prayed and striven with God for some object, be it bread for your hungering children, or be it advice in bitter perplexities, or be it a little alleviation and rest in thy pains, or be it a small drop of comfort in your anguish, and do not immediately receive it, there again is the devil at hand—whispering : "Is it not written, 'Whatsoever ye ask the Father in my name, He will give it you?' Now, poor beggar, have you got your bosom full of God's gifts ?" Thus mocks the tempter, and surely did the Lord not keep his hand on our faith, you would not be able to escape these fiery darts unscathed.

The most dangerous method in which the devil can manage the word of God, as a weapon against us, is this. He tears out individual texts from their connection, and instead of interpreting them according to the analogy of faith, he gives them to us mutilated, perverts their sense, and thus seeks to impose them upon people. Now, just here it is, if anywhere, we must encounter him with like weapons, and lead the battle against him with the sword of the word. If he says : "It is written, 'Where sin abounded, grace did much more abound,' therefore, slacken the reins, let passions boil ; what boots it ?" then reply :

"It is written again, 'Shall we continue in sin that grace may abound? God forbid. How shall we who are dead to sin live any longer therein?'" Again, if the devil says: "It is written, 'It is no more I that do it, but sin that liveth in me;' therefore, keep quiet, and be not so anxious about your misdoings." Then give him the retort: "It is also written, 'O wretched man that I am, who shall deliver me from the body of this death.' God's children must mourn for their sins." Should Satan say: "It is written, 'It is not of him that willeth, nor of him that runneth, but of God that showeth mercy,' therefore abide in the world, and enjoy its feastings and frolic, until God calls you." Then say in reply: "I know it; but it is written again, 'Work out your salvation with fear and trembling, for it is God that worketh in you both to will and to do of His good pleasure.'"

Once more, if the tempter cries: "It is written, 'Known unto God are all His works, from the beginning of the world;' therefore, desist from prayer and supplication, your lot is determined. What you ought to have you will certainly receive;" let the reply be: "It is written again, 'Ask, and ye shall receive, for every one that asketh receiveth.'" Still further, if the dragon declares: "It is written, 'This is the Father's will which hath sent me, that of all which He hath given me I should lose nothing, but should raise him up at the last day;' therefore, live as you list, and do what your heart lusteth after. What has Moses to do with you? You are insured to salvation!" Then answer back: "Again it is written, 'My sheep hear my voice, and I know them, and they follow me." Behold, my brethren, it is thus you can disarm the devil, and in the might of God obtain a triumph over him, and make a show of him openly.

The battle-field is changed. Quick as lightning is the Son of God snatched away from the pinnacle of the temple by the power conceded to Satan over Him, and transported to the top of a high mountain. Yet not merely in the body, but in a spiritual manner likewise did He see himself planted suddenly as

on the dizzy apex of a high tower, and suddenly there stretched
out before Him a boundless prospect of unparalleled charm
and dazzling beauty, in the magic mirror of a wonderful vision.

What happens?   Quick as thought there appears before Him
in His horizon all the kingdoms of the world most brilliantly
illuminated ; and all their glory, pomp, pleasures, and decorations
pass before His eyes in the most fascinating images, and most
captivating scenes.   The limits of time and space retire ; that
which was distant is brought near, that which was locked up is
opened, that which was covered is unveiled ; and all this, as
St. Luke says, "in a moment of time."   An unheard of illusion
it was.   Like to one vast glowing picture, there lie spread out
to view the most delightful realms of earth, and all around Him
is displayed the enchanting panorama of its splendid cities and
most princely palaces.   Here was proud Rome, the victorious
mistress of the world, and sovereign over a hundred kings ;
there, the spicy mountains of the East, and Persia's loveliest
rose-gardens.   Here was Ophir, with its rich mines of gold
and diamonds ; there, India, that wonder-land, decked in all the
variegated colors of an endless spring, and traversed by streams
of milk and honey.   Yet, not kingdoms and cities merely, but
other wonders still pass before the eyes of Jesus.

Besides the kingdoms of the world, the devil shows Him also
the glory of the world—all that the world has of witchery and
fascination—whatever delights and ravishes the senses—and
whatever the children of this world call their Paradise and their
heaven.   All this Jesus now sees lying before Him.   Here, glittering palaces unbosomed amid fragrant gardens and fields ; there,
chariots and horses, the pomp and retinue of courts.   Here,
galleries of art and temples of dazzling wisdom ; there, laurel
crowns of fame and monuments of glory.   Here, sumptuous ban-
quets in halls resplendent with gold ; there, festive crowds listening to magic symphonies and rapturous choirs of music.

In short, all—all that makes the hearts of the children of men
leap in their bosoms, and the blood thrill in their veins, and the

eyes glow with joy and desire, all this rushes at once before His vision in the most vivid imagery, and God alone can tell what the pure eyes of Jesus must have seen at that moment. We may be sure no bewildering scene, no sense-intoxicating image was then left uncovered before Him by Satan.

Something like this which Jesus experienced on the summit of this high mountain, do we also at times pass through. Those especially among our brethren, who by nature are of a lively temperament, and possess an enthusiastic disposition, and a quick fancy, will be able, no doubt, to tell us something of these magic visions. People of this character are most readily approached by such snares of the devil, because their susceptible natures and ardent sensibilities appear to promise him a certain victory —and if he does conquer, he at least succeeds in winning away such people to his magic mountains far more easily than others. For the attainment of this object he ordinarily employs some external means. These means, for example, he finds in the sphere of the fine arts,—so far as they have entered into the service of the world and sin. Now it is an attractive picture ; now a bewitching poem ; now a sweet tone or a heart-stirring melody, by means of which he carries on his magical incantations.

Oftentimes there is needed only a few chords or some single notes, perchance of a flute, which float out from the distance, in tender vibrations scarcely audible unto the solitude of our still chamber, and the charm is at once wrought—as at a fiat of the Almighty, there lies spread out before us in a moment a whole paradise of intoxicating felicity, and, as, through the rent of some overhanging curtain, our eyes look away into an heaven upon earth. The joys of our youth, to which we had long since bidden farewell, again draw near in most enchanting pictures, and pleasures to which we, perhaps years since, had become crucified and dead by the grace of God, re-appear in the most winning forms and in the most attractive lights. Here, then, hang wreaths of perishable glory ; but how lovely do they seem once

more ! how fascinating ! There, then, are opened before us halls
of worldly revelry and vain mirth ; and how pleasant do they
look again—those gay circles ! how is the poor heart again captivated ! Here, then, are unlocked to sight the brilliant assembly
rooms of the fashionable world, filled with shout and song, with
harp melodies and mazy dances, and there the eye wanders over
flowery fields of worldly art and sweet poetic dreams.

In short, every thing beautiful and costly which the world
possesses, suddenly, as at the touch of a magic wand, bursts
upon the mirror of our fancy in the most lively pictures, and
scenes and forms ; and however vain it may all be in itself, however nugatory and worthless, there lies upon it all a charm, a
play of coloring, such beauty and enamelling, as if one were
actually looking over into a paradise ; and in presence of such
fascinating visions the sea of sensibility, and longing, and of
desire begins to heave and swell as if a storm was working in
its inmost depths. It is at such moments you stand upon the
high magic mountains, and the devil is showing you the kingdoms
of the earth and their glory in a moment of time.

And for this reason it is, that our secular music, as it is now
constituted, has become so dangerous a thing because the devil
is so ready and skillful in using it to call up such seasons of sensual intoxication. In the operas and the arias, the symphonies
and the concerts, of this world, the devil finds a powerful charm
whereby to transfigure the vain splendor of earth into the glory
of heaven. Experienced Christians have acknowledged that
they, in moments at least, through such ungodly and secularized
music, have been so mightily and so irresistibly captivated by the
devil, that they, like real inebriates, have for the time lamented
their departure from Egypt, and envied the children of this
world, if not for their revellings and banquetings, yet for their
more refined enjoyments and more polished pleasures. And, it not
seldom happens, that this most potent of all arts, forms one of
the wings by means of which the power of the tempter lifts
us to those magic mountains from whence the kingdoms of

this world, and all the glory of them, are arrayed before our fancy in such transfigured splendor, and overlaid with such a golden mist and glory, as to transport all our senses into a dream of perfect delight and ecstasy, which would surely overcome us on the spot, if Almighty Grace, our mother, did not cover us with her shield.

DISCOURSE XII.

THE LAST ASSAULT AND ISSUE OF THE CONTEST.

"Then was Jesus led up of the Spirit into the wilderness, to be tempted of the devil," etc.—MATT. iv. 1-11.

In that very moment when the kingdoms of this world stood before the eyes of Jesus in the magic mirror of that enchanting vision, the devil smote upon his breast, and losing his composure, and, in spite of all his affectation of majesty and dignity, forgetting the part he was acting and betraying himself, exclaims : " All this is mine. I give it to whom I will; to thee will I give it, if thou wilt fall down and worship me."

" All this is mine !" Great God, how shockingly this sounds; and alas ! here the father of lies has spoken the truth. By a holy decree of God has it become his ; this world, for which, at a subsequent period, the great High Priest would not pray. He is its prince, its head, its god—its liege lord. The vast majority on earth are his—the largest number of souls draw in his yoke—most lands pay him tribute, and upon the walls of most cities his black banners are waving. Who can count them —those hundreds of millions, whose souls he keeps fast locked, barred, and imprisoned in the thousand fold fetters and bonds of sin and darkness, and in countless spiritual dungeons and cells, be it of Islam or of heathenism, of the strong delusions of the Talmud, or of the dogmas of the Seven Hills ; of heaven-storming rationalism, or of pantheism and atheism ? Yes, without any vain parade, may he say 'it is all mine ;' for that small part which is not his but God's, this cottage in a garden of cucumbers, this worm Jacob, this despised remnant of Israel, becomes lost as it were, in the gigantic domain of this fallen prince of angels, and floats about in the same like a drop in the boundless ocean.

And what is there in the world which the devil has not usurped and prostrated to the expansion and the strengthening of his kingdom, and made subservient to his satanic designs, especially in these our days. To him belong the most of our pulpits and cathedrals ; his are the newspapers and daily journals ; his the public assemblies and associations ; his the sciences and the fine arts—all these things has he had skill gradually to draw into the service of his own cause. Who inspires the poetry in that flood of romances and comedies which is now inundating the world with its thousands of lies, and godless conceptions ? Who plays and manages the music in those voluptuous operas and frivolous arias, in which the melody that ought to be praising the name of the Lord, steps forth as a dangerous murderess of souls, and breathes a refined poison into all hearts ? Who holds his seat in the pompous institutes of the later philosophies, and from these redoubts and bastions, deals his deadly strokes at the gospel of peace ?—and who is it that has concocted and brought into the market this fashionable religion of the present day, this sweet magic potion—a mixture of sentimental atheism and indolent, corrupt, and God-estranged morality, which has lulled the people into a profound slumber, from which the thunders of the judgment alone will awaken them, alas, too late ? Is it not the father of lies—the old serpent—the dragon out of the abyss ?

Let no one then be astonished that the devil speaks of a giving which is in his power : "All these things will I *give* to thee if thou wilt fall down and worship me." There are satanic gifts as well as divine gifts, and the world swarms with men who are indebted to the devil for their enjoyments, their pleasures, honors, titles, and dignities. Yes, and he has his wages and his premiums for those who follow his banner, and he knows how to reward well their zeal in his service in various ways ; and not seldom is it permitted him of God to overwhelm reprobate men so abundantly with the pleasures and the glory of this world, and to lead them about so freely upon the rich meadows of carnal indulgence, that in the end the very last traces of humanity are obliterated from those vessels of wrath, and they go to hell like brutes.

"All these things will I give thee if thou wilt fall down and worship me." Thus the tempter to our Lord. Just imagine the Son of the living God bending the knee worshipfully before the Old Serpent ! This is the most wicked, the most monstrous proposal which was ever made to a being in this world. Indeed it appears an entire forgetfulness of the part he was acting, and hardly consistent with the cunning and craft of this greatest of magicians, this prince of sorcerers, and of a genius so gigantic as Satan is.

But let us only realize the critical and perilous condition in which Satan found himself at this moment, and we shall no longer be surprised at his shameless and accursed demand. The veils are falling off, and the devil suspects with increasing certainty with whom he has to deal. The brilliant triumphs which the Lord has hitherto achieved over him, and his most subtle arts, scarcely leave him the slightest doubt that Jesus is the Christ. Disconcerted beyond measure on account of his unsuccessful operations against this great adversary of his kingdom, and no less disturbed at the dangers which threaten his rule, he resolves, with angry impetuosity, upon a last decisive stroke ; but already his reflection faltered by passion, his coolness and moderation, have sunk in those fiery waves of despairing rage, which wildly and fearfully surge through his soul.

Indeed now, for the first time, after having ascertained the character of his adversary, he becomes clearly conscious of the intense earnestness and the momentous significance of the struggle in which he is engaged, and he clearly perceives that one of them must fall. " Either Thou," he thinks, " or I—either I overcome Thee, or I am overcome." But, nevertheless, his last attack, however much of art and energy it displayed, was of all the most unskillful, and resembles the charge of a desperate warrior, who gives up his cause for lost, and daring every extremity, rushes wildly and blindly into the ranks of the foe, and flings himself upon their swords. The last stroke which the devil aimed at Jesus was an act of desperation which was designed, in fact, less to overcome the Son of God and drive Him from the field (of which, indeed, there remained but little hope), than by way of farewell to offer Him yet one grievous insult and affront, and to give him to understand, as with a contemptuous stamp of the foot, that He must not imagine that he had succeeded in bowing the neck of His adversary.

In such desperate mood of mind, and foaming with rage, the devil begins his incantations, passes his magic mirror before the eyes of his adversary, opens to Him one prospect after another into the most fascinating regions of wordly pleasure and glory, and exclaims with grinning scorn, and wild, devilish contempt : " Behold there all this that thou seest, these enjoyments, all these delightful possessions, which cannot but be pleasing to thee, these shalt thou have if thou wilt fall down and worship me—up then, seize the tempting prize—down in the dust and worship thy Lord and monarch." It might also be supposed that, from the circumstance of Jesus having withheld the miraculous proofs desired of Him, the devil had drawn the inference that Jesus was not the God-man, but only some great saint, yet still a man upon whom, as such, he could make still more exorbitant demands, and approach with less disguise and with greater daring and firmness. The above hinted explanation, however, appears to lie nearer the truth. The satanic demand was, as before observed, an act of despair—an outbreak of blasphemous rage and devilish scorn, rather than of proper temptation.

Believers also have often to suffer from the devil precisely

the same which their Master suffered in the wilderness, in that
the wicked one persecutes them also with the most horrible
and godless demands, and projects thoughts into their souls
so wicked and abominable, that they quake before them with
horror. But take comfort, and despair not, ye tempted souls.
The devil assails you with such buffetings and blows, out of
pure vexation and rage, because he cannot succeed in destroying
you altogether. Regard these temptations as the ebullitions of
a weak enemy, who, because he cannot overcome you with sword
and sling, flings at you mire and filth, in order, at least, to fret
you, and in this way he would fain wreak his spite, because he
can do it in no other.

Let us witness, now, the ISSUE OF THE CONTEST.
Scarcely had Jesus heard the blasphemous request, scarcely had
He cast a glance into the magic scene of glory and pleasure
which the devil had the boldness to parade before Him, when
it became perfectly evident with whom He had to do. "These
are thy goods, thy kingdoms," thinks He, "and is it worship
thou askest? Thou art betrayed, subtle spirit; the mask is
fallen. I know thee." With abhorrence and contempt the holy
soul of our spotless High Priest turns away from the images of
vanity and delight which Satan had conjured up before Him.
He seizes the brazen shield of the word of God, on which all the
fiery darts of the devil are quenched, and exclaims with the
majesty of the Only-begotten, to whom all power is given in
heaven and on earth : " Get thee behind me, Satan, for it is
written, ' Thou shalt worship the Lord thy God, and Him only
shalt thou serve.' "

The devil ventured not to speak a second time concerning
worship ; he was beaten, and the Lamb of God, pure and without blemish, came forth from the contest in triumph, a victor.
In the obedience of faith with the sword of the Spirit,
which is the word of God, He laid the dragon low in the dust.

The temptation which Jesus so victoriously repelled occurs not seldom also in the life of His children. We have already remarked how the devil can also exhibit to us, in his magic mirror, all the kingdoms of this world and the glory of them in a moment of time. Ah! yes, also the holiest on earth will be obliged to acknowledge, that in the life of the children of God there may come hours and moments, when a thousand pleasures and enjoyments, goods and connections, to which they had deemed themselves long since entirely dead, suddenly float around them again in the most charming magic light, and present themselves to the eyes of their fancy. Then once more does it grow stormy and tempestuous upon the sea of sense and passion, and the devil then leaves no means untried wherewith to engulph the poor soul in these raging floods.

In such moments is it also said to us quickly, unexpectedly, ere we can recollect ourselves, " All these things will I give thee, if thou wilt fall down and worship me ;" and lo! it is only a trifle that is demanded in order to win all these glories and golden mountains—only a slight trespass, which, perhaps, no man would ever discover ; only one rapid foot-fall before the wicked one, only one passing act of homage, and all is ours. And oh! ye dear ones, David and Solomon are not the only instances among God's children, of persons who have paid this homage in order once more to drink from the intoxicating cup of this world's joys. Yet in whatever way this homage may be paid, we compassionate these prostrate brethren, and despise them not. No—we despise them not, for we know our hearts, and know what we are, and understand how the wicked one can paint the world so fair, and color its vanities so charmingly as to captivate the strongest. We know this, and sigh through all the hours, " Lord lead us not into temptation."

Indeed, the wicked one is not to be mistaken when he assails us with such bewitching and such shameful propositions. The enjoyments and possessions which he offers us so eloquently, and the ways and means which he proposes for the attainment of the same betray him. In temptations of this sort he comes not as an angel of light, but unmasked and unclothed, plumply and openly, boldly and firmly. Thus we soon know with whom we have to deal, and this makes the conflict all the easier. Unharmed, like Jesus, we shall indeed never perhaps quit the field. Without having felt any excitement of sinful desire, shall we rarely turn our glance away from those enchanting scenes. Happy will it be for us if we can but escape ere lust has conceived and brought forth, and are enabled to leave the plain unsubdued and uncrushed. Let the weapon with which Jesus so readily beat back the last attack of the tempter be in like cases also our own. It is written, "Thou shalt worship the Lord thy God, and Him only shalt thou serve." Against this word, when it is taken as a word of God and opposed in faith to the wicked one, will his strongest lances be shivered like straws, and as often as he sees this piece of armor glistening around our breast, all hope will vanish at once of ever being able to tempt us to the slightest worship or the most momentary homage of him.

Then the devil leaveth Him, and behold angels came and ministered unto Him. Such was the final issue of this great and momentous conflict ; and, surely, never could the Devil have yielded a battle-field in more unhappy mood—never quit a foe with such lacerated and infuriated soul—as he then must have left the most formidable adversary of his kingdom. To be routed so utterly, and to be compelled to ground his weapons covered with such shame, this was to him as intolerable as it was novel. Like a dark cloud of the night, which the storm-wind drives, he hurried hence, rolling around his fiery eyes and gnashing his teeth in despair ; and to the mountains and to the hills might he have called, that they should fall upon him and hide him from the sight alike of heaven and hell ; that he might neither hear the triumph of the angels above him, nor the sullen murmur and mournful howlings of the hellish host below over such utter shame and prostration.

But with our Lord it is well. Oh, how well must it have been for Him, when, after a forty days' sad desertion, not in the wilderness merely, but in the very midst of the powers of darkness (for Luke says that He was forty days tempted of the devil), he now suddenly is again restored to His element, and finds Himself among the dear angels of God, who come to worship and to wait on the great Conqueror. Then was fulfilled the word which the dying Jacob uttered of old with prophetic spirit: "Judah is a lion's whelp. From the prey, my son, thou art gone up. He stooped down, he couched as a lion, and as an old lion who shall rouse him up." This rest, however, was not the end of the combat, but only a short truce. The devil, observes Luke, departed from Him for a season. It was not long before he stood again in full array against Jesus upon the plain; and he has followed Him with his slings and his darts until this great Samson on Golgotha crushed him with His own folly, and for ever wrested the sceptre out of his hands. When the blood of the Lamb of God stained the wood of the accursed tree, then it was that the serpent's head was effectually bruised.

Our life, too, dear friends, will prove a conflict, even unto the end. There will not, indeed, be wanting to us days of rest and festival hours in the wilderness; but the full, unbroken Sabbath awaits us yonder. So long as we dwell in these pilgrim tents, so long will the Devil not sheathe his sword, and the roaring Lion not cease "to go about seeking whom he may devour;" and although he may be forced to give up the hope of conquering us, yet will he not desist from wreaking his anger upon us; and through assaults and buffetings of various kinds, will he cause us to feel his hatred and his contempt. Yet we fear not. With Paul we will exultingly say, "Thanks be unto God who giveth us the victory, through our Lord Jesus Christ." The victories of our great Surety are all ours through faith. We have already conquered before the battle. We triumph now, though the field is yet dusty with the strife, and the fiery darts are whizzing around our heads by thousands; and even in defeat we are and shall continue conquerors, and are more than conquerors through Him that has loved us. Blessed truth ! precious faith ! Where this faith lives, there courage cannot fail when the trumpet sounds for the battle ; and should we sink in the strife in this faith, will our tottering knees be soon strengthened. "Happy art thou, O Israel ! who is like unto thee, O people saved by the Lord, the shield of thy help, and who is the sword of thy excellence ; and thine enemies shall be found liars unto thee, and thou shalt tread upon their high places."

DISCOURSE XIII.

THE PERIL AND SAFETY OF THE CHURCH.

"Though the waters thereof roar and be troubled, though the mountains shake with the swelling thereof, [yet*] there is a river, the streams whereof shall make glad the city of God, the holy place of the tabernacles of the Most High. God is in the midst of her; she shall not be moved: God shall help her, and that right early."—PSALMS xlvi. 3-5.

Our Psalm is a leap with God over the wall; a soaring above the heights of the earth; a joyful dance before the Ark of the Covenant. No tone of complaint, no trace of anxiety, is to be found in this song of triumph; though it may have been sung in time of distress and affliction. The song breathes only the joyfulness of faith, and confidence is its soul. "God is our refuge and strength, a very present help in trouble;" so the Psalm begins. "The Lord of hosts is with us, the God of Jacob is our refuge;" thus it ends. It boasts of the secure condition of the people of God; and of this we will speak, according to the indications of our text, in this last morning of the ecclesiastical year. We consider the true church, according to its form:—*a city*; its situation—*in the sea*; its consolation—*she shall be glad*; its safety—*God is in the midst of her*.

I. There is nothing more vexatious and intolerable to unbelievers, than that we draw so marked a line between the children of God and the children of the world, and are accustomed to

---

* The word *yet*, only implied in the English version, is expressed in the German.
TRANS.

represent the number of the former as so very small and inconsiderable. But we cannot help it. *We* do not make the difference ; it is made by God himself ; and is deeply rooted in the nature and essence of the two parties ; and the mouth of Truth itself says, in several places, that the number is small of those who are saved. Truly all that are called are not chosen ; and not every one belongs to the true church who bears its colors. Even you, our enemies, are used to say that of those who would be Christians, but few are sincere. And you may be in the right. After deducting the Canaanites, the false brethren, the foolish Virgins, who have lamps but not oil ; clouds without water ; and the Issachars, who are their own product, and not that of the Spirit ; there remains in truth but a small seed—a twinkling star in the vast clouded firmament ; a cottage in a garden of cucumbers. That which makes a true Christian is not a decent conduct, and the ornament of a regular observance of the outward forms of religion ; it is not the retiring from the diversions of the men of the world, and the language of Canaan ; it is not the bowed head and the sullen look. Even an orthodox faith is not sufficient. "There are many persons," says somebody, "who, with a little heavenly light, wander towards hell." Poverty of spirit, and the having nothing, willing nothing, and desiring nothing but Jesus, and Jesus only—the man upon the cross, His blood and His grace—and this from the bottom of the soul : *this* is the stamp on God's coin. Let no one, then, mingle chaff and wheat together ; let no one attempt to unite what God has put asunder.

The Great Shepherd's lamp-fold, that rose among thorns, that grain of salt amid corruption, is called in our text "a city ;" and that *a city of God*. The figure is familiar, and I would only say a few words by way of illustration.

Truly, it is a strange city ; little and insignificant ; and yet of an extent like the world in which we live ; stretching from one pole to the other. But it will be one day gathered together from the dispersion, and seen in one spot, in all its beauty and splendor. Everything belonging to a city is found in this little city of God. If you inquire after her foundation, it is a Rock that cannot be moved. If you ask after her wall, it is one of fire and life, the Lord is a wall of fire round about her : "The angel of the Lord encamps round them that fear Him." If you ask for her bastions, defences and palisades, they are the perfections of our God that are round about us : His wisdom to guide us ; his omnipotence to protect us ; His long-suffering to bear with us ; and His grace, to justify and save us. Only one gate has the city, and that is strait ; only one way that leads to it, and that is narrow. Whoever attempts to enter by another way, by stealth or by storm, over the walls or through the roof, he is a thief and a robber. When we look out of our windows, our eyes fall on beloved mountains, on holy places. Here lies Golgotha, there the Mount of Olives ; here Gethsemane, there Bethlehem Ephrata—all dear places, that ever lie close about us : our city, therefore, is Jerusalem.

The city has its festivals : for instance, when a poor sinner repenteth ; its assemblies, when the brethren live together in unity, and Jesus is in the midst of them ; its concerts, when they speak together in psalms, and hymns, and spiritual songs, and Jesus touches the harp-chords of their hearts ; and its spectacles, when they sit at the foot of the cross, beholding the Man with the crown of thorns, and His holy blood, as, making atonement for sin, it drips from His wounds.

The city has likewise its market-place ; there it is proclaimed, " Come, ye that have no money ; come, buy and eat ; yea, come, buy wine and milk, without money and without price." It has also its council-chamber, where one presides who knows how to give good counsel. Its police, too : this every citizen has in his heart—the controlling power of the Spirit. Has it, also, its watchmen ? Surely it has : they stand on the walls and blow the trumpet, and raise the shout when they see the Bridegroom coming. . And here and there stand guards upon the watch-towers, placed there by God, to see what hour the great clock of time has struck. And what say they—these guards of our days? "Midnight is the hour! Past midnight," they cry from the housetops, and the whole city is full of the things which are to come to pass.

In this city, now, as the text says, is found "the holy place of the tabernacles of the Most High." Now, indeed, every house where dwells a child of God, is also a house of God : for the Lord dwells with His own, under one roof. Nay, every believer is a living temple. It is written, " I live ; yet not I, but Christ liveth in me." By the holy tabernacles we are to understand the various conditions and states of the soul, in which the saints are placed by the ordinances of God. There is one, well lodged in the lofty rock of pure faith, where, untroubled about the ebb and flow of the feelings of his heart, and raised far above all the alternations of spiritual temperature in his soul, he sings, with Asaph, " Whom have I in heaven but Thee ! and there is none upon earth that I desire beside Thee." Another must make shift in the cave of Adullam, and must, year out and year in, eat his bread with tears, and find no consolation. Some dwell in the spacious pavilions of a sweet, heartfelt communion with the Lord, basking in the sunshine of His love, and deeply feeling the refreshing beams of His countenance shining into their souls ; so that they can exclaim : " It is good for us to be here—here let us build tabernacles." Others, on the contrary, are pent up in narrow, dark cells, and are compelled to dwell between darkness and doubt : their daily task is combat and conflict, labor and pain ; and their breath a gush of sighs : so that they must be heartily glad when a faint ray of hope shines upon their gloom.

Oh ! various are the dwelling-places in the city of God. One sits under the juniper, another under the apple-tree ; one in the desert, another in the garden of roses ; one in the cool arbor, another, like a fugitive, trembling dove, in the cleft of the rock ; one in the tent, another in the vineyard ; and wherever else they may sit and house. But all have their windows to the East ; and wherever each happens to dwell with his soul, in whatever condition or situation, he there dwells happily. God has directed him ; and therefore his dwelling is holy—a dwelling of God. Ah ! indeed, and this would be so, even were it a narrow dungeon, or a dark pit, if only the pit be in the city of God. For we know whither we are going : our stay on earth is but a short sojourn ; beyond Jordan, better tabernacles are waiting to receive us.

Lastly, our text speaks of "streams that flow into the city of God :" and we know that the house of David and the citizens of Jerusalem have one main fountain, which is free and open, against all impurity and sin, and its name is Immanuel. Four nails and a spear have opened it : now it flows with exceeding abundance ; and though people have bathed in it, and drunk of it, for thousands of years, yet its waters have not diminished. Around this fountain of health, the city is continually assembled, with buckets of faith and bowls of prayer ; and every cripple and beggar is allowed to draw from it as much as he pleases for his daily use. Our fountain never dries up, never freezes ; and if, at times, it seems as if we, with our buckets, struck upon a hard ice-crust instead of into the water, yet is this *only* a seeming ; our thirst is notwithstanding quenched, and the water only flows secretly and covertly into our souls.

This well of Jacob nourishes and refreshes us as it pleases it ; sometimes sensibly, sometimes secretly ; sometimes in immediate influxes, sometimes through various channels and intervening pipes—as, through the word or sacrament, through the mouth of the brethren, or through their experience and course of life ; sometimes through a sign or image of nature, as, Noah, through the rainbow ; sometimes through a providence in our life, or through whatever else may happen. In a thousand little brooks, it pours its healing waves through the holy city ; and it so happens that almost every citizen of Jerusalem, aside from the general fountain, has yet a special brooklet welling up at his door, to refresh him. One experiences the hearing of a prayer, in which he possessed, as long as he lives, a private treasure, and a fountain in his chamber, which every day revives and invigorates his courage. Another feels some promise singularly established and sealed in his heart ; so that to the end of his days it is to him bread and water, and a pilgrim's staff in his right hand. One has a consoling verse, which makes music for him all his days, and is more to him than David's harp to King Saul. Another sees a vision, and hears a voice, or whatever else he may see, or hear before his inward ear, perceive or experience within : and this is a fountain in his house and chamber, which raises his head and keeps his leaves fresh and green, when the dry year has come, and the dear time has broken in. In a word, hunger and thirst are not to be thought of on the Rock of Zion. Bread is given unto each one, and his water is sure.

II. After having taken a view of the city, we now inquire after its situation ; and we learn from the text that it lies in a roaring sea, and that the surf beats against its walls. So has it always lain ; and at all times has it been compared with the ship on the sea of Galilee, in which the disciples cry, " Lord, save us ; we perish !" But the Lord commanded the storm and the waves, so that they passed over in safety. At one time the sea has beaten more furiously than at others; nay, there have been times when it really appeared as if the city were entirely swallowed up, and buried in the deep ; and ere one was aware of it, it rose like a green and lovely island up from the surrounding waters, and laughed at the winds and the floods.

In our days the city of God still lies in the sea, and in the very midst of it, as it never lay before, God knows ! The enemies of the Cross all around are this sea. Who can discern the bounds of this ocean, which has cast us up ? who can fathom the depth of their enmity, rancor, perfidy, and malice ? Here and there is there a storm upon the sea, and wild commotion. Hear how the waves of false philosophy and godless exposition foam up more and more frantically against the sacred walls ! See how the floods of hatred to Christ roll more and more madly and furiously over the face of the earth! Behold how the enemies more and more eagerly exert all the powers of intellect—all arts, to wage a war of extermination against the kingdom of the Lord—against the poor company of Israel, and his cause! Already we see here and there a foaming of rage, and here a gnashing of teeth, against the fold of Christ; as if the complete outburst of their fury could no longer be restrained. Invention is at a loss to find new terms of abuse and reprobation to heap upon them; they are already spoken of as plague-spots, which afflict mankind, and which, if no other means can be found, must be extirpated with fire and sword.

A frightful and unbroken cry of "Crucify! crucify!" sounds through the world against Jesus and his people. Crucify! cries Fashion, which is already almost ashamed of the Christian name, as a blemish, and has raised Anti-christianity to the rank of the religion of the polite world. Crucify! cries polite Etiquette, in the assemblies and circles of the great, whence Christ has long since been banished, and where no Christian can enter toll free, and without scorning and upturning of the nose. Crucify! cry a thousand priests of Baal, who will have nothing but morality; no Christ, no cross, no blood, no grace. Crucify! cry almost all the journals, while they without ceasing open their batteries against true Christianity. Nay, to whatever side we turn our ears, to books and writings, to companies and circles, to the assemblies of the great and the polished, or the drinking-rooms of the vulgar and the low, to the workshops of the mechanics or to the cabinets of men in office, and the counting-houses of the merchants—nay, even to lectures of professors, or the sermons of preachers—wherever we turn—ere we hear one "Hosannah to the son of David," the fatal Crucify, crucify, rudely or politely, covertly or openly, a hundred or a thousand times assaults your ears. Thus do matters stand: so rage the waves of that sea whose breakers roar around the city of our God.

But, my brethren, it will yet be worse. God's watchmen proclaim it from the battlements, and more than one sign of these times indicates that the prophecy is hastening to its accomplishment. The paper waves will one day become billows of fire, and the hissing of the sea, roaring and howling. Vast tracts of the ocean around Zion lie even now still and motionless : only in the depths below, it boils, and storms, and rages. A fearful mass of rage and rancor has gradually collected against the Cross and its followers, and this powder magazine waits but for the match, to blow up with a fearful explosion. The thousands that have already become Anti-christians, must still devour their gall and bitterness. The waves of Babel, which lie round Jerusalem like a calm, deep, treacherous sea, still lurk behind the dams ; their fury is yet stayed. But who can tell how much longer ? Everything indicates that the time of a universal break of the dams and bars is at hand, and that the great hour of temptation is no longer distant. The sea is already prepared for a dreadful commotion : birds of ill omen, the precursors of the storm, already fly about with piercing cries that forebode nothing good. I will not name the blood-thirsty Inquisition in the West ; how it rises with renewed vigor from its tomb, and is exerting itself to the utmost to reëstablish the tribunals against heretics. I will not name those missionaries, who with mad fanaticism rage through the neighboring kingdom of France. I will not name Jesuitism, how it is again carrying on its intrigues, and in some parts is aiming at such a degree of power and influence, that there is but too much foundation for the alarm with which the church looks upon its efforts. I will not speak of the blood-red sky in the South, of which no politician can calculate what it may bring forth, or how it may yet spread the glare of its fires. I will not dwell on the notes sounded by the trumpet of God, which in this time of agitation announces serious events. Enough ! there is no want of indications of the most alarming kind, of screaming storm-birds on the ocean of our times ; and tokens of the most manifest character unite to presage to the city of our God a day which shall burn like an oven, and glow like a furnace.

It is true, that many mountains still stand round about us, as ice and water-breakers, and many a hill to protect the city of God. Thus in our country we have as a bulwark against the invasions of Babel, and against Anti-christian attacks, an Evangelical King, who is steadfastly attached to the true faith ; and against the false prophet without, and his fanatical operations, we have horses and horsemen from many quarters. As a dam against the floods of false doctrine, we have the Bible Society, with its far-spreading branches ; and for the enlargement and fortifying of our city of God, we have the invaluable mission, and hosts of Evangelical teachers. To nourish, strengthen, and refresh us, we have our beautiful Divine Service, and the preaching of the unadulterated Gospel. For our encouragement, we have beloved men of God, who zealously blow the trumpet around us, and encouragingly take us by the hand. But who will be our security, that, before we are aware, these mountains shall not also fall, those hills give way also, and all our supports sink into the breach ? Then the waves of the sea might have their free course, and the city of God might be destroyed. Destroyed ? No ! not so ; God forbid !

III. Hear what the sweet singer says in our Psalm : " Though the waters thereof roar and be troubled, though the mountains shake with the swelling thereof ; [yet] there is a river, the streams whereof shall make glad the city of God, the holy place of the tabernacles of the Most High." Oh ! what words of comfort ! Are they not like a golden rainbow in the clouds, and like a float to the net, to keep it above water ? They are sufficient at once to overcome all faint-heartedness, and to put to flight a whole host of misgivings. It is not the word of man, but the word of God, delivered by the mouth of man ; and hence the power with which it is endowed. " Yet !" Oh, a precious " yet !" This " Yet" of our God, is more than these mountains and hills, which it, in fact, renders unnecessary. If we have this " Yet" in the hand of faith, what should alarm and make us uneasy? With this "Yet" we take from the storms their terrors, and from the fiery waves their fearfulness. With this "Yet," we may stand with confidence on our walls; and, however gloomy the prospect, however the thunder-clouds may lower and the deep roar, we proclaim this "Yet" of our Lord; and though the storm were never so great and awful, so severe that voices should call to us on all sides, "You are fools, to hope where no hope is," we will not be confounded: our watchword is "Yet, Yet;" and we answer, "What is impossible must become possible, sooner than that the city of God shall not be glad with its streams." He has spoken the word, and He is the Amen.

And now, consider what unheard of things are here promised to the congregation of God. Not only that they shall abide in the hour of temptation, and be preserved from despondency and backsliding: but they shall even be glad with their streams, and bloom yet more fair than in times of peace. There are but few rejoicing Christians, yet we learn that it is no sin to be joyful in God. He who has no occasion to mourn, may lift up his head, and need not bow it down like a bulrush. We have cause and reason enough to be glad in the Lord, and to pass through life with a joyful spirit. For what do we yet want, we who are in Christ; and in Him have all that heart can desire; we who go clothed in the purple of our King, and in his robe are glorious before the eyes of God; we who know that our names are written in the book of life, and that our souls are in hands from which nothing and nobody can pluck them away; we who have the assurance that He has always loved us, and that He will keep that which we have committed to Him against that day; we who are certain that all our enemies already lie vanquished under our feet, and that one day, adorned with the victor-crowns of our surety, we shall cast anchor on the golden coast of the promised Land? Nay, if we could, we might sit from morning till evening at the harp, and none could justly reproach us for being so glad. If we could, our whole life might be a dance, like that of David before the Ark of the Covenant ; and we might be drunk with the wine of the house of God, and, as Zechariah says, " make a noise as through wine, and be filled like bowls, and as the corners of the altar." God would have nothing against it ; He would have pleasure in it.   But the eye of our faith is so dim, and the hand of our confidence takes such loose hold ; we look more to ourselves than to Christ, and will not seek in Him alone, but would also find something in ourselves : and hence it comes, that with all our riches, we are so poor in joy ; and that our treasure which we have through grace, is like a talent buried in the earth, from which we do not even get the interest ; and our life is miserable, like that of a poor beggar, and yet we are told, " All is yours."

This wretched life, however, shall one day cease in the city of God on earth ; and, wonderful to tell ! just at the moment when it should seem to be only beginning in earnest—namely, when the sea around foams and rages in the height of its fury, and the mountains shake with the swelling thereof.   But thus, too, it often fares with the individual Christian.   When fierce temptations assail him, so that all his supports give way, and all the mountains and hills of his own power and will, and of his own righteousness, are overthrown, so that he must wholly lean on Christ, and be content with His grace ; then, and not till then, he becomes glad.   And so has it fared with the church of God on earth up to this very day.   Never has she blossomed more fair, never has she shone in the night with brighter splendor, than in evil days, and of the time of persecution.   Read the history of the church ; it is even so.   The most glorious stars in the firmament of the church, the most joyful confessors of the faith, became great amid storms and tempest ; and never has the Bride of the Lamb on earth stood forth more gloriously adorned than in the times of martyrdom, and of the martyrs whose footsteps still shine up to this day.   Their souls were naturally weak ; and when we are weak, then we are strong : then nothing

remained to them but to go out of themselves, and to hide themselves in Christ; and in Christ we can do all things. And,
indeed, if the Lord be ever out on the field among His people
with His Spirit and His gifts, it is in such days of distress and
affliction, when the sea roars and rages, and the mountains
shake. Then He opens more wide the flood-gates of His divine
power, and His refreshing streams flow more abundantly, and
keep equal course with the sea of troubles and afflictions; the
more violent the latter, the richer are the former, for the city
of God shall be "glad with its streams."

And so, probably, matters will not change with the city of
God in our vale; which, on the whole, actually appears right
meagre, poor, and miserable, and is closely covered and hidden.
Yes, truly; so long as the good days last, so long ye may
go about languid and faint; so long ye may be so full of complaints with your riches, and so bowed down with your treasures,
so cold in the embraces of your Bridegroom, so lukewarm and
indifferent in the confession of His name; so long you are
permitted to continue your disputes and dissensions, to carry
on your petty wars of opinion, and to indulge in idle speculations. But, I answer for it, at the first sound of the trumpet
that shall announce to you the approach of the hour of temptation, at the first deluge of the waves of the great struggle,
which shall break in upon our valley, everything will be
suddenly changed, and the city be glad with her streams.

Dissension will cease, and there will be a holding together
and unity in love, such as will astonish the world. There will
be no more disputing about the restoration of all things; or
whether there will be a third place, etc.; but all will regard
one place only, Jesus! Jesus!—and be anxious only about
complete restoration to His favor, His blood, and His wounds;
and in this strong-hold that which was separated will again be
united. Then the covering will be removed, and the gentle
dove in the clefts of the rock will be seen to soar as with eagle's
wings, and sucklings shall be as the horses caparisoned for the

battle ; and, as the Prophet says, they shall devour and subdue
with sling-stones. For, "though the sea roars and is troubled,
and the mountains shake, there is a river the streams whereof
make glad the city of God !"

IV Oh, what a glorious prospect for the city of God, though
the sky is darkened, and the clouds lower and threaten ! How
secure does the fair city lie, though in the midst of the sea,
whose waves dash furiously against her walls ! The ground of
her security, however, is not in herself, but in that Rock on
which she is founded. "God is in the midst of her," sings the
holy Psalmist, and "helps her early :" "God is in the midst
of her," as He is in each individual member ; always working,
not always felt ; always active, not always to be traced ; incessantly sustaining, frequently without our knowledge ; constantly
blessing and fructifying, not always according to our wish, and
often in secret. But He is always at hand. "This is my rest
for ever ; here will I dwell."

Blessed, my brethren, are the eyes that see what we see.
Behold, one pole shouts it to the other ; the east proclaims it
to the west, "God is in the midst of her." Oh, how majestic
is the step with which He this day again marches through the
world, not that He may judge the world, but that He may
surround it with the bulwarks of His holy city, and, over
mountain and sea stretch forth the curtains of His habitations !
The prince of this world is cast out, and we see with rejoicing
how the strong, pressed by the Stronger, is forced to yield one
province after another. Not a hoof remains behind of what the
Father has given to the Son. How does the faithful Shepherd
call His sheep, and they hasten from every desert, and every
rock, to fall on His breast and repose in His bosom ? How
diligently does the great Reaper ply the sickle in His harvest
field, and bring in the sheaves in abundance, as if winter were
at hand, and haste were necessary that the last fruits might be
brought home ! Islands, that for thousands of years have awaited

His coming, quiver with joy at the sound of His feet ; and dark
heathen plains grow light, because their Light is come, and they
greet with hosannas and hallelujahs the day-spring from on
high. The Hottentot sees the golden bark of the dearest of all
guests land on his shores, and with bended knees welcomes the
Lord of glory. The man at the North Pole grows warm upon
the mother-heart of the most faithful Shepherd, and his ice-
bound world blooms like a paradise, now that the Prince of
Peace has entered. Yes, His footsteps are bright and glorious ;
and mighty voices proclaim from land to land : " God is in the
midst of her."

Nor has He forgotten *us*—no, not even *us*—and though He
walks about more lightly of late, and less in the noon-day than
in former times, yet His footsteps are still in the valley, and we
hear the tinkling of the bells that hang to his priestly robe. If
but a few were added to his flock during the past year—and
you well know, my beloved, that in this point we must not prescribe to Him, but leave Him to take His own course ; for herein
He faithfully follows a plan delivered to Him in a holy Council
before the world began—yet He has given manifold evidences of
His presence in other ways. He has strengthened the weary
hands of the one, and upheld the sinking knees of another. The
suckling in spirit has He borne in the arms of His love, and
counseled in due season those who struggled in doubt. He has
brought one from the night of temptation into His light, and
has bestowed upon another the crown of victory, after the fight.
One he has made to hear His glad voice, saying, " Be of good
cheer, thy sins are forgiven thee !" so that being now healed, he
goes on his way rejoicing ;—while by another providence he has
relieved the heart of a second from its heavy burden. Thus
there are, doubtless, many in the midst of us to-day, with cheerful, yet penitent countenances, who acknowledge with joy and
humility, " The Lord hath done great things for me. Yea, the
Lord is in the midst of us—therefore have I not been removed."
And truly, my beloved brethren, is not it an irrefragable proof

that Immanuel was in the midst of us, that we have not been removed, that we still remain together on Jesus's bosom and under Jesus's banner, though the devil daily roars around as if he would devour us?

And see! how many a bed of pain is in the midst of us, where the bush of thorns has burned the whole year through, and yet has not been consumed; how many a miserable family, where all was wanting, and yet the barrel of meal did not waste, nor the cruse of oil fail; how many a pilgrim who knew not what way to take, and yet now has passed Jordan; how many a Jonah, who had already gone down to the very bottoms of the mountains, now stands joyful and glorifying God on the shore! For the prosperity of our Christian Institutions; the happy success, far beyond all expectation, of our efforts in the cause of God, behold monument on monument, witness upon witness, praising His grace, and loudly proclaiming, in the triumphant language of our Psalm, "God is in the midst of her!"

And so long as a tent of Kedar shall stand in our valley, He will not depart from our valley. Jerusalem is His habitation and His rest forever. Therefore let us not fear, since the Rock of Jacob is with us, and such a bulwark is raised around us. He who bears arms against us, contends with God; and it is dangerous to take the field against Him. Sooner shall the thorns overcome the fire, and the chaff resist the storm, than hell triumph over us, who have such a Defender.

"He helps her early," sings the sacred minstrel: and truly this is the manner of our God. His help generally appears as the dawn of the morning after the night. His light, says the Psalmist, breaks forth as the morning; and "weeping may endure for a night, but joy cometh in the morning." After the gloom of repentance He gave us the kiss of love; after the night of combat, He crowned us with victory; His glory shone upon us in the cave of Adullam; and after wrestling till break of day, Jacob received His blessing. Therefore, let us not be afraid, if a day of darkness and clouds should come over us; He helps

us early ; and so often as our sky is overcast, it is only that the
sun may afterwards shine on us with more welcome and vivifying
splendor. And in the darkness itself there is a blessing, a salutary seed in affliction. The **church of God** is like a palm-tree,
which flourishes the **more vigorously the more** it is pressed down.
Every embarrassment is to her but as the weight to the clock,
which keeps it going ; and the **most violent storms are to the**
church but a brisk wind in the sails, which impels the vessel more
rapidly towards the harbor. And beyond her **strength she is**
never tried—beyond her own, indeed, **she may be, but not**
beyond that which He lends us—and as for **the desolation of**
Zion, it is not for a moment to be thought of.   The city stands
fast and immovable, like the Mercy on which it is founded, and
the Faithfulness which bears it up.   " **Not a bone of Him shall**
be broken," is it written of our Immanuel.   This word is in
force even unto this day.   We are " bone of His bone :" who
shall hurt us ?

May the Lord strengthen us in the faith, that we may walk
cheerfully under the dark sky of this world, looking up to the
glorious **stars of promise** that He has placed amid **the clouds !**
In this faith may He inclose us as in a fortress, so long as we
weep in this vale of fogs and storms !   In this faith we repose
amid the waves of **temptation,** like Noah in his Ark.   In this
faith we are secure like a hero in his **armor.**   **Who will venture**
to attack us ?

> A ship by winds and waves in vain assailed ;
> Adventurer bold, whose courage ne'er has failed ;
> Gold in the fiery furnace made more bright ;
> A shield of adamant the foes to fright ;
> Hero of God, that ne'er has lost the field ;
> A child of grace, by foreign power upheld ;
> Born where hell's sad and dreary confines lie,—
> *Such* is our FAITH, in which we live and die !

DISCOURSE XIV.

THE BELIEVER'S CHALLENGE.

"Who is he that condemneth? It is Christ that died; yea, rather that is risen again; who is even at the right hand of God; who also maketh intercession for us."—Rom. viii. 3.

THIS rings, indeed, fresh and lively, brethren; this is Easter-music, and the resurrection jubilee. Oh, that we could, one and all, conclude this festival with such a shout of triumph! Behold the sum of all the consolation brought to us by Passion-week, Good Friday, and Easter, expressed in these cheerful and cheering words. Let us then examine their meaning more closely, and direct our attention to three points. We shall consider, I. The defying challenge: II. Who may join in it: III. Upon what it is founded.

I. "Who is he that condemneth?" Hold! who cries there? We look round, and, behold, there stands before us a man with a cheerful countenance, and uplifted head; he stands there, firm as a battlement, his arm resting on his side, as if he would say: "Who will venture now to try it with me?" His eyes sparkle; victory lies in his features; great confidence in his attitudes; and serene defiance on his brow. Who is He? It is one from Judah—a Christian. How! a Christian so daring? Oh, yes; these people are lambs and lions too; like the Captain of their salvation, of whom it is said: "And as a sheep before her shearers is dumb, so He openeth not His mouth." And in another place : "The Lion hath roared, who will not be afraid ?"

Yes, indeed, Christians can be very daring and very proud ; and they dare to be ; for is not that pride, when they cast your honors back in your face, and say : "O, world, thine honor I want not ?" And is that not daring, when they bind your reproach and shame about their head, like a princely diadem, and parade therewith as with a crown ? Is not that pride, when, in utter indifference, they pass by your places of amusement, as those that are accustomed to something better than your empty pleasures ? And is not that daring, when, in chains and bands, and amid storms of fiercest persecution, they can laugh and sing, to the chagrin of the world and the devil, as Paul and Silas did in their prison ? Yes, Christians are free and courageous people, for the Lord is their boast and their pride. But if they look off from Him, and upon themselves, aye, then their glory shrivels together, and there is an end of their daring and their proud carriage ; then the head reclines down as a bulrush ; the eyes are cast down, and the man becometh tame as a lamb, and dares not open his mouth through shame and confusion.

But where have we left our man of defiant tone ? There he stands, and looks about with sparkling eyes, as if he had something against heaven and earth, and calls till every ear tingles : " Who will condemn ?" That rings bold. Who is the man that dares thus to boast ? By nature, one godless without parallel ; an enemy to Jesus Christ and His saints ; a persecutor and murderer of the churches, who, with a malicious joy, can feed on the blood of the innocent ; a proud, self-righteous disciple of the Pharisees, and a fearful instrument of Antichrist. There you have him as he *was* ; and would you know what he *is* ? Hear it from his own mouth : " I am the chiefest of sinners ;— oh, wretched man that I am ! who shall deliver me from the body of this death ? I see a law in my members warring against the law of my mind, and bringing me into captivity to the law of sin. The good that I would, I do not ; but the evil which I would not, that I do. And, lest I should be exalted above measure through the abundance of the revelations, there was given to me a thorn in the flesh, the messenger of Satan, to buffet me, lest I should be exalted above measure." Now you know him.

What, then, is the man about ? What rash act would he perform ? Oh, incomparable daring ! Behold, there he goes. —Whither, then ?—Yes, ye well may wonder !

Behold, there looms up in the distance a high mountain towards heaven ; the whole mountain as a flame of fire ; dark vapor-clouds around it ; thick smoke and thunder and lightning upon its top ; and the tone of a mighty trumpet, so that the rocks do quake ! And the Lord descends upon the Mount Sinai ; but upon its peak there blazes a fire, and the smoke thereof mounts up like the smoke of a furnace, so that the whole mountain trembles:—and now hark : " I am a jealous God, and a consuming fire !" And again : "Thou shalt, and thou shalt not ! Thou shalt, and thou shalt not !" And again : " Cursed is every one that continueth not in all things that are written in the book of the Law to do them." " Whosoever hath sinned against me, him will I blot out of my book." " Tribulation and anguish upon every soul that doeth evil." And again : "He that offendeth in one point is guilty of all." And again : " A fire is kindled in mine anger, and shall burn to the lowest hell ; and all the people shall say, Amen." And, behold, there is a great eye over the mountain, like a torch of fire, which looks and watches that no tittle of this eternal law may fall ; and a dreadful sword glitters like lightning beside it, against the transgressor ; and the mountain itself is so holy that God forbids even to touch it : "Take heed to yourselves, that ye go not up into the mount, or touch the border of it ; whosoever toucheth the mount shall surely be put to death." But let it be so—so holy and so dreadful as it will, yon man advances straight towards it; he touches it, climbs up, makes straight into the darkness, looks without trembling into the roaring din, and cries, as if he would outcry both **thunder and trumpet**: "Who is he that condemneth?"—And **the Eye** of flame consumes him not!—and Moses accuses him not! **All is dumb, as if a Deity** had cried! —What mean these things?

He quits Mount Sinai, and goes—whither? Oh, presumption! He plants himself on the abyss of hell; oh, spectacle of horror! a burning lake; a fire which never is quenched; monsters who never die; a rattle of everlasting chains; howlings of the damned! Whew! A shudder comes over the frame—the **hair** stands on end!—but *he* looks in, as into a magic lantern, or into a painted picture, from which one has nothing to **fear.** Presumptuous man! Behold, he walks amid a thousand devils; their prince is the fallen Morning-star; **the Old Serpent,** Satan—a deceiver, and cunning without equal; the accuser of men, who day and night eyes their sins in order to bring them before God; a crafty fellow, who sees astonishingly far into the human heart; who does not suffer any to dissemble to him; whom the strictest external religion cannot deceive; but who, as we see from the history of Job, is able to hunt out whether one serves God for naught, or for the sake of profit. A dreadful enemy! who should not be afraid of him? But our audacious friend looks him courageously in the face; glances around boldly upon the fiendish hosts, opens his mouth, and shouts into the abyss below, so that a hundred echoes ring along the gloomy vaults: "Who is he that condemneth?"—And,—oh, wonder! —the devils gnash their teeth—and are dumb!

Now he steps into the habitations of the dead. Oh, see, whole hosts of **accusers, of witnesses,** against him. Paul, Paul! dost thou not quake **into** nothing at such a sight? Behold, here is one whom thou hast murdered; another, and that one there, thou castedst into chains and bonds; this one thou lockedst up in the night in a dungeon; and that one thou laidst upon the rack, and tookest delight in the streaming of his blood.

Behold the testimony against thee! they bear it on their body! Their wounds, their mangled limbs, their stripes, their scars, call down curse and death upon thy head. Now, indeed, thy chivalry will have an end.—Oh, not at all!—"Come on, whoever has aught against me! Ye bloody corpses, whom I brought to death, up! who dares—who accuses me? who will condemn? who will condemn?"—Dares none?—*None;* the godless has won the suit!

He looks about to see who will take heart to stand forth against him; and behold a sore witness comes forward; incorruptible, downright, penetrating, and unsparing; he resides in his own breast and knows everything, even that which takes place in the hidden corners of thought and feeling;—"Conscience" by name. With hundred thousand charges, comes he forward, leaves not a sound hair on him—makes him—God knows—*what* a wretch! There is no disgrace and no wickedness which he does not heap upon his head; and he swears by the living God that he has testified truly. Now, Paul, reach your back here, and receive the brand: here the ceremonies end.—Nay, by no means: "Frighten some one else, thou unseen beadle," he cries; "we are nothing moved at thy thundering! Silence, invisible accuser! stay at home with thine accusations, thou scrupulous witness! thou speakest the truth, I know; and yet, Who is he that condemneth?"

And what happens next? Ha! what a sight! The curtain rolls up, the heavens flee; the earth departs; the mountains quake; the hills melt; and the world, with all that is therein, is one flame; and, behold, there stands a throne prepared and decked with all the insignia of terror; and one sits thereupon whose eyes are flames of fire, whose feet are brass, and righteousness His girdle and crown. We know Him, and yet we know Him not; for He is no longer the hunted one, who has not where to lay His head; He is no longer the lamb that is dumb before its shearers. He bears the sceptre of universal dominion; the key of the Almighty, to open and shut heaven and hell at His pleasure ; and His wrath is horrible—a fiery furnace, to consume the adversaries like straw. Whole hosts, thousand times ten thousand are plunged into the abyss of hell, are delivered over to the devils forever—forever—and there is no pity and no mercy !

There are among them the honorable, whose names shine among the benefactors of the nations—"Away with you, I know you not !" There are the lordly ones there, who have won battles, taken cities, blessed kingdoms : "Away with the nobles ! I never knew them !" There are the sanctimonious, against whom no human being dares testify ; who endowed churches and schools ; spent days in praying and singing ; on whom scarcely a speck can be found, so careful and cautious were they : "Away with these sanctimonious ones ! I am displeased with their righteousness ; away ! into eternal fire prepared for the devil and his angels !" Oh, dreadful, horrible ! the hard rocks might well crumble into dust and ashes in dismay. Behold, how the whole atmosphere is full of nothing but howling and gnashing of teeth ; and the arrows of wrath fly by thousands, enough to obscure the light of heaven. And there a man rushes boldly and rapidly through all the din ; steps up to the bar of judgment, lifts his head and cries so that the whole judgment-seat echoes therewith : "Who—who will condemn ?" Who is the presumptuous one ? Who commits this unexampled piece of daring ? Ha ! we know him already ; he has already challenged everything, and now proceeds to the utmost extreme ; he places himself in the light of those eyes which search heart and reins, to see whether they might find aught in him, that they may try to find something against him. "Up ! who dares ? Who will condemn ?" he cries, and there is none to condemn ! The devils curse, the damned shriek over the injustice ; out of hell voices cry : "He was more godless than we."—What boots it ? This godless one goes through free, and there is no one to condemn !

II. Ah! what a glorious condition, to know ourselves irreproachable and justified before God and all creatures; and, in the face of heaven and earth, of God and man, of angels and devils, to be permitted joyfully to exclaim: "Who will condemn?" and find heaven and earth compelled to be silent!

But who may do it? Thou, perhaps?—and thou? Indeed, try it once, and cry, "Who will condemn?" Behold, instead of one, a thousand sentences of condemnation will rattle down upon thy head, and curses will overwhelm thee, as with a terrific shower. Thou art known, friend; thy weak points are observed; thou dwellest among sleeping lions; woe to thee, if they awake; they will devour and tear thee in pieces! These lions are, thy conscience—the Law—and the accuser in hell—the inmates of thine house—and others, too many to name. Only wait until the hearing of the witnesses, and they will all condemn thee. Ha! the sins of thy youth alone would destroy thee, and though no one should condemn thee—we, who only know thee a little, are able to hurl thee down headlong, and by our testimony against thee to draw down the sentence of death upon thy head. Thou, therefore, be quiet, and rejoice that hell has not yet swallowed thee up!

Well, then, who dare say, with Paul: "Who is he that condemneth?" Answer. None, but he who can say with Paul: "Christ is *here*." * This gives the fitness. That is easily seen—is it not? But hold; rejoice not too soon. All depends upon how the little word "here," is to be taken. You think, for example, that if one can only say, "Christ is here"—in the head—that is enough. Indeed, beloved brethren! then all the devils might cry: "Who is he that condemneth?" For, in this sense, they too can say: "Christ is here." I tell you, that that Christ who dwells nowhere else, you may take to hell with you. "What! beautiful views and glimpses, all this clear light and knowledge with us to hell?" Yes, beloved brethren;

* Instead of the words, "It is Christ who died," Luther has, "Christ is *here* who died," though without sufficient authority in the original.

innumerable is the crowd, who, with mere head-knowledge wander to hell. "But how is it, then, if Christ be *here*?"—In the mouth, do you mean? Why, if that were sufficient, the case would not be so hard; we preachers should then have a peculiar advantage, and might dispense with repentance, regeneration, and all such bitter and hateful things; but the Christ that is here, and nowhere else, will not intercede for us in our time of need.

When Paul says, "Christ is *here*," he lays his hand upon his *heart*. Can *you* do that, too? Now, then, cheer up! "Who is he that condemneth?" Just prove it—hand on the heart! Now I ask you before God, what is beneath it? Christ or Belial, and the world? Here the two parties divide. They who cannot say, "I live; yet not I, but Christ liveth in me," they step to the left—they are cursed. The others shout with joy, "Who is he that condemneth?" They may do it, for Christ is *here!*

But now, would you gladly know whether Christ is here or not? The answer is found in the words; a good tree brings forth its fruit in its season. Hear these words: *each fruit in its season.* One must not expect to find the fruits of the new man all together, and at once, at each moment; by so doing we unnecessarily destroy our peace. There are Christians who think, any hour that they set themselves down to seek for the signs of a state of grace in themselves, they must find the same altogether, piece for piece, plainly stamped from number one on. And because this is very seldom the case, they never attain to inward peace: and this is a misunderstanding. "Every fruit *in its season;*" this is the rule here, according to which you must search.

For example, when you stumble, then is the season for the fruit of repentance; see, then, whether it hangs on the tree. When the conscience rages, then is the season when the fruit of longing after the blood of the sacrifice must show itself; observe whether it appears. When a child of God suffers need, then must the sweet grapes of love redden to ripeness. When you are cast among the children of this world, then a certain sense of discomfort, a not-at-home feeling, a certain home-sickness, is the fruit which ought to be found ; according to the saying : " In the world ye shall have tribulation," etc.

He, then, who observes that the tree of his inner man sends forth such heavenly fruits, each in its season, let him not be uneasy that they are not all at all times there ; but rejoice, and say, to the honor of Christ : "Christ is here." It is true that Christ may often retire so far into the depths of the soul, that scarcely a trace of His existence there can be perceived ; but if He is there once, He is there forever. If a regenerate person should again become a natural man, another regeneration by God's Almighty power would be necessary ; but to think such a thing possible would be nonsense. But no Christian has ever so fallen away as that a time never comes, when the leafless tree again puts forth its fruit, and when one could say : " Christ is here." A storm often restores an apparently dead tree to all the lovely bloom of spring. And even should it last until death in this state of decay and saplessness, when this general alarm is sounded, the old soldiers will certainly place themselves in rank and order ; and, like young heroes, march joyfully to Jerusalem under the good old banner of the Lamb.

III. He, then, who can say, "Christ is here," may also say, "Who will condemn ?"

But upon what ground ? This we learn from Paul. On what does he stand, when he gives out his bold challenge, "Who is he that condemneth ?" On works ? Deeds ? Noble feelings, and the like ? God forbid ! The ground on which his feet rest, is, first, a cross ; and then the broken ruins of the grave. He cries, " Christ is here who *died* ; yea, rather, that is *risen* again." Again, with his right hand he points to a throne above, and a priestly sanctuary, and says, " Who is he that condemneth ?

Christ is here that died ; yea, rather, that is risen again, who is even at the right hand of God, who also maketh *intercession* for us." There, you have the whole foundation upon which our guiltlessness and undamnableness rest ; and truly the foundation is adamantine !

We found our confidence, therefore, first of all, on the bloody mount and the timbers of the cross. As truly as my Lord died in this place, so truly am I on this spot freed from condemnation ! On this spot, all the accusations of men and of devils appear to me entirely absurd ;—all the reproaches of conscience falsely applied ;—all the menaces of the law, as mere scare-crows ; —all curses, as false shots. Ask me, and from this place of offering will I send you word : "Is there nothing more wanting ?" No, nothing more at all. "Art thou afraid of no sin ?" No, of none. "Art thou not terrified when thy heart condemns thee ?" God is for me, and He is greater than my heart. "If thou wert without sin, wouldst not thou be more assured than thou art now ?" Not in the least ; my assurance grows not with my sanctification ; it rests on the offering of Christ. "But if thou wert altogether holy, wouldst thou have yet less to fear than now ?" I am entirely holy ; * and aught less than nothing is not conceivable ; and I fear nothing.

Have you any other questions to propose ? Ask on ; we are but too glad to be reminded of these things ; and for the answer we are at no loss. "Yet God is angry at sin ; and should He not also be angry at thine ?" His wrath *has* burned ; this cross is witness. Who hung thereon ? I, in my Head, and drank my curse below. "But may not His wrath be kindled against thee anew ?" I *have* experienced His wrath, in that measure in which I shall deserve it, when the last sin shall have been committed ; consequently the whole sum with which my life concludes, and I give up the ghost. No thought of wrath may move against me more, or God denies himself, and becomes

---

* His idea is, that God sees him IN CHRIST as holy.—TRANS.

unjust, inasmuch as He gives me more than He has threatened, and I have deserved. "Can, therefore, no punishment overtake thee?" No punishment whatsoever—no judgment whatever—no condemnation whatsoever; in short, nothing hostile, for all has been paid off, once for all, upon the cross. And if ever I should go so far—which may God forbid!—that I, who have tasted of the good word of God and the powers of the world to come, should fall away, and crucify the Son of God afresh, and put Him to an open shame, and should become a field bringing forth thorns and briers, and nigh unto cursing; still, notwithstanding all this, no fire could touch me, except such a one as the hand of Love kindles upon me, in order to renew me to repentance. Hear! Hear! This I maintain, that God can never more be displeased with me without being at strife with himself, for the very extremity of His displeasure was poured out upon our bleeding Surety.

So are we delivered forever from all judgment, and from all examinations, suits, and inquisitions: and, hid behind our great Sacrifice we cry: "Who is he that condemneth?" and enter at last—however holy or wicked we may have been—immediately from our death-bed—without stay, circumstances, or ceremonies, into heaven to take our place; and no door-keeper dare presume to subject us to an examination; we are marked on the forehead and the hand with a cross. That is our passport and credential, before which all the police of heaven must bow, and that of hell no less.

But let us not be mistaken, my brethren; our position upon Golgotha would still be insecure, and we only with muffled tones give forth our challenge, "Who is he that condemneth?" if we did not perceive by the side of the cross, that banner of victory which flutters over the *open tomb* of our Head; and if we could not, like Paul, after his "Christ is here, who died," add with exulting joy, "yea, rather, who is *risen* again." If thou art in distress, and shouldst be distrained, and findest a friend to go security for thee, thou wouldst rejoice; but with trembling still, until thou knowest that thy creditor has accepted the security. In like manner, all came to this, that the sacrifice of our representative should be acknowledged, received, and approved by God as valid and sufficient. But behold how, as it were with drums and trumpets, God has proclaimed from heaven His consent and assent, and stamped upon the receipt which was written for us, to acknowledge the payment of Jesus, the impress of a signet which can never be blotted out—namely, in the Resurrection, of our security. If, then, our hope in the sacrifice of Christ be vain and perverted, no one else—I say it with reverence and respect—is responsible, but God himself, who is the author of this hope.

If we regard the satisfaction as insufficient for our salvation, then God must have left our Surety in the grave, or taken Him away secretly, or have intimated the same in some other way ; but could never have made an Easter-day for us, nor presented before our eyes the Surety crowned with such glory ; for from all this pomp and splendor no other conclusion can be drawn than this, that the Almighty is perfectly satisfied with the security given. Were He, then, about to condemn us, we should hold up to Him the stones of the rent rocky tomb, and say : "Lord, these stones testify that Thou thyself hast encouraged us to cast ourselves altogether upon Jesus. Lord ! these stones are the seal which Thou hast affixed to the documents of our atonement. Lord, these stones would cry out because of injustice, if Thou shouldst disappoint the hopes which Thou thyself hast created in us, of thine own accord ;" and truly, even if God hesitated, yet when He looks upon these rocky fragments—by which He has solemnly promised us forgiveness in the wounds of Jesus—*necessity* would be laid upon Him to pronounce us righteous, in order to remain holy, true, and faithful—that is, to remain God. Behold, *such* is the security of our affairs. "Who is he that condemneth ?"

Hear what Paul says : "If Christ be not risen, ye are yet in your sins :" but now, he means to say, ye are no longer in your sins. "How! does Paul mean to say, no more under the curse and wrath?'" No! he means also, no longer in your sins. Oh, mystery of godliness! The risen One are *we*. "Who? We?" Yes, yes, we poor sinners! Not a ray of light that is seen in Him, not a virtue which shines around Him, that is not ours. Behold, how He stands there; a youthful champion upon His open tomb—such we stand before God. Not such we *shall* stand; but such *we stand*. He has suffered—*we also!* He was taken away from judgment—we *with Him!* Nothing damnable rests longer upon Him—nothing damnable upon *us* also. Here is a picture of purity and beauty—*we no less!* He is clothed with nothing but obedience and light; the same light, the same obedience adorns *us*, also. He dares venture, clothed in pure linen, into the light of the Eternal fire-eyes, without any fear lest the least grain of dust should be found upon Him— *we venture, too!* He is the righteousness of God himself; *we are, also*, for His righteousness is given to us. "But our old Adam? What of him?" He lies before God in the grave of an everlasting oblivion. Oh, ecstasy of joy! We are not merely pardoned delinquents; we are beloved and honored saints of God; and as from the cross we should cry, "Who is he that condemneth?" so from the theatre of our Redeemer's triumph, we cry: "Which of you convinceth me of sin?"

And what we cry to-day, the same will we cry to-morrow, and the day after, and on to the end. Everything possible supposed—stumbling and defects, falling away and straying, new sins, and new shame—yet, out of every fall, out of every overthrow, we will venture to cry: "Who is he that condemneth?" Our Surety is not gone far over land; we see Him every moment; and where? in what attitude? We see Him, either as King upon the throne; or near the throne, as Advocate and Intercessor; and joyfully shout: "Christ is here, who not only died and rose again, but who sitteth at the right hand of God, and maketh intercession for us."

If I see Him sitting upon the throne, what, then, have I to

fear from a Judge who is interested to the utmost in my salvation, and who allowed himself to be thrown overboard, rather than let me perish in the storm? My Friend and Brother will not condemn me. I set myself boldly beside Him upon his resting-place, and cling to Him, for we know each other; He is my Shepherd, and I His sheep. If in spirit I behold the Father sitting upon the throne, my Jesus stands close by. Why then should I tremble, when He, who, as God, is God's eternal Son, is my Advocate? If I sin, behold, even before I repent, intercession is made for me. If I fall, lo! ere yet I have risen, Jesus stands for me before God; shows His wounds, which also flowed for me, and says: "If a rod must be broken, break it upon me, this poor sheep cannot perish; this I have promised him." Behold, thus the Surety intercedes for His sinners before the Father—that is, He puts himself in their place; in all cases steps in for them; and inasmuch as the Intercessor is God himself, it is plain of itself, that in the moment in which the advocacy and intercession takes place, it is accepted.

Behold, my brethren, such is the nature of our security. Up! then, and let us enjoy the delights of Easter; and in the presence of our enemies be glad, and rejoice in our victory.

Come, then, all ye who have anything against us! Come on, ye devils out of hell! Ye angels—ye mighty heroes, with your bright, pure, holy eyes! Moses, thou earnest watchman, hither from thy cloudy mount! Come, ye human accusers, ye living and ye dead! Thou internal witness, take thy seat upon thy throne! We will make your work easy, ye hostile spirits! Before ye accuse, we will confess: yes! we *are* altogether vile and corrupt—not a fibre in us that is good—not a breath without sin; the sand of the sea tells our sins and the number of them; Lebanon, that rises up to heaven, their height and weight; the scarlet, their color! Yes, we confess it, from hour to hour, the mountain of our guilt grows higher; its greatness is gigantic! and we have, not once, but a thousand times, deserved curse and damnation. But, nevertheless, what have ye to do with us?

behold under our feet this tree, and these stones ; and, over our head, this royal throne and this priestly seat ! Come on, then ! "Who is he that condemneth ?" Ha ! the curse sticks in your throat ! Away, ye hateful accusers ! Be dumb ! be dumb ! Hark ! a voice of thunder is heard from heaven : "Touch not mine anointed : Speak comfortably to Jerusalem !" Hear ye it ? The tongue must dry up that would judge us. "Who is he that condemneth ?"

"Who is he that condemneth ?" That is our watchword : in want and in death ; in the time of falling and of rising. "Who is he that condemneth ?" "For if when we were enemies we were reconciled to God by the death of his Son, much more, being reconciled, we shall be saved by his life." "And not only so, but we also joy in God through our Lord Jesus Christ, by whom we have received the atonement." Amen.

FRED. AUG. GOT. THOLUCK, D.D.

BIOGRAPHICAL NOTICE.

Dr. Frederic Augustus Gottreu Tholuck, was born at Breslau, the capital of Silesia, on the 30th of March, 1799; so that he is now about sixty years of age. He is of poor and humble parentage, and labored, while a boy, as jeweler, until some friends helped him to enter upon a course of study. He was naturally inclined to pantheism, from which he was saved, in great part, by the influence of the learned Neander. When awakened to the need of Christ, in his twentieth year, and truly converted, he determined to give himself to the profession of theology. At the age of twenty he become Professor at Berlin, and at twenty-seven (1826) he was appointed Professor of Theology at Halle, where he has remained ever since. Through his influence, mainly, this ancient seat of learning was recovered from rationalistic sentiments, which almost exclusively prevailed there a quarter of a century ago.

Professor Tholuck sustains a reputation as Lecturer in Theology, second to that of no one in Germany; but at the same time he is even now a laborious student, writes extensively for religious periodical publications, composes elaborate works, and preaches at least once in two weeks, to the members of the University. It is only by habits of the most rigid regularity and caution that he keeps soul and body together.

The published writings of Professor Tholuck are very numerous; among which are several volumes of Sermons, and Commentaries on different parts of the Bible. The chief peculiarities of his discourses are, a remarkable elevation and richness of evangelical sentiment; no display of abstruse thought or dry discussion; liveliness and exuberance of fancy; vigor, sprightliness, and boldness of expression and a peculiar fervor, and tenderness, and childlike simplicity, which warm and attract every pious heart.

Professor Tholuck has had no children, and is exceedingly attached to the students; perhaps the more warmly from the fact alluded to. He not only freely invites them to his house and table, but almost invariably has some of them at his side in his morning and evening walks for recreation, whom he entertains by his wit, wins by his affections, rouses to thought by odd and startling questions, and edifies by his piety.

In personal appearance, Professor Tholuck is modest, unprepossessing, and quite original. He is of delicate, stooping frame, medium size, meagre and emaciated, extremely nervous and excitable, and at times almost blind by excessive study. A recent writer from Germany says of him: "Although it may be true, as some maintain who heard him twenty years ago, that his eloquence has lost a little of its brilliancy and edge, it must have gained in depth and subdued pathos, more than an equivalent for what it has lost. Nay, one should not speak of loss; it is a result of growth—the brilliant flower is not lost; it ripens into solid, luscious fruit. It is a repetition of the same process of development by which the impetuous 'Son of thunder' matured into the white-haired 'Apostle of love.'"

The Sermons which follow will convey some idea of the originality and freshness of his thoughts, and the richness of his eloquence.

DISCOURSE XV.

THE BETRAYAL OF JESUS.

BELOVED FRIENDS: We have with our Saviour fought through the fight in Gethsemane, and our eyes have seen him marching in the van victorious. As the uprising sun, before which a morning tempest had suddenly encamped, after its thunder was spent, mounts majestically in the heavens—unclouded and spotless—so walked he forth from the inclosures of the garden. With like dignity we see him standing again in presence of his betrayer and his judges. And yet in this day's discourse we intend not to leave the spot where the bloody sweat had fallen, and where, through the lonely night, there thrice rang out, in earnest tones, those memorable words, "Father, not my will but thine be done." Our purpose now is to direct attention to the last address made by our Saviour to the traitor. It is to be found in Luke, xxii. 47, 48.

"And while he yet spake, behold a multitude, and he that was called Judas, one of the twelve, went before them and drew near to Jesus to kiss him. But Jesus said unto him, Judas, betrayest thou the Son of man with a kiss?"

Let us first glance at the act of the traitor—at the cunning, the inward compunction, and the deep turpitude evinced therein ; and then at the words of our Lord—at the serenity, the love, the majesty which they manifest.

A long struggle, perhaps of many weeks, yea, it may be, of months, came to its decisive close at that moment, when Jesus extended to Judas the sop, and to the disciple who lay on his bosom, replied, "He it is to whom I shall give the sop, when I have dipped it." "And after the sop," it is said, "Satan entered into him." So long as he kept up the conflict with his black thoughts, he was still in the power of God—now advancing—now retreating. But from the moment the resolve ripened, he fell wholly under Satan's control, and at every step trod the sloping path down towards the abyss. He goes out into the night—and what a contrast !—there in the lighted chamber they are celebrating the last feast of love ; and he—he goes out into the *night*—and unto the children of night. Already had the preliminary arrangements been made, and there only remained the execution.

Now mark, in the first place, the *cunning* of the act. As a general rule, it is admitted, that "the children of this world are wiser in their generation than the children of light." The serpent in Paradise was also crafty. Alas ! that when once the heart has been enslaved to sin, the noble gift of reason, which God has given man, should also become degraded to the same vile service ; and that, instead of that *wisdom*, which it is ever wont to produce while the heart remains true to God, it should generate only policy—a policy which works in the service of hell. Oh, be not deceived, ye who imagine, that by reason and science ye will be able to secure yourselves from sin. "Where your treasure is, there will your heart be also," said the Saviour ; and where your heart, the inmost tendency of your will is, there will your reason be. And know ye unto what ends it will serve ? *Before* the commission of your deed, it will devise the necessary means for its accomplishment ; *during* its commission, it will spread a veil over its enormity ; *after* its commission, when conscience begins to storm, its business will be to lull it to silence by crafty apologies and lying justifications. These are the ends it will serve. So was it with Judas. Because his heart was not right with God, therefore was his reason blind to the *nature* of the act he was on the point of perpetrating.

It was not, however, blind to the *means* necessary for its execution. He decides to act under cover of night. This was sagacious both for the sake of his enterprise, and for the sake of his conscience. It was sagacious for his enterprise ; for had it been undertaken by day, how many swords, besides that of Peter, would have leaped from their scabbards in Christ's defence? The Saviour had servants who would not have hesitated a moment to risk their lives in his behalf. But the prudent traitor chose for his work the time "when men slept." And the time when men sleep, is the chosen time for the enemy to sow tares. This was also politic in regard of his conscience. "If I can only betray him in his sleep," thought he to himself, "then there will be no need of looking him in the eye." And would not this be an advantage gained? It is, indeed, a shameful betrayal, to surrender a friend—and in this case, how much, yea many, many times more than a friend—into the hands of his enemies while asleep. But how can it be helped, if conscience be so cowardly that it dare not look the man in the eye? "Betray him in sleep." Ah, that is a wise thought. The friends of Jesus betrayed, and at the same time, one's own consciences.

But this first contrivance, at least, miscarries. In the house through which the way to the garden runs, Judas is informed that the eye of the dreaded was awake—that Jesus was with the disciples in the garden. How now, Judas? How wilt thou now secure thy prey? How cheat thy conscience? Cunning must invent some new plan. What the cowardly soul expects of itself, that it expects also from the Lord. Judas fears his flight. How shall he make sure of his prey? It will not do to approach him with the audible sounds of treachery—he may not call aloud, "This is he—seize him." Softly must he steal on his way, unsuspected, like the snake gliding under the grass. The armed troop remain behind at the garden door, and the traitor advances alone, as if it were the visit of a friend at the

13*

hour of night. Ah, Judas ; amid all these various manœuvres, has nothing within, meanwhile, spoken to thee ? When the first step failed, was there no rebuke of conscience ?

Sin ever treads upon uncertain ground. Especially is it wont to take alarm, and feel insecure after the first effort has miscarried. It takes long years of hardening, before the sinner comes to feel the ground so firm beneath his tread as not to tremble at his first failure. Novices in crime cannot endure to be thus frustrated ; they are startled by it, and fancy they see the ministers of God's justice close at their heels. They shrink back at every step, as if there were traps right and left, and each moment brought them to an abyss. Here you perceive how difficult it is for the sinner to rid himself of the conviction, that sin has no right in the world—that it is already judged—that the divine administration has set a curse upon it, that it is nowhere safe, and exists only as an outlaw. Judas, art thou only a novice in the business, or hast thou learned to flout thy conscience ? Oh, couldst thou not even then have paused to reflect and amend, when thou foundest awake and watchful the eye of Him whom thou didst hope to arrest in sleep ? Couldst thou not then have discerned the finger of thy God directing thy notice within ? Alas ! it is all in vain. Conscience may have spoken never so loud ; for Judas its voice was but a challenge to exert himself the more skillfully to deceive it, as he proceeded.

Observe ye not, how in this kiss of Judas, there is evinced a cunning which would fain not only deceive Jesus, but even his own conscience itself ? That kiss shows conclusively, that he had entered upon this whole work of treachery with great inward compunctions, and that as he encountered the waking eye of his Lord, these compunctions stung him more deeply to the quick. That kiss was a token of respect and love, and with it he hoped to lay his rebuking conscience asleep. But there was also another advantage counted on. Judas thought by his greeting to avoid the necessity of encountering in Jesus the eye of a Judge, and to enjoy the chance of once more beholding in Him, as a friend, a friend's look. But, Judas, hast thou then, the heart to look into the eye of thy *friend*, when thou darest not meet the eye of thy *Judge*? Oppressive enough may even this effort have been to him ; but oh, would that he had chosen not to take a last look at all into that eye, neither as being the eye of a judge, nor as being the eye of a friend. Still, there was no other choice. Perhaps, you think, he never understood that expression of exalted love in Christ. Oh, had this been the case, then would his guilt have proved infinitely less. But, no. Traitor as he was, he had belonged to the number of those whom the Father had drawn to the Son, and therefore is his guilt so heavy. "These that thou gavest me I have kept," says the Saviour, "and none of them is lost, but the son of perdition." So, then, even Judas had been given by the Father to the Saviour, and the Father had drawn him to the Son ; but he would not suffer himself to be drawn ; and it is precisely this which makes his deed so dark. Yet, even then, some gleam of Heaven's light might have shone upon him from out the eye of Jesus ; but the sin in progress gives the lie to any hope of favor, even had it dawned. Afterwards, however, when the deed is done, it vindicates again its own right. That heaven's light then becomes a fire-brand in his bosom ; and that fire-brand he took into his soul with this last look. In the subsequent anguish of his despair, this last look into the eye of Jesus finds utterance. "I have betrayed innocent blood. I have betrayed innocent blood." There, you see how the innocent blood is turned into a sea of fire, which has rolled up its flames within his heart, and it was this last holy, mild look of Jesus which testified to that innocence.

Thus it is seen, that even though man may part from his conscience, it nevertheless does not part from him. Oh, if there be any among you who have forsaken conscience, even though it may not be altogether, but only in reference to some one particular lust, and if you discover that conscience has not forsaken you, oh, recognize therein, I entreat you, the good angel of God

And, Judas, even so, thou mayest still recognize it ; thou mayest
yet retreat. When the rebuking glance of love smote Peter
after his denial, then " he went out, and wept bitterly." And,
Judas, thou mayest still do likewise. But, alas ! how much
more difficult had this become for him now, than it was an hour
before ; now, there is a host of bailiffs in the rear ; and accomplices in his own crime bar retreat. With every step forward,
the path of sin grows more precipitous ; each act committed,
yea, the very warnings of conscience itself, those good angels of
God, turn into avenging furies, which drive the man onwards
with increasing velocity. Now, the entire host of the ministers
of justice are behind Judas. The very steps which the man has
taken in his evil course, become the officers which are to arrest
him, if he wishes to turn back ; and which now keep urging
him to the end, even though it might be against his will. And
this *involuntariness* in iniquity, is it not one of the most fearful
aspects of human wickedness ?

The fact of Judas betraying the Son of Man with the token
of reverence and love, while it testifies to his compunctions at
the deed, also gives proof of its deep *turpitude*. Every step
onward in his course of sin—yea, the very means employed to
purchase quiet of conscience, becomes even more reprehensible
and monstrous. That sweet token, consecrated among all mankind to love—to take just this, and use it as a signal for treachery—who does not shudder at the deed ? Does not sin appear
to us all the more horrible—and justly, too—when it adopts
sacred means for its unhallowed objects. Theft, by a reprobate
child, assassination in the church, poisoning by means of the
consecrated wafer, even such is betrayal by a kiss. It is the
deceit, the hypocrisy in the thing, which shocks us, although
it must be said in the instance before us, that a rude act of
violence perpetrated by a disciple of Jesus, would have been
still more revolting. Oh, Judas, what a firebrand to thy conscience must this kiss of thine have become ! Thou child of
perdition, say, when thou just touchedst those sacred lips, which,

by means of this thy kiss, were seen to turn pale in death, did there not come up to remembrance before thee those precious moments, when thou stoodest listening to words issuing from that holy mouth—such as no other human lips ever spake to thee?—moments when thou couldst look into that holy, mild eye, without fear of conscience, and with a heart most blessed. Ah, yes, that kiss, it could not but have been a firebrand for thy conscience.

Let us now turn our saddened glance away from this deed, to apply the words of our Saviour on the occasion to ourselves. We saw Him arising a few moments before in deepest agitation of spirit from His bitter conflict in the garden. And now mark the deep, divine repose evinced in the language with which He received the traitor. "Judas, betrayest thou the Son of Man with a kiss?" There is no ebullition of anger here; indeed, no ebullition of passion ever disturbed the placid mirror of that holy soul, but there is not even an expression of sorrow over that bitter cup, which, with and through that kiss, was presented to His lips. He looks not at himself, but only at the lost child; He considers not His own suffering, but only the crime of His betrayer. Perceive ye not already in these words what a deep calm had followed upon the loud storm? what undisturbed repose had succeeded to the mighty commotion that had agitated His breast. Here, again, we become impressed with that appearance of mystery, which His wonted repose of manner, and perfect self-possession ever imparted to all His words and deeds through life.

It is the last word He ever exchanges with this son of perdition, and this is still a word of love. And there had been so many words of love! yet, like drops of water falling on hot stones, they had become dissipated in a moment. Already had Christ bidden him, "What thou dost, do quickly;" and does it not seem as if with these words Jesus had given up the wretched disciple for lost! as if the Saviour had thereupon dismissed him to hell? But He has for him yet one word of questioning love.

He might, indeed, instead, have hurled into his soul one questioning word of thunder ; He might have called down upon him
a woe of horror, but, He chides not, He imprecates not, He only
asks ; and may we not say, that, so long as a *question* is put to
the soul, there is an *answer* from it possible ? that at least some
echo of it might be heard in the deep recesses of the heart?
That most fearful word in the sinner's life—"Too late"—even
up to this time, the Lord does not seem to have spoken it
respecting Judas ; although we might have looked for it after
hearing that order : "What thou doest, do quickly."

In like manner, the merifcul heart of the Saviour still inter-
rogates every child of perdition—even though he may be standing on the very verge of destruction ; and so long as Jesus continues to question, so long then is an answer possible—a way
to return open.   Oh, ye who have not hitherto hearkened to his
questions, would that ye might, even at the last moment, give
ear to them. But alas ! it happens, that for those who have heard,
again, and again—but all to no purpose—the very ability to
hear grows so dull—so dull that the questions of Jesus sound
in the soul only as muffled thunder-peals. And these questions
of love have no more the power to *waken*—but only to *alarm*.
And how sad is the impression, when we recount those affectionate appeals, which, from the beginning onward, God addresses, during a whole life, to the heart of one who has wandered from the path of righteousness, and become apostate. At
the outset there was the modest, and partially-decided "Yes,
Lord," audibly responded ; then in proportion as sin became
bolder, this "yes" would grow more uncertain and feeble, and
at last, how it dies away altogether, or is changed into a defiant
"No." When the Lord, on an earlier occasion, put the question
to the disciples, "Will ye also go away ?" then Judas could understand it, and could give it the right answer. That was the first
question of love. Oh, how did his heart appear at this LAST !

It was no thunder tone of denunciation—it was no impreca-
tion of woe, which the Lord poured forth on Judas. There was

love with him still—nay, if you please, a certain degree of confidence preserved in this warning question. But along with this, how distinctly also is wounded majesty heard to speak. There is here no weak, sentimental love. Jesus does not say, "Oh, thou dear disciple, how could you do this to your dear Master?" The words are few and earnest, and they bear the impress of a majestic, yet dishonored, royal love—"Judas, betrayest thou the Son of man with a kiss?" That which we just now perceived to be the height of enormity in this act of treachery, viz.: the desecration of the universally consecrated token of love into a cover for treason—this in particular is it which the Saviour here seizes upon and holds up to view; and still further, he alludes to the special dignity of Him, who was given over to death by this token. Human relations here receded into the back-ground. Though it is the Friend—the public Benefactor, who is betrayed —yet of all this not a word. "Thou hast betrayed the *Son of Man*"—the man without spot or sin—Him through whom alone human nature obtains its proper humanity.

See with what majesty the Lord speaks of himself. He plants the traitor, not before a human tribunal, but before the throne of God; for it is not merely against human hearts, and human feelings that he is transgressing, but it is against the heart of God himself—since he was betraying the only begotten of the Father. Just at the moment when human feelings in the Saviour might have obtained the readiest utterance—then spake out in Him only the feeling of violated majesty. Ah, that word could be for Judas no more an angel of deliverance: for this it was too late; and because it could not be for him an angel of deliverance, it became for him an angel of vengeance. It brought the entire weight of his guilt down upon his conscience at once—even the guilt of treason against the great King. When that conscience cried, "Thou hast betrayed innocent blood"—then was he forced to add, "and that innocent blood was the blood of the Son of man—the Saviour of Israel; and under the garb of love didst thou betray him"

And what does all this teach us? Does it apply only to criminals, and not at all to such righteous people as we are? Is there, then, no one among us who is seeking to betray his conscience? Have you never discovered that, as with Judas, so with you, every step in sin turns behind you into an executioner of Justice, which draws you onward in your headlong course? Have you not heard those questions of love from Jesus, which follow the sinner even until he stands but one remove from the abyss? Are there none here who have become—and are daily acting the part of traitors to the love of the Son of Man? We may not, perhaps, have approached so near the abyss, upon that precipitous path along which Judas plunged—yet it must be said that every man is on that path, who betrays his conscience, or is wittingly a traitor against the love of the Son of man. Oh, ye secure ones—ye who, as often as the divine call, "To-day if ye will hear his voice," presses on your heart, begin to storm, and say, "To-morrow will be time enough," oh, let that word of alarm, "Too late," fall with fresh force on your conscience. Learn from the instance of Judas, how when a man despises the grace of Jesus, God's angels of deliverance become to his hardened heart the ministers of vengeance. Behold in his example, how a sinner, who has rushed onwards, careless, and secure, without reflection, when he comes to the precipice and *desires* to retreat, can go back no more, but is hurried over into the abyss below, by the very despair of his own conscience. He that hath ears to hear let him hear! He that hath ears to hear let him hear!

DISCOURSE XVI.

THE CHRISTIAN LIFE, A GLORIFIED CHILDHOOD.

BRETHREN in Christ, what a beautiful characteristic is it of our faith, that it is so simple in itself, and begets in us a like simplicity. Where, outside the sphere of the Gospel, do we hear *singleness of heart* praised as a high virtue. To us, nevertheless, who are in Christ, this divine simplicity shines with the brilliancy of a jewel, as the crown of all virtues, without which the rest appear dull and dim.

The Gospel makes us single-minded, when it proclaims to us that "*one* thing is needful," and, together with this, imparts an inclination towards the one eternal magnet and centre, to which all our endeavors should be directed. It carries on the work also, when, after that God in Christ has become the centre of our efforts, it again simplifies all our virtues and duties, by summing them up in this one injunction: "Become as little children." Where, in all antiquity, have you heard a precept like this? And does it not sound to your hearts as a greeting from home? Does it not move upon your souls, awakening there holiest longings and sweetest anticipations?

This happy destiny of Christians to become as children, let us this day once more bring before our contemplation; and consider anew the so-often heard, but, alas! so often forgotten precept of our Lord in Matt. xviii. 3 :

"Verily, I say unto you, except ye be converted, and become as little children, ye shall in nowise enter the kingdom of heaven."

The Christian life is a glorified childhood: such is the truth which these words teach us.

That in childhood certain attributes are manifested which exhibit to us the fundamental tendencies of a Christian spirit, is inferrible from the fact that our Lord at several times, and in various though kindred aspects, set before His disciples little children as their example. And does it not readily occur to you that what the Apostle Paul affirms of love, viz.: "It believeth all things, it endureth all things, it hopeth all things," involves just the conception we form of a truly good and pious child? Indeed, may we not say, that so far as it regards the three ground-tones of the Christian life, good children might be taken as our instructors, viz.: as teachers in *Faith*, teachers in *Love*, teachers in *Hope?* For a general apprehension of the meaning of our Lord's precepts, I certainly know of no statement more expressive than this, that good children are to be our examples in *faith, love,* and *hope.*

It will be understood, meanwhile, that the comparison here does not hold good in all respects. That in the child, as well as in the adult, the old Adam, the poison of selfishness, exists from its earliest unfolding, is a truth well known ; and we may not suffer ourselves to be deceived in regard to it, by the evil appearing in forms which belong to that sphere in which childhood lives and moves. Whether it be the mighty conqueror, who, from envy ravages whole territories with violent hand, or the child, who, from envy, spoils its playmate's toys, the old Adam is the same, even though it is clad in a child's garb. Accordingly, the language of our Saviour cannot be taken as exhorting us to become children in all points ; and at the very outset, we are to bear in mind, that in the stage of childhood there also exists something which we are not permitted to transfer into our Christian life. This fact has also been set forth with sufficient definiteness by the Apostle where he says ; "Brethren, be not children in understanding ; howbeit, in malice be ye children, but in understanding be ye men." From this you perceive why we are not at liberty to say absolutely—the Christian life is a childhood, but are obliged to add the qualification, a glorified childhood. With the assistance of our Saviour, let us now proceed to consider more closely the nature of this glorified childhood, as it manifests itself in the *faith*, in the *love*, and in the *hope* of the Christian.

The Christian life is a glorified childhood in FAITH. *The child confides in his superiors unhesitatingly;* he trusts, nothing doubting, his parents and teachers. Is there, I ask, a more touching sight than to see a group of children, who, with thirsty, inquiring eyes, are hanging to their mother, or to their father, and imbibing every word from those hallowed lips as a gospel. Nothing, I am sure, would prompt me to strive, whatever my creed might be, with more earnestness and greater conscientiousness after religious truth, than to be planted in the midst of a company of child-like hearts. In conversation with adults, I think to myself, " They need not take all I say on trust ; they can see for themselves, whether I am giving them bread, or a stone." But the little darlings, they cannot be so discerning ; they are entirely confident that they are receiving from me nothing but bread. Oh, thrice cursed be that man, who gives children a stone instead of bread ! Well has the old German proverb said : " He who deceives a child, is as if he had ravished a virgin." For are not children's souls virgin-souls ?

As now children trust, without suspicion, their superiors who speak to them, so do we, whom the Son of God has purchased with his precious, noble blood, have like faith in our Lord. Woe to him who sows distrust in the soul of the child towards the word of its mother. Cursed also be he who plants a doubt of our Lord in our souls. We hang on him with a true, thirsting eye ; let other masters, if they choose, give their disciples stones for bread—a serpent for fish—a scorpion for an egg ; the word of our Lord is always the bread of life—whether I understand it or not. If I understand it, then it nourishes me. If I understand it not, then is there something stored up for me in the future. At any rate, this I am certain of, from the mouth of my Lord no other word has ever flowed but a word of life. He who has attained to this child-like faith in his Lord, is like one who has run in from a wide sea into a safe haven.

This faith of the child we are speaking of, is a precious stone—a diamond—but it is not yet polished; therefore, it does not glisten. The child does not know *why* it believes, and therefore it becomes the prey of error; *the natural child-faith is a faith without light.* Hence, again, the exhortation of the Apostle: "Be no more children tossed to and fro by every wind of doctrine." The blind child-faith is that which believes, because others *have believed and testified.* The *glorified* child-faith is that which believes because it has *known.* The blind child-faith is that of the Samaritans, when they believed in the word of the woman who said to them, "Come, see a man who told me all things that ever I did: is not this the Christ?" The glorified child-faith is that which these same expressed afterwards, when they said, "Now we believe, not because of thy saying, for we have heard him ourselves, and know that this is indeed Christ, the Saviour of the world." The blind child-faith was that of Peter, when he believed his brother Andrew, as he told him, "We have found the Messias." The glorified child-faith is that with which Peter afterwards spoke, "We have believed and have known, that thou art Christ, the Son of the living God."

Listen, ye youth; here you have a knowledge of the great object of faith, which is not learned from parchment, nor acquired in the lecture-rooms and in the schools; for it existed long before your lecture rooms were built, and your schools were founded; yea, ere yet books were written in vindication of the faith, did glorified child-like souls exclaim, "We have believed and known, and have sealed this witness with our blood." I am here speaking of that knowledge which comes from the light obtained in that school, where we all have been trained—both learned and unlearned—even the school of experience. All of us alike once *believed* the great history of our Redemption, as it was pressed on our ear from the lips of trusted fathers and mothers. Now have we come to *know* it, because it has stood the test of experience. That is to say, we have found therein the key to the great problem of the human heart ; for it has conferred the light of truth on our intelligence, and a new power of sanctification has it imparted to our wills, inasmuch as grace has effected what no law of the world could accomplish ; it has made it sweet for us to hate ourselves, and to give ourselves daily unto death, and it has caused us to taste in our own consciousness something of the powers of the future unseen world. So we still hang on his lips with good confidence like little children ; and as often as he speaks, each blessed word he utters calls forth in our hearts the responsive Amen. And since we have come to be trained in the school of experience, we can also say, that we *know* what has been delivered to us through Him.

The Christian life is a glorified childhood in LOVE. *The child loves with an affection that is without distinction.* Does not the child approach every man with confidence ? and is not confidence, in all cases, a bond of attraction and of love ? Let there be but a human eye—a human face—and the child smiles on it ; it loves without distinction. The child of the prince reaches out after the hand of the beggar ; the wise child will permit itself to be led by the hand of a simpleton ; the pious child will cling to the breast of a villain :—although in this case, indeed, it sometimes happens very wonderfully that a direct inner voice awakens in the child's heart most of all an anxious suspicion and fearful dread ; the proximity of a dark spirit is not merely *known*, it is at times also felt by it.

And now may not we also say, that we Christians love, as children, without distinction ? Truly to us likewise is every human face a holy thing ; only in this respect we have an advantage over the child ; for as the child believes without light, so also does it love without wisdom. It understands not why it so loves mankind, and is therefore as blind in its love as in its faith. But we in whom the love of humanity has been ennobled by the

Spirit of the Lord—we know why it is we should love mankind without distinction. With glorified vision we read upon every human brow the inscription — that solemn inscription which makes every human countenance sacred—" God hath made of one blood all nations of men, that they should seek the Lord, if haply they might feel after him, and find him though he be not far from every one of us."

Do ye read this superscription, my hearers, do ye read it upon the forehead of all your friends—your relations—your domestics —yea, do you read it abroad among the ragamuffins, with whom misery and vice has obscured the lettering? Is it not so, that every man appears other than I represent him—other than an immortal spirit who is able to find God? But when *the* glorified love has entered the heart, this knows at once *wherefore* it loves man ; and it knows, too, *unto what ends* it loves him. Oh, man, is this thy nobility, that thou art a creature, capable of seeking and finding God? how then can I evince my love to thee better than by helping thee to seek God? Alas ! how feebly is it re- cognized—how rarely do people consider, that, in all our com- munications there is no service of love we can render each other more essential, than to assist in seeking and finding God. It is a a blind, a carnal, and not *the* glorified love, which we cherish, when we love men without any reference to this eternal end of their creation. Always should it be our aim, in our social inter- course, to keep alive and manifest some reference to that great object for the attainment of which we are here upon the earth.

From this duty no one present can rightly exempt himself: not even thou, my brother, who art complaining that it is not in thy power to help any one. In such a case, thou thyself canst not yet have found thy true aim. No, not even thou ; for if thou hast not discovered that, which thy brethren summon thee to help them seek, canst thou not declare, dear brother, at least what thou *hast*—yea, more, confess what is *lacking*? for even this will prove a blessing to thyself and others. By means of thy very doubting will thy brother's faith be made clearer—and the

stones of thy stumbling will prove building stones for the structure of his truth.   Oh, let there not, then, be this reserve in
regard to the highest concerns of humanity among men, who
have sprung from one blood, and are travelling to one end.   And
is it not something unnatural beyond measure—deny it who can
—when among Christians, who call Christ their Saviour, the
cheeks are observed to blanch the moment a person begins to
speak earnestly of this Saviour, and when men at once sink
their voice to a whisper as often as they mention God ?

If now that *glorified* love for all men, without distinction,
manifests itself in this, that it strives to lead them to God—yet
it lies in its very nature to make some distinctions also—and
this *out* of love, because otherwise it cannot conduct to God.
The eternal distinctions, which the word of God himself makes,
between truth and falsehood, light and darkness, the children of
this world and the children of the kingdom—these we cannot
wipe out.   Away with that insipid, carnal love, which never has
the force to exercise a moral judgment.   True, we must leave it
to the Searcher of hearts to judge the heart—but it is ours to
judge respecting word and deed, so surely as it stands written :
"Try the spirits, whether they be of God."   That inward shudder, with which the otherwise so artless child, shrinks from a
face on which sensuality, pride, revenge, has stamped its impress,
is it not to us something holy ?—does it not seem like an inspiration of the Deity ?

How then ?   This moral judgment in the child, which reminds
us of the denunciatory woes of a loftier spirit, ought it not to
be exercised by us also—by us to whom this spirit has imparted
a glorified love ?   Yea, verily, we *must* exercise it.   Unto the day
must we say, "Thou art day ;" and unto the night we declare,
"Thou art night."   We must make distinctions.   Only be it
remembered that, when love makes distinctions, it makes them
for the purpose of removing them.   We say to sinners, "ye
stand without," but it is to draw them within ; we say, "ye are
fallen," but it is that they may look round for the hand that

shall lift them up ; we say, " ye are the enemies of God," but it
is in order to be able to preach at the same time, " Be ye reconciled to God." " Knowing, therefore, the terror of the Lord,"
says the Apostle, " we persuade men ; but we are made manifest
unto God." Behold here, that glorified love, with which the
Christian life embraces everything which is human.

The child-life is a life in HOPE. *It hopes without bounds.* The
child perceives in the present no thorns ; and so it is capable of
abandoning itself without reserve to the floral beauty which
greets its vision on every side—and should it, indeed, cast a
glance into the future, even there it only sees reflected the
flowers of the present. How lovely, also, does the child appear
before us in this its hopefulness ! As for the adult, to whom the
present has furnished so many thorns, with what sadness does he
observe them strewed into the far distance along the whole
course of the future—and in his crystal tears how does every
individual sorrow multiply itself a thousand fold ! What a
refreshment is it, therefore, to the heart to see for once a man, a
child, that can so cordially hope ! Joyous hope makes a person
so amiable !

Now, whatever is amiable in the child's life—its believing, its
loving, and so also its hoping—all this, fellow Christians, has the
grace of Christ offered to you—and it proffers it to you in a glorified form. That ceaseless hoping, indeed, as childhood hath it,
is no more the hope with which the disciple of Jesus looks into
the future ; as the faith of the child is without light, as its love
is without wisdom, so also is its hope without foundation. But
of us, who have become children in Christ Jesus, the word of
God demands that we be "ready to give to every man that
asketh us, a reason of the hope that is in us." It is essential,
then, to the Christian hope, that we know *why we hope.* Accordingly, let me first ask you—have you become children in Christ
Jesus ?

Have you also *this* seal of your adoption, that you can with *a
right hearty hope* look out upon the whole course of the future as

it lies before you?—yea, even away beyond the dark limits which separate between time and eternity? Christians are children of hope, for they trust in Christ—who, as the apostle says, is in his own person "the hope of glory." Christians are children of hope, for, as the apostle says, "The God of hope has filled them with all joy." Christians are children of hope, for, as the apostle says, "God, according to His abundant mercy, hath begotten them again into a lively hope."

> Faith lays the foundation,
>   Love the rising structure builds;
> Hope puts on the top-stone,
>   Then scans aloft the eternal fields!

Yet once more, have ye become children in Christ Jesus—go to, then! Prove that this holy hope dwells in your hearts, even a hope which can look out upon the whole path before you with the fullest composure and trust—even to the latest end. Yet further—dear brethren, let me ask is our hope, in like manner as our faith, and our love, *a glorified* hope? Can ye tell on what foundation it rests? Here, remember, I am not speaking of that unconcerned carelessness, with which a trifling spirit glances into the future. Christians are not men who do not *care*, but men who *cast their care upon the Lord*. Christians are not men who see no thorns upon the track of life. Oh, no; they are men who perhaps see far more thorns than all others do; but they are men who know from their own experience, that where Christ's grace is granted, all thorns at last swell and burst open into roses. In short, Christians are men who believe in the words, "If God be for us, who can be against us? He that spared not His own son but delivered Him up for us all, how shall He not with Him also freely give us all things?" Observe here the foundation of the Christian hope. He who spared not His own Son for our sakes, must be cherishing kind intentions toward us; and, if a man would tread his path in hope, he can properly require for this nothing more than the hearty, well-

14

grounded conviction—"God means well with me—God has thoughts of peace toward me."

O ye, who are wandering in the world without hope, without any clear, joyful out-look into the future of time—as well as into that of eternity, let me say, you are wanting in nothing so much as in the hearty and assured consciousness—"God means well with me." And why are you wanting in this? It is because the Holy Spirit has not yet sealed upon your hearts the truth, "that God was in Christ reconciling the world unto himself." He, who can declare it, not simply with his mouth, and to whom in the inmost depths of his soul it has become a strong verity—that God has followed erring man into the very thorns of life—*he*, I say, must be a man of joyful hope. Christians are men for whom this is a solemn truth; yea, and not only this; in their hearts the love of God is poured forth like a stream, as the Apostle says—"And hope maketh not ashamed because the love of God is shed abroad in our hearts—by the Holy Ghost which is given unto us."

Who will wonder then if Christians are a joyous people as children are? How much rather ought we to be astonished at ourselves, if we are still sad! No. The Christian life is a transfigured childhood: Like children, we believe without suspicion; like children, we love without distinction; like children, we hope without limitation; and together with this has the Spirit of grace given to our faith, *light;* to our love, *wisdom,* and to our hope *an everlasting foundation.* Honor—and praise—and worship be unto Him who hath done such great things for us. Amen

DISCOURSE XVII.

THE TOUCHSTONE OF HUMAN HEARTS.

Those of us who have had much acquaintance with Christians, especially with those of the olden time, will have observed how customary it was for them to confirm remarkable experiences of the spiritual life, with the saying : "Then was again fulfilled what the Scripture saith." Such, too, was the habit of the Apostles, and in just this sense did they often refer to the words of the Old Testament. Herein, then, is exhibited a deep conviction of the world-wide comprehensiveness of the truth of God's word. Of this broad character is whatever stands on record, respecting the doings of man, or the ways of God, more particularly during the period of our Lord's manifestation on earth ; so that along the course of history, we are prompted ever and anon to exclaim : "There has the Scripture been fulfilled." With one such expression will our meditations this day be occupied— with a Scripture saying, which first proved true in the history of Christ, and has again and again been verified through all subsequent times. I refer to the prophetic exclamation of the aged Simeon, when, in the days of the legal purification, the parents brought the child Jesus, for the first time to the temple. It is found in Luke ii. 34, 35 : "And Simeon blessed them, and said unto Mary his mother, Behold, this child is set for the fall and rising again of many in Israel ; and for a sign which shall be spoken against. Yea, a sword shall pierce through thine own soul also, that the thoughts of many hearts may be revealed."

We will first explain the entire passage, and then direct your attention particularly to its last clause. It is hardly possible to imagine a more solemn scene bearing the impress of substantial truth, than that into which these words of the Evangelist translate us. The bare thought of that little company, which, as we are told, had gathered about the child Jesus, is enough to awaken in us the liveliest emotions. It is said that there were assembled there those who were "waiting for the consolation of Israel." These, of course, were but a small fraction of the great multitude then gathering in Jerusalem—a select few only, in whose hearts there burned this one desire : "That the Deliverer would come out of Zion, and take away ungodliness from us." The number could not have been large, and most of these, it is likely, were aged people. Simeon and Hannah, at least, were far advanced in years. A touching thought is it, also, that they oftentimes found themselves collected precisely here in the temple, in order to pray in company. Besides, to Simeon was it expressly promised, that he should not die before he had seen the salvation of the Lord. And now the long-desired child of heaven approaches, borne upon the arm of its mother. But how are they to recognize it ? It is, indeed, a holy thing, but no halo of glory surrounds its head. It is a king without a diadem. The grace of God, nevertheless, resolves the difficulty. To Simeon is the truth supernaturally revealed. Under the impulse of the divine Spirit, he now advances, and significantly addresses himself, not to the father, but to the mother. It is no sweet, flattering speech, however ; no bright, smiling vision of future triumphs which he utters. Simeon calls the babe a rock ; but a rock whereon a part of Israel would be broken. His prophetic eye also discerns the sword, which should, ere long, pierce the mother's aching heart, in order, as he says, *"that the thoughts of many hearts might be revealed."* With these words, which refer particularly to that time when the sword actually pierced the mother's heart, the prophetic speech concludes. We lay them at the foundation of our now-commencing series of discourses, and derive from them this doctrine :

THE MANIFESTATION OF CHRIST IS THE TOUCHSTONE OF HUMAN HEARTS, THROUGH WHICH IS FIRST REVEALED WHAT IS IN EVERY MAN.

Let us consider this subject, first, in its more general aspect, and then as it is particularly manifest in the history of our Lord's passion.

The manifestation of Christ is the touchstone of human hearts, by which that which is in every man is first clearly revealed. There are some, but not many, who have the power of readily detecting what is in men. Almost every individual knows what is in himself. But what do we mean, when we say there is something in a man? This expression strikes deeper than many may imagine. Rarely is it used merely in reference to the talents or gifts which a man may possess. It rather pertains to the *manner* in which these gifts are employed. We understand by it, not so much what a man *has*, as what he *is*. The disposition, the will, is intended. And this is just what the Scripture means, when it says, that "the hearts of men were revealed through Christ." For, according to the saying of our Lord, it is out of the *heart* that evil thoughts proceed, and of the thoughts and ways of the heart it is affirmed, that it is evil from "its youth up." The heart is the seat of affection. The worth of a man is determined by what he loves. We love, indeed, only that with which we have some inward affinity—that in which we find *ourselves* again. Whatever object you love most, determines your worth. The incomprehensible good, which is above all other good, because it is the foundation and source of all other good, even God, *He* is, above all things, worthy of our love. This we unanimously admit. For who is there that does not admit it ? But will any one, treating the whole matter as something vague, affirm : "Thou lovest Him, in a certain sense, and so, too, thou lovest Him not?" Is not our love for Him as impalpable and hidden as He is himself? Is it not the mystery which every soul performs in its most retired chambers, as within closed doors?

My friends, I will not now stop to show that although the flame of love to God may glow in the heart, deeply concealed, yet it must manifest its fervor in works. I will ask but this, can God still be called a hidden, unseen object of love, now that Christ has come into the world? John says: "Whosoever loveth Him that begat, loveth Him also that is begotten of Him. No man hath seen God at any time. If we love one another, God dwelleth in us." Here, you perceive the whole matter at a glance. Although we may persuade ourselves a thousand times that we are cherishing a love to the unseen God, so long as we have no affection for those whom He has begotten again through Christ, and whom He has made to reflect His grace and truth, there is no true love in us—all our professions are empty words. There is not one of you, my brethren, who would not raise an outcry against the man who should desert the brother in whose veins there flowed the same ancestral blood as in his own. Such a person we would all term a monster, to whom there is nothing sacred in the name or in the memory of *father*. And can we, then, in truth, love our Father in heaven, and at the same time withhold our affections from that brother in whom reigns the same spirit of grace and truth through which we have been begotten anew?

But I go yet further, and say, that our love for an individual who might be manifesting only a somewhat lively religious striving—or an inclination even of the heart towards God—is also a touchstone by which our inward thoughts are revealed. For certain it is, that all contemplation of, and longing after God among men, finds its perfection only in Christ. If this be so, can we regard the yearnings of any human heart which thirsts after light and life from God, in any other aspect than as standing in connection with Christ? "Whosoever is of God, heareth

God's voice," says our Lord, and then he explains the assertion
by affirming that no one finds God, save he in whom God's Spirit
is already operating ; and that no one can come to the Son,
save he who is drawn of the Father. Behold there stands the
aged John in his eightieth year, and exclaims with all the fire
of his youthful ardor : " And we beheld His glory—the glory
as of the only-begotten of the Father, full of grace and truth."
And again, in his first epistle : " For the Life was manifested,
and we have seen it, and bear witness, and show unto you that
eternal Life which was with the Father, and which was manifested unto us." If this be the character of Christ—if Christ
is the manifested life of God—if He is the visible Son of the
invisible Father, why may I not then say, that in the feelings
which we all cherish towards the Son, we are truly indicating
whether we are sincere in our professions of love to the Father.
Yea, indeed, ever since *He* has come into the world, who once
could say, " Learn of me, for I am lowly in heart ;" and who at
another time dared to utter that which never yet had passed the
lips of mortal : " He that seeth me hath seen the Father also ;"
ever since that period the only-begotten of the Father, full of
grace and truth, we assert, has been set before us as a touchstone, which is to make known what of truth there may be in
our love to God, and what there is in ourselves.

We have learned from Simeon a word of prophecy that con-
veys this thought. Let us receive the same from the very mouth
of Him who was the lowliest among the children of men. It is
a remarkable utterance to which I now refer you. When its
meaning for the first time dawned upon me—when, for the first
time my soul clearly apprehended its deep import—with what
wonderful power did it seize me ! How was I startled as my
eye saw into the true source of all love to Christ, and of all
alienation from Him ! And here I speak to your own experience.
We read in John : " And the Father himself, which hath sent
me, hath borne witness of me. Ye have neither heard His voice
at any time, nor seen His shape. And ye have not His word

abiding in you ; for whom He hath sent, Him ye believe not.   I
receive not honor from men.   But I know you, that ye have not
the love of God in you."   The thoughts here are strung together
in a loose connection ; and it may be that their real drift has
escaped many of you.   What the Lord charged upon the Jews
is this : that they loved him not, because they had not the love
of God in themselves.   He asserts that to love God truly—to
carry His word in our hearts, and yet not to feel drawn towards
Him, was an utter impossibility.   Such is the doctrine plainly
taught us by one whom we reverence as the archetype of all
humility.   Besides, these assertions stand not isolated.   The same
truth rings out in other statements : " If God were your Father,
ye would love me ; for I proceeded forth and came from God."
Ye neither know me nor my Father.   " If ye had known me, ye
should have known my Father also."   And had there not been
in Christ this perfect interpenetration of the divine and the human
—had He not been the manifestation of God in the flesh—how
could He reconcile with His humility the fact, that He exacted
this degree of love : " Whosoever loveth father or mother more
than me, is not worthy of me ?"   What mortal has ever asked
to be *so* loved ?   Accordingly then, supported not only by the
word of a Simeon, but also by Christ's *own* words, I dare affirm,
with the fullest emphasis, that the degree in which the manifestation of Christ prevails over, attracts, and appropriates a man,
measures precisely the degree of his love to God.

But perhaps a distinction will be insisted upon here, on the
ground that we have Jesus no more before our eyes.   But let me
ask, is not the declaration, " We have seen his glory," ever new
and fresh upon earth ?   Has it ceased to be uttered ever since
the last eye-witness of Jesus was laid in his grave ?   It might
be so if it was with our bodily eyes alone, that we were to behold
His glory.   But with such eyes Caiaphas also beheld him.   And
Christ has affirmed : " They have eyes and see not."   Only with the
eyes of the spirit can we behold Christ's glory ; and with these
eyes of the *spirit* we can behold it still.   And that we are able

to see it now the same as ever—is not this the proof of what we call the inspiration of His evangelists? If the record of the evangelists concerning Christ, impresses believers afresh in each successive age, with the same original power, as did the very things which they formerly, with their own senses, saw and heard; and if he who reads Christ's words now exclaims, precisely as did those who first heard them: "Never man spake like this man;" do ye ask any further proof of the fact, that in spite of all human weaknesses, God's hand was nevertheless guiding the pen of those who have written to us of Christ? If, then, the majestic form of Christ yet abides upon earth, it is here in the record, and remains here as a touchstone, by which the hearts of men may be revealed for all time to come.

But, in still another sense is he also present; for he has said that he would yet come again, in order to take up his abode with us. Are not believers his temples, his body, his members? Is Christ not perpetually present in all those who are born of his Spirit? That we are weak members, this we, indeed, confess; but, yet, he who is of Christ, must be regarded as led by Christ's Spirit. He cannot but have in himself something of Christ's ways and character. And this is why I say again, Christ resides in his followers also, as a touchstone of human hearts. He who has true love for Christ, can never hate his disciples. He who has no heart for his disciples, can never love Christ. "If they have persecuted me, they will also persecute you; if they have kept my sayings, they will keep yours also." Thus spake the Saviour, and in this way did he inseparably bind together his own lot and that of his disciples. Weaknesses, individual mistakes, errors, we dare not disavow, for who of us has them not? May a man, then, hate his own flesh and blood? But he who is of Christ is my flesh and blood; yea, more, he is one spirit with me. Indeed, we go yet farther. All the religious life and striving of humanity is only a striving towards Christ; for, let me ask, is not Christ the crowning point of all religion— the end and aim of humanity, so far as it is religiously stirred

14*

and longs after God? He has himself intimated that, in every man who discovers and lays hold upon him, there must already exist something akin to himself: "He who is of God," he says, "heareth my voice." The man, therefore, who strives after God, by however circuitous and devious a path, he is an object of my love; and in all phases of humanity, the extent to which any person attracts me is determined by the earnestness with which he seeks after God, or the devotion with which he clings to him in Christ. All other motives for love are subordinate to this.

And, now, how is it with us in this regard? How does it stand in respect to our love for Christ, and for all his members, be they ever so weak; yea, for all those who, though in the most imperfect manner, are still making religion the central object of all their endeavors? Have we all attained to such a personal relationship to the glorified Son of God, that we are able to say, "Christ is the highest object of my affection! I love him as he demands to be loved! I love him more than father and mother!" Are those who cleave to Christ with the greatest devotion, however wanting they may be in other worthy human gifts and talents, still the dearest to you among men—the persons to whom you feel, most of all, closely attached? We will not here ask after your confession of faith. We will accept your love as sufficient. For he who can respond affirmatively to the question, "Lovest thou Christ better than father and moth-. er?" need not avow his creed. He to whom Christ is of more worth than any other child of Adam, such as the rest of us are, is, on this ground, truly a Christian. But, oh, how are the hearts of the children of this age laid bare, as, on the one hand, may be seen those to whom adhesion to some one little article of their own favorite creed is of more weight than the undoubted manifestations of a Christ-loving heart! and, on the other hand, there are thousands upon thousands who are ever ready to make a great ado when a person goes *too far*—as they term it—in religion; but who have not one word of complaint or dissent in respect to the multitudes who do not go far enough! What a touchstone of the human heart have we here! How imperatively does the age demand that all who have only a love for Christ—that all who are truly in earnest about religion, should hold fast to each other. If ever the saying, "He that is not for us is against us," be applicable, it is applicable now—now, when Protestant Christendom is beginning to part into two camps—when the contest is no longer about particular articles of faith—but the mooted question is, whether the State shall have a church, Christendom a Saviour, and humanity a God in heaven. Now, verily, is Christ the banner, and all who can kneel in faith before his cross should join hands. Now, once more, Christ is in every respect the sign everywhere spoken against, and through which the thoughts of many hearts are revealed.

When Simeon spoke these words, he had in view the last moments of our Saviour's conflict with the world, and in reference to this scene, we have yet to consider *how Christ was a touchstone of the human heart*, through which what was in man became first revealed.

Never, at any period, have the contents of the human heart been so brought out by action and endurance, as they were in the conduct of men towards him who dared to affirm that, those who saw Him saw the Father also, in their conduct towards the Son of God himself, in his deepest sufferings.

The essential character was there exhibited, both as regards his foes and his friends. What may be in man's heart was already indicated in the fact, that a being like Jesus could have enemies at all—and *such* enemies! Direct your glance with me a moment to this point. Humanity has passed through many scenes, which are sufficient to undeceive any person, who will know nothing of human nature but its original goodness and excellence. Let me refer you to one of these. Scarcely fifty years have passed since there was heard in Europe, among a cultivated and Christian people, the cry—and whose blood does not curdle in his veins, even now, at the remembrance of it?—" It will never go well with mankind, until the last king is throttled with the intestines of the last priest !" As we have just said, whose blood does not curdle in his veins at hearing such a hell-cry ? And yet, this is not so horrible as that which happened in regard to Christ. When men suffer innocently—even the best of men—we yet do not forget that they are, after all, sinners ; although a very small portion of their own guilt, be it no more than a simple lack of wisdom, may have been proven in the sufferings of the innocent victims. So, too, how often does the burden of the curse which remote ancestors had provoked, first fall with crushing weight upon their descendants. And, however we may shudder at the monstrous cruelties of the French Revolution, let me ask, were not the crying sins of whole generations of bygone kings and priests expiated in that blood-bath ? Yet, it must be added, sins from which, indeed, the descendants themselves were by no means altogether exempt. See, now, wherein lies the difference between the impression made by the sacrifice of Christ, and that made by all the scaffolds upon which innocent humanity has bled. Here stands one, of whom it may be affirmed, without fear of contradiction, "He had done no sin, neither was any guile found in his mouth." That Being who said, "He that seeth me, seeth the unseen Father," *him* have men put to death on the cross as a malefactor !

Here, then, is the human heart first truly laid open, even unto the inmost depths of that corruption which festered in it. If human nature could do this, what is it not capable of perpetrating ? But this same nature, which was in the breast of Caiaphas, Judas, and Pilate, is in mine also.

I go yet further. What is in the human heart is revealed to us also amid the circle of Jesus's friends. What an image of weakness and infirmity, even after the sincerest and most ardent protestation, is presented to us in the case of Peter ! In respect to that being of whom Peter had testified : "Whither shall we go ? thou hast the words of eternal life ; thou art the son of the living God ;" even in respect to *Him*, could this same Peter declare in the hour of danger, " I know him not !"   But it was not *Peter's* nature alone that was here disclosed by the touchstone. The very trials which dwelt in the breast of Peter the fallen, dwell also in my breast.   Besides, Peter stands, not alone by the cross, as the only type of our common infirmity.   Do you not there see the rest of the disciples, how they all crowd timidly together at an equal remove from their Lord ?   Not one of them has the courage to speak a bold word in behalf of the man of their heart, who hangs near on the accursed tree.   If in the critical hour of trial Peter denies his Master, so do the rest all betray fear in like manner.

It is not necessary, however, that I should dwell only on the *melancholy disclosures* of the human heart called forth by the suffering Saviour.   He was a touchstone to reveal to us, not only to what a degree the human heart was capable of obduracy, and shallowness, and inconstancy, but he also shows us how this same human heart may be rendered teachable and tractable under the influences of divine grace.   For in spite of all the disciples' weakness, it was still plain that their faith had a firm foundation on which it fastened.   What lay on the other side of the cross was at this time hardly even surmised by them. When Christ was borne to the grave, then was their *hope* borne to the grave also ; but, oh, blessed experience, their *faith* was not borne thither with it.   See how wonderfully this fact is indicated in the instance of Nicodemus.   He who ventured to approach a living Christ only by night, now that he is dead, hesitates not, as we see, openly to bury him by day ; and, when all hope is over, he confesses him publicly before the world.   And then, when the grave has opened—when the cross, this star with shorn rays, touched with the beams of the Easter morning sun, once more is clothed with radiance, how does the hope that was buried with their Jesus, rise together with him !   How does the little spark of faith, almost smothered by the burden of the cross, shoot up again heavenward in a flame that was never more to subside.   In view of these things, may we not affirm that if one great drama of humanity was enacting *upon* the cross, there was still another at the same time acted out *beneath* it, of hardly less significance ! Thus it happened that *over against* the noblest manifestation of human nature, as well as *in* it, and *through* it, there is made known to us what is in man.

If it has been shown that the manifestation of Christ was a touchstone of the hearts of men, oh, how should our love towards him, and also towards his true believers, kindle with fresh earnestness ! for it is according to the measure of our affection for Him, that we shall be judged in the end. Oh, thou blessed Saviour, thou hast demanded that we love thee better than father and mother. Thou wouldst not have demanded this of us, had not thy glory, thy grace, and thy truth been indeed deserving of such affection. Reveal thyself to us, then, oh, thou worshipful Redeemer ! Reveal thyself to us in thine incomparable glory and beauty, in order that we may be strengthened to love thee with that all-excluding love which thou requirest ! And fill us anew also with love towards thy members on the earth ! Yea, may all who in this world but confess thy name, and are subject to thee in love and sincere devotion, be also sacred to our hearts ; for thou, Lord, art the only begotten of the Father, full of grace and truth ! Amen.

DISCOURSE XVIII.

THE FATHER DRAWING MEN TO THE SON.

My devout brethren, must it not strike us very painfully, to hear the words "My Saviour," "My Redeemer," repeated from so many thousand lips, and yet, if we ask a person, face to face, "How knowest thou that He is indeed *thy Redeemer?*" silence is the only answer we receive? And, strange to say, the very persons whom we are most sure to find in this state, are just the ones who dispute the most vehemently about Christ, and to whom much that is related of Him in the Scripture, and believed by the church, is utterly unintelligible. It is on such occasions that the word of the Lord comes to remembrance, which He spake when He once heard people of this sort disputing about Him in the temple ; a weighty word in a time like this, when religious truths are so much controverted and so little understood, so much contended for and written upon and so little experienced.

The saying of the Lord, which I refer to, we read in St. John (vi. 43-45) :

"Jesus, therefore, answered, and said unto them, Murmur not among yourselves. No man can come to me, except the Father which hath sent me draw him : and I will raise him up at the last day. It is written in the prophets, And they shall be all taught of God. Every man, therefore, that hath heard, and hath learned of the Father, cometh unto me."

In entering upon the consideration of this text with you, well might I exclaim : "Put off thy shoes from off thy feet, for the place whereon thou standest is holy ground." What deep mystery of mercy is that into which we are led ; that He who hath created us, purposes by the powerful yet tender drawing of His Spirit, to lead us to His Son. That the coming to Christ here spoken of, is not simply an outward coming, is clear. All those to whom Jesus addressed these words had already approached Him on their feet ; but He spake of their coming to him with their hearts. In another expression of His, He implies that no man cometh unto Him who does not hunger and thirst : viz., where He says, "I am the bread of life : he that cometh to me shall never hunger ; and he that believeth on me shall never thirst."—(John vi. 35.) The coming, therefore, of which He speaks, is that in which a man begins to taste and enjoy Him as a REDEEMER. In *this* manner it is, He says, that "No man can come unto Him, whom the Father has not drawn ;" that is, as the subsequent words explain it, who has not been *taught* by the Father, who has not *heard* and *learned* of the Father. This *drawing* of the Father to the Son, we will now proceed to examine more closely, in the light of truth.

I. *It is in appearance a gracious gift for a chosen few, and, yet, in truth, it is as wide and universal as the atmosphere.*

II. *It goes through nature and human fortune; it goes through the human spirit, and human heart.*

III. *The Father draws, only we do not follow. The Father teaches, only we do not learn.*

I. It is, in appearance, a gift of grace for a chosen few, and yet, in truth, it is as wide and universal as the atmosphere.

How like a holy mystery does that expression steal over the

soul—*The drawing of the Father to the Son.* Who does not feel, that in these words there are contained unsearchable depths? We understand not the mystery, only we encounter it ; and the deeper, I may say the more inwardly we push matters home, the greater is the impression made on us of there being here a gift of grace, which others have not, solely because the Father has *not drawn* them; because, as we well express it, they are not constitutionally qualified for such experiences.

When we see the indifference of all other men towards the mystery of godliness ; when we see how happy and how satisfied they are to live in the world without the Father and without the Son ; they appear to us as men of a different order ; and it seems to us incredible that the reason why they know nothing of the mystery of godliness, is simply because they choose not to know it—incredible that the cause why so many know not the drawing of the Father, is simply this, that they would not suffer themselves to be drawn. As it is certain that every one who comes to the Son, has also been drawn by the Father, it follows with equal certainty, that he who does not come to Him, comes not because the Father has not drawn him. Is not this the unmistakable meaning of this declaration of our Lord? When Jesus said to them : "Murmur not among yourselves, no man can come to me, except the Father which hath sent me draw him," does He not manifestly make a difference between those whom the Father draws, and those whom He does not draw? Does it not sound as if He meant to say : "Good people, what signifies your laboring and disputing ? If God has once shut the narrow gate, you will surely never open it ?" Thus it appears ; and yet had it been so intended, would there not seem to lurk in these words a cold, unfeeling scorn ? and who can tolerate the idea of scorn from the mouth of Christ ? Who can refrain from asking : "Had it been so meant, why, then, is it written, ' and He upbraided their unbelief ?' " Why, then, did He again and again enter the company of those who were unable to open the narrow door, which the Father had closed ? You

perceive that this word of our Lord is a perplexing one ; but
has He not himself given us the key to the meaning ? If
the drawing of the Father is nothing else than precept and
instruction, and if it is written : " *He that hath heard, and hath
learned of the Father cometh unto me,*" is it not manifest, that
there may be a teaching of the Father, where the man does
not learn ; and a drawing, where the man does not permit himself to be drawn ? And if it is so, can we still doubt that those
words, "*except the Father draw him,*" were by no means intended
to imply a difference between some whom He draws, and others
whom He does not draw ? When He saith : " *Every man, therefore, that hath heard and learned of the Father cometh unto me,*"
does He not thereby give us to know that the Father is always
teaching, but men will not learn ; that the Father is always
drawing, but men will not suffer themselves to be drawn ?

No ; though it may produce salutary alarm, to preach that
doctrine of the Reformed Church which still many millions profess—the doctrine of an absolute predestination, according to
which the one half of the sinful world is drawn by the free
mercy of the Father, to the Son, by which they are made to
reflect His undeserved mercy ; whilst the other half, through
just anger against sin, being left to their fate, become a mirror
of that which all sin hath, in truth, deserved ; though I say
there may be, also, a certain unspeakable power in the preaching of this entirely unconditioned Omnipotence in God, which,
by an absolute decree, snatches the elect, and saves them from
out of the mass of those who are lost—yet, too strongly and too
undeniably does the divine word make known to us a God, who is
the Saviour of all men, and a redemption, whose light spreads
itself not a step less widely than the dark shadow of sin which
covers all mankind ; for it affirms that human nature, from all
eternity, *has been laid upon* Christ ; yea, that the creation of the
world itself rests upon Him. If God (as the apostle Paul says)
has "*chosen us in Christ,*" before the foundation of the world,
and consequently before Paradise and the Fall, then must Christ

be the fundamental idea, the turning point around which the whole development of the human race revolves; then, to His account must everything be reckoned; then must the drawing of the Father to the Son be extended as far as the human race goes; then must it be as wide and universal as the air itself.

II. And *it is thus universal, for it* goes through all nature, and all human fortune—it goes through *the human spirit and the human heart.* Oh that I could rightly waken in you the conviction, that He whom you call your FATHER in heaven, is actually so near to his people, that He can draw them with his hand—that He can speak to them with his mouth! Oh that you could believe that his heaven is not closed, that his throne stands not merely beyond the clouds—his Spirit is nearer to you than you are to yourselves! I will not now speak to you of those mysterious drawings in the depths of the heart—of those drawings which you carry about with you, and which preach to you from within, "*Be ye reconciled unto God.*" Let me first speak to you of that drawing of the Father which pervades nature and all human fortune.

Indeed, in respect to nature, it might, perhaps, appear, if we listen to what she boasts respecting her entertainments, that, instead of pointing to a Redeemer, she rather tended to render Him unnecessary. Is it not nature that so enthralls man with her quiet charms, that when, with heart agitated by storm and trouble, she persuades him to cast himself upon her full breast, and *there* find the ATONEMENT? But if we inquire more deeply into that which they call the atoning power of nature, am I mistaken if I consider the discourse which she holds with us rather as a preaching of repentance than as a gospel of reconciliation?

For those who seldom emerge from the din of business, there is, indeed, an appearance of repose in those hours when they step forth alone into the temple of nature. It is true, this vast nature of ours is itself, also, one wide workshop; but then how quietly, with what unchangeable regularity, does her work proceed! This we cannot but feel, and are so thrown back upon ourselves, and the first impression therefrom is beneficial. But, is it not, also, a humiliating and chastening impression which arises as soon as we begin to recollect ourselves, and begin to ask, Why is it not then in *me* also equally peaceful? Why does there not prevail in me also this quiet regularity of nature? Especially does this inquiry force itself on us, if we are constrained at the same time to own that we are spirits, created in the image of God, and ought, therefore, voluntarily to obey the eternal laws of our CREATOR, even as nature obeys them, from an eternal necessity. *These* are thoughts, I say, which must occur to every person when he comes to sober reflection. But, alas, man hastens out thoughtless, and thoughtless he returns home; and persuades himself that he has won inward peace, when it scarcely lasts him a single hour; and he perceives not that for the human spirit the enjoyment of nature does not supersede the necessity of atonement with God, but only causes this necessity to be all the more felt. For, that *something* is wanting to us, we all feel; but deeper and more earnest meditation is demanded, in order to perceive what that defect is, and to learn from nature the meaning of what the royal preacher affirmed, that "*that sin, and sin alone, is the reproach of any people.*"—Prov. xiv. 34.

Still more plainly does this preaching, and with it the drawing of the Father to the Son, go through all history and human fortune. Is not the history of the human race, as a whole, and the history of every household, and the lot of each individual life of man, a drawing of the Father to the Son, which preaches to us that we need a REDEEMER? When the prophet inquires, "*Wherefore doth a living man complain—a man for the punishment of his sins?*"—(Sam. iii. 39) would it be too much to infer that all and every misfortune would be done away from the life of man, could we but get rid of sin? Can we be mistaken here? No, surely not. With all the frailty and danger accompanying a man's earthly life; in spite of pestilence and earthquake; in spite of disease and death ; take sin away, and the earth would become at once a Paradise ! Gather up in one all the tears which have been shed upon earth, since the time when the Cherubim, with the flaming sword, placed themselves before the Paradise of Innocence, and say, have not by far the greater part been tears over sin, and its consequences ? Take also those wounds which have not been inflicted by the sins of man, but through the frailty of our earthly nature, or through the elements warring against man, and destroying the creations of his industry ; yea, take all that has been inflicted by those two angels of wrath that we fear the most, disease and death, and, oh, how much more easily would these be also endured, were sin only taken out of the world ! Imagine only how much lighter would be the burden, if men loved each other as they ought ; if no mourner had to shed tears for himself alone, and all mankind were of one heart. And ought it not be so ?

But this is not all. How great a share has sin also in those evils which appear to us to be quite out of our own power— disease and death ! Do not the traditions of many nations ring of a time when man lived a simple and natural life ; and the poison of disease was almost unknown ; and the destroying angel of death, who now breaks off the buds in the morning, and tears off the bloom at noon, came only as the reaper, that mowed down the well-ripened fruit at latest evening, in order to store it in the garner ? It is written, "*Death came into the world by sin ;*" and, looking away from that which happened at the beginning of our race, how great a share has sin, even now, in the hastening of death ! How does it gnaw at the life of man, in order to make it still shorter than it would otherwise be in our decrepit system ! Truly, there goes through all human fortune a voice preaching to us that *sin is the destruction* of man ; and *this* voice —this is a drawing, which from the Father leads to the Son.

Yet, in vain goes this drawing through everything external to man, through nature, and human fortune, so long as it does not draw and constrain us *here*—within. But lightly as the sunbeam,

and like it, shining and warming, goes also the drawing of the
Father to the Son, through the human spirit and the human
heart. Ye, whose calling is science, to whichever of its faculties
you may belong, ye cannot study profoundly without perceiving
how all reflection upon human things irresistibly constrains and
drives the spirit, till it at last arrives at the great centre of all
things—even GOD—and how the thinking mind can repose in no
other God than Him whose hidden glory is revealed in the face
of JESUS CHRIST.

Ye, who search out the necessary laws of thought, ye must, above
all others, have felt, how the key-stone to all worldly wisdom is
wanting, so long as it has not found its final aim in GOD, in that
Spirit at which the light of our thoughts was first kindled. And
again, ye cannot but deeply feel that the mysterious impress of GOD,
which lies veiled in the human spirit, was never revealed to human
thought, until the WORD OF GOD became flesh, and gave us, instead
of *" the unknown God,"* the name of GOD, our FATHER in Heaven.

Ye, who have been directing your studies to the fine arts and
military glory of a perished world—ye must have discovered
that it perished from the fact, that it did not as yet enjoy the
highest revelation of the GODHEAD ; and these objects, constitut-
ing as they do the noblest efforts of that age, will only then
become intelligible to you, when they are viewed as a striving
after that Light and Life, which has disclosed itself to the world
in the SON OF GOD.

Ye, who have applied your minds to those institutions by
which society and civil right are maintained among men, must
have perceived how all political communion is refined and ennobled by the spirit of Christian morality, and that even right
itself, finds its highest fulfillment in love ; and furthermore, ye
must have seen, how all the driving of the law-giver with the
rod of Moses, applied from without, can never render a people
truly happy, so long as their hearts have not been softened under
the mild shepherd's rod of JESUS CHRIST, to obey the law with
gladness and from the strong impulse of holy affection.

Ye, who search through the healing powers of nature, in order to build up and preserve the holy temple of the Spirit, the body, ye must have deeply felt, what a phantom our natural life is, when the quickening breath of the Eternal, is not therein perceptible ; and what an empty corpse the body is, to which ye have dedicated your life and labor, when it is not the temple of an immortal inhabitant ; and how the frightful death-mask can only be changed into an angelic face, by being viewed in the light of Him, who has spoiled Death of His might.

Thus does the drawing of the Father to the Son traverse the spirit of man so universally, that one might almost say, it is harder for a reflecting mind to avoid the God who is revealed to us in Christ, than—to *find* Him.   And all sciences—what are they but the satellites of the Eternal Spiritual Sun, from which they receive light, in various degrees proportionate to the several distances at which they circle round Him.   To him who hears the instruction of GOD, in his own spirit, they all are but sermons on the indispensableness of that redemption, of which we are made partakers in CHRIST JESUS.

And what shall we say of that restless, unsatisfied heart of man, whose yearnings are as intense as its conflicts ?   We tremble before that inner judgment-voice which we call conscience, when she upbraids us with our misspent days, our broken vows, the sins of our youth, and our secret transgressions ; and now we begin to understand that the **voice of conscience was only the voice of the Father**, aiming to lead us to the Son, who is the sacrifice for our sins !   Formerly, indeed, we ventured now and then to listen to the voice of conscience, with only half an ear ; to make terms with it, to muffle its tones ; this we ventured to do, holding, as we did, conscience to be only the voice of our own heart.   Shall we venture to do so now, after we have learnt that it is the voice of the FATHER, desirous of leading us to the Son ?   How holy does the voice of conscience become in the light of that saying, " No one can come to the Son except the Father draw him !"   Is there now any one here, with a bosom full of accusations which will not be silent ? with a branded conscience, whose marks cannot be effaced ?   Is there any one here, who needs an Advocate ?   There stands the Advocate, O man, **to whom, in the very** anguish of thy conscience, the drawing of the FATHER is urging thee !

That unsatisfied longing, which has been gnawing at our hearts day and night, we had looked **upon as a nervous** disorder, a spasmodic twitching of our own heart : and have sought to chase it away, as one would scare flies, by the sounding laugh and merry thoughts, by the **noise of** company, by riot and revelling. And now we learn, it was the voice of the FATHER, seeking His child !   "Hear, O Heavens, and give ear, O Earth, the ox knoweth his owner, and the ass his master's crib ; but Israel doth not know, my people doth not consider." (Isaiah i. 2.)   Is not that disquiet of heart which finds no rest, except in God, is it not as a great mind has said, " the remains of the Image of God, in the heart of man ?" for why else do we remain uneasy, and dissatisfied with all aside from God, if it be not that we were created for God ?   When at last the heart has found that peace in the Son of God, which the world cannot give, then how does it perceive that their yearning sighs which breathed forth unchecked so long as Christ was not enjoyed, were nothing else than the holy drawing of the Father, which have been conducting it to the Son.   All this time had it been turning hither and thither, ignorant of what was properly wanting ; **and then only** did it come to understand its need, when it was proffered to it in CHRIST.   And on finding peace in Him, **how** plain does it become to us, that each **pulsation of the** beating heart, each convulsive movement of the disordered conscience, was all the drawing whereby the Father would lead **us** to the Son.

III.   Yea, verily, " *the Father draweth us, but we will not follow ; the Father teacheth us, but we will not hear !*"   If the drawing of the Father to the Son is actually as broad and free as the air of heaven—if all who are excluded from the mystery of

godliness are excluded only by their own fault, how humiliating
is the thought, that it has nevertheless at all times the appearance of being intended peculiarly as a gift only for a chosen few !
when, in truth, the election of God is commensurate with the human race itself.   Oh that the power of human speech—oh that
the might of God's Spirit might assist me in convincing you of
the truth of Christ's declaration, that all your experience from
within and from without, is pervaded by the drawings of the
Father's love, which would fain lead you to the Son : for you
cannot believe this assertion unless your heart prompts it—unless you listen thereto attentively.   You see a poor child in the
wood, or in the desert ; he stands perplexed, then runs, now right
and now left ; his eye detects not the path which leads towards
home ; and though behind him, and above him, and on all sides,
a father's voice is calling to him, yet his ear hears not.   Such
is man in the midst of the voices of God, which are calling
to him out of the height and out of the depth—from within
and from without.   Ye children of a Heavenly FATHER "To-
day, if ye will hear his voice, harden not your hearts."
Should you step forth into nature, oh, close not your ear on the
great question she puts to you, " Oh, man, why is it not as calm
and quiet in you as in me ?"   For as you wander forth in those
peaceful scenes, and nature's holy stillness turns your thoughts
back upon yourself, then, in contrast with her sweet harmony,
how deeply conscious do you become of your own inward discord
and schisms !   Or suppose it is the history of mankind which
is the object of your deep reflection, or at least that paragraph
of it which is filled up with your own biography, what a sermon
do you hear preached even out of the narrow compass of your
own individual experiences, as soon as you begin to inquire what
your life might have been, had it not been deranged and broken
up by your sins and the sins of others ! and in it all believe that
you discover the drawings of the Father, by which he has been
daily endeavoring to lead you to the Son.

Ye votaries of knowledge, even your studies must become to

15

you a divine worship. Estimate yourselves fittingly. You are too noble to devote yourselves to intellectual labors, for the sake of finite objects, for office and for honor, when, if prosecuted with an upward glance to God, they would in all points be leading to Him. Truly you have not yet learned the holy significance of science, so long as it appears to you impossible to pursue it as a divine worship. And that disquiet—that unsatisfied longing—that oppressiveness which your heart feels, let it henceforth appear to you in another light than that in which you have hitherto been wont to regard it : it is a drawing of the Father. And if you consider this unstilled yearning of soul in this light, you will turn for relief to no other helper than that all-sufficient One, to whom the Father desires to draw you. We have the assurance of Christ that there is an inward voice in our own hearts, which is a drawing of the Father ; in proportion to the blessedness of the results which follow upon listening to it, will be the greatness of our responsibility, if we remain deaf to its solicitations.

Verily, O my God, I know that no man can find the way unto Thee except under thy guidance. Take then, O most merciful FATHER, thy weak and erring child by the hand, and I will follow, whithersoever Thou leadest. I acknowledge it as a boundless mercy of Thine, that Thou stoopest from above to instruct us in our hearts respecting the things which belong to our peace ; therefore, I tremble greatly lest I should not hear when thou speakest. Nay, I will attend, and be observant as an obedient child, whenever Thou raisest Thy voice to me, and by Thee will I be entirely guided ; for I know that wheresoever Thou dost choose to lead me, there it is good to be.

JULIUS MÜLLER, D.D.

339

BIOGRAPHICAL NOTICE.

JULIUS MÜLLER, a brother of Karl Ottfried Müller (the celebrated and now deceased Archæologist), was born at Brieg in Silesia, April 10th, 1801; in which place his father was a preacher. He studied with great assiduity at the Gymnasium in Brieg, and afterwards at the Universities of Breslau and Göttingen,—and first entered upon the study of Law, which he abandoned, after many struggles, for that of Divinity. Under the guidance of Neander, Tholuck, etc., he came to a firm and peaceful faith,—and in the year 1825, became Pastor at Schönbrunn and Rosen, where he continued seven years. While there he wrote a review of a work on the Catholic Church of Silesia, which attracted much attention and admiration.

In 1831, he was appointed second University Preacher at Göttingen, and in connection with this office, began lectures on Practical Theology and Pedagogics. It was here that he preached his sermons on the Christian Life. In 1834 he was appointed Professor Extraordinarius of Theology, and in 1835 Professor Ordinarius at Marburg. Here he lectured four years, especially on Dogmatics and Morals, and with distinguished success—and was then appointed Professor at Halle, where he now is. His great work is "The Christian Doctrine of Sin." He has published very able articles in the "Studien and Kritiken," and other Journals, one in answer to Strauss —and has written also an able work in defence of the Evangelical Union against the attacks of the exclusive Lutheran party, who are endeavoring to subvert it.

Professor Müller belongs, theologically, with Neander, Nitzsch, Tholuck, etc.:—i. e. among the liberal evangelical theologians as opposed to exclusive Calvinism, exclusive Lutheranism, and the indifference of Rationalism. He is a man of earnest, serious, reverent and pious character, and is one of the most profound and scientific Theologians in Germany; possessing a shining and disciplined intellect of great argumentative grasp. Next to Professor Tholuck, his bosom friend, he forms the chief attraction of the University at Halle; and throughout Germany, owing to his practical wisdom, his piety and great moral worth, he stands a kind of umpire amid the theological conflicts of the day. By some misfortune he early lost one eye, and quite recently a shock of apoplexy has injured his memory, and threatened to interfere materially with the prosecution of his labors. His loss or disability would be widely and deeply felt. In personal appearance he is tall, dignified, and fine-looking, with the bearings of a courteous and amiable Christian gentleman.

As a preacher, Professor Müller occupies a high rank. In reading his sermons, however, it should be borne in mind, that the *sermon* in Germany, is not so high a thing *intellectually* as the sermon with us. Not so much discussion and thought are expected—nor would they be appreciated. Hence there is a wide interval between the *Sermons* of Müller and his Theological Treatises and Lectures, in respect to the *mental* power displayed. They show, rather, how much heart he has, and how a learned theologian can speak on the gospel to young men and to the people. His style is polished and tasteful, though not sprightly, his arrangement clear and distinct, and he glides in a graceful and happy way from one part to the other of the subject under remark. None of his Sermons (with a single exception) have appeared in English; a circumstance which affords us the greater pleasure in submitting to the public those here furnished.

DISCOURSE XIX.

THE SUPERIOR MIGHT OF GOD'S SERVANTS.

IF there be, my respected hearers, any one among those about our Lord while on earth, who deserves the name of a MAN, in the noblest sense of the word, it is John the Baptist, whom the Christian Church of our country to-day commemorates.* When Christ, on one occasion, called Peter a rock, He significantly and encouragingly alluded to that which Peter was afterwards to become. The Peter who attempts to walk upon the waves, and then is frightened, and begins to sink, as soon as he sees the storm striking him ; who protests that he will go with his Master to prison and to death, and a few hours afterwards thrice denies Him—*this* Peter was at that time, certainly, as yet no rock. Then, on the contrary, Jesus, in order to show the Jews what they were not to look for in John, asks them : "What went ye out to see—a reed, shaken by the wind ?" He spoke not of the future, but of the past and the present. He pointed to that strong, invincible firmness in John, with which he preached repentance to all the people, without asking whether he pleased or displeased them thereby, and with which he rebuked the sins of the mightiest, without fearing their anger or their vengeance. Such a man of God certainly deserves to have his memory celebrated, and his actions held up for a model, in the Christian Church.

* Preached on St. John's Festival.

Or shall we believe that this unbending firmness and vigor in
the assertion of the truth, belongs properly to the virtues of the
Old Testament, which are foreign to the order of the new Covenant ; and that Christian virtue is properly Love, and that love
precludes this severe earnestness, and reveals itself only as gentleness, pliancy, and patience ? Oh, let us guard ourselves, my dear
friends, against any such perverted opinions ; which are so much
the more dangerous, the more they carry the seductive appearance of truth. The right kind of love does not exclude John's
method of dealing, but strengthens it. It does not weaken the
firmness ; it does not destroy the earnestness ; it does not break
the energy of one's activity ; but it exalts and ennobles these
qualities. That love is a false sentiment, which knows not how to
be strong, which always speaks only of yielding an acquiescence;
which cries without intermission, "Peace, peace," when there
is no peace. Such love is ordinarily a pretext for indolence
and weakness. True love, on the contrary, acts on the principle, that the real good of the person loved can spring only from
truth and righteousness. It, therefore, begets in every soul
which it animates a deep, repelling hatred of everything bad
and perverse. Therefore, it bids us rather perish than act
against God's will, or even be silent towards an iniquity which
we are called to withstand.

In a peculiar degree do we, in our time, need to look at that
high model of free, manly feeling ; when the word is so abundant
in empty talk, and so meagre in strong action ; when there is so
much apparent enthusiasm, and so little honest devotion to the
truth ; when multitudes are so passionately chasing after outward freedom, and trouble themselves not at all about that
inward freedom, without which the outward has no value and
no significance. It is this inward freedom which gives to the
servants of God that invincible power over the children of the
world, and of just this superiority the life and death of John
affords a glorious example. Let us more closely consider this
example, during this hour of devotion.

"But, when Herod heard *thereof*, he said, it is John, whom I beheaded: he is risen from the dead. For Herod himself had sent forth and laid hold upon John, and bound him in prison for Herodias' sake, his brother Philip's wife: for he had married her. For John had said unto Herod, It is not lawful for thee to have thy brother's wife. Therefore Herodias had a quarrel against him, and would have killed him: but she could not. For Herod feared John, knowing that he was a just man and a holy, and observed him; and when he heard him, he did many things and heard him gladly. And when a convenient day was come, that Herod on his birthday made a supper to his lords, high captains, and chief *estates* of Galilee. And when the daughter of the said Herodias came in, and danced, and pleased Herod and them that sat with him, the king said unto the damsel, Ask of me whatsoever thou wilt, and I will give *it* thee. And he sware unto her, Whatsoever thou shalt ask of me, I will give *it* thee, unto the half of my kingdom. And she went forth, and said unto her mother, What shall I ask? And she said, The head of John the Baptist. And she came in straightway with haste unto the king, and asked, saying, I will that thou give me, by and by, in a charger, the head of John the Baptist. And the king was exceedingly sorry; *yet* for his oath's sake, and for their sakes which sat with him, he would not reject her. And immediately the king sent an executioner, and commanded his head to be brought: and he went and beheaded him in the prison. And brought his head in a charger, and gave it to the damsel: and the damsel gave it to her mother."—MARK vi. 16-28.

The text, at first view, appears but little suited to bring before our minds this invincible power of the servants of God, in their struggle with the world. It seems rather to remind us of their weakness, and of their frequent overthrow in this struggle; for it exhibits to us, at first, the solitary prison of the servant of God, and at last his bleeding head. And yet this weakness, this deficit is, in fact, only in appearance. Outwardly, John lies beneath his foe; spiritually, he vanquishes him, masters him by force, carries him off in triumph against his will. And in order to convince you of this, we only need to regard more attentively what the Evangelist narrates in our text. Let us, therefore, learn from him the superiority of the children of God over the children of the world. We follow, in this discussion, the *inner* order of the events which our text describes.

Herod, the Tetrarch of Galilee, whom his subjects styled a king, had robbed his brother Philip of his wife, the vain Herodias, and married her after his own wife had fled from him. Philip is compelled to submit to this violence of his overbearing brother. The powerful in Galilee are silent at the wicked deed, or applaud it with abject flattery. The nation is amazed at this double and threefold transgression of the law, but fear shuts their mouths. Before all these, his subjects, the tyrant felt no fear, because they feared him. He knew that they loved the pleasures of sense—the earthly life—above everything else, and so he wanted not means to bind them by fear, and even by hope, to his evil deeds.

But there was one over whom these means avail nothing; because He is lifted far above all earthly fear and hope. One man alone compels the criminal prince to tremble before Him. It is the Prophet of the wilderness, who goes clothed with a garment of camel's hair and is girt with a leathern girdle, and whose food is locusts and wild honey. Whether it was that Herod had asked Him for His judgment, in the hope of using the great credit which the Baptist enjoyed among the people, to palliate his detested deed in their eyes, or whether it was that John felt it to be his duty, unasked, to chastise the powerful sinner, he at any rate tells the king plainly: "It is not lawful for thee to have thy brother's wife." His words bear the impress of the calmest self-possession, and they must have operated so much the more powerfully on the mind of the king. Do you ask, whence John acquired this boldness? Was it, perchance, that he stood at the head of a numerous party which could have protected him against the wrath and vengeance of Herod? Oh! sin not, through any such distrust, against the pure spirit of John, which was far from being actuated by such low motives. Defenceless, there he stands, a lamb in the midst of ravening wolves; but inwardly, strong in the superior might of a true servant of God. To God had he consecrated his life, ready to die in His service, when it should be his duty. Therefore, was he free in the highest sense of the word, free in the midst of a thousand slaves. Therefore, was the tyrant not able, with all his power, to prevent him from uttering a truth that struck him to the earth.

John's mode of dealing shows the way to that true freedom which makes us invincible in conflict with the world and its powers. Let us imitate his example, and not follow the wild and unintelligible shout of the multitude, who go chasing after the phantom of a mere outward freedom; let us not be misled by the beguiling voice of those betrayers who promise us liberty, and are themselves "the servants of corruption." He alone is free, who carries that within him which lifts him altogether above the earthly life, and surrenders himself with a pure heart to the will of God. "If the Son, therefore, shall make you free," says Christ, "ye shall be free, indeed." No power of the world has conferred on us this freedom, and no power of the world can wrest it from us. He who cannot look into the earnest face of death without trembling, he is not truly free; and were he never so free in outward circumstances, yet is he a slave to the earth. His life does not belong to him, but he belongs to his life. For life does not truly become our own, until we are prepared to give it up for the sake of God. Out of the highest renunciation, springs the most perfect possession. "Whosoever," says Christ, "will save his life, shall lose it; and whosoever shall lose his life for My sake, shall find it."

But, if we have once obtained this freedom, what power can prevent us from testifying, in our vocation, to the truth; from testifying to the truth, even, when to the respected and powerful, be it in the greater or smaller spheres of life, it is a stone of stumbling and a rock of offence—because by it their sin and folly are chastised? Say not that, "In most cases, it is not to be expected we can, by bold censure, succeed in altering the evil; that if the sin is once done, it cannot be undone; and that even though the warning word were to precede the crime, it would be, for the most part, in vain; and, on the other hand, that by such a free confession of the truth, we might very easily destroy or endanger our own circle of influence, which it is our duty most carefully to preserve, and might thus be depriving the world of many blessings." Oh! how vain does this prudence which dictates such declarations, appear before the simplicity of John! He knew very well, that by his censure he would not be able to undo the iniquity of Herod, once committed. He also knew Herod too well, to expect that, on account of *his* word, he would dissolve his incestuous, adulterous alliance. But it *was* of the utmost importance to him that Herod, and that all the people should know that God is "not a God that hath pleasure in wickedness," and that such crimes are an abomination in His eyes. The more powerful and respected the transgressor of the law was, so much the more important did it seem to him for the servant of God to mark out and expose in his conduct, all that belonged to sin, and that ought not to be imitated by the people, but rather be abhorred and shunned by them. Or again, shall a regard for our sphere of influence prevent us from testifying to the truth, when we are opposed to some earthly power? Oh! let not any one deem himself so indispensable in the world, as to suppose that his place could be supplied by no other, and that the good cause, in a larger or smaller circle, would at once go to ruin, if he were no longer acting in it! Here, too, let John serve as an example for us. He was operating benignly upon a large part of the nation; he was waking thousands from the sleep of sin, and urging them powerfully to rise and seek God. And this whole ministry of his, so rich in blessings, he boldly staked, rather than shrink from his duty of chastising the prince. To be obedient to the known will of God—oh! let a preference for this lift us superior to every earthly consideration. Let us never commit the sin of doing evil that good may come. Then shall we also, like John, become strong and invincible in our contest with the world. Yes, when our influence in the cause of truth apparently falls to the ground, we shall then be exerting the strongest influence. In being cast down, we conquer.

This truth John also experienced. Herod, burning with wrath against the bold reprover, casts him into prison. But can he thereby hinder the influence of that spoken word? And did the people honor the imprisoned witness for the truth any the less than when he was free? Must not the words which they had heard from him, have sunk all the deeper into their hearts, for the fact that they saw the witness suffer for the truth's sake? But also in relation to Herod himself, how much stronger does he appear than the king! Though in his chains, he is free; his soul is not fettered, though his body is; yea, from out of his prison, he rules his very gaoler. Herod, it is said, "feared John, knowing that he was a just man and an holy, and observed him: and when he heard him, he did many things, and heard him gladly." The vengeance of Herodias seeks to entice him to the murder of the holy man; and there is something in himself that makes him desire the death of John. But these, also, awake in his soul better impulses which drive back the murderous thought into its darkest corner, and he is tied by a mysterious dread and reverence for his prisoner.

Do you find this mingling of feelings in Herod's mind strange and contradictory? And yet, in this respect, he but resembled by far the greater number of the children of the world. Ruled by carnal impulses, impelled by avarice and ambition, by vanity and lust, capable, in certain circumstances, of committing the awfullest crimes, they are yet by no means closed against salutary convictions. A silent awe bows them almost involuntarily before true piety and Christian virtue. If they stand in near connection with such servants of God, holding the relation of friend with friend, of husband with wife, of child with father and mother, of church member with pastor—they will listen to them in many things, especially where obedience is not too hard, and they will hearken gladly to their warning word, when it does not rebuke too severely their darling inclinations. But, though deeply sunk and governed by earthly lusts, still in the innermost, stillest chambers of their heart, there still dwells a secret approbation of the good, which is dispelled only with an entire hardening.

Do you know, my friends, what is the thread by which you to-day are to lead the children of the world to salvation? Then let him who would be a servant of God lay hold of it boldly, not for the purpose of giving predominance to his own will, but for

the purpose of furthering the kingdom of God upon earth. For
to this work you are at all times called, in whatever rank, in
whatever relations of life God has placed you. We are all
to follow our Saviour. To this end were we born that we, like
Him, might testify to the truth by word and deed. The great
mass of men are, as I have remarked, in a wavering condition ;
but though, as a rule, they follow the impulses of selfishness, yet
a nobler thought sometimes wins a momentary victory over these
impulses, which is without a lasting salutary effect. This, those
children of darkness know well, who with determination devote
themselves to the evil one, and they are, therefore, unweariedly
active in drawing others deeper and deeper into their net. So
Herodias, who, like a wicked angel to the soul of Herod, strives
to blow up the glimmering spark of murderous thought into
a blaze.

Shall, then, my friends, our love to God be less active for the
salvation of souls, than is wickedness of the wicked for their destruction ? Dare we resign to those spirits the arena of conflict,
and withdraw with hopeless abandonment into inactive stillness,
and bury the talent which God has intrusted to us ? Far be it ; let
us rather work untiringly while it is day, "for the night cometh,
when no man can work." Are others the evil angels of the children of this world ? We will be their good angels. Let us combat delusion and sin without fear or hesitation, wherever they
meet us. Let us freely proclaim the truth and the will of God,
and seek to gain for them a recognition among those who, in
their life, deny both. Let us defend the truth, even unto death,
and the Lord will contend for us. Let the renunciation of this
holy conflict be as impossible for us as for the glorious hero of
faith, who, when in the face of impending destruction, boldly
declared, "Here I stand—I cannot otherwise—God help me !"

Believe me, we have still in the hearts of most persons a secret
confederate, who, at the favorable hour, opens an avenue for our
entrance, so that our word at length suffices to overcome the
stiff resistance. And if it happens to us as to John with Herod,

who heard him gladly, and listened to him in many things, but in his inmost heart remained unimproved, oh, let us always regard it as a great gain if, by our coöperation, we can succeed in bringing to pass any good at all—in guarding against anything evil, in compelling any error to yield to the light of truth. Let us not despise the fragment because we cannot gain the whole ; let us not trample upon the germ because no blade of grass is springing up from it. If we have at any time won any place in the heart of a wicked man, let us courageously maintain it, and hope for greater victories in the future.

But if John cherished such hopes, you say, they have, as it seems, cruelly deceived him. This is shown by the sad conclusion of his history. Herod celebrates his birthday in the circle of the great men of his kingdom. The brilliance and noise of the festival crowds his secret connection with the prisoner back into the deepest recess of his soul. The daughter of Herodias steps into the festal hall, and delights the assembly with her mazy dance. The king, drunk with rapture, frivolous in promise, invites her to ask of him a favor, and promises to grant her request, even to the half of his kingdom. The daughter of Herodias, shrewdly weighing the importance of the offer, departs to consult with her mother, and then comes back to the king with the horrible petition, "I will that thou give me, in a charger, the head of John the Baptist." Herod is appalled and troubled. Mighty voices in his soul wax loud in behalf of the persecuted servant of God ; his better feeling struggles against the thought of murder, saying, "Sin lieth at the door ;" but give it not its will ; overcome it.

Yet Herod's struggle is in vain ; there is no deep earnestness in it. The hour of temptation has weighed him, and found him wanting. Because he has not sincerely given himself up to the divine truth, devilish wickedness has bound him in its snares. Instead of rueing the sin of his foolish promise, he adds to it another tenfold worse. He gives the bloody command—the head of John falls, and the bloodthirsty vengeance of Herodias is satiated. Thus Herod hardened his heart against the holy monitions of God, so that now upon him, as his later history informs us, the judgment of a divine hardening was inflicted. The murderer of the prophet ripened into the reviler of the suffering Son of God. That which might have rescued him—his salutary subjection to the influence of John—he himself, with audacious hand, destroyed by the murder of this righteous man.

Yet no, not wholly ; for this subjection has now turned into a gloomy, horrible foreboding. "When Herod," as the Evangelist tells us at the beginning of our text, "heard of Jesus, he said, 'It is John, whom I beheaded ; he is risen from the dead.'" This one word affords us a deep insight into the discomposure of Herod's mind. The murdered still exercises a silent power over the soul of his murderer. The latter finds no rest from him, amid the regal splendors of his life. Horrible thoughts haunt him, like apparitions. When he hears of the wonderful deeds of the Saviour, he dreams of the re-appearance of his beheaded victim. Thus, too, Sadducean unbelief in the immortality of the soul, blends with the strangest superstition. Oh, could we penetrate the secret of many a heart—could we follow many a persecutor of the pious and righteous into his calm, solitary hours, and into his sleepless nights, how often should we discover a parallel to this, and become convinced that he whom the world regards as the vanquisher, is, in fact, the vanquished ! A secret anxiety comes over him, as often as he thinks of his evil deeds, and of the wide-spread harm which he has done. Upon his soul it lies with a heavy weight, and when he seeks rest he finds none ; for the very avenue to Him in whom alone rest for our souls is to be found, he has himself effectually closed.

Yet another victory did John achieve over Herod, after his death. History has passed judgment upon both. The kingdom of Herod has long since perished ; every trace of his activity has long since vanished from the earth, while that of John has become a mighty pillar in that most glorious edifice whose duration is eternal ; and his word to-day is still operating with saving power upon millions of hearts. The name of Herod, history has handed down among the names of the murderers of the Son of God— among the names of Pontius Pilate, of Caiaphas, of Judas Iscariot—among the names upon which the curse of the human race rests—names which one repeats when he wishes to designate whatever is most repulsive and monstrous. The name of John, history has preserved among the names of the pious of the Old Testament—yea, in inseparable connection with the most holy name of the Redeemer of the world.

My friends, can we hide from ourselves the fact, that we live in a deeply agitated, excited time ; when opposition and hatred against the word of God, and against His church, come forth unveiled and resolute ; in a time which threatens the kingdom of the Lord with open warfare ? The servants of God know, indeed, that no hair shall fall from their head without the Father's will—that to them all things shall work for good—but nowhere is a promise given them that, in their struggles with the world, they shall be exempted from all injury to body and life. On the contrary, they are admonished by the instance of John— by the fate of the prophets and apostles, and by the death of the Lord himself, to prepare themselves for all extremities. But this, again, they are assured of, that the works which they have done in God the world cannot destroy ; the continuity of their blessed influence upon coming generations it cannot arrest. The whole course and action of the world is splintered and self-contradictory. The errors and sins of men are in ceaseless conflict, not only with the good and true, but also with each other. The pious endeavors of the servants of God, on the contrary, mutually strengthen and sustain each other. With them nothing happens in vain—nothing is lost. What in itself appears weak and small, becomes great and mighty through its close connection with similar works of countless others. Children, and children's children, dwell with thankful love upon the names of pious ancestors. The grateful recognition of good deeds always comes, though often late. The justice which a contemporary genera tion, blinded by passion and party rage, denied to them, is allowed them by the more considerate judgment of an after age. And though the circle in which they labored be ever so small, "the memory of the just is blessed."

But the perfected victory of the children of God over the children of the world, lies not within the sphere of the earthly life, but beyond its bounds, in a higher future. Yes, we will frankly confess, that the whole life of the Christian remains an unsolved riddle, if there were no such future. Yet, let us never hear it urged, by way of reproach, that Christians, when they cannot establish the truth of their assertions from the present state of existence, appeal to the future. How could they do otherwise? The full justification of their faith and life lies, in reality, beyond this present state. John dies in prison by the sword of the executioner; but his soul goes to God, and receives in His Paradise the blessed reward of his fidelity; while to his persecutors, death brings only the miserable wages of their enmity against God. "For we must all appear before the judgment-seat of Christ, that every one may receive the things done in his body according to that he hath done, whether it be good or bad." Then will the Lord take his faithful servants to himself, that they may see his glory, "For where I am," he says, "there shall also my servant be." But the children of the world, who have persistently resisted his call to repentance, and have persecuted Him in his church, he will give up to the tormenting darkness to which they have devoted themselves, "For," says the apostle Paul, "it is a righteous thing with God to recompense tribulation to them that trouble you; and to you, who are troubled, rest with us, when the Lord Jesus shall be revealed from heaven!"   Amen.

DISCOURSE XX.

THE WALK OF CHRIST UPON THE WAVES.

" But the ship was now in the midst of the sea, tossed with waves; for the wind was contrary. And in the fourth watch of the night Jesus went unto them, walking on the sea. And when the disciples saw him walking on the sea, they were troubled, saying, It is a spirit: and they cried out for fear. But straightway Jesus spake unto them, saying, Be of good cheer; it is I; be not afraid. And Peter answered him and said, Lord, if it be thou, bid me come unto thee on the water. And he said, Come. And when Peter was come down out of the ship, he walked on the water, to go to Jesus. But when he saw the wind boisterous, he was afraid; and beginning to sink, he cried, saying, Lord, save me. And immediately Jesus stretched forth *his hand*, and caught him, and said unto him, O thou of little faith, wherefore didst thou doubt? And when they were come into the ship, the wind ceased. Then they that were in the ship came and worshipped him, saying, Of a truth thou art the Son of God."—MATT. xiv. 24-33.

As the prophets of the old covenant, my hearers, often gave a symbolical stamp to their actions, in order to portray the future and its great events to the people, as in a picture, so we see Christ also not unfrequently availing himself of the same practice. When, for example, he withered up the fig-tree, which bore leaves, indeed, but no fruit, he intended thereby plainly to indicate the impending fate of the people, Israel. For however brilliant and promising was the jubilant reception with which they received their King when he rode into Jerusalem, he yet sought in vain among them for the fruits of a holy, earnest devotion, of an honest and faithful dependence on Him. A similar symbolical character we detect also in the transaction, whose record you have just been listening to. For though the first and most direct lesson to be learned from the walking of Christ upon the storm-tossed sea of Galilee, is the dominion which He, as the Son of God, exercised over nature ; yet the fact is at the same time the token of a still greater lordship which belonged to Him, and which He has continued to exercise ever since he appeared upon the earth—I mean His dominion over the spiritual life of men. Now whilst this event, so apprehended, is full of significance for all times, it must be, to us, especially at this crisis, in the highest degree important and consoling to observe, in this picture, a vivid representation of Christ, as the ruler over all the great movements now happening. And who can fail to perceive the deep meaning which Peter's attempt to walk, like his master, upon the billows of the sea, has for us ? Do we not here receive hints worthy of the most serious regard, as to the manner in which we are to conduct ourselves in this agitated time, in order to keep from sinking under its waves ? In this sense, and from this point of view, we propose to make use of the events which our text narrates. Let the walking of Christ and of his disciple Peter upon the lake of Gennesareth, be the subject of our medi-tation. The order of the text will give the order to our dis-course.

Upon the lake of Gennesareth, we descry in the darkness of night a vessel. It bears a company which is well known to us. It is the disciples of Christ, whom their master, the evening pre-vious, had bidden to sail across the lake alone. And does it not seem as if everything were against them, now that they are deserted by him ? The lake is stirred by a violent wind, which blows contrary. Already have they struggled many hours with the waves, and still they find themselves in the middle of the sea, which at other times they have often crossed, in less than an hour.

Who among us, **beloved friends,** can fail to perceive that this stormy, billowy sea, **is a most** striking image of our time, which, in its **deep** and universal agitation, has hardly a parallel in the history of the human race ? We are now no longer engaged in

a contest of isolated opinions and views, which indeed has always
been waged. The highest principles, whose antagonism strikes
its roots deep into the innermost depths of the human soul, have
entered the list against each other for an irreconcilable combat,
which has now for many years continued to rage. For a time,
indeed, it appeared, as if the storm, at least in the civil life of
the nations, had been hushed ; yet it was but a deceitful appearance like that appalling stillness, which sometimes upon the sea
interrupts for a moment the war of the storm, as if the elements
were gathering strength for a redoubled violence. While the
surface was calm, it heaved and swelled in the depths ; and these
wild commotions and passionate struggles, which have broken
forth in our day, did they not all issue from the pregnant womb
of the season just past, and thence derive their nourishment ?
And when we now look around us, what a spectacle does the
present exhibit ? Is not confusion everywhere in conflict with
confusion, error with error, selfishness with selfishness ? Do not
corruption and mischief threaten us on all sides ? Do not the
powers of the abyss appear to have been let loose, to instigate
men into irreconcilable hate and strife, one against the other ?
Oh, my friends, let us hide nothing from ourselves ; thick darkness lies over our earthly future, so that no human eye can discern it. The ship of our life, of its repose and its bliss, is every
moment in danger of being swallowed up by the waves or of
being shattered upon unknown rocks.

Yet there, upon the lake of Gennesareth, the darkness begins
to yield to the approaching light. The fourth watch is come ;
the grey of dawn appears ; those charming heights—which
toward the west encircle and crown the sea, while the craggy
masses of rock towards the east grow the darker ; soon will the
first streaks of the morning red glide over the lake ; suddenly,
and together with the twilight, lo, He suddenly appears—the
long wished-for master, walking upon the sea. Wonderful spectacle ! The tossing wave sustains His foot, as if it were the
solid ground ; the insurgent billows acknowledge, amazed, their

mighty sovereign, Him who once bade them "be still," and they
were still. With a firm and sure step, He walks there upon the
flowing element, towards the distressed boat. The towering
waves may sometimes, indeed for a moment, hide Him from
the eyes of his disciples, but they cannot block His path to the
goal.

What then took place, Christian hearers, takes place again to-
day. Over the foaming waves of agitated thought and feeling,
which makes us fearful, he walks calmly as their Lord and
Sovereign. They may rise against, but they cannot overmaster
Him. They may sometimes conceal Him from the sight of his
disciples, but they cannot check his course. They must at
length own Him as their Master, and serve his will. Do you
not see Him walking in might through the press and tumult? Is
not the darkness retiring at his approach? Comes He not attended with a dusky light, with blushes of the morning glow,
which proclaim the coming day? Have not thousands upon
thousands of hearts been awakened out of deep sleep in the
midst of this stormy time, and recognized Him as the way to
the Father—as the truth and the life, and found in Him a new
and nobler existence? And what wonder is it, if just now, while
he is drawing near, the waves should foam more wildly, and the
storm rage with greater violence? Who will think it strange
if the resistance to Him and his Gospel should rage more
fiercely? if men should defame and scorn all living faith in Him,
either as a childish delusion, that belongs to an era long anti-
quated, and which mankind, now waxen mature, has outgrown,
or should blaspheme and ridicule it as a hypocritical imposition?
Yea, if whole nations should more and more resolutely turn
away from this faith. Against the rising light, the powers of
darkness, error, and falsehood, are compelled to collect their
forces, in order to defend their tottering kingdom against the
Stronger who comes to conquer it.

Shall we therefore fear that he will be defeated in this contest?
What, my friend! Is he not Jesus Christ, the same yesterday,

to-day, and for ever? / The same whose words shall not pass away, even though heaven and earth pass away ? The same who says to the rapt Apostle, " I am the first and the last ; I am he that liveth and was dead ; I am alive for evermore ?" After the floods of time shall have long submerged the idols of this generation in its dark depths, he will still be walking calmly upon its waves, as he did of old, and as he does now. When the names of those who in their vain wisdom deem themselves to be far above Christ, and think his Gospel to have been worn out and no more needed, His name will live upon millions of lips and in millions of hearts, and children will lisp this name, and the knees of men will bow at the mention of this name, and pain will vanish, and mourning will cease, and tears will be dried, and the deepest wounds of the heart will be healed in the name of Jesus Christ. For there is salvation in no other : " for there is no other name under heaven, given among men, whereby we must be saved." So it was then, when Peter spoke these words ; and so it will be to the end of days.

Upon the disciples, however, the sudden appearance of the Lord, near the vessel, makes an entirely different impression from what would have been expected. The circumstance so miraculous and supernatural appears to them, in the grey twilight, as something strange and fearful. As they see the form advancing towards them, upon the waves, they cry out in terror, " It is a Spirit !" and anticipate with fright the sinking of their vessel at its approach.

When He meets us, as the mighty ruler of the world, as He whom the Father has made the Lord of the dead and of the living, to whom he has given power " to execute judgment also, because he is the Son of Man"—does there not often fall upon pious souls, a fear and trembling before Him and his irresistible power ? He always stands before them, as Judge, in a threatening form ; and if they hear the gospel of his love, and impelled by a deep, longing, desire to draw near to Him a disquieting sense of His majesty frightens them back. They still see Him only in the dusk, therefore their fear transforms the Redeemer into a destroyer.

But is anything more needed to banish this fear from the soul, than that He should come nearer to us and talk with us, and let us recognize him, as he there talked with his disciples, and said : "Be of good cheer, it is I, be not afraid." How sweetly sound these words ! How comforting their import ! Yes, this is the sweet voice with which He everywhere speaks to us in the Gospel. Fear not ! That is the tone from the beginning to the end. So He calms the timorous hearts and kindly allures them to himself—fear not, it is I. "Come unto me all ye that labor and are heavy laden, and I will give you rest." Rest for your souls, the heavenly peace which you so much need amid the dangers of this time, the divine comfort which will not suffer you to sink in the floods—this shall you find in Me. Oh, learn to know me, as I also know you and your weakness and anxiety—your struggles and strife, so fruitless without me ! Am I not come that ye might have life, and have it more abundantly ? Am I not the physician of the sick—the Saviour of the lost—your tender-hearted high priest, who takes compassion on your weakness ? "All power is given to me in heaven and upon earth ;" but I possess it for your good ; "for unto this end has my Father given me power over all flesh, that I might give eternal life to as many as he has given me." Now, oh, how that majestic sovereignty before which we trembled, turns into our highest consolation. Now we feel assured He will rule over the world —will rule in our hearts, not with iron sceptre, but with the mild shepherd's rod of love. Thus it is, he wins men to his service, and to him whom he has won, he imparts eternal life out of his divine fullness ; "Because I live," he says, "ye shall live also ;" and "where I am, there shall also my servant be."

Thus Peter thinks, also—Peter, the man of fiery spirit and quick resolve. He sees the Master walking upon the sea ; an urgent desire seizes him to be at His side, and to walk with Him upon the waves—"Lord, if it be Thou, bid me come unto Thee on the water !" And when Christ bids him "come," he steps forth without hesitation from the vessel, full of firm assurance, and strides towards Jesus. With trembling joy, he perceives how the flowing element is compelled to afford him, also, a safe path ; the waves may roar, but they frighten him not ; the depths may open, but him they cannot swallow. Already does he seem to be sharing with his Master in His dominion over nature and her rebellious powers.

My friends, if the Gospel of Christ presents us with sure, firm principles for estimating the movements of the present, if it intrusts to us the word that solves the riddle of our time, the word which the prudent men of the world, the obtrusive physicians of the sick generation, in vain seek for, is it not natural that a powerful impulse should be roused in ardent souls, to rush with a spirit for contest into the midst of the confusion of the time, in order to help to end it ? in order to dissipate the delusions of folly and passion, and rule with power over the wild waves of discordant opinions ? And can we blame them for this desire ? It is the example of the Lord himself which allures them to it, as it did Peter ; for Christ also did not withdraw Himself from the apparently inextricable confusion of His day ; but He entered into the raging sea of passionate strife, interfering between embittered parties, in order that by living, personal intercourse with all on every side, He might, through the divine clearness of His soul, bring light and order into the dark time and its wild movements ; in order that He might point susceptible hearts to the one thing needful for founding a new—more beautiful edifice, in the impending overthrow of everything old. And it is faith in His word that empowers them for this undertaking, as then it empowered Peter. This faith is the weapon with which they will contend against the resistance of hostile powers ; it is the light that shall enlighten them in the darkness. And their assurance, that they shall stand firm in the billowy sea, and safely advance to the goal, is grounded upon Him alone. Should we not, then, rejoice, when, with sympathetic

16

participation in public interests, they seek to apply their excellent gifts for the furtherance of the common weal, and extend to it their pious activity? Must we not anticipate a rich blessing from their efforts? Will they not work mightily for the salvation of many? Yes, if all blossoms were to become fruits, and all fruits were to ripen! But the most beautiful blossoms of pious impulse, of noble resolve, are swept away by the storm, and the most promising fruits of enterprises well begun drop off, pierced by the worm, before they can ripen.

This, Peter too was obliged to experience. With a bold, confident spirit he has begun his walk upon the sea; but all at once he sees a strong gust of wind coming which rolls up yet mightier surges. Upon this he becomes terrified, his faith wavers, his courage fails: "Will not the roaring flood swallow me up?"—and ere he has time to collect himself, he begins to sink.

Our Lord, on one occasion, said to His disciples, after He had invited them to faithful, self-denying imitation of Him: "For which of you intending to build a tower, sitteth not down first, and counteth the cost, whether he have *sufficient* to finish it? Lest haply, after he hath laid the foundation, and is not able to finish it, all that behold it begin to mock him, saying, This man began to build, and was not able to finish. Or what king, going to make war against another king, sitteth not down first, and consulteth whether he be able with ten thousand to meet him that cometh against him with twenty thousand? Or else, while the other is yet a great way off, he sendeth an ambassage, and desireth conditions of peace. So, likewise, whosoever he be of you that forsaketh not all that he hath, he cannot be my disciple." This the Lord says to Peter, who so often, as in our text, trusted in himself to a degree beyond his ability for execution; this He says also to the countless number who are like him. Oh, my friends, it is no easy matter to step into the midst of the confusion of this time, in order to struggle against it, and tread with firm step upon a ground which appears to shake constantly under our feet, and not to lose the path where all is veiled in the grey cloud; and whoever enters upon a calling which obliges him to this struggle, or whoever is otherwise compelled freely to devote his activity to it, let him consider well what he undertakes, and whether he has the courage and the perseverance to carry it through successfully. Can we hide from ourselves the fact, that our time is productive of temptations, to which even the strong succumb? that it leads the bold individual who rushes into its conflicts, upon smooth, slippery paths, where it appears well-nigh impossible not to slide and fall, and keep himself clean from all wrong and sin? that it places him, as it were, upon the heaving waves and bids him there stand firm? And when you have once stepped out upon the wild sea, for the purpose of helping to bind and rule its tumultuous commotion, and you then see the storm breaking loose and the waves tower against you, will not anxiety and doubt seize upon your soul, will not your faith totter and fail? And then just as your faith vanishes, you will, like Peter, begin to sink, for it was Faith alone that held you up; with him, you will lose all power, and the whirlpool of a selfish chase, ruled by folly and passion, will draw you with violence into its horrible circle, that it may engulph you in its dark depths.

At such a crisis there is only one means of rescue; it is that which Peter seized upon. When he began to sink, he cried: "Lord, help me!" And he did not cry in vain. Jesus is already by the side of the sinking one, and stretches out His hand and grasps him, and punishes his weakness only with the mild reproof: "O thou of little faith, wherefore didst thou doubt?"

Woe to those who, after having begun in faith the conflict with the rushing stream of dominant errors, prejudices, and passions, thereupon lose their faith, and with it the strength of God, and then, with a spirit of defiance, continue the contest in their own strength, thus trying to perfect in the flesh what they have begun in the spirit. Such persons continue to sink deeper and deeper in guile and ambitious scheming. What in the beginning was God's cause, becomes in the end a mere thing of a party. In the place of child-like, trustful simplicity, there enters worldly calculation and cunning. They wear the armor of the ungodly, and contend with carnal weapons, and eventually become of their mind. They propose to overcome evil with evil, and are thereupon themselves overcome by evil, and are caught in its snares. In such temptation and need, let us, therefore, like Peter, fly to Jesus for refuge, and cry, "Lord, help me." Though we may not have faith enough to finish that great struggle in his name, yet, let there never be wanting that small measure of faith which will enable us, in our embarrassment and weakness, to seek help from Him. Let us entreat Him that He would draw us out of the entanglements in which we have rashly involved ourselves, without a stain upon our conscience ; and that He would not suffer us to be tempted beyond our ability, but with the temptation would also provide a way of escape. Let us pray that he would rescue our soul from death, and our foot from sliding upon the tottering path, and set us upon a rock, where we may stand in safety.

And, surely, if we pray sincerely we shall, with the disciple of the Lord, experience that He is near to all " that call upon Him in truth ;" that He lovingly assists the weak, and despises not the anxious cry of the sinking. If we trustfully grasp His hand, and (in humility) commit ourselves wholly to his guidance, ready to sacrifice every gain, to suffer every disgrace, if only we can secure His approval, I say, if we do this, He will open ways for us through the raging waves of temptation, and will lead us out of the wild tumult upon a quiet and safe path. But while his help does not fail us, He yet administers to us His mild word of rebuke : O thou of little faith, wherefore dost thou doubt? Wherefore didst thou let the victory slip when thou already hadst it in your hand ? Would not a firm faith, which looks not upon the storm and the billows, but upon God, have continued to keep thee erect, as heretofore, in the struggle ? Would

not a child-like simplicity of heart have guarded thee yet longer
from sinking into the sins and the corruption of the time ? No,
it was not that the temptations were not too great, but thine
own faith was too small.

With the humbled and rescued Peter, Christ now enters the
ship where the other disciples are. The wind lulls, the waves
cease to roar ; upon the peaceful surface of the sea the boat
glides softly and swiftly to the opposite shore.

Yes, it is He alone who, as He can control and rule in the
raging sea of the troubled time, can also quiet the very storm
itself of the spiritual life. Upon His Gospel and its divine power,
rests all hope for the future. If rescue does not come from
hence, there is no rescue for us at all. If faith does not again
wax mighty in this disordered time—a faith which can quench
the consuming fire of selfish passion, and teach us to honor the
will and the word of God above everything else, then truly there
is no help. By whatever other methods men may seek to heal
their wounds, if these methods are not penetrated by the power
of faith, it is all idle delusion, and can only serve to bring about
the deceptive appearance of a cure, while the poison of the
wound corrodes more and more fatally within. Were our hopes
resting only on such means of human strength and prudence, oh
then, indeed, should we be obliged to prepare ourselves for the
approaching death-night of a melancholy bewilderment, and utter
dissolution of all human relations ; and, with a bleeding heart,
we must look upon the dark future of the rising generation.

But does not the morning dawn upon the sea of Gennesareth,
which bears that vessel with Christ and his disciples ? Comforting picture of our time ! Yes, it is the grey of morning, which
appears, however, to fearful, anxious souls, as the twilight of
evening. We are not approaching the night, but the day—a
more beautiful day—where living faith and true piety shall again
thoroughly penetrate the life of the nations ; where, after having
once and again " hewn themselves out broken cisterns which hold
no water," they shall, with deeper longing, betake themselves

again to the fountain from which stream forth the waters of
everlasting life.

And does it not begin to break forth? Do you not see
the lofty One, walking in calm majesty over the lifted waves,
which are forced to crouch at his feet? Do not the rays of the
morning red shine before Him, and proclaim the advancing conquest of his heavenly light over the earthly darkness? Has not
his Father given Him a great multitude as his portion, and the
strong as his spoil? Has He not become too powerful for thousands who once withstood Him; and has he not overcome them
by his love, so that they now lie at his feet, and know no higher
glory than that of being His possession? Ah, will not many
among us, who now withstand Him, one day also bow their knees
before Him, and say: "Lord, to whom shall we go? Thou hast
the words of eternal life, and we believe and are sure that Thou
art that Christ, the Son of the living God!" Yes, as there in
the vessel, when He entered it and all became still, the men fall
before Him and exclaim, "Of a truth, Thou art the Son of God,
so will we worshipfully bow before Him, who is in the midst of
us, where two or three are gathered in His name."

Of a truth, Thou art the Son of God, O Lord, and thy Father
hath given all things into thy hand—hath called the whole
human race to become thy possession. And Thou dost pity all,
and art willing to be the helper of all in the necessities of their
earthly life, and dost kindly call every one of us to Thee, as
Thou didst call Peter. Oh that we may willingly obey the call
of Thy love, and faithfully continue in Thy holy communion.
Then will the storm and the billows not terrify us. We see
Thee walking upon the boisterous sea of our agitated time. We
follow Thee with confident courage, and if we sink, and cry in
distress, "Lord, help us!" then dost Thou reach forth Thy hand
to us, thou faithful Saviour, and dost rescue us, and strengthen
us for new conflicts, until with Thee we reach the safe shore of
everlasting peace, when for us the day breaks to which no night
again succeeds. Amen

DISCOURSE XXI.

THE RELATION OF RELIGION TO BUSINESS.*

It is an old and famous maxim, my beloved friends, that the middle way is the best ; a maxim to which the highest value is wont to be ascribed, not only in the business of life, in the education of youth, and in the government of nations, but in reference to the study of external truth. Nevertheless, neither the antiquity nor the wide-spread authority of this principle can blind us to the mournful errors into which it misleads us, when we come to make it universally applicable. To be sure, it commends itself to us as an easy and convenient procedure, in the strife of opposite views and aims, if nothing farther were needful for us, in order to hit upon the truth, but each time to seek out that which lies in the middle, between the contending antagonisms. But how does the ease and simplicity of this procedure help us, if its result is still so unsafe ? For can we conceal from ourselves the fact, that among men not always one one-sided principle contends with another, but just as frequently truth with error, good with evil ? When the word of eternal truth— the Gospel of Christ—was still obliged to contend with heathen delusion, which withstood its progress, into what dark, bottomless depths of error must those have fallen, who sought to gain a middle ground between the contending powers, who ventured

---

* A friend and admirer of Prof. Müller, not connected with the preparation of this volume, kindly furnished the translation of this and the following discourses.

upon the mad attempt to harmonize and reconcile the Gospel
with Idolatry !   And if we to-day, as at all times of the Christian Church, see on the one side, enthusiastic zeal for the kingdom of God, for truth and righteousness, on the other, cold
indifference, or even embittered hostility, woe to us, if we think
that we must place ourselves in the middle, between the antagonistic sentiments and endeavors.   For that crushing word of
Christ strikes us ; Alas, that you are neither cold nor hot !
" Because thou art lukewarm, and art neither cold nor hot, I will
spue thee out of my mouth."

But however insufficient that principle is found to be, when it
will exalt itself as a universal rule for ascertaining right and
truth, still there lies indisputably at the bottom of it a great
truth.   For how do those errors commonly arise, which, with
destructive violence, take a deep hold of the whole life, and by
their appearance of truth, draw countless numbers after them ?
Is it not in this way, that some one-sided notion of the objects
of our knowledge passes itself as complete, and excludes every
other ; that an isolated thought which has its truth in its connection with others, in its definite place in a great circle of
thoughts, breaks loose from this connection, in order that it may
alone rule the soul, so that, despising every limit, with vehe-
mence it pursues the single tendency to the extremest point?
Thus, it happens, that we see, everywhere in the world, antagonistic one-sided combatants in strife with one another—opinions,
feelings, spiritual tendencies, of which the one is just as far aside
from the right and the true as the other.   Here the Gospel
points us to the true medium ; but not in this way, that out of
the antagonistic deviations, and their comparison and mutual
approximation, we can calculate out the evangelical truth which
is between them, but so that we must have first found this truth,
in order to recognize these deviations as such, and rightly to
estimate them.   Therefore, if we trust with sincere confidence,
to the guidance of the Gospel, it leads us upon the narrow but
safe path, between and through the seductive by-paths at the

right and the left. It makes known to us the convincing truth of the Christian faith, as the medium between unbelief and superstition ; it guides us on to the mild earnestness of Christian holiness, as the medium between a light, frivolous, worldly temper, and a dark, world-despising severity. And as in the general course of life, so the more our heart is penetrated by the power of the divine word, the more we live and move in it, so much the more does the Gospel manifest itself in the special relations of life, so that the Gospel everywhere places its true adherents in the middle between antagonistic errors. May our meditation to-day, from a particular point of view, contribute to strengthen and confirm us anew in this conviction.

"Now it came to pass, as they went, that he entered into a certain village : and a certain woman named Martha, received him into her house. And she had a sister called Mary, which also sat at Jesus' feet, and heard his word : But Martha was cumbered about much serving, and came to him, and said, Lord, dost thou not care that my sister hath left me to serve alone ? Bid her, therefore, that she help me. And Jesus answered, and said unto her, Martha, Martha, thou art careful, and troubled about many things. But one thing is needful, and Mary hath chosen that good part, which shall not be taken away from her."—LUKE x. 38–42.

It is a very simple event which the Evangelist narrates to us in our text, so simple that one might almost doubt whether it were worthy to be preserved among so weighty discourses and transactions. What passes between the sisters, in a similar way often occurs in domestic life. The thought, too, which the Lord expresses in connection, in its great simplicity, appears to us to offer no material for varied discussion. But as nothing is of trifling value to Christian souls, which affords them a glance into the mind of their Lord, as in nearness to the Son of God the apparently insignificant becomes significant, so, then, are here very important lessons which our text presents to us, in the conduct of the sisters, in the discourse of the Lord, as in His previous silence—instructions upon THE TRUE RELATION OF THE ASPIRATION AFTER HEAVENLY THINGS TO OUR EARTHLY BUSINESS. These instructions, let us then, in this hour consecrated to devotion, farther consider with one another ; and follow the course which is taken by the narrative of the Evangelist in our text.

Well known to us is the house into which the narrative of the Evangelist conducts us—the house of the brother and sisters, Lazarus, Martha, and Mary, into whose trusty circle our Lord so loved to retire, when the bitter hate of His enemies grieved Him, and their persecution pressed Him. So we do not first learn the different tempers of heart of that sisterly pair which receives the Lord, in our text, out of this description ; it only completes the picture which is sketched by some other narratives where we see them act. Martha we know as one of those peculiar, strong characters which appear to be destined for a restless activity and employment in outward life. Still, lonely contemplation, continuous thought, are not for her. Quick, often somewhat precipitate, the thought ripens into the word, the resolve into the act ; and every impulse, every impression which she receives from without at once becomes for her a stimulus to react upon the outward world. Mary, on the contrary, seems to us to be one of those lovely souls which hide in themselves a rich, inner world, with which they love to busy themselves in still thought, and for which they seek to gain a new enrichment by every contact with the outward world. If their knowledge is of narrow compass, its connections are still closer ; are they sparing of words, yet their whole nature expresses deep, strong feeling ; are they slow, unskillful in action, yet there manifests itself in their actions that thoughtful earnestness, which often exerts the greatest power over other souls, without themselves being conscious of it.

Out of these diverse tempers of the sisters, arises the great difference in their deportment with reference to Christ, as our text pictures it for us. Martha only thinks how, as a hostess, she can best entertain the worthy guest, the revered prophet from Nazareth. Therefore "she was cumbered about much serving" him ; busily she hurries hither and thither, to care for everything needful, and if she sometimes hearkens to the discourse of the Master, this happens, certainly, only as she is hurrying by. Quite otherwise Mary. Hardly has she heard that the Lord is disposed to teach, when she is already sitting at his feet and listening to His words. She knows well that He has not come that He may be sumptuously entertained, that it is His food to do the will of His Father, and to finish His work. Here she forgets the earthy cares and business, the outward world is for her vanished, her whole soul sinks itself into the unfathomable depths of divine grace and wisdom, which the word of the Master opens for her. For of this, the connection of the events leaves no doubt; not of earthly but of heavenly things, did Christ speak to Mary, of the holy will of His Father, of His immeasurable love, which sent the Son for the redemption of sinful men, of the new kingdom which He has come to found upon the earth, and of the imperishable glory which shall one day be the portion of the citizens of this kingdom.

But what says Christ to this different deportment of the sisters? Does he blame Martha's earthly activity? Does he bid her do as Mary does? No, my friends; of this the Evangelist says not a word. Nothing entitles us to believe that the Saviour expressed disapproval and dissatisfaction with Martha. Yea, we may decidedly assert that He did not; otherwise Martha could not afterwards have claimed his help against the, according to her judgment, inactive sister. And what could have prompted the Lord to reprove her? That she was so vigorous and indefatigable in her earthly business, can, in His eyes, only have redounded to her honor; with approval, he looks upon her industrious activity; for he perceives in her action, a well-meaning, loving heart, an honest endeavor to do something agreeable to Him. As love sanctifies everything that it touches, so it lends to this domestic industry a higher sacredness and significance. What prevents Martha from sitting, like her sister, at the feet of the Redeemer is surely not a contemptuous indifference to the word of the kingdom of God, but zeal to honor the lofty guest. And if, besides, her whole nature was disposed to this restless industry, shall we not have confidence in the friend of Jesus, and believe that in her soul, in the midst of outward activity, so many a divine thought dwelt, that often the heart prayed, while the hand labored? Oh, surely, with a mild, kind look the Lord followed Martha, in her busy employment.

So He looks, who is with His church always, until the end of the world. He looks to-day with approval, when his disciples are unweariedly active in their earthly calling. For he is not come to disturb and destroy the earthly life, in its natural relations, but to ennoble and to perfect. The activity of men in so far as it aims to improve as much as possible, their outward condition, to give their earthly existence, in all its directions, more proportionate and graceful forms; their endeavor to subject the outward world to themselves, and to stamp upon it, everywhere, the impress of the human mind, which is called to the dominion of nature,—all this Christ will not destroy, but confirm. Far from us be the thought, that His redemption work is to place itself in any contradiction with the work of creation, in which His Father endowed man with many gifts and powers, and together with the gifts and powers, has implanted the impulse to put them into their appropriate activity. Rather will the Redeemer cherish, sanctify, ennoble human activity in the improvement of the earthly life, while he purifies it from the displacing, obstructing influences of sin, while that to which a natural impulse incites us, which an outward necessity commands us, he exalts to a duty of obedience and of love to God, and so communicates to it a higher meaning, and a new, a deeper motive.

And does not the whole history of the human race, since the coming of the Son of God in the flesh, testify most decidedly, that from Christianity a power went forth, to form the earthly side, also, of human life, according to the most varied tendencies, in a peculiar way; that the Gospel became for the human mind a mightier spur to fresh activity, to erect over the ruins of the ancient world, a new, magnificent edifice? The whole culture

of the modern times, what it has brought forth in science and
art, in the wide circle of the state, as well as in the narrow
circle of family life—has it not its deepest roots in Christianity,
even though it will not itself be conscious of it, and even though
it may be immeasurably far from being completely penetrated
by the Christian spirit ?

It is the nature of all Fanaticism to fancy the earthly and the
heavenly, as in necessary antagonism, and just for this reason
can its workings be not otherwise than destructive. In dark,
morose feeling, or in gloomy, anxious, shyness, it turns away
from the rich world, as if it were not God's creation, but the
devil's work, as if all its charm, all its beauty were only hellish
enticement. To attain to eternal life, it thinks it necessary to
renounce the stirring activity of temporal life ; to give place for
the working of divine Grace in the soul, it seeks to annihilate
all the feelings of human nature ; to behold the heavenly, it
will entirely close the eye to the earthly. It will become acquainted with the shining and warming strength of the sun ; but it
regards not its workings upon earthly objects, which are enlightened and warmed by it, but stares fixedly at its light, till at
length the eye of the soul is blinded.

But is this not the reproach which touches the second of this
sisterly pair, Mary ? Is she not one of the souls which, in the
consideration of heavenly things, forget and neglect activity in the
earthly ? It is not to be denied that these calm, thoughtful
souls, easier than others, fall into this error. Perhaps Mary,
too, has sometimes been obliged to struggle with the temptation
to yield herself, in a too great degree, to inactive contemplation.
But if she had succumbed to this temptation, if that morbid
disinclination to earthly activity had really overmastered her
soul, would not Christ, who knew well what was in man, have
warned her with emphasis and earnestness ? Would He have
allowed that Mary, following a perverted inclination, should
place herself at His feet ? Or was His strong, holy, love to men
like our love, which is often too weak and too unholy to be able,

by the severe truth, **to give** the loved one, even when his soul's
good requires it? No, my hearers, if Christ suffered Mary,
putting everything aside, **to listen to** his teaching—what do I
say, suffered?—if He expressly *praised* her choice, it was surely
free from every fanatical perverseness; and if Mary heard His
word with devotion, and preserved it in her fine, good heart,
that word, in turn, must have preserved her from such error.
Did He who had the words of eternal life, appear in her house,
then she had indeed nothing more pressing to do than to listen
to Him; but we may not doubt, but that when refreshed by a
deep draught from the fountain of living water, she again returned
with renewed zeal, and with redoubled love and fidelity, to her
daily work, and to its only apparently unimportant labors and
business.

No, not Mary, but Martha it is, who mistakes and disturbs
the true, divinely-pleasing relation between the care for heavenly
things and earthly business. It is she, who for the moment
wanders from the right way, not indeed into fanaticism, but into
the opposite by-path, into a culpable subordination of the heavenly to the earthly. And is it not just this danger which
chiefly threatens those souls which are inclined to unremitting
outward activity? Is it not this danger in which the faith of so
many, yet in the germ, has perished, choked by earthly **cares?**
In the beginning, we may believe, Martha conceived of her
household management in its right relation to the higher aspiration after eternal good. But, as it often happens, in busy employment itself, she loses the measure for judging it. Outward
business and its aims appear to her more and more, as properly
the principal thing. Her mind is taken **captive** by them, instead
of mastering them; the labor appears ever to grow, the more
hastily and unquietly she carries it on; she thinks that she cannot alone be done with it; vexation awakes in her heart that
her sister is not busy with her; it is to her inconceivable how
her Master can suffer it; finally, she cannot longer restrain herself—not without an expression of displeasure, however much

we may imagine it to have been softened by the tone of the voice, she turns complainingly to the Lord : " Lord dost thou not care that my sister hath left me to serve alone ? bid her therefore that she help me."

Poor Martha ! How quickly have earthly cares succeeded in obscuring her eye, and making her forget that there is something that is much weightier than the transient things with which she has to do. Instead of subordinating to this one thing, all earthly business and efforts, that they by means of this subordination may be sanctified, she lets herself be misled into giving to them her soul, as a complete possession. Yea, more : instead of modestly recognizing and honoring the tender feeling of her sister, the more hearty expressions of her glowing love to the Lord and to the word of life, she becomes impatient towards Mary, and will force upon her her own way of feeling and of acting. Hardly has passionate disorder won a place in her soul, when it loses the modest consciousness of its proper restriction and seeks to exalt its ways for a universal touchstone and for an imperative pattern for others.

But He to whom she has brought her unseemly complaint, checks the serious fault at the right time with soft but earnest correction : " Martha, Martha, thou art careful and troubled about many things, but one thing is needful ! Let us carefully observe, my friends, what sort of conduct it is which the Lord censures in these words. Is it the being busy with earthly things, in general ? or busy industry in this employment ? Not at all, but only the passionate disorder and error of the soul, to which Martha has allowed herself, by this means, to be hurried away. More clearly and definitely than in our translation this is expressed by the original text : " Many are the things," says Christ, reprovingly, " which put you into anxious care and tumultuous excitement." That her soul was so wholly possessed by the busy stir of earthly things, that it would perceive nothing higher —nothing more important—this it is in Martha that displeased the Lord ; this it is which displeases him to-day in his disciples

who allow themselves to be so often carried away by the error of
Martha. This it is which separates a countless number from him,
all those who in this transient state of Martha's heart behold the
picture of their whole life. Does your soul regard earthly things
as the highest, and the business which relates to them as your
weightiest employment? Then is your soul like the waves of the
sea which are driven and blown by the wind; it is given up to
eternal disquiet and transient change. For manifold and varied
are earthly things, and whoever gives himself up to their dominion
—his soul is dragged hither and thither, in all directions, by hope
and fear—by joy and sorrow—by desire for gain and by pain at
loss. And how should the grace of the Lord and his peace
make their dwelling in such a disturbed soul? O my friends,
whatever earthly calling may be allotted to us—however spiritual in its functions—however blessed in its effects, if its employ-
ments drive us forwards in breathless haste upon life's path—if
we think that we can find no more time, sometimes to stand
still and to think where we are and whither we will go, and
to reflect on the heavenly and eternal concerns of our immortal
soul—if prayer has lost its power and the divine word its charm
for us, then we have cast away our life upon a fearful error—
upon a fleeting dream; then are we with all our apparent richness in bodily and spiritual goods, really poor, very poor. We
have, like Martha, much care and trouble, but the highest good
which alone gives to our life its worth and significance, is wanting.

One thing is needful! Only one does Christ recognize as re
ally essential, as the highest and most pressing necessity, and that
is the seeking for the kingdom of God and its righteousness, the
endeavor to gain the grace and the approbation of the Heavenly
Father. This is the precious pearl which a merchant found, and
"went and sold all that he had and bought it." This is the
heavenly and eternal good, which we should seek with the entire
devotion of our soul, with the resolute subordination, day by
day, of things earthly to things heavenly The time is short.

Therefore, those who weep should be "as though they wept not ; and they that rejoice, as though they rejoiced not ; and they that buy, as though they possessed not ; and they that use this world, as not abusing it ; for the fashion of this world passeth away." Whoever will be a disciple of Christ, ought not to forget that here upon the earth he is a stranger and a pilgrim ; for as our Lord had not where to lay his head, so his friends here "have no continuing city, but seek one to come."

One thing is needful. If earthly things, which are infinitely various, and stand in manifold contrasts with one another, involve the soul that passionately clings to them, in a confused, restless chase, heavenly things, on the contrary, are harmonious in holy unison, and alone able to bring true unity and abiding peace into the life of him who devotes himself to them with his whole soul. The discord in which the changing and contradictory impressions of the outward world involve us—this the one thing that is needful is able to end. The wounds which the earthly life inflicts upon us—this one thing is able to heal them.

One thing is needful. Oh that no one among us would neglect that earnestly warning, that kindly alluring word of the Lord ! That as the sunbeam penetrates the icy surface of the ground, and in the depths wakes a new life—that with the same power, this word would melt, and penetrate to its innermost depths the hard crust with which the long habit, perhaps, of chasing after merely earthly goods has invested the heart— might penetrate, and so waken that hidden longing for the heavenly, which often sleeps, to be sure, but only seldom wholly dies out ! That this word, too, would sound in our soul when the distractions and pleasures of sensuous life would take possession of our heart ! That this warning voice of the true Shepherd would keep us in the hour of temptation, when we are on the point of yielding to sin ! That it would rouse us when sin has succeeded in lulling us into that secure sleep, from which a too late awaking will be terrible.

Yet, not with a depressing menace should our meditation conclude. The last word of the Lord contains a joyful, elevating promise. "Mary," He says, "has chosen that good part that shall not be taken away from her." According to its nearest reference, this word of the Lord teaches us that Mary acted in a praiseworthy manner, when she preferred to place herself at the feet of the Redeemer, in order to listen to His discourse, and that the remonstrance of her sister should not rob her of the present possession of this fortune. But through this meaning, this word lets us into a deeper and more comprehensive sense, which intimates that the heavenly good that Mary chose, is of eternal continuance, and affords its possessor an imperishable blessedness, which no power of the world can tear away from her.

This divine promise—it is also given to us, my friends. If we, like Mary, seek what is above, where Christ sits at the right hand of God, and lay up for ourselves treasures in heaven which moth and rust cannot corrupt, and thieves cannot break through and steal ; if we, like her, hear the word of everlasting life with eagerness, and keep it in a refined, good heart, "and bring forth fruit with patience ;" if trust in God through Christ, and love to God and obedience to God have become for us the inmost and most powerful motives to a faithful and assiduous fulfillment of our earthly calling—then in our life the right, divinely-approved relation between the aspiration after heavenly good and our earthly business, is restored ; then have we chosen the good part which shall not be taken from us. Misfortunes and sickness, the caprice of the mighty, and the secret arts of cowardly antagonists, the enemy's violence and the friend's treachery, they can tear from us all our earthly possessions— what is safe in this stormy time?—but of the *highest* good they cannot rob us ; hardly can they disturb us in its enjoyment. The all-subduing power of death, which tears from our arms the dearest friends, and to which our own earthly life, sooner or later, must yield—this power finds here its master. In death, even, the good part remains to us, and accompanies us through death into immortal life, only there to manifest in us its blessed power and glory. * * * * *

Contemplative souls like Mary, may also, like her, find their highest pleasures at times, in penetrating in quiet reflection into the unfathomable depths of the will and the grace of God; but let them, like Mary, avoid the by-path of fanatical inactivity; let them never forget that these beautiful, festal hours of still contemplation, become a selfish enjoyment when they do not serve to strengthen them for active life, to inspire them to fulfill, more and more faithfully, their earthly calling. Those souls, however, who, like Martha, never enjoy life, and are never in their element if they cannot work and manage in vigorous activity, need not relieve themselves of their unwearied labor in outward life; but let the consciousness everywhere accompany them which Martha, indeed, lost only for the moment—that they walk before God's countenance; let them studiously nourish and strengthen this consciousness out of the living fountain, in earnest, holy contemplation, that their activity may neither be perverted into an empty superficial, nor into an unquiet and passionate pursuit. And if they have become weak, and, troubling and impeding themselves and others have gone out of the right path, let then the word of the Lord, "One thing is needful!" lead them back again, as easily as it did Martha, into their original place, and to the divinely-approved order of their life. Amen.

DISCOURSE XXII.

THE LONGING FOR HOME.

You are familiar, my friends, with that singular longing which sometimes strongly seizes the mind of a man, especially in the period of youth, and strangely affects his feelings. Human situations and circumstances float before him, such as he is, perhaps not able himself very nearly to describe, but which concerning he can say this, that they are much more beautiful and perfect than all that he can see around him, or all that his previous experience has shown him. All the circumstances there, are noble and magnificent. He sees lofty forms walk before him, and a magical radiance rests upon them. Untroubled bliss, deep satisfaction, beckon the longing youth, and in unchecked activity he is to reveal the strength and fullness of his soul. This longing sets him whom it possesses at variance with the outward life, which then appears to him poor and colorless. He would re-make it according to his own ideas; but because he does not succeed in this, he turns away from it, discontented and impatient. All activity in it is repulsive to him. As often as he can, he retreats thoughtfully into the still world of his dreams and fancies.

Men blame the mind that weakly gives up to this longing; and surely with justice. They warn the youth to repress this exaggerated, dreamy feeling—to content himself with the actual world, as it now is—to build up for himself in it, as well as he can, his life's fortune, and, at the same time, make himself as useful as possible to others. But this counsel evidently is easier given than followed. Besides, one hardly finds much heed among those whom this longing has once possessed. Yea, the most promising among the youthful minds will generally contend most decidedly against the view of human life which lies at the basis of this advice. They do not willingly submit to come down to the cold wisdom, which once for all renounces everything higher, and more perfect, and only finds itself at home in the narrow limits and poverty of common life. They think that with their longing after something unconditioned and perfect in life, they stand higher than those moderate persons by whom they are pitied as visionaries. Yea, they boast of having on their side the most glorious, the most eminent minds of all times. Ever, they say, has the mainspring of their immortal deeds, the fountain of their lofty works, been a great, bold thought, which appeared to common-place men only as the fruit of a foolish extravagance—the enthusiastic striving after some high goal, whose attainment these held to be absolutely impossible.

We shall not here enter into this dispute for the purpose of accurately dividing the right from the wrong on both sides ; but so much is certain, that is a perverse beginning, to repress that dim longing, instead of giving to it the right object ; to destroy this obscure and indefinite seeking and striving, instead of guiding it to an understanding of itself, and leading it to its true goal. One should show such souls that what they seek is properly the full revlation of eternal life. For in this alone, will all human life appear in its true, pure, godlike form. In it alone, will all our longing and aspiring find their perfect satisfaction. Not upon the earth, but in heaven, is our home, and therefore is man here a creature who seeks. He finds no rest, so long as he knows not the heavenly home, and even when he has become acquainted with it, his longing is not yet stilled, since the full possession of the heavenly inheritance is still in the future. Let us linger by this truth in our meditation to-day.

"Therefore we are always confident, knowing that whilst we are at home in the body, we are absent from the Lord. For we walk by faith, not by sight. We are confident, I say, and willing rather to be absent from the body, and to be present with the Lord. Wherefore we labor, that whether present or absent, we may be accepted of him." 2 Cor. v. 6-9.

With simple and touching words the Apostle, in our text, expresses his longing for the Christian's heavenly home. He regards, however, this longing in no wise as anything peculiar to himself, but speaks of it as a universal attribute of the Christian life. In this he not the less testifies from his own experience, though in the name of all true Christians, to the salutary influence of this longing, to its consoling and cheering power. From these two points of view then, let the longing for Home be the subject of our meditation. When we have first perceived the necessary place of this longing in the inner life of the Christian, it will not be difficult to persuade ourselves of its salutary influence.

I. That the longing for home belongs essentially to the Christian life, is, my brethren, by no means so universally acknowledged, as would be expected by a pious soul which, unconcerned in the strife of opinions, is endeavoring to shape its inner life according to the directions of the Bible. Voices, louder and bolder than ever, are lifted up in our times, which dispute the right of the longing, and the hope from which it springs and with which it is inseparably connected, to a place in the harmonious connection of the inner Christian life. "To afford full satisfaction in the complete knowledge of God," we hear it said, "is the essential design of Christianity." "In Christianity, the Divine has appeared in time, and the soul breaks through, even now, this restricting barrier. Whoever believes in Christ *has* the eternal life, and needs to long for nothing beyond the present. It is only unbelief, or weakness of faith, which waits for the future, instead of grasping and holding fast the eternal in the midst of the earthly life, and of being perfectly content with its full, living, presence for the soul."

These lofty words bear a certain semblance of strength of faith and fullness of faith, which, however, can deceive only the ignorant. Or has the eternal life in Christ whose perfect possession these persons so confidently ascribe to themselves, just now appeared upon the earth? Has the church of Christ hitherto known nothing of it? There is no one who would venture to make so foolish an assertion. And yet the longing for the consummation of the kingdom of God has ever been earnest in the church. Yea, experience testifies incontestably, that it has everywhere least of all failed where faith and love have been the strongest. Those who have here participated in eternal life in communion with God, have, without doubt, most heartily longed for its fulfillment beyond the present existence. And assuredly if any Christian feelings have found in the songs of the church a sincere, touching, heartfelt expression, they are its glorious hopes ; and these are its holy longings.

But whether the church of the Lord has a divine right to such a hope and longing, or whether in this any human fancy, and strange delusion has misled it, let the Apostles of the Lord first decide. Paul has been styled preëminently the Apostle of faith ; and this justly. The unconditioned, the justifying and saving power of faith in the grace of God in Christ, is the great subject of his preaching, of which he knows how to testify with words of flame. And yet the same Paul, who possessed in his faith an inexhaustible spring of the holiest peace, according to his own acknowledgment, as our text in the original reads, had a "desire to depart from the body and to be at home with the Lord." Just for the reason that Christ is his life here, even during his stay on earth, is dying for him gain. The life of believers, as he writes to the Colossians, is hidden with Christ in God. Its real nature as it appears to the eye of God, remains concealed from the world by an impenetrable veil, as Christ himself, by his return to the Father, has withdrawn himself from the view of the world. But when Christ, our life, shall appear, then will His disciples appear with Him in glory. Yea, the Holy

Ghost with all His gifts and influences, the Apostle, in several passages of his Epistles, declares to be the pledge of an imperishable inheritance, whose full **possession God so guarantees to his** church ; and of the possessors of the first fruits of this heavenly harvest, he says that they wait for the adoption, the redemption of their body. The assertion, which was heard at that time, that the resurrection is already past, in a spiritual way, and that no farther resurrection is to be expected—this assertion the Apostle rejects as profane and vain babbling.

And how harmonious with these testimonies of Paul is what the Apostle of Love says of the relation of our present participation in the kingdom of Heaven to the full enjoyment of this kingdom. Who can deny that, with strong and bold words, which are so much the loftier the simpler they are, he praises the blessed communion which here even unites the disciple in whose heart love reigns, with his God and his Saviour ? And yet he regards it only as the introduction to a higher communion. Little children, he prays, " abide in Christ, that when He shall appear we may have confidence and not be ashamed before Him at His **coming.**" And that the consummation of the kingdom of God, which then appears, is so infinitely more glorious than all that believers here possess that it must hence of necessity awaken their deepest longing—this the weighty words of John do show : " Beloved, now are we the **sons of God, and it doth not yet** appear what we shall be. But we know that when He shall appear, we shall be like Him ; for we shall see Him as He is."

And what shall I say of Peter, who makes this longing of the Christian church the very kernel of hope? Strangers and pilgrims, he styles the believers, and points them encouragingly to the heavenly **bliss and glory which shall** follow their earthly life ; and speaks, with earnest desire, of the future revelation of Jesus Christ, whom, although they had not seen, they love, and on whom they believe, though they see him not.

Finally, He himself whose word is **the** highest source and measure of all our knowledge, whose spirit guided the Apostles

into all truth—He declares that whoever sees the Son and
believes in him, hath everlasting life ; but immediately adds, in
order to define more closely the nature of this possession, that
such a one He will raise up at the last day. And so He often
speaks to His disciples of the time when they should become
participant of a more perfect and glorious communion with Him.
Yea, His last words, which He spoke before His death, in the
circle of His disciples—they must have awakened in their souls
the deepest longing for the heavenly home. " I will that they
also whom thou hast given me, be with me where I am, that
they may behold my glory which thou has given me." And
when to the Prince of life upon Golgotha, the night of death
approached, there, even, His gracious word opened the gate of
paradise to the longing glance of His companion in death.

Surely, my friends, if pious Christians in all times have longed
for their home in the heavens, the Apostles have incited them to
this aspiration. And if the Apostles have awakened this longing, their Lord and Master has himself authorized them to do so.
But if there there are in our time those who boast of having the
everlasting life and will yet know nothing of this longing, of
this hope, they may thank another for their imagined riches.
The eternal life in Christ they know not.

What the word of the Lord and His Apostles teaches, is confirmed when we view attentively the nature and inner connections
of the life which His Spirit produces in us. While we dwell in
the body, says the Apostle Paul, we are separated from the
Lord, in a foreign land ; for, adds Paul immediately, as the
reason, "we walk by faith, not by sight." This, my brethren,
is a great and weighty word. Is not Faith the fountain of the
new life and its continual supporter, a certain assurance of
what we hope for, a firm conviction of what we see not ? Do
we not know through it, that in our pilgrimage, the Lord
is at all times near us ? And yet, however close may be the
union of the believer with Christ, it is yet to be regarded as a
separation, compared with the perfect communion with Him,

17

of which he will be participant when his faith shall be transformed into sight. And if faith, in its innermost nature, is nothing else than the veiled bud of sight, how shall we not long for the unfolding of this bud to a most glorious blossom? If we see now the glory of the Lord only through a glass, in a mysterious way—who will not aspire, with the Apostles, to see face to face, to know even as we are known? Yes, what signifies this seeing in the glass, if that which appears to us therein in twilight, is not one day to be revealed to us in serene clearness? Would not the whole life of the Christian remain a strange fragment, full of facts which point to the Highest, the Divine, and yet again so inexplicably incomplete, if a future consummation did not await it? What mean these seeds full of promise, if they are to ripen into no harvest? And who gives us light to understand the history of the true Church of Christ? Who solves for us the hard riddle of its inward and outward strife, of its strength and its weakness, of its growth and its decline? And why all this struggle, if it leads to no real victory? To this triumph in the future everything points in the earthly development of the Church of the Lord—that community of the true believers and saints, which we term the invisible church. By this alone can its struggles and sufferings be explained. A time is to come when everything incomplete shall attain a perfection, and every fragment appear as a beautiful whole; when every discord shall be resolved into harmony, and every hidden glory be revealed; when every holy desire find full satisfaction. Then shall our faith, which to the children of this world appears now as an offence—now as a folly, be solemnly justified by sight. Then shall the fountain of all evil, sin, be forever sealed. Then shall those who have truly loved one another in the earthly life, know of no separation more. Then shall the troubles and the hindrances which spring from the society of the world vanish. Then shall the purified be free from all the pains and distresses of this perishable body.

My friends, it may again, in our days, become a disputed point, whether the natural intelligence in itself finds sufficient ground for maintaining the immortality of the soul. But in the sphere of Christian faith, the reality of a blessed future can never be a subject of debate. One needs, in truth, to have taken only the first steps in this holy sphere, to become aware how here all paths run towards a goal which shines alluringly from the world beyond : how all is only a beginning that points to a future consummation. It is true, Christ continues to come in a way invisible, hidden from the world, so often as His Spirit is poured out anew among men ; but just for this reason will He one day, in the fullness of time, visibly appear in divine glory. It is true, His disciples with Him have arisen to a new life ; but just for this reason will He one day awaken them to the full and complete purification and transfiguration of their being. It is true, His judgment walks through the history of the world, an ever new separation of the good and evil, and of those who belong to both, an ever new condemnation and destruction of the perverse, ungodly action of the world ; but just for this reason shall this judgment one day attain to its complete realization. It is true, the powers of the future world, and of the everlasting life, are already efficient in the present life of the believers ; but just for this reason shall they one day, when nothing longer hinders them, pour themselves over the perfected ones, in exuberant and blessed fullness.

Whoever will wrest from the Christian this object of his hope and longing, declares a war of extermination against his whole faith. This it is which the Apostle says : " For if the dead rise not, then is not Christ raised : and if Christ be not raised, your faith is vain ; ye are yet in your sins." Upon the rock of this Apostolical declaration, the bold pretence is shattered, of those who boast of holding, yea of perfecting the Christian faith, while seeking to destroy the Christian hope. The faith and the hope of the Christian are an indivisible whole. Whoever dares to put asunder what God has joined together in his everlasting counsels ;

whoever, with presumptuous modesty, renounces the whole, and will
content himself with a part—he does not truly possess even this
part, but a self-made phantom that in the hour of trial dissolves
before his eyes. Whoever hath, to him shall be given; and whoever hath not, from him shall be taken away what he thinks he
has. If our hope is vain, our whole faith is a cheat and a lie.
"If in this life only we have hope in Christ, we are of all men
most miserable," for we are the most deluded. But we know whom
we have believed; we know that He cannot deceive us. We
calmly trust to His promise that he has gone to prepare a place
for us, and that He will one day come and take us to Himself,
that we may be where He is. How can we help longing for this
blessed consummation?

You see, my brethren, that whether we regard the express
testimonies of Christ and his Apostles, or look into the inner
nature of the Christian life, the same conviction meets us, that
this longing belongs to the Christian mode of thought and temper of heart.

II.—But if this be so, we should anticipate that the *effects*
of this longing could not be otherwise than salutary. And
that this expectation does not deceive us, the progress of our
meditation will render certain.

The first effect of the Christian longing, is the strengthening and
animation of our zeal in the work of sanctification. "We are
confident," says the Apostle, inspired, "and willing rather to
be absent from the body, and to be present with the Lord—
wherefore we labor, that whether present or absent, we may be
accepted of him." What the Apostle here testifies to from his
innermost experience, all Christians have also experienced who
have shared his glowing aspiration after the heavenly home.
This aspiration has been to them a powerful spur, by patience
in well doing, to seek for everlasting life. Yes, so close and so
essential is this connection between both, that we can recognize
a truly Christian longing for home, such as filled the heart of the

Apostle, only when it bears these holy fruits in the life of the man. As the sun cannot do otherwise than enlighten and warm, so the longing for home in the mind of the Christian cannot help revealing itself in a redoubled endeavor to walk in a way well pleasing to God.

Or shall that sickly sensibility, which, with its repulsive caricature, mimics the holiest feelings of the Christian, and with its lie nestles in the truest and simplest expressions of a pious soul, shake our conviction? Or those disordered states of men who, by their own guilt have made life intolerable, and now long for death, fancying that one needs only to die in order to be blessed? Do all these really aspire after the home with Christ, after perfect communion with Him? Far from it; but the present form of earthly life to which their heart is fettered with iron chains, they hope to find again, a little improved, on the other side of the grave. They will make that immortal which is devoted to transitoriness. Their selfish and worthless chase, as it is turned away from God, their diseased fancy bears over to the next life, in order then to find blessedness in the undisturbed enjoyment of this wretchedness. But if this be the nature of their hope, their longing, so far as they are earnest in it—who will wonder that it has no sanctifying influence upon their life?

How entirely otherwise is it with the hope and longing of the believing Christian? Among the divine promises which irradiate his future life—is there one precious above all others—is there one that wakes his deepest longing—it is the promise that his communion with Christ which here ever continues a disturbed and imperfect communion, shall then be perfected; that in this communion he shall be participant of a knowledge of God, before which his present knowledge sinks away, as the inarticulate thoughts of a child before the ripened weight of the man. Can you, my friends, imagine a loftier destination for man, than this which the Gospel points out for him—the destination to perfect communion with the Son, to the blessed intuition of the Father? So lofty is this destination that we need not at all wonder if many regard the hope of attaining it as wicked presumption—as a fanatical delusion. For truly, there is required the whole childlike simplicity and boldness of the Christian faith, in order to hold fast the promise of the Lord, in defiance of all doubts and apprehensions, in the midst of the pitifulness and worthlessness of earthly life. "And every man that hath this hope in him, purifieth himself, even as He is pure." For only to those who are pure in heart, is the promise given that they shall see God. So there is an immeasurable chasm between Christian hope and longing, and every service of sin.

And upon this point no one in whom this hope and longing is actually living, can be deceived, or in his innermost consciousness, doubt. When the imperishable glory of his home comes near his mind and enkindles that deep longing in him, his whole life appears to be consecrated. He feels himself elevated above the common and paltry bustle of the world—above its foolish chase after perishable enjoyments. Destined to see God, it is unworthy for him to bear the yoke of earthly cares and passions. Upon his way to this heavenly home, he dare not pollute himself with sin. He carefully guards against all that could displease Him, after the closest communion with whom he aspires ; as this holy longing lifts him above many temptations which become dangerous to others, so it strengthens him for the struggle with those which still menace him. And if, forgetful of his eternal home, he becomes weak and gives up to slumber, it is the re-awakening remembrance of this home which admonishes him to rouse himself again, and anew to press towards the "mark for the prize of the high calling of God in Christ Jesus."

Everywhere in the Christian life, are the purifying and consoling influences of the Gospel closely connected. As that alone is able truly to console us, which at the same time works with sanctifying power upon our will ; so whatever truly sanctifies us will not be without a consoling and blessing influence upon our hearts. The longing for our heavenly home—comfort and peace for the earthly life is its other not less essential effect.

To those, indeed, who have only an outward acquaintance with Christian faith and the Christian temper, this will by no means be clear. It rather seems to them to be exactly the reverse. They think, that to whoever longs for a heavenly home, the whole earthly life must necessarily be painful; that nothing can longer give him joy; that he everywhere sees only misery and want.

Let us ask the Apostle, whether the earthly life became to him tormenting darkness, after he had caught a glimpse of the blessed light beyond its borders? It is true, a strain of holy sadness presses forth irresistibly from the words of our text. The same strain chimes mildly and earnestly, through all the epistles of the Apostle. You hear it reëcho from the epistles of the other disciples of our Lord; and if you will listen, you can easily hear the same in the inner life of every pious Christian. But this still sadness by no means excludes joy and peace—of this Paul himself is a proof, when he so often, in the most hearty and lofty words, discloses to us the deep peace and divine joyfulness of his soul; when he also in our text expressly testifies: "We are always confident." And this comfort which never leaves him, he places in the closest connection with his longing for home. "We are confident," he repeats, with emphasis, "and willing rather to be absent from the body, and to be present with the Lord." * * * * * *

Surely, my friends, the walk through the earthly life is very calm and peaceful when one has nothing to fear, but everything to hope; when, by faith, the sting is taken from death, by the fear of which countless men are slaves for their whole life; when the natural dread of this great, wondrous event is swallowed up in the joyful courage of Christian hope, which sees in death only a birth into a more perfect life. Those who long for home are already dead, in the midst of the earthly life. They are familiar with the idea from which others flee in terror, that the time will come when their eye, too, will grow dim, their heart stand still, their last thought sink into the darkness of unconsciousness; that

then the coffin and the grave will close over their dissolving
frame. They *are* dead. They have within them experienced
and survived death. They know that to them beyond death,
life is made sure, in communion with Him who says to His
disciples : "Because I live, ye shall live also." And when, from
their home they shall glance back to the checkered world, there
rests upon it a mild, peaceful light, which harmonizes all its
discords, and reveals to them here even in the works of His creation, as in a mirror, the glory of God which they shall one day
fully see. Nature has to them a livelier radiance, and prophesies
of its future transfiguration. More grateful are the forms of
those human relations in which the penetrating glance of aspiring love to the Eternal One, easily discovers the seeds of a
higher, imperishable development. That passionate dependence
on the goods of the earthly life, that immoderate joy, that
rapture in their possession, you may not, indeed, expect from
them. They have become acquainted with something better
than this world can proffer. The calm, blessed consciousness
that they are called to something infinitely higher and more
glorious, constantly accompanies them. But are they, therefore,
less capable of appreciating and enjoying earthly beauties and
blessings, because, in the view of death and the future life, they
have found and ever hold fast their right measure ? And how
much easier are the pains and toils of this perishable life borne
when the eye of the soul is directed to its eternal home ! Oh,
then, with the apostle Paul, we hold, "that the sufferings of
this present time are not worthy to be compared with the glory
which shall be revealed in us." Then we enjoy, in the midst of
affliction and need, a holy peace by the power of living hope,
"as dying, and behold we live, as chastened and not killed, as
sorrowful, yet always rejoicing."

And whether the great hour comes early or late, when the
gates of the Father's house open, the hour when the Lord
beckons to the weary pilgrim to come out of the body—oh,
how calm and courageously do we enter, then, into the mys-

terious, silent night of the valley of death, leaning on the hand of Him who has for our eternal salvation, trod this narrow, dark path. As a child upon a perilous way clings to its mother, so do we cling closely to Him, who has taken from death its power through His death, and has brought life and immortality to light through His resurrection. Only a few steps are to be taken in that valley of pain. For only a few moments does our outward nature struggle against the dissolving power of death. Then it is over. The dark shades disappear, and into the enraptured eye beams, in the mildest, most blessed radiance, the Eternal Home!—Yes, "we are always confident" whether in life or in death. With calm longing, our glance rests upon the blessed home which lies before us, and life appears to us peaceful, and death sweet. The thorns of our pilgrim-path no longer wound us, and the entrance to the Father's house is no more narrow and fearful. The waste blooms into a garden of the Lord, and the dark valley becomes a light, lovely path. With refreshing peace within, praising God with heart and mouth, we joyfully walk toward the beloved home.

From Thee, our Father in Jesus Christ, our Lord, comes this longing. It is thy attracting power in the heart which all Thy children experience. To Thee it leads, and confirms us in communion with Thee. When shall we come that we may behold Thy face? Oh, surely Thou wilt not leave Thy dear promises unfulfilled. If we trustfully walk in Thy way, Thou takest us to Thee in death, and keepest us calm in Thy communion, until one day, at the end of the world, Thou leadest us into Thy glorious kingdom, where all longing ceases, where full peace and eternal blessedness awaits Thy children. Amen.

APPENDIX.

THE DELIVERY OF SERMONS,

BY DR. ADOLPHE MONOD.*

ALTHOUGH the art of recitation depends more on practice than on theory, it nevertheless has certain rules, which must be presented to the mind before you can address yourselves with profit to the exercises which are demanded, and which form the object of this course. In commencing the lectures of the year, I think it my duty to lay these rules before you, or rather to recall them to your memory. In so doing, I limit myself to such general views as may be comprised in a single discourse, and, at the same time, are of universal application.

GENERAL VIEWS OF THE ART OF RECITATION—ITS IMPORTANCE—ITS DIFFICULTY —ITS NATURE—INVESTIGATION OF A QUESTION.

It is scarcely necessary for me to call your attention to the IMPORTANCE of a good delivery. Among all human means, there is no one which contributes more to fix the attention of men, and to move their hearts. The discourse which, delivered with forced emphasis or with monotony, leaves the hearer cold and seems to court inattention, would have attracted, convinced, and melted, if it had been pronounced with the accent of the soul, and the intonations which nature communicates to sentiment and reason. It is vain to say

---

* This Lecture was delivered by Dr. Monod, to several classes of Theological students at Montauban. A translation of it by Dr. James W. Alexander, appeared in the Princeton Review, some fifteen years ago, and at the time excited remarks of a very commendatory nature. The wish has been expressed that it might be had in a more available form, and read, especially by young ministers, generally. Dr. Monod, as the most accomplished orator of our day, in France, if not in Europe, certainly deserves to be heard with the respect due to a master in the department of sacred eloquence. For vivid originality and native truth, there are few compositions on the subject to compare with this Lecture. The very accurate rendering referred to above, is here, in the main retained; a few changes, mostly at the kind suggestion of Dr. Alexander, having been made.

that this is an affair of mere form, about which the Christian orator should not much concern himself. Even if delivery were a secondary thing with the orator, which indeed it is not—inasmuch as the state of the mind has more to do with it than is commonly thought—it must always have a commanding interest for the hearer, from its powerful influence on his thoughts and inclinations. Hearken to two men, who ought to be at home in this matter—Demosthenes and Massillon. The greater the difference between the kinds of eloquence in which they respectively excelled, the more forcible is the testimony which they both bear to the power of delivery and oratorical action. Demosthenes was asked what was the first quality of the orator? "It is action," and the second? "Action," and the third? "Action." Massillon expressed the same judgment, when he replied, on a certain occasion, to one who asked him which he thought his best sermon, "That one which I know best." Why so, unless that which he knew the best was that which he could best deliver? We may be allowed to believe that these two great masters of the art exaggerated their opinion in order to make it more striking: but its foundation is perfectly true. It is not merely a true opinion; it is an experimental fact, which cannot be contested.

There is nothing in what we have been saying which should startle a pious soul. True piety does not forbid the use of the natural faculties which God has allotted to us; but commands us to use these for His glory, and for the good of our race. What Bossuet so well said of God's inspired servants, applies with greater reason to all others: "True wisdom avails itself of all, and it is not the will of God that those whom he inspires should neglect human means, which also in some sort proceed from Him." The motto of the mystic morals is *abstain;* that of evangelic morals is *consecrate.* And surely the latter is above the former: for to abstain, it is enough to distrust; but to consecrate, we must believe. Exercise yourselves, then, gentlemen, without scruple in the art of elocution and delivery; but let it be in a Christian spirit. Let the art of recitation be with you, not an end, but a means. If in your application to this exercise you have no higher aim than recitation itself, and those praises which the world lavishes on such as speak well, you are no longer a preacher; you are no longer even an orator; you are an actor. But if you cultivate elocution as a means of glorifying God and doing good to man, you fulfill an obligation; and the greater the zeal and labor which you bring to the task, the more may you implore with confidence that grace without which the most eloquent is but "a sounding brass and tinkling cymbal."

This labor is the more necessary, moreover, because the DIFFICULTY of the art which occupies our attention is equal to its importance. This is proved by experience: those who recite well are few. There is, however, a distinction to be observed between the recitation of the actor, and that of the orator. The former is much more difficult than the latter; and good orators are not commonly great actors, at least in tragedy. Scarcely one appears in an age. For the actor has two things to do, of which the orator has but one. To the latter, it suffices to express the sentiments which he actually experiences; but the former must express the sentiments of another. Now, to express these, he must first make them his own; and this necessity which has no existence in the case of the orator, demands of the actor a study altogether peculiar, and apparently constitutes the most difficult portion of his art. To transform one's self into a person altogether foreign; to become invested with his manners, character, passions, and language; and, nevertheless, to remain master of himself and with the mind free, since it would be a weakness in the actor to confound himself with his part, so far as to forget himself and his acting: this demands a prodigious faculty, and one which seems to depend on certain natural dispositions which are altogether peculiar.* It seems as if there were a separate organ for the dramatic art; and it has been remarked that illustrious actors have not always been men of commanding intellect. So that we may make the same distinction between the orator and the actor, which Cicero makes between the orator and the poet: *nascuntur poetæ, fiunt oratores.* We may thank God that we depend less on organization, and that this power of imagination is not indispensable to us: our task is, at the same time, more noble and less complicated. To communicate our thoughts and feelings in a suitable, just, and expressive manner, is all that we demand.

But how does it happen, then, that speakers, whose delivery is good, exist in no greater numbers? Leaving out of view forensic and parliamentary orators, how comes it that there are Christian preachers who sometimes pronounce their discourses without action, and even without just inflection, and this when neither the sincerity of their belief nor their interest in the subject can be called in question? There is the greater reason to be astonished at this, because the same men often manifest in animated conversation many of the very qualities which we miss in their pulpit exercises, so that they need nothing in order to make them excellent speakers, but to be themselves. It is a difficult question; but let us attempt its solution.

It must be borne in mind, in the first place, that there is a wide distinction between preaching and conversation, however grave, interesting, or animated. A discourse, in which it is attempted to develop one or more propositions, one person being sole speaker for an hour, before a numerous audience, has, and ought to have, something of continuity and elevation which does not belong to mere conversation. We are no longer in the sphere of simple nature. There must be some calculation of measures, management of voice, and strengthening of intonations; in a word, there must be *self-observation;* and where this begins, the speaker is no longer in that pure simplicity where nature displays and acts itself forth unreservedly. Preaching likewise demands certain powers, both physical and moral, which are not possessed by every one, and which are not required in conversation. The two cases, therefore, are not parallel; and this may suffice to show how the same persons may succeed in one and fail in the other.

This first difference, which is in the nature of things, produces another which pertains to the orator. In attempting to rise above the tone of conver-

---

* Some curiosity will be felt, perhaps, to know in what great actors themselves have made their talent to consist. "What they call my talent," Talma somewhere says, "is perhaps nothing but an extreme facility in raising myself to sentiments which are not my own, but which I appropriate in imagination. During some hours I am able to live the life of others, and if it is not granted to me to resuscitate the personages of history with their earthly dress, I at least force their passions to rise and murmur within me."

sation, most preachers depart from it too much. **They inflate** their delivery, and declaim instead of speaking; and when the pompous enters, the natural departs. We must not, indeed, expect too much; but whether it be the influence of example, or traditionary bad taste, or the case of a method in which capacity of lungs goes for labor of reflection and energy of sentiment, the fact is that there is scarcely one among us, who does not betray some leaven of declamation, or who preaches with perfect simplicity.

We may read, recite, or speak extempore. If we read, it is almost impossible to assume a tone entirely natural; either because the art of reading well is perhaps more difficult than that of speaking well, or because the preacher who reads, when he is supposed to be speaking, places himself thereby in a kind of false position, of which he must undergo the penalty. It will be better to rehearse after having committed to memory; the preacher speaks throughout after his manuscript, it is true, but he *speaks*, nevertheless. Where the speaker has prepared his thoughts and even his words, it is a matter which the auditor need not know, and which a good delivery can ordinarily conceal from those who are not themselves in the habit of speaking in public. The mind, the voice, the attitude, all are more free, and the delivery is far more natural. But can it be completely so? I do not know. Art may go very far, but it is art still; and there is a certain tone of semi-declamation, from which there is scarcely any escape; a tax, as it were, which must be paid to method; to that method which we are, however, far from condemning, and which seems to have been practised by some of the servants of God, in whom He has been most glorified. Finally, will it be possible to avoid the inconveniences just mentioned, and shall we certainly attain a simple delivery, by abandoning ourselves to *extempore* speaking? I believe, indeed, that this is the method in which one may hope for the best delivery; provided, always, that the speaker has so great a facility, or so complete a preparation, or, what is better, both at once, as to be freed from the necessity of a painful search for thoughts and words. Without this, it is the worst of all methods, for matter as well as for form. But even where one has received from nature, or acquired by practice a genuine facility, and has premeditated, with care, the concatenation and order of his ideas, and has even been aided by the pen (which is almost indispensable, in order to speak well), there will nevertheless always remain something of that constraint which arises from the research of what is to be said: and while the solicitude about mere words absorbs much of the mind's forces, the orator will hardly preserve freedom enough to secure, in all cases, the tones of nature. In this way simplicity will be injured by causes different from those which affect one who recites from memory, but scarcely less in degree. It is a fact, that with men who abandon themselves to extempore speaking, false and exaggerated intonations are not rare, at those **moments when they are not perfectly free, and** completely masters of their diction.

I have mentioned freedom of mind. It is this, more than **all the rest,** which brings the preacher into the natural position, and, consequently, into the true intonation. If he could be perfectly at his ease, the greatest hindrance of a **just and** natural elocution would be removed. But **it is** this which is chiefly wanting, both in those who speak extemporaneously what has been meditated without extraordinary pains, and even in those who rehearse a discourse which they have learnt by rote. When they find themselves before an auditory, they become agitated. They fear to displease; or, if they are under the influence of higher sentiments, they fear lest they shall not make an impression on their **hearers; or,** finally, they experience a vague embarrassment of which they **take no** distinct account themselves, and from which certain pious ministers **are** not altogether exempt. Sometimes, it is the concourse which intimidates **them; sometimes, it is the small number of** hearers; nay, perhaps, a single **hearer,** more enlightened, more fastidious, or higher in rank, than the rest; **—alas,** for poor human heart!—From the moment that this miserable timidity **enters the** soul all is lost. The mind's vision is troubled, the thoughts are confused, the feelings **are blunted, the voice** itself is less firm; the laboring breath fatigues the lungs, and forebodes an approaching hoarseness. If the orator speak extempore, he will be in danger of stopping short; or, by a sort of calculation which takes place almost without his own knowledge, he will seek **to hide** the poverty of the matter under the show of the manner, and will vent common-place, ill-developed, **though, perhaps,** just ideas with a solemn voice **and a declamatory tone, which will leave his** hearers as cold as himself, and **which, once adopted, or rather** submitted to, will hold him enchained till the **end of his** discourse.

We hear much of the talent and facility for speaking. **I am far from admitting** the principle, which (whether justly or not) is attributed to Jacotot— **that** all capacities are equal. Yet, it is an error which, like most others, is **only the** exaggeration of a truth. God has shown himself in the distribution of His gifts, less frugal and less unequal than it is common to think; and as **there is scarcely any soil from which culture may not extract at least necessary food, so there is scarcely any mind,** which, under proper direction, may not learn to speak in a correct, interesting, and impressive manner. The immense differences which we observe between speakers proceed less than is imagined, from a natural inequality, and much more than we imagine, from that *other* inequality which depends on human will and human effort. This seems just, and as it should be; and it is true, doubly true, as to *pulpit* eloquence, in which the moral element holds so considerable **a space.**

But, to return to the subject which gave occasion to this reflection: the power with which certain men speak, and the excellence of their delivery, arise in a great measure from their ability to put themselves perfectly at their **ease in a position where others are embarrassed. If confusion** paralyses the **faculties—self-possession** multiplies **them. Of two** men who encounter **any danger,** it is not always the ablest who best extricates himself; it is commonly he who keeps himself cool; and the greatest genius is good for nothing when frozen by fear. Of what avail would the best faculties be to you, without self-possession? But he who is at his ease says just what he intends, and just as he intends; reflects; checks himself in a moment, if necessary, to seek a word or a thought, and from the very pause borrows some natural and expressive accent or gesture; takes advantage of what he sees and hears, and in a word brings into use all his resources; which is saying a great deal; for "the spirit of man is the candle of the Lord, searching all the inward parts."

You will, perhaps, tell me, that this confidence to which I exhort you, is rather a favor to be wished for, than a disposition to be enjoined; that it is the happy fruit of temperament, or of success, or of native talent; and that it is not every one that chooses who *can* be at his ease. I grant that it depends partly on temperament; and this is a reason for fortifying it, if it is naturally timid: so on success; and this is a reason why the young man should use all pains to make a good beginning: so on talent itself; and this is a reason for improving that which may be possessed. But there is another element which enters into this case of manner, and I both wish it for you, and enjoin it upon you;—it is *Faith.* Take your position as the ambassador of Jesus Christ, sent by God to treat with sinful men; believe that He who sends you will not leave you to speak in vain; labor for the salvation of those whom you address, as if it were your own; so forget yourself to see only the glory of God and the salvation of your hearers; you will then tremble more before God, but less before men. You will then speak with liberty, therefore with the same facility and propriety which you possess in the other circumstances of life. If our faith were perfect, we should scarcely be in more danger of falling into false or declamatory tones, than if we were crying out to a drowning man to seize the rope which is thrown out to save him.

I attribute, therefore, the inferiority of many preachers, in oratorical delivery, partly to the difficulty of public and continuous discourses, but partly, also, to the want of certain moral dispositions. Hence it follows, that it is by assiduous labor and by spiritual progress, that they must become able to carry into the pulpit the same powers of speech which they enjoy elsewhere. But this particular question has diverted us too far from our subject; it is time to return, and give some account of *what constitutes* THE ART of recitation, or acceptable delivery.

The basis of every art is nature, but nature in a state of embellishment. The basis is nature; poetry and eloquence do not rest on conventional rules; it is the heart and the mind of man—of man as he is—which must be depicted, and which must also be interested. But it has for its basis nature *embellished,* —*idealized: imitates* it, but it does not *copy.* When Barthélemy describes to us the massacres of September, in terms which cause us not so much to understand, as to behold with our own eyes; when his bloody muse has no other ambition than that of inspiring the same horror which the hideous spectacle, to which he delights to drag us, would itself have produced; Barthélemy, with all his genius, has been false to his art; here is neither painting nor poetry, but butchery.

I would not subject myself to the prepossession of a mere artistic view, in treating of the recitation of the preachers. Yet, it may be said, in general, that this recitation should partake equally of imitation and of nature. Listen to those who speak well; observe them, at times, when they are not observing themselves; retain their intonations, and transfer them to your delivery. But while you adopt, elevate them; *imitate,* but do not *copy.* Do not *talk* in the pulpit. Too great familiarity is almost as great a fault as declamation; more rare, indeed, but nevertheless occurring among certain preachers, and especially such as are uneducated. It is the tone of good conversation, but this tone ennobled and exalted, which seems to me to be the ideal of oratorical delivery.

From these general **considerations, I pass to** those exercises which are soon to occupy us; and the remainder of this discourse will be employed in giving some DIRECTIONS, first for the *physical*, and then for the *moral* part of elocution.

We have just said, and we shall have occasion to repeat it, that the *Physical Part* of delivery is secondary, because it is instrumental. In public speaking, as in all the operations of the human understanding, the organs are the mere agents of the mind. But these agents are indispensable, and in proportion as they obey the understanding, other things being equal, will the delivery be effective. We must not, therefore, despise the physical part of delivery. We shall, nevertheless, be brief on this point, where every one will be able, with the aid of a few suggestions, to guide himself.

The *voice* should be exercised frequently and carefully. Endeavor to render your voice at the same time distinct, strong, sonorous, and flexible; this can be attained only by long practice. Labor to acquire the mastery of your voice. He who possesses this faculty will find resources even in a refractory voice, and will produce great effects, with little fatigue. But most public speakers are the slaves of their voice; they do not govern it, so much as it governs them. In this case, even though it has the most precious qualities, it is but a rebellious instrument. No one need fear any injury to the chest from those daily exercises which are necessary, in order thus to subdue and discipline the voice. If moderate, they will on the contrary strengthen it; and experienced physicians recommend recitation and singing to persons of delicate habit. The most favorable time for these exercises, is an hour or two after a meal; the stomach should be neither full nor empty.

After the care of the voice comes that of *pronunciation*. There is a natural pronunciation; by which I mean that utterance of the elements of speech which is common to all languages; and there is a conventional pronunciation, or that which each nation adopts for the words of its own tongue.

The student should begin by making himself perfectly master of the natural pronunciation, and learn to give every vowel its appropriate sound, and to make the organic motions belonging to every consonant. The latter point is the more important. If the purity of the vowel sounds conduce much to the grace of discourse, it is especially the articulation of the consonants, which gives it distinctness, vigor, and expression. A man who articulates well can make himself heard at a distance without vociferation, even though he lay little stress upon the vowels; and this is the method to which actors have recourse, when they make dying persons speak with a subdued voice; they explode the consonant while they retain the vowel sound. But one who articulates badly will never make himself heard at a distance; and adding force to the vowels will but increase the confusion. It is, further, in the utterance of consonants that the most usual impediments and other faults occur; and there is scarcely any one, who may not, on strict observation, detect himself as faulty in some particulars. One speaks thickly, he pronounces the *r* with the uvula and in the throat, instead of uttering it with the tongue, against the palate.

Another *lisps*; in pronouncing the *s* he protrudes the end of the tongue between the rows of teeth, and makes the English *th*, instead of a pure sibilation. Many fail in the *ch* (English *sh*), substituting an *s*, or a sort of *f*, or an awkward *ch*, produced by an oblique portion of the tongue. There is no one of these faults which may not be corrected by perseverance.* You remember the example of Demosthenes, whose principal efforts were directed to the development of his voice, and the utterance of the letter *r*. It is to be wished, that it were more customary to exercise children, at an early age, in the proper formation of sounds and use of their organs; there might thus be obtained without trouble, results which at a more advanced age cost immense pains and valuable time.

There remains another point, which is almost entirely neglected by public speakers, and which has, nevertheless, great importance; it is the art of *taking breath at the right time*. A man who takes breath properly, will fatigue himself less in speaking three or four hours, as certain political orators do, especially in England, than another in half an hour; and the orators who are able to speak so long, are either men who have studied the management of their breath, or men who speak much, but who speak well; for in this case, respiration regulates itself, without separate thought, just as in conversation. But it is by no means the same when one recites a discourse from memory; especially if it is the discourse of another; for in writing we take care, without being aware of it, to adjust the length of the periods to the habitudes of our lungs. But the exercise in which it is most difficult to breathe aright, as being that which is furthest removed from the natural tone, is the exercise of reading; and it is remarked that one is wearied much sooner by reading than by speaking. There are very few persons who can bear half an hour of reading without a slight inconvenience of the organ; but there are many who can speak an hour without trouble. The point of the difficulty is this, to time the respiration so as always to take breath a moment before it is exhausted. For this purpose, it is necessary to breathe quite often, and to take advantage of little rests in the delivery. It might be feared lest this necessity should injure the utterance and make it frigid; but, on the contrary, the rests which are thus employed by one who is exercised so as to use them properly, are as expressive as the voice itself; the slowness which they communicate to the discourse is only that slowness which gives more weight and vigor to the thought; so this happy infirmity becomes an additional power.

It is, lastly, by breathing seasonably, that the speaker will avoid a fault which is very common and very great; that of letting the voice fall at the end of sentences, which renders the recitation at the same time indistinct and monotonous. This is the abuse of the rule which is pointed out by nature. It is natural to lower the voice slightly at the moment of finishing a sentence, at least in most cases; for there are certain thoughts which, on the contrary, demand an elevation of the voice at the close. But the fall is made too perceptible, and is taken from too great a height, so that there are often three or

---

* The difficulty with regard to the *r* is one which is least easily removed. Yet it may be effected by pronouncing *d* instead of *r* for some time. Excellent teachers declare this expedient to be infallible.

four words which the hearer catches with difficulty, or does not catch at all. This would be bad enough, even without the additional evil, that the expression is weakened at the same time with the voice. As a general rule, the voice should be kept up to the end of the sentence, excepting only that slight depression and, as it were, reflexion which denote that the sense is terminated. But to do this, you must breathe in time; as it is, because the lungs are exhausted that you must lower the voice; for, where there is no breath, there is no sound.

I come now to some directions as to the *Moral Part* of delivery.

The expression sufficiently shows the point of view under which we consider the whole art of recitation, and in which we find the fundamental principle which supports all our rules. The principle is this: delivery has its residence, not in the mouth, but in the *sentiment* and the *thought*. It depends less on the *voice* than on the *soul*. I should have been in danger of being misunderstood if I had not begun by making some reservation in favor of the vocal part of delivery. This I am far from wishing to sacrifice. But now I assume an instrument fully exercised, an organ flexible and strong, a good pronunciation, distinct articulation, and easy respiration. When this previous training is accomplished, and when the moment has come for actual speaking, remember that the delivery is above all an affair of the soul; and make it as independent as possible of your organs. It is at bottom, the soul of the speaker, which addresses the soul of the hearer. The organs of speech, on the one part, and the organs of hearing on the other, are but intermediates between the mind of him who speaks and the mind of of him who hears. The more free one makes this communication, the more one forgets the organ, so as to bring out nothing but the soul, the better will be the elocution. Let the soul, the entire soul, with its constant unity, as well as with its infinite movements, look through the utterance, like the bottom of a stream, through perfectly limpid water; so limpid that it seems not to exist. The organs should be such docile and faithful interpreters of the thought, as to seem not to be present; they should obey to a degree of self-concealment. This is their glory and their mission; and the realizing of this ideal would infer the perfection, as well of the organ, as of the sentiment. This is according to our fundamental principle, viz.: "*It is the soul that should speak.*" We proceed now to deduce from this certain general directions:

I.—The delivery should be *true*, or just; it should give to each thought and each sentiment the tone which belongs to it. Why is such a tone proper to such an emotion of the soul? Why, for example, do we raise the voice at the beginning of a sentence, and let it fall at the end, when we ask a question to which an answer is expected? Why do we invert the method, in that species of questions which require no answer, and which are only another form of affirmation? Why does a certain intonation mark a simple assertion, another a doubt, another surprise, another anger, and the like? This is a question which we cannot answer. We are assured it is so in nature: to observe and to reproduce it, is the business of elocution. But to explain the secret relation which exists between the movements of the mind and the inflections of the voice, is more than any one can do, if we except Him who formed both the human soul and the organs which serve to communicate its impressions. That there are, in regard to this, fixed and well-determined laws, is sufficiently proved by the two following observations. In the first place, all men, without excepting those who never practise public speaking, recognize just inflection, when they hear it : the dramatic art is founded on this remark. In the second place, there are certain inflections which may be called primitive, and which remain invariable ; when we pass from one nation and idiom to another, notwithstanding the infinite diversity of all that is conventional.

But how are we to discover these accents of nature ? The first means, which offers itself to the mind, is to observe them in others ; it is excellent ; but we cannot employ it in every case. We do not always find an occasion to hear precisely this or that word, or sentence, about which we are embarrassed, pronounced by good speakers. I suppose the case therefore where we are left to ourselves. How are we to discover the accents of nature ? I answer, we must seek them in the soul. We must begin by discerning the inward impression ; and this impression, well caught, will conduct us to the intonation. This is the first consequence of the general principle which we have laid down above, or rather it is only the principle itself put into practice.

It is not meant that random trials must be made of all sorts of intonations, or that bursts of voice must be uttered at hazard. We must sit down, reflect, comprehend, feel, and silently interrogate the mind and heart. It is not till after this inward labor, that the essays of the voice will be useful : they will succeed in clearing and animating the movement of mind which gave them birth. By these means, one may gradually arrive at the true tone, which once found, and especially found in this way, will abide in the soul's memory, and will return and present itself at the moment of necessity. A very useful method of aiding in this research, is to translate the thought into other terms, more familiar than those of the discourse ; or, which is still better, to inquire how one would utter an analogous sentiment in the ordinary course of life. This care in tracing the language to the thought, and questioning the soul concerning the inflections of the voice, is the more necessary, from the fact, that the same sentence or the same word, is susceptible of a multitude of inflections, which the mind alone can distinguish, perceiving as it does the most delicate relations, while the diction and the pen have but a single expression for the whole.

Take a word—the most insignificant you can find—a proper name, for instance—and this, if you please, a monosyllable, as *Paul.* For writing and for language, there is but this one word, *Paul ;* but there are ten, twenty, an infinity, for the soul, and the organ it inspires. By the mere way in which an intelligent speaker, or better still, one who speaks without observing how, utters this name, and without waiting for him to add anything, you will be able to discern whether he be about to praise or to blame ; to tell good news, or bad ; to encourage a design, or to depart from it ; to call one afar off, or at hand ; to question, or to repel. We should never end, if we should try to enumerate all the thoughts which may be included in the utterance of this little name. Now, amidst this infinite variety, what rule shall guide us ? What other than that the mind, well exercised and correct, will find in delivery, the tone which suits the occasion and the moment of speaking? I cannot, then, repeat too often, speak *ex animo* (*out of the soul*). Perhaps you think this is a matter of course, and that the advice is unimportant. But practice will convince you that it is not so.

Let me be allowed to cite the authority of a man, who, received from God a rare genius, which, unfortunately, he squandered on vanities—I mean Talma; listen to his own exposition, given in private to some of his friends; for he wrote nothing of importance on his art. It will be seen that his mode of preparation was that of which I have been speaking; and it may be believed, that one of the causes of that reform which he wrought in theatric delivery, was the care which he bestowed, in searching for inflections in his soul, and in employing his organs only as docile instruments, destined to reproduce the internal impressions.*

The intonations being found, we must give it a degree of intensity greater than one would employ in conversation. From this comes the *energy* of public discourse. It is needless to say, this energy should bear a proportion to the nature of the subject. It will be at one time the energy of argument, at another the energy of passion; but it will always be the energy of propriety and of truth. This utterance, at once accurate and firm, these inflections, true and struck out with precision, have a peculiar charm for the hearer, and can make a discourse interesting from beginning to end, even in the least animated parts.

II. The delivery should be simple, or natural. In speaking from the soul, one will speak simply—for the soul is simple. It is only the presence of man which can make us affected; when alone we are always simple, for the single reason, that then we are ourselves. The accents of the soul are those of nature. It is these which we are to reproduce; and we must take care not to substitute for these the accents of conventional artifice, or of arbitrary choice. It is necessary that the hearer should recognize himself, and that the instinct of his nature should be satisfied with each of our inflections. In other words, we must speak, and not declaim. I have already said, elevate, ennoble the tone of conversation and of common life; but while you elevate, do not forsake it. An able painter does not slavishly copy the traits of his model; he idealizes them, and transfers them to the canvas only after he has subjected them to a sort of transfiguration in his brain; but even while idealizing them, he so imitates them, that they may be recognized at once. Thus it is that a portrait

---

* "It has been imagined, even by enlightened minds, that in studying my parts, I place myself before a glass, as a model before a painter in his atelier. According to them, I gesticulate, I shake the ceiling of the room with my cries; in the evening, on the stage, I utter the intonations learned in the morning, prepared inflections, and sobs of which I know the number; imitating Crecentini, who, in his Romeo, evinces a despair scored beforehand in a passage sung a hundred times over at home, with a piano accompaniment. It is an error: reflection is one of the greatest parts of my labor; following the example of the poet, I walk, I muse, or even seat myself on the margin of my little river; like the poet, I rub my forehead, it is the only gesture I allow myself, and then you know it is by no means one of the grandest. Oh! how a thing becoming historical, remains true! If any one should inquire how I have found the greater part of my greatest successes, I should reply, 'By constantly thinking of them.'"—(*Musée des familles.* 6 vol. p. 124.)

may be a perfect likeness, and yet more beautiful than the original. The same thing occurs in good speaking. The tones of common parlance are embellished, and yet they are perfectly recognizable, because their essence is carefully preserved. But to declaim, to take a new tone, because one is in the pulpit—in fine, to speak as no one ever speaks, is a grievous fault; while, strange to say, it is a fault very common, very hard to avoid, and which, perhaps, none of us escapes altogether. For it is far easier to assume a sustained and unaltering tone, than, step by step, to follow thought and sentiment in their infinite sinuosities; and then, there are never wanting hearers of bad taste, for whom the pomp of language is imposing. Nevertheless, consulting only the human effect of your preaching—if this consideration were not unworthy—the man who *speaks* in the pulpit will rise above him who *declaims*. Even those who at first suffer themselves to be dazzled by the cadence of periods, and the outbreaks of voice, at length grow weary, and are less pleased with the artificial preacher than with him whose very tones make them feel that he thinks all that he says. And what shall I say of the real and useful effect produced by these two preachers? How much more directly, nay, exclusively, will the latter find his way to the heart and conscience! How will his vehement parts be relieved by the calm and simple tone of his habitual manner! How much more truly will he be what he ought, in the sight both of God and of man, by continuing to be himself, and not stepping aside from truth in announcing truth!

Yes, if you would have a pulpit delivery which shall be dignified and Christian, and which shall make deep impression, speak always with simplicity. Say things as you feel them. Put no more warmth into your manner than you have in your heart. This honesty in speaking—allow me the expression—will constrain you to introduce a more sincere and profound warmth than you would ever have attained in any other way. It will, besides, have a salutary reaction on your writing, and even on your soul. For, displaying things as they are, it will bring your faults to light, and admonish you to correct them.

I have spoken of the pulpit. If it had been proper here to speak of the stage, many similar observations might be made. Great actors no longer *declaim ;* they *speak.* Talma, whom I have so often named, began by declaiming, as do others. An interesting circumstance made him feel the necessity of adopting a new manner, more conformed to nature: and from that day he became another man, in regard to his art, and produced extraordinary effects. Those who have heard him will tell you that the extreme simplicity of his playing astonished them at first, and that they were tempted to take him for a very ordinary man, whose only advantage over others consisted in a magnificent voice. But they were soon subdued by the power of nature; and the vivid impressions by which they were seized, made them understand that the very simplicity of his acting constituted its force, as well as its originality.*

* "We were," it is Talma who speaks, "rhetoricians and not dramatic personages. How many academic discourses on the stage! How few words of simplicity! But, one evening, chance threw me into a parlor with the leaders of the Gironde party; their sombre and disquieted appearance attracted my attention. There were written there, in visible characters, great and mighty interests. As they were too much men of heart to

III. The delivery should be *varied*. We know how monotonous it is in general; and though every one feels the grossness of the fault, few succeed in avoiding it. The best means of doing so, is to observe our principle of recitation *from the soul*. The soul is all full of variety. If there are no two leaves on a tree exactly alike, still less are there two sentiments in a human soul which are perfectly identical. Listen to a man engaged in animated conversation; you will be confounded at the marvellous flexibility of the human mind, and the infinity of shades to which it can adapt itself by turns. All this the vocal organ will deliver, if it confine itself to follow the movements of the soul. It must, therefore, be conceded, that there is no reason why any one should be monotonous in recitation. Take account of the sense of each sentence, of each member of a sentence, you will discover a perpetual mobility in the thought, and will need only to infuse abundance of truth into your delivery, to insure for it abundance of variety. There is, in particular, a kind of variety which will be found in this way, and which will spread itself over all the rest; I mean variety in regard to *rapidity of delivery*. It is natural to speak sometimes slow, and sometimes fast: sometimes, even very slow, and sometimes very fast. Here is a word on which one must dwell a moment; here, on the other hand, is a sentence which must be exploded, rather than recited, and which must be pronounced with all the rapidity of which the organs are capable in consistency with precise articulation. An elocution which levels these inequalities, and in which every sentence takes its turn with a measure always equal, and almost with the same rhythm, contradicts nature, and loses half its resources. This monotony must be broken, at all hazards. Better even would it be to employ excessive action and abrupt transitions, though this extreme must also be avoided, because it gives the delivery a theatrical air, or rather because by exaggerating the nature it falsifies it. In general, we speak too fast, much too fast. When any one speaks, the thoughts and sentiments do not come to him all at once: they rise in his mind by little and little. Now, this labor and this delay should appear in the delivery, or it will always fail of being natural. Take your time to reflect, to feel, to let ideas come; and do not make your elocution precipitate, except when determined so to do by some peculiar consideration. This *necessary* rapidity will give greater movement and vivacity to the deli-

allow these interests to be tainted with selfishness, I saw them manifest proofs of the dangers of the country. All were assembled for pleasure, yet no one thought of it. Discussion ensued, they touched the most thrilling questions of the crisis. It was beautiful. I imagined myself present at a secret deliberation of the Roman Senate. 'It is thus,' thought I, 'that men should speak. The country, whether it be named France or Rome, employs the same accents, the same language; if then they do not declaim here, neither did they declaim in the olden time, it is evident.' These reflections made me more attentive. My impressions, though produced by a conversation devoid of all violent manner (*emphase*), became profound. 'An apparent calmness in these men,' thought I, 'agitates the soul; eloquence, then, can have force, without throwing the body into disorderly movements?' I even perceived that discourse, uttered without effort or outcry, renders the gesture more energetic and gives more expression to the countenance. All these deputies, thus assembled before me, appeared far more eloquent than at the tribune, where, finding themselves a spectacle, they thought it necessary to utter their harangues in the manner of actors, of such actors as we then were, that is to say, of declaimers, fraught with turgidity. From that moment I caught new light and saw my art regenerated."—(*Musée des familles, ibid.* p. 250.)

very; but that other rapidity, which arises only from **embarrassment** and want of intelligence or reflection, confounds all the inequalities **of thought,** and engenders a manner which is effeminate, dull, lifeless, and **uninteresting.**

IV. Together with variety, the delivery should present another condition, without which this variety will itself be without connection and support; it is that of *unity*. The delivery should be one. In other words, we must use an effort to have a *récitation d'ensemble*, which results again from the principle which we laid down in the outset. For, if the words are manifold, the thought is one and indivisible in the mind. If we were pure spirits, we could communi cate it to other spirits of the same nature, without decomposition. But being constrained to clothe it in words, we are constrained to dismember it, and, from being simple in our soul, it becomes multiplied in language. To seize and transmit to the hearer this sole thought, to rise from language to the soul, and from the multiplicity of words to the simplicity of intellect, is the great work of a good delivery. Collecting, then, into one general sentiment, the various sentiments of which I have said so much, it will deserve the defini tion which has been given of the Beautiful, "Unity in variety, or variety in unity."

This is not to be accomplished, however, always in the same manner. In general, we shall, in a well-constructed sentence, avoid giving prominence to this or that word; causing the whole of it, rather to stand forth alike, and supporting it to the end. For it is the genius of our language to accent constantly, but lightly, the end of every word, and consequently also the end of every sentence. There are, nevertheless, certain cases where one is obliged to give a saliency to some words, or even to a single word, because this word comprises the capital idea. Even then, however, such words should predominate over the sentence, but not absorb it. It is the thought which should always appear, and always in its unity. A delivery which is broken, jerking, rising and falling by turns, is bad indeed.   .   .   .   .

I might add other counsels, but these are such as experience shows to be most useful; and by means of the illustrations which we have commenced, you will yourselves be able to make other applications of one general prin ciple, to which we must continually return, and in which are embodied all the directions we have given.

I have said nothing about gestures. It is a subject by itself, and one which I have not time to treat at present. Let me merely say, that the preacher should make few gestures, and these of a very simple kind, and further, that they should be dictated by the emotions of the soul, as well as by the inflections of the voice.

To sum up what I have said, if you wish to attain to a good delivery, begin by preparing your mind and your heart. Then, by reflection, with the aid of observation, search for the inflections of the soul, and oblige your organs to conform to these, humbly and exactly. As to the rest, be persuaded you will speak all the better, the more you sink yourselves; that the best delivery is that which turns attention away from the orator, and fixes it upon what he says; and finally, that the highest point of the art, especially in the case of the preacher, is to cause himself to be forgotten.